Mytica

THE IRON COAST

LIMEROS

THE GRANITE COAST

Ravencrest

The Temple
of Valoria

Castle
Damora

THE IMPERIAL ROAD

BLACK HARBOR

PAELSIA

THE
SILVER
SEA

TRADER'S
HARBOR

Basilius's
Compound

FORBIDDEN MOUNTAINS

THE WILDLANDS

KING'S
HARBOR

The Temple
of Cleiona

AURANOS

Castle Bellos/
City of Gold

Hawk's
Brow

Elder's
Pitch

THE RADIANT COAST

N
W   E
S

GATHERING DARKNESS

GATHERING DARKNESS

BOOK **3** IN THE

FALLING KINGDOMS

SERIES

MORGAN RHODES

razOr
bill

An Imprint of Penguin Group (USA) LLC

A division of Penguin Young Readers Group
Published by the Penguin Group
Penguin Group (USA) LLC
345 Hudson Street
New York, New York 10014

USA / Canada / UK / Ireland / Australia / New Zealand / India / South Africa / China

Penguin.com

A Penguin Random House Company

ISBN: 978-1-59514-705-9

Printed in the United States of America

10 9 8 7 6 5 4 3 2 1

CAST OF CHARACTERS

Limeros: The Conquerors

GAIUS DAMORA	The king
MAGNUS LUKAS DAMORA	Prince and heir to the throne
LUCIA EVA DAMORA	Adopted princess; prophesied sorceress
CRONUS	Captain of the guard
MILO & BURRUS	Palace guards
LORD GARETH	A friend of the king
LADY SOPHIA	A friend of the king

Auranos: The Defeated

CLEIONA (CLEO)	Imprisoned princess
NICOLO (NIC) CASSIAN	Cleo's best friend and palace guard
NERISSA FLORENS	Rebel aid
PETROS	Rebel aid
GALYN	Rebel sympathizer and tavern owner
BRUNO	Galyn's father

Paelsia: The Rebels

JONAS AGALLON	Rebel leader
FELIX GAEBRAS	Rebel
LYSANDRA BARBAS	Rebel
GREGOR BARBAS	Lysandra's brother
TARUS	Young rebel

Kraeshia: The Guests

ASHUR CORTAS   Prince
AMARA CORTAS   Princess

The Watchers

ALEXIUS   Watcher
MELENIA   Council member
TIMOTHEUS   Council member
DANAUS   Council member
XANTHUS   Exiled Watcher

PROLOGUE

The young man woke up surrounded by fire and chaos.

Swords clashed nearby in a violent battle in the shadow of the mountains. The sharp cries of the dying sliced through the cool early morning breeze. He could smell the acrid scents of both fear and hate from those who fought for their lives. He tasted the copper tang of the blood that had sunk into the ground.

It was the taste of blood that had awoken him.

He pressed his hands against the dry earth, flames licking at his bare skin, and tried forcing himself to his feet. He failed, his body screaming from the effort.

As his vision cleared he took a better look around. He was at the edge of a camp that was currently under siege. To his left, about fifty paces away, was a forest. It was dry and sparse and dying, but it offered more protection than his exposed position by the battleground.

Two men—one short, one tall, both wearing red guard uniforms—approached him, their swords drawn.

"What do we have here?" the short one said. "A slave thinking he can escape?"

"I'm no slave." His voice cracked, and his throat felt as dry and brittle as the ground beneath him.

"Forget your clothes somewhere, boy?" the taller guard said.

He glanced down at his bare skin. "Something like that."

"Doesn't matter," the tall guard snapped. "You won't need clothes when you're dead. We'll make this quick."

The tall guard brought his blade down hard, but the young man managed to roll out of its way just in time. He pushed himself up to his feet, his legs as weak as a newborn colt's. Muscles screaming, he staggered toward the forest line.

"We don't have time to chase after one runaway slave." The tall guard spoke loud enough to be heard above the noise of battle.

"You'd rather have your throat cut by a rebel back there?" the short guard said.

"The king would prefer—"

"I don't give a damn what the king would prefer. Let's go."

The forest was sparse, but the young man found a dry bush to hide behind. Its branches scratched his sensitive skin, but he stayed quiet and still. The guards ventured closer, whacking at the meager foliage with their swords.

He looked down at his hand and flexed. How long would it take before he got his strength back? He'd already waited an eternity to be free.

I've awakened before my time.

"Maybe we should let him go," the shorter guard said, his previous bravado vanishing as fear entered his voice. "Maybe he's the one who set the fire back there. He could be dangerous."

"Don't be a coward. Strays can lead to more trouble, and more strays. I want his blood on my blade before we do anything else."

They drew closer, and he stumbled away from his hiding spot. As he fled, he tripped on the tangled roots of a large oak tree and fell, hard, to the ground. The guards swiftly found him, and he scrambled backward until he hit the tree's thick trunk.

"You must feel so pathetic right now," the tall guard sneered. "Hiding in a forest, naked, begging for your life."

He did feel pathetic. It was not an emotion he savored. "I'm not begging."

"Oh, you'll be begging soon enough. I promise." The guard gave him a smile that revealed just how much he enjoyed inflicting pain and suffering on those who were smaller and weaker than him.

"What do you think?" the tall guard asked his companion. "Shall we take his hands before we kill him? Or his feet, so he can't try to run again?"

"Perhaps we should bring him back to the dungeon to rot with the other captured rebels."

"That's no fun." He touched the tip of his sword under the young man's chin, forcing him to meet the guard's cruel gaze. "Who are you, boy? A slave who would bow to my whip while working on the king's road? Or are you a rebel who mistakenly believes he can change the destiny of this kingdom?"

"Neither." His lips were parched and his breathing was shallow.

The sword wrenched his head up higher, biting into his flesh. "Then who are you?" the guard asked.

"I . . ." he began, very softly, ". . . am a god."

"A god, are you?" The guard snorted with amusement. "I'm curious . . . how much do gods bleed?"

"Wait." The shorter one's voice was trembling. "His eyes. Look at his eyes!"

The tall guard withdrew his sword and took a shaky step back. "What—?"

The young man unclenched his fist and looked down at his right hand. Etched into his palm was a triangle. Its edges glowed with the same blue light that now emanated from his eyes.

"You're a demon," the guard whispered. "That's what you are."

"I already told you what I am. But perhaps you weren't listening." He pushed himself back up to his feet. The symbol on his hand grew brighter as he held it out to the guard. "Shall I show you instead?"

Suddenly, a single flame appeared on the dry ground in front of them. It flickered, then shot up and licked the guard's boot. In a thin line, the fire snaked around his ankle and then began to wrap itself around his calf and thigh. He batted at it and touched it with his hand, which only made it grow even mightier. It clawed at his wrist and writhed around his arm like a bracelet.

"What's happening?" The guard reached out for assistance, but his short friend staggered away from him.

"Does it hurt yet?" the young man asked calmly. "If not, just give it a moment. It will."

The flames spread until the guard's legs, torso, arms, and, lastly, his confused, fearful face were all ablaze. The fire then turned from orange to blue.

That was when the guard began to scream.

The other guard stood frozen in place with horror, watching as his friend blazed like a torch in the early morning light. Suddenly, the flames grew wilder, leaping up thirty feet into the air and taking the guard with them. Finally, the guard stopped screaming.

Like a glass sculpture landing on a marble floor, his body shattered into a million pieces.

He turned to the guard he'd spared. "Run."

Eyes wide with terror, the guard turned and fled.

With what little energy he'd had now depleted, he collapsed to his knees. The symbol on his hand faded to only a trace, a mark resembling an old scar. The ground still smoldered where the tall guard once stood, although there was nothing left of him but an already fading memory.

Finally, his pain eased. His thoughts became clear, and a small smile lifted the corners of his mouth.

"Only the beginning," he whispered as darkness rose up to cover him like a thick cloak.

Soon he'd make them all burn for what they'd done to him.

CHAPTER 1

JONAS

PAELSIA

"I've got a bad feeling about this."

Rufus's voice was as distracting as a persistent horsefly. Jonas sent his fellow rebel an impatient look through the darkness.

"Really. Which part?"

"All of it. We need to get out of here while we still can." Rufus craned his thick, sweaty neck to scan the line of trees surrounding them, guided only by the light of a single torch they'd shoved into the loose soil. "He said his friends would be here any moment."

He was referring to the Limerian guard they'd captured after discovering him straying too close to the edge of the forest. He was currently tied to a tree, unconscious.

But an unconscious guard wasn't any use to Jonas. He needed answers. Though he had to agree with Rufus on one thing: They were swiftly running out of time, especially since they were so close to a village infested with the king's red-uniformed minions.

"Of course he said that," Jonas said. "It's called a bluff."

"Oh." Rufus raised his brows, as though this hadn't occurred to him. "You think?"

A week had passed since the rebel attack on the road camp in eastern Paelsia beneath the Forbidden Mountains. A week since Jonas's most recent plan to defeat King Gaius had gone horribly awry.

Forty-seven rebels had descended upon the sleepy campground at dawn in an attempt to seize the road engineer, Xanthus, and the Limerian heir, Prince Magnus, to hold as hostages against King Gaius.

They'd failed. A flash fire of strange blue flames had burned everything in its path, and Jonas had barely escaped with his life.

Rufus had been the only other rebel waiting at the meeting spot later that morning. Jonas had found him standing there with tears streaming down his dirty face, trembling with fear and rambling about fire magic and witches and sorcery.

Only two of forty-seven had been accounted for. It was a crushing defeat in far too many ways, and if Jonas thought about it too much he could barely see straight, could barely function beyond his guilt and grief.

His plan. His orders.

His fault.

Again.

Desperately trying to push aside his own pain, Jonas had immediately begun to gather information about other potential survivors—anyone who'd been captured alive and carted away.

The guard they'd found wore red. He was the enemy.

He had to have answers that could help Jonas. He *had* to.

Finally, the guard opened his eyes. He was older than most other guards, with graying hair at his temples. He also walked with a limp, which had made him easier to catch.

"You . . . I know you," the guard muttered, his eyes glittering in the meager torchlight. "You're Jonas Agallon, the murderer of Queen Althea."

He threw these words like weapons. Jonas flinched inwardly, but showed no sign that the most heinous lie ever told about him caused him injury.

"I didn't kill the queen," he growled.

"Why would I believe you?"

Ignoring Rufus's squeamish expression, Jonas walked a slow circle around the restrained guard, trying to determine how difficult it would be to get him talking.

"You don't have to believe me." He leaned closer. "But you're going to answer some questions for me now."

The guard's upper lip drew back from his yellow teeth in a snarl. "I'll tell you nothing."

He'd expected that, of course. Nothing was ever easy.

Jonas pulled the jeweled dagger from the sheath on his belt. Its wavy silver blade caught the moonlight, immediately drawing the guard's attention.

It was the very same weapon that had taken his older brother from this world. That vain and pompous Auranian lord had left it behind, embedded in Tomas's throat. This dagger had become a symbol to Jonas, representing the line he'd drawn in the sand between his past as the son of a poor wine seller who toiled every day in his father's vineyard, and his future as a rebel, certain he would die fighting for what he believed in most: freedom from tyranny for those he loved. And freedom from tyranny for those he'd never even met before.

A world without King Gaius's hands wringing the necks of the weak and powerless.

Jonas pressed the dagger to the guard's throat. "I suggest you answer my questions if you don't want your blood to be spilled tonight."

"I'll do more than bleed if the king learns I've done anything to help you."

He was right—the crime of assisting a rebel would undoubtedly lead to torture or execution. Likely both. Though the king enjoyed making pretty speeches about the united kingdoms of Mytica with a broad smile on his handsome face, he did not receive the nickname "the King of Blood" by being fair and kind.

"One week ago, there was a rebel attack on the road camp east of here. Do you know about it?"

The guard held his gaze unflinchingly. "I heard the rebels died screaming."

Jonas's heart twisted. He clenched his hand into a fist, aching to make this guard suffer. A tremor shook through him at the memory of last week, but he tried to focus on the task at hand. *Only* the task at hand.

Rufus raked his fingers through his messy hair and paced back and forth in nervous lines.

"I need to know if any rebels were captured alive," Jonas continued. "And I need to know where the king is holding them."

"I have no idea."

"I don't believe you. Start talking or I promise I'll cut your throat."

There was no fear in the guard's eyes, only a mocking edge. "I've heard so many fearsome rumors about the leader of the Paelsian rebels. But rumors aren't facts, aren't they? Perhaps you're nothing more than a Paelsian peasant boy—not nearly ruthless enough to kill someone in cold blood. Not even your enemy."

Jonas had killed before—enough that he'd lost count. In a foolish war that tricked Paelsians into allying with Limerians against

Auranos. In the battle at the road camp. He'd only fought in order to strike down his enemies and bring justice to his friends, his family, and his fellow Paelsians. And to protect himself.

There had been meaning behind those deaths, even if that meaning had been jumbled and unclear. He fought for a purpose, believed in something.

He took no pleasure in taking lives, and he hoped he never would.

"Come on, Jonas. He's useless," Rufus said, his voice twisting with anxiety. "Let's go while we still can."

But Jonas didn't budge, and forced himself to focus on the task at hand. He hadn't come this far to give up now. "There was a girl who fought in the battle named Lysandra Barbas. I need to know if she's still alive."

The guard's lips twisted into a cruel grin. "Ah, so this is why you're so driven for answers. This girl belongs to you?"

It took Jonas a moment to understand his meaning. "She's like a sister to me."

"Jonas," Rufus whined. "Lysandra's gone. She's dead. Obsessing about her is only going to get us killed, too!"

Jonas cast a glare at Rufus that made the boy wince, but it was enough to make him shut his stupid mouth.

Lysandra wasn't dead. She couldn't be. She was an incredible fighter—skilled with a bow and arrow like no one Jonas had witnessed before.

Lysandra had also been opinionated, demanding, and incredibly annoying from the first moment he'd first met her. And if she still lived, Jonas would do anything to find her.

He needed her—both as a fellow rebel and as a friend.

"You must know *something*." Jonas pressed the dagger closer to the guard's throat. "And you're going to tell me right now."

No matter how high the stakes, Jonas would never give up. Not until his very last breath.

"This girl . . . ," the guard said through clenched teeth, "is she worth your life?"

Jonas didn't have to think twice. "Yes."

"Then I've no doubt she's every bit as dead as you are." The guard smirked despite the trickle of blood now sliding down his throat. He raised his voice. "Over here!"

A crunch of dirt and a snap of branches were all that warned of the half-dozen Limerian guards that now burst into the small forest clearing. Their swords were drawn, and two of them carried torches.

"Drop your weapons, rebel!"

Rufus swung his fist at an approaching guard, but missed by a mile. "Jonas, do something!"

Rather than drop the dagger, Jonas sheathed it, then drew the sword he'd stolen from Prince Magnus last week before Jonas had managed to escape. He hoisted it up in time to block a blow aimed directly for his chest. Rufus tried to fight back, punching and kicking, but it wasn't long before a guard grabbed hold of his hair, yanked him backward, and put a blade to his throat.

"I said," the guard hissed, "drop your weapon. Or your friend dies."

The world skidded to a stop as the memory of Tomas's murder once again crashed into Jonas. It had happened so quickly—no time to save him, no time to fight or even beg for his life. And then Jonas recalled another memory that would be seared into his soul forever: that of his best friend Brion, slain by the same killer while Jonas watched, helpless.

With Jonas momentarily distracted, a guard took the oppor-tunity to slam his fist into his face. As hot blood poured from his nose, another guard wrenched the blade from his grasp, nearly breaking his fingers. Another kicked the back of his knees and slammed him down to the ground.

The world spun and sparkled before his eyes as he fought to remain conscious.

He knew it would end now, that he'd been on borrowed time ever since his most recent brush with death. There was no magic here to save him this time. Death no longer scared him, but the timing was wrong. He had too much left to do.

Just then, another figure entered the torch-lit clearing, causing the guards to spin around.

"Am I interrupting something?" said the young man. He looked a couple years older than Jonas, with dark hair and eyes. He wore a dark cloak, the hood back to show his skin was deeply tanned, and he gave an easy smile that showed straight white teeth, as well as his apparent nonchalance at the fact that he'd just casually strolled into the middle of a battle. He scanned the area, starting on one side with Rufus, who was still being held in place, then making his way over to Jonas, who braced himself against the mossy ground with two swords pointed at his throat.

"Get out of here," a guard growled. "Unless you want trouble."

"You're Jonas Agallon," the boy said, nodding at him as if they were meeting in a tavern instead of the middle of the forest in the dead of night. "This is quite an honor."

Jonas never asked to be famous. But the wanted posters clearly sketched with his face that had been tacked up throughout all three kingdoms had ensured otherwise. Despite having few victories and more false accusations than actual crimes, his name had quickly become legend.

And the high reward his capture offered sparked the interest of many.

The older guard had been cut free from his ropes and was now gingerly rubbing his wrists. "You've been following this rebel scum?" he asked. "Does that make you aspiring rebel scum? We'll save a spike back at the palace for your head as well. Seize him!"

The guards lunged for him, but he just laughed and dodged their grasp as easily as a slippery fish.

"Need my help?" the boy asked Jonas. "How about this—I help you, you help me. That's the deal."

He moved so well there was no way he was only a curious bystander. Jonas had no idea who he was, but right now he really didn't give a damn.

"Sounds good to me," Jonas managed.

"Then let's get started." The boy reached down and pulled out two thick blades the length of his forearms from beneath his cloak. He spun and sliced, moving faster than any of the guards could counter.

Jonas's head was still swimming, but he managed to elbow the guard behind him directly in his face. He felt and heard the crack as the guard yelped in pain.

He jumped to his feet and grabbed his sword, thrusting the hilt behind him to catch the guard in his soft gut.

The new boy took down the guard holding Rufus. Now free, the unskilled rebel just stood there in place, staring at the violent scene for a frozen moment; then he turned and ran out of the clearing without looking back.

A part of Jonas was disappointed in Rufus, but another part was glad the kid finally had a chance to escape a fight he hadn't been ready for since day one.

He might even stay alive if he played it smart and stayed out of trouble.

With the other guards now dead, scattered, or unconscious

in the clearing, Jonas grabbed hold of his original prisoner and slammed him back against the tree.

The smugness in the guard's eyes finally turned to fear.

"Spare me," he gasped.

Jonas ignored him, turning instead to the boy who'd just saved his life. "What's your name?"

"Felix," he offered with a grin. "Felix Gaebras. Happy to meet you."

"Likewise. Thanks for the help."

"Any time."

If Felix hadn't intervened, Jonas would be dead. No doubt about it. He'd given him a chance at another day, one in which he might make a difference. For that, Jonas was damn grateful.

Still, he'd be stupid not to be wary of any stranger who knew his identity.

"What's your price?" Jonas asked.

"Price?"

"You said if you help me, I help you."

"First thing's first." Felix approached, nudging Jonas out of the way and taking the guard by the throat. "I've been eavesdropping. Rude, I know. But I heard you say you didn't think Jonas was ruthless enough to kill someone in cold blood. Well, what's your first impression of me?"

The guard drew in a shaky breath. "What do you want?"

"Answer the question. His friends—are any of them still alive?"

The guard trembled. "Yes. A handful were brought to the palace dungeon to await execution."

"How many's a handful?"

"I don't know exactly . . . three, four? I'm not sure. I wasn't there!"

Jonas winced. Three or four? There were so few survivors. . . .

"Names?" Felix pressed harder on the guard's throat.

He sputtered, his face reddening. "I don't know. I'd tell you if I did."

"How long till they're executed?" Jonas asked, trying to keep his voice steady. The thought of people he cared about trapped under the king's thumb turned his blood ice cold.

"It could be a few days, or maybe a few months. Please, spare my life! I've told you all I know. Show mercy to me now, I beg of you."

Felix regarded him for a long, silent while. "How about I show you the same mercy you would have shown us?"

One swipe of Felix's blade, and the guard was silenced forever. His body slumped to the ground to join his fellow fallen guards in the flickering firelight, and Jonas found he couldn't look away.

"You know I had to do that, right?" Felix said, his voice as cold as stone.

"I know."

There was a hardness in Felix's eyes that was foreign to Jonas. They showed no flicker of remorse for what he'd done, nor did they show any joy.

It was true: The guard would not have shown them mercy. He would have executed them without a moment's hesitation.

"Much gratitude for saving my life," Jonas said as Felix wiped his blades on the mossy ground before sheathing them.

"You're welcome." Felix peered into the dark forest. "I think your friend ran away."

"He'll be safer staying far away from me." Jonas studied the bodies littering the area, then turned back to Felix warily. "You're an assassin."

With his fighting skills, his ease with a blade—it would have been obvious to anyone that he was a trained killer.

The coldness faded from Felix's eyes as he grinned. "Depends on the day, really. One does what one must with the talents they have."

That would be a confirmation. "So now what? I have far less gold than the wanted posters offer for my head."

"Somebody's a bit of a pessimist, isn't he? With the king's eyes everywhere lately, looking for anyone causing trouble, what I want is someone watching my back while I watch his. Why not partner up with the infamous Jonas Agallon, I say?" He glanced in the direction Rufus ran off. "I'm not seeing much competition. You need me. Simple as that."

"You want to be a rebel?"

"What I want is to cause trouble and create mayhem wherever I can." Felix's grin widened. "If that makes me a rebel, then so be it. How about I start by helping you save your friends?"

Jonas continued to eye Felix with wariness, his heart pounding as fast as it had during the fight. "The guard was only telling us what we wanted to hear. We've no way to know if my friends are really in the palace dungeon."

"There are no guarantees in this life, only strong possibilities. That's enough for me."

"Even if they are there, the dungeon would be impossible to breach."

Felix shrugged. "I kind of like impossible challenges. Don't you?"

Despite his best efforts to ignore it, hope had begun to well up in Jonas's chest. Hope often led to pain. . . .

But hope could also lead to victory.

Jonas studied the tall, muscular boy who'd just taken out five guards single-handedly. "Impossible challenges, huh?"

Felix laughed. "The most enjoyable ones. So what do you say? Shall we be partners in anarchy?"

Felix was right about one thing: Jonas didn't have a long line of skilled rebels waiting to fight by his side.

He relented, grasping hold of the fluttering hope inside of him and smiling. "Sounds like a plan."

Felix grabbed Jonas's outstretched hand. "And I promise I won't run off into the forest with my tail between my legs like your friend back there."

"I'd appreciate that." Plans and schemes were already racing through Jonas's head. The future suddenly seemed infinitely brighter.

"Tomorrow we get started on freeing your friends," Felix said. "And sending as many of the king's guards to the darklands as we can."

As far as friendships went, Jonas thought, this was an excellent beginning.

CHAPTER 2

MAGNUS

AURANOS

Magnus had no appetite for a celebratory feast, yet that's exactly what greeted him the day after he returned to the Auranian royal palace in the City of Gold. He'd just endured a grueling ride back from Paelsia and was now required to attend a banquet honoring his victory against the rebels.

Guests drank without restraint as bottle upon bottle of sweet Paelsian wine flowed like spring water. Not so long ago, Magnus would never have indulged in such frivolous things, which were forbidden in his homeland of Limeros.

But things had changed. Now, he'd decided, he would indulge whenever possible.

He arrived late. A few hours late, actually. He couldn't care less about punctuality, but as the guest of honor he was supposed to have made a grand entrance, and it seemed as if he'd missed his initial introduction. He managed to enjoy three goblets' worth of sweet wine before he was interrupted.

"Magnus." The sound of the king's voice cut through him like a blade. It was the first contact he'd had with his father since his return; Magnus had been purposely avoiding him.

He turned to meet his father's cold, appraising gaze. King Gaius had dark brown eyes, just like Magnus's, and their hair was the same nearly black shade—the king's had not yet shown any sign of graying. His father wore his finest formal surcoat, made from richly woven charcoal gray cloth and bearing the Limerian symbol of intertwining snakes in red silk thread on the sleeves. Magnus wore a nearly identical coat, which was much too stiff and restrictive for such a warm day.

Standing with the king were Prince Ashur, a visitor from across the sea who had by now far outstayed his welcome in this kingdom, and a beautiful girl Magnus didn't recognize.

"Yes, Father?" Magnus's sheer hatred for the man before him caused his throat to constrict. He fought with all his strength to not let that hatred show on the surface.

Not here. Not yet.

"I'd like to introduce you to Princess Amara Cortas of the Kraeshian Empire. The princess has joined her brother Ashur as our most honored guests. Princess, I present my son and the heir to my throne, Prince Magnus Lukas Damora."

How Magnus wished he were anywhere else. Meeting new people and appearing cordial was such an unpleasant chore, even when he was in a relatively good mood. Which he wasn't.

Magnus tipped his goblet to the Kraeshian siblings.

He had heard rumors of Princess Amara's beauty, and now he saw all of them proven to be true. Her pitch-black hair was swept up into a tight coil at the back of her long, graceful neck; her skin was as dark and as flawless as her brother's and her eyes a pale, silvery blue to match his.

Magnus forced a smile and bowed his head. "An honor, princess."

"No," Princess Amara said, "it is *my* honor to have been welcomed into your father's palace so graciously after giving barely any notice at all of my arrival."

"My sister is full of surprises." Ashur's deep voice held the edge of a Kraeshian accent, just as his sister's did. "Even *I* wasn't made aware of her arrival until late last night."

"I missed you terribly," she said. "I couldn't bear to wait until you decided to return home. You left us with no idea of how long you'd be gone."

"I like Mytica," he replied. "Such a charming little cluster of kingdoms."

Magnus noticed the slightest twitch in the king's cheek at the word *little*. Perhaps Prince Ashur had not meant it to sound dismissive, but . . .

It sounded dismissive.

"You're both welcome to stay in my little kingdom for as long as you like," King Gaius said, his tone free of any noticeable animosity.

One thing Magnus endlessly admired about his father was how he always managed to slather on the charm when necessary. It was a talent Magnus had yet to acquire.

"Where has your lovely wife gone?" Princess Amara asked Magnus now. "I only had a chance to meet her briefly, when I first arrived."

Now, there was a word that made Magnus's cheek twitch. *Wife.* He glanced around the crowded banquet hall, at the several hundred guests seated at long tables, mounds of food and drink set before them, swarms of servants ensuring no glass was fully emptied. A quintet of musicians played their instruments in one corner like a cluster of noisy crickets.

How different this was from the austere ways of Limeros, where there were few parties and it was rare to ever hear the sound of music. And how swiftly his father had altered his previous tastes and interests, adapting to new laws and rules in order to blend in with his surroundings. He was deceptive: a chameleon hiding in plain sight.

Magnus supposed it was easier to adapt to Auranian ways than to force a newly conquered kingdom to change their lives overnight. That would only lead to more rebellion than his father already had to contend with, and the Limerian army was spread thin across the entire continent.

It was all going according to the king's plan.

Or perhaps his father had begun to enjoy music and banquets and golden thrones more than he'd ever admit out loud.

"My wife? I don't know where she is," Magnus replied, taking a sip of his wine and beckoning a serving girl over to refill his goblet. He looked around the room again. All the faces blended together, and he couldn't see the pale golden color of Cleo's hair anywhere in the crowd.

"I'm sure she's very happy to have her new husband back by her side after such a long time apart," Amara said.

"It wasn't all that long." *Quite frankly, not nearly long enough,* he thought.

"Even a single day apart is far too long for two young people in love," Ashur said.

The wine Magnus had drunk nearly rose in his throat. "What a delightful sentiment, Prince Ashur. I had no idea you were a romantic."

"Ashur is the most sought-after bachelor in all of Kraeshia." Princess Amara hooked her arm through her brother's. "He's refused several potential brides. Father fears he'll never settle down."

"What can I say?" Ashur replied. "True love has yet to find me, and I'll settle for nothing less."

"Which makes you that much more desirable. Even here, you've easily managed to capture every woman's attention."

"Lucky me."

"If you'll excuse us," King Gaius interjected, "I must have a word alone with my son. Please, enjoy the rest of the banquet."

"Much gratitude, your highness," Amara replied. Touching Magnus's arm, she said, "I hope to see you again soon."

Magnus smiled and, despite the girl's unquestionable beauty and grace, the gesture felt so false it was actually painful. "I insist that you do."

As Magnus followed the king out of the crowded room, several guests tried to catch his attention, offering greetings and congratulating him on his victory in Paelsia, where he thwarted the rebels from halting the construction of the Imperial Road.

Magnus then noticed the sharp glare of Nicolo Cassian, the young palace guard stationed by the great hall doors.

"Did you keep her warm for me while I was away?" Magnus said to him in passing, feeling the first flicker of pleasure all day as Nic's expression grew more hateful, his face turning so red it almost matched his hair.

Nic would really have to learn to control his emotions if he wanted to stay out of trouble.

The foolish boy was in love with Cleo. And, as far as Magnus knew or cared, Cleo felt the same toward him. Yet he sincerely doubted that Cleo's eye could be caught by a lowly guard, even one she considered a friend.

The king took him to the throne room, a grand hall with high ceilings and chiseled marble steps that led to an enormous and ornate golden throne studded with rubies and sapphires. The Auranian tapestries and banners that had previously hung above the throne had been discarded for those of Limeros, but the room had otherwise remained just as it was when King Corvin Bellos ruled this affluent kingdom.

The king's guards stood just outside the heavy doors, leaving them alone in the cavernous room.

Magnus regarded his father in silence, willing himself to stay calm. He didn't want to speak first for fear he'd say something he'd regret.

"We have a problem, you and I," the king said as he took a seat upon the throne.

A breath caught in Magnus's chest. "What do you mean?"

"The Kraeshians." The king's expression soured, his features turning sharp and unpleasant in an instant. "Those little fools think I don't know why they're here. But I do."

This was not what Magnus had anticipated. "And why are they here?"

"They're here on behalf of their emperor father, who hungers for more power and destroys everything in his path to get it."

"Is that so? And what do you propose to do about it?"

"I will let nothing disrupt my plans. And if those two spies find out how close I am to seizing my treasure, I know they'll try to steal it."

Worry and doubt flooded his father's eyes. Magnus had never before seen such weakness in him, this man whose confidence was perpetually blinding, no matter what he was saying or doing.

The king had lofty goals to match his incessant greed and ruthlessness. He sought the Kindred, the four crystals that held the essence of *elementia*—elemental magic. They were lost a millennium ago, but any mortal who possessed them would become a god.

Magnus had seen magic side by side with death in the shadows of the Forbidden Mountains, and he knew with deep certainty the Kindred were real.

And they would be *his*, not his father's.

"Anyone who would dare try that would surely regret it, no matter who they are," Magnus said.

The king nodded, and the shadow of uncertainty faded. "The battle at the camp—I've been told you handled yourself well. Sometimes I forget how young you are."

Magnus bristled. "I'm eighteen."

"Eighteen is still very young. But you've grown so much this last year. I can't tell you how proud I am of all that you do, of all that you've had to endure and rise above. You are everything I ever dreamed you would be, my son."

There was a time when hearing such words from his father would have been like receiving a sip of water just before dying of thirst.

Now, after everything he'd learned, he knew this was only a manipulation uttered by the man Magnus hated more than anyone else in the world.

"Thank you, Father," he said tightly.

"I was disappointed to hear of my kingsliege's fate." Before Magnus could comment, the king continued. "But he was unskilled in battle. It's no surprise he fell so easily to a rebel's blade."

The image of Aron Lagaris's pale face and glossy, dead eyes flitted through Magnus's mind.

"He will be missed," he said evenly.

"Indeed."

The king stood up and descended the stairs to stand face-to-face with Magnus. Magnus fought back the urge to reach for his blade. He had to be calm.

"Melenia hasn't contacted me in weeks." The king's voice held frustration as he spoke of the mysterious immortal who allegedly advised him in his dreams. "I don't know what she's waiting for, and I need to know how to use Lucia's magic to light our path. After all this time, your sister can still barely control her *elementia* and I can find no one trustworthy enough to tutor her."

"Lucia's prophecy remains true. She is the one who will lead you to the Kindred, not Melenia. Lucia is the key to all of this and I will always have faith in her—more than anyone else."

His words stuck in his throat all the more because they were the truth.

He still believed in Lucia, even if she no longer believed in him.

The king clasped Magnus's shoulders. "Of course, you're right. Lucia will lead the way. It is my destiny to possess the Kindred's magic for myself."

No, Father, Magnus thought. My *destiny*.

"I'll keep an eye on the Kraeshians," he said. "If they show any sign of wanting what's ours, we can deal with them together."

The king nodded and pressed his hand against Magnus's scarred cheek, a smile lifting the corners of his mouth. "Yes. Together."

Magnus left the throne room. He walked swiftly down the hall until he reached a place where he could pause, unseen by his father, and will himself to stop shaking with anger. With frustration. The need to avenge his mother's murder and bring his father to justice crawled over his skin like ants.

The wine he'd had was no help at all; it had only blurred his vision and his mind.

He needed air. Badly.

He continued down the hallway until he found an exit to a large balcony overlooking the palace gardens. Illuminated only by moonlight, even he had to admit they were excruciatingly beautiful. The sweet scent of roses wafted up to where he stood on the balcony, about thirty feet above. His shoulders hunched, he clutched the cool marble banister and inhaled.

Suddenly, a small movement caught his eye. Down in the gardens, along the mosaic pathway winding its way through the lush area, he saw three figures: his adopted sister, Lucia, walking with the Kraeshian prince and princess.

He found he could not look away.

"Someone looks rather unhappy tonight."

The voice cut through his concentration and tightened the muscles in his back.

Without turning around, he said, "I thought I was alone out here."

"And yet, clearly, you're not."

"I would *like* to be alone out here."

"I'm sure you would. But I was here first. Actually, I was here for sixteen years before you arrived and murdered practically everyone I know and love, so I believe that definitely grants me the right to this particular balcony."

He turned to face the girl standing in the shadows and was shocked that he hadn't noticed her immediately. Known as the Golden Princess to the citizens of Auranos, Princess Cleiona's hair was so pale it nearly glowed beneath the moonlight. She had eyes of aquamarine, as vibrant as a lake's surface under a summer sky.

Perhaps he hadn't seen her because her dress was so dark: bluish, like the deepest shade of dusk in the moments just before nightfall.

Cleo emerged from her cloak of shadows and joined him at the balcony's edge. Following his gaze, her eyes locked on Lucia and the visiting prince and princess.

"I'm sure you'll be pleased to know that I've become rather well acquainted with Lucia in your absence," Cleo said.

"Have you, now."

"Yes. I might go so far as to call us friends. She's very special, your sister. I see why you love her so much."

Taken at face value, it was a cordial observation.

But taken another way . . .

Magnus knew that rumors about his unrequited desire for Lucia were circulating the palace. Servants always enjoyed gossiping about people of higher stations. And sometimes they gossiped *to* those of higher stations.

"I'm very pleased to see that Lucia has been up and around the palace during my absence," he said, ignoring Cleo's unspoken accusations. "Have you met Princess Amara yet?"

"Briefly," she said crisply and without warmth.

"Is she also to become one of your *friends*?"

Cleo's demure smile remained, but her eyes stayed cold. "I certainly hope so."

He couldn't help but be amused by this girl. Princess Cleiona Bellos was an incredibly deceptive creature.

But there was something besides lies and passive aggression in her expression tonight. He saw fresh pain there—an edge of it that she couldn't hide.

He waited for her to speak again.

Cleo returned her attention to the garden. "They buried Lord Aron today."

His mouth went dry. "I heard."

She played with a long tendril of her hair that had come loose from its pins. "I knew him all my life, through good times and bad. To know he's gone now . . ."

Her grief over the fallen boy was misplaced. Aron deserved

neither tears nor heartache from anyone, but Magnus understood grief. He'd felt it himself when his mother was killed. He still felt it, like a dark, bottomless hole in his chest.

Lord Aron had been betrothed to Cleo when, without warning, King Gaius changed their plans and bound Cleo to Magnus instead.

"How did he die?" she asked now, her voice soft.

"While battling the rebels who attacked the road camp we were inspecting."

"And a rebel killed Aron?"

"Yes."

Cleo turned and looked at him directly. "He died in battle. That sounds so . . . brave."

"Yes, it does."

"Aron was many things, but brave was never one of them." She turned away. "Perhaps I had him all wrong. If he was courageous in the end—"

"He wasn't." All the acidity Magnus had felt this evening poured out of him through those two words.

Cleo regarded him with shock.

"Apologies," he said, attempting to rein in the poison that threatened to leak from him in a horrible gush of truth. "Lord Aron acted in battle exactly according to his experience, which was lacking. He had no chance. I only regret that I wasn't able to save him."

Such lies. He wondered how she'd react if he told her the truth—that Aron was an insipid bootlicker, a pathetic wimp who'd sooner bow down before a conquering king and do whatever was asked of him without question than defend his or his people's honor.

Aron only got what was coming to him.

Cleo watched him now with a frown.

"This topic has upset you," she said.

Magnus turned toward the garden to shield his face from her. His sister and the Kraeshians were gone. "I feel nothing other than eagerness to end this conversation. Unless there's anything else you wish to know tonight?"

"Only the truth."

"Excuse me?"

"I feel that there's something you're holding back."

"Believe me, princess, even if I were, it's nothing you'd want to know."

She looked at him intently as he absently brushed his fingers against the scar that stretched from the top of his left cheek to the left corner of his mouth. He despised such close scrutiny.

There was a time when Lucia had been able to see through his masks, the invisible ones he'd perfected over the years to hide his emotions, to keep a necessary distance between himself and those around him. To appear as a younger version of his father. Now that his sister had lost that ability, he had the deeply unnerving sensation that Cleo had learned how to see past his masks as well.

"Tell me more about what happened in Paelsia," she urged.

He met her gaze again only to find that she'd drawn alarmingly closer to him. "Careful, princess. Remember what happened the last time we shared a balcony. You don't want that to happen again, do you?"

He expected to see disgust flash in her eyes at being reminded of their wedding tour, when they'd been forced to share a kiss in front of an eager, cheering crowd.

Their first kiss and, as he'd promised her at the time, their *last*.

"Good night, Prince Magnus."

Without another word and only a chill in her voice to indicate her reaction to the memory, Cleo turned and exited the balcony, leaving him alone in the darkness.

CHAPTER 3

LYSANDRA

AURANOS

Lysandra pounded on the bars of her cell until she finally earned the attention of a passing guard.

"When is Gregor coming back?" she demanded.

"What do you care? Mind your own business, girl. You might stay alive longer."

Why did she care? Because Gregor was her brother—something the guards didn't know. And because she loved him, and wanted him to be safe and strong so they could escape this overcrowded dungeon stinking of filth and death.

Gregor had been arrested after attempting to assassinate Prince Magnus in Limeros during his wedding tour. He'd claimed to have had contact with an immortal Watcher named Phaedra through his dreams—a confession that most would consider to be the ravings of a madman. But it seemed as though King Gaius didn't share that opinion. Gregor wouldn't have been spared execution for so long if the king didn't believe him valuable.

The guard still stood there, staring at Lysandra through the bars with growing interest.

She glared back at him. "What?"

"Pretty little girl, aren't you? Such prettiness in an ugly place like this."

"I'm not a little girl."

Keep looking at me like that, she thought, *and I will claw out your eyes.*

"You're a rebel." He squinted at her. "Not too many girls I know like to fight."

She wouldn't give him the satisfaction of a response, keeping her mouth shut until he left to speak to another guard. Their voices were low, but Lysandra watched as their expressions grew more smug and self-satisfied with every word.

Lit only by torches set into the hallway walls, the darkness of these sunken dungeons was oppressive. The metal bars were coated in slime, the walls caked with filth. The hard dirt floor spread with straw made for an uncomfortable bed during the few fleeting moments Lysandra had been able to sleep since her arrival. Echoing down the corridor were the horrible sounds of other prisoners, those who laughed at nothing, cried at everything, or talked to themselves like men and women who'd lost their minds long before their lives.

It was a nightmare.

But she would stay strong. She had no other choice.

The second guard looked over at her and nodded. "Very well. We need some entertainment today. Get her."

The first guard unlocked her cell and roughly dragged Lysandra out by her hair. Her first instinct was to fight, but she held back. This might be her chance to escape, and if so, she needed to pretend to be weak and docile. Locked behind the stone walls and iron bars she had no chance, but if he were to take her outside, she might be able to flee—although the thought of leaving without Gregor gutted her.

But he didn't take her outside. The guard led Lysandra down the dim and narrow corridor to another cell. He shoved her through the door and she fell to the floor hard enough to bruise her knees.

Though it was very dark, she knew someone else was in there.

The two guards stood on the other side of the iron bars, grinning. One threw something metallic into the cell and it landed a few paces away from her on the dirt floor.

A knife. She flicked her gaze up to the guard.

"You like to fight, rebel?" he asked. "Give us a show."

Suddenly, another prisoner came surging out of the darkness, rising to her feet and shoving Lysandra hard in her chest, causing her to stagger back into the wall. She was a girl, taller and more bulky than Lysandra, with a dirty face and matted hair. She snatched up the blade and stared at it for a moment with a wild look in her eyes.

"Go on, then," the guard urged. "Whoever wins gets to eat today. Let's see some blood."

The other girl's gaze snapped to Lysandra's. Then, with a cry, she charged at her, clutching the knife.

Lysandra was hungry and weak, but she hadn't lost her mind—not yet. She'd arrived here two days ago with three other rebels who'd survived the battle—Tarus, Cato, and Fabius.

She knew King Gaius had ordered them here to be publicly executed, to be made an example of. She didn't expect to be pardoned for her crimes. And she didn't expect anyone in shining armor to break in to rescue her.

But those had been her expectations her entire life. She was different from other girls who dreamed of strong husbands and a houseful of drooling babies. She'd been a warrior from the beginning. She would be a warrior till the end.

And that end was *not* going to be today.

She dodged the knife easily and shoved the girl away.

"What's your name?" Lysandra asked.

"My name?" the girl said, her gaze narrowing. "Why?"

"I'm Lysandra. Lysandra Barbas." Introductions could make friends of strangers, and this girl—she wasn't her enemy. They were both prisoners here; they had common ground.

"I don't care who you are." The girl lacked skill but was determined in her attempts to stab Lysandra.

"Need a little help, rebel?" The guard opened the door and shoved another prisoner in. He was short and skinny and wore a fearful expression.

Before Lysandra had a chance to say anything, the unmarked girl attacked and cut Tarus's arm.

Seeing the gash on his flesh was enough to incite Lysandra. She launched herself at the girl and punched her in the stomach, making her grunt with pain.

"Are you all right?" Lysandra barked at Tarus.

He clutched his injured arm. "Yeah. I think so. Be careful!"

The tip of the blade darted at Lysandra's chest. She dodged it, and this time she punched the girl right in her face. Blood trickled from her nose.

"Stop it," Lysandra hissed. "You're better than this! Don't give them the show they want. Don't let them win!"

The girl's eyes were red with tears of rage. "I haven't eaten in days!"

"Take her down," the guard snarled. "Kill her. I've put my silver on you, rebel. Don't make me a loser."

The girl continued to strike at them relentlessly until Lysandra finally knocked the blade out of her hand and grabbed it for herself. The girl fell hard to the ground and scrambled back into a corner, raising her hands to shield her face as Lysandra drew closer.

"Please! Please, no. Spare me. I'm sorry—I'm sorry!"

"Kill her!" the guard demanded.

Lysandra shot them a look of hatred. "No."

"She would have killed you."

"Perhaps. But she doesn't deserve to die just for trying to survive another day in this cesspit."

The guards stormed into the cell and disarmed Lysandra, then dragged her back to her original cell, throwing Tarus in with her.

"You can keep each other company while you wait for your turn to die."

In the darkness, Lysandra pressed herself up against the wall with Tarus next to her. He began to sob softly; she put an arm around his shoulders to pull him closer.

"I know this is hard," she whispered, "but I'll get us out of here. I promise I will."

"How?"

That was a very good question. "Working on it. Give me time."

"If Jonas can find us, he'll save us. I know it."

"Jonas is dead." The words tasted as bitter on her tongue as they felt in her heart, the cold, painful thought making her eyes sting with endless grief. "If he wasn't killed in the battle, he'd have been captured just like us and we would've seen him or heard about it."

Tarus's eyes hardened. "I don't believe it."

"I don't want to believe it either, but holding on to hope that he's going to find us . . ." She let out a shaky sigh. She wouldn't let herself believe in Jonas because she knew she couldn't handle the disappointment if he didn't show. No, she'd rely on herself only, just as she always had.

Silence fell upon them and remained until Gregor was finally brought back, staggering, into the cell. He fell to his knees and Lysandra rushed to his side, taking his face between her hands to make him look at her.

He was dazed, his face bruised and bloody.

Fury ripped through her at the sight of someone she loved so horribly abused.

"Damn it." She tore a piece of cloth from her shirt and tried to clean his wounds. "Damn them! I'll kill every last one of them!"

"It's all right, little Lys. It'll be over soon."

Tears began to stream from her eyes and she angrily swiped them away. "Don't say that! We're getting out of here and we'll leave this stinking place far behind us. We found each other again for a reason. We're not going to die here. Just tell them what they want to hear so they'll stop hurting you."

"There aren't enough truths in the world to get them to do that."

It pained her to hear the defeat in his voice. This was so unlike the brother she'd grown up with—her rock, someone who showed strength even during the hardest of times. She'd always envied him that, ashamed of her own weaknesses.

"What did they want today?" she asked.

"Same as every other time." He leaned against the stone wall. "The king wants to know what Phaedra told me about the Kindred. He asks me the same questions again and again, but my answers never satisfy him."

Not so long ago Lysandra wouldn't have hesitated to tell Gregor he was a fool to believe in immortal creatures from a different world or magic crystals. What a laugh.

But no one was laughing now.

"She'll visit me again," he whispered. "I know she will. And then she'll tell me what to do."

Lysandra lowered her voice. "Did you tell them what Phaedra said about the sorceress?"

It pained her even to say such a thing aloud, but it was what Gregor believed. Helping him hold on to his beliefs might give him the strength he needed to hold on to life.

He squeezed his eyes shut. "I tried to say as little as I could. I need to be patient. Phaedra will visit me again. She wouldn't abandon me like this."

If this Phaedra really existed, then Lysandra hated her for what she'd done to her brother. For what she'd said to him.

"When the sorceress's blood is spilled, they will finally rise. And the world will burn."

Who would rise? There was no such thing as magic, only foolish people who believed in foolish things to better explain what they didn't understand.

"So tell the king that—about this sorceress and her powerful blood," Lysandra whispered. "Let him scurry off to find some girl to blame! Get the attention off you."

"You'd wish something horrible like that on someone else?"

She flinched. Would she wish for something cold and brutal to happen to some innocent girl, all to save someone she loves?

She wasn't sure anymore.

Gregor touched his forehead, then brought his hand in front of his face and looked at the smear of crimson on his fingertips. "Blood is the key to all of this, little Lys. Remember that. Blood is life. Blood is magic."

"If you say so." She tried to keep her frustration out of her voice. Gregor had been through so much; she only wanted him to rest and regain his strength and his mind. "Do you know the identity of this sorceress your dream-girl told you about? Any idea at all?"

"No," he admitted. "But she exists."

Lysandra let out a shaky sigh. "That doesn't help us very much."

Tarus spoke up from the corner. "My grandmother once told me of a prophecy about a sorceress. One who can wield *elementia* more powerfully than anybody else. She's the one who can recover the Kindred."

"Your grandmother sounds like a great storyteller," Lysandra said.

Tarus shrugged. "Maybe it's not just a story. Maybe it's fate."

Paelsians might not believe in magic, but they did believe in fate. They believed in accepting the harsh realities of life in a land that was wasting away day by day—empty stomachs, dying children—as if such horrors could not be prevented.

Lysandra had never subscribed to such fatalistic beliefs. She knew there was only one person who could change your destiny, and that was yourself.

"Phaedra will visit me again. She'll tell me how to help her." Gregor's eyes shone with tears, then he squeezed them shut again. Lysandra's heart ached.

"Watchers visit mortals' dreams," said Tarus, getting Lysandra's attention. "Sometimes. Rarely—I mean, it doesn't happen a lot. But it's possible."

He must have seen the skepticism written all over her face. Still, Gregor seemed so certain. She couldn't just dismiss his words as the ramblings of an insane person. She might not believe in much, but she believed in her brother.

And all of this was clearly important to the king, which made it important to her as well.

"Why do you think it's possible?" she asked.

Tarus's expression grew pensive. "I met a witch once, an old friend of my grandmother's. She could light the fireplace just by staring at it."

Lysandra had heard similar accounts but had never witnessed anything like that for herself. "How old were you?"

"Five? Maybe six? But I know it happened."

Childhood memories wouldn't help them. They needed facts. They needed action, a plan of escape.

Her brother had fallen asleep. Perhaps he was dreaming of beautiful immortals, but she was left awake with a thousand questions and doubts.

"Forget about Watchers, Lys. Jonas will save us," Tarus whispered. "I know he will."

She wasn't so sure. But if there were any magic in this world for wishes, that was exactly what she'd wish for.

CHAPTER 4

CLEO

AURANOS

Cleo was regarded with uncertainty by the people who had lived in the palace before, when times were good, who hadn't given King Gaius reason to cast them out or kill their families. They remembered what it was like when King Corvin sat on the throne, a kind king who would never rule with an iron fist clenched around the throats of his subjects.

Cleo saw the confusion in their eyes, questioning how she could bear living on in her father's palace with a smile on her face only a few short months after his death. How she—a self-indulgent girl once known for her love of parties, friends, and wine—could be forced to wed the son of her enemy without constantly, desperately looking for a way to escape.

But these people had never really known Cleo. And they had no idea how far she would go to reclaim what had been stolen from her.

Some sought revenge against their mortal enemies with the edge of a sword. Her plan for vengeance began with the edge of a smile.

And if she was careful, no one, not even the man who'd crushed everything and everyone she loved into dust, would ever think of her as a true threat. .

She'd recently begun to believe that the handsome rebel who'd both kidnapped her and kissed her might be able to aid her. She hadn't seen Jonas in over two months, but she thought of him often and worried about his fate. She had no idea whether he lived or died.

But she knew she couldn't rely solely on him.

Cleo emerged from the palace and found Lucia in the palace garden. She forced herself to remain calm, to ignore her racing heart as she steeled herself and approached the other princess, who was cutting red roses from their stems and placing the blossoms in a basket.

What an ordinary pastime for a secret sorceress.

"Good day," Cleo said as she came up alongside her.

Lucia's shoulders stiffened, but she continued to pick her flowers. "Good day."

There was no friendliness in the greeting, which sent a whisper of worry through Cleo. They'd parted as friends only a few days ago, but, what with Magnus's return and the lavish victory banquet, Cleo hadn't had a chance to speak with her alone and solidify their bond since.

No matter. Cleo had decided. They would be the best of friends.

Cleo conjured up her natural talent for being social and charming—a skill she hadn't required in some time.

"Is there something you wish to say to me?" Lucia's tone was alarmingly suspicious.

This would not be easy.

But Cleo remained composed. "Only that I hope I've said nothing to offend you. I was under the impression that we'd grown close after . . . what happened the other day."

Lucia's expression darkened. "I don't want to talk about that."

"I understand how difficult it must be for you." *To wield elementia so powerful that you can kill a living creature,* Cleo thought.
"But I'm here for you. I know I can help you."

Lucia's eyes shone icy blue beneath her raised brows. "Do you
honestly believe *you* can help *me*?"

Oh, no. A short separation was all it had taken for Lucia to raise
up her walls against anyone who might potentially be untrust-
worthy. Cleo would have to work very hard to break them down,
stone by stone.

"I know what I saw," Cleo said gently. "And I helped you. Just
my presence was enough to help you contain your magic."

Lucia wouldn't look her in the eye. "I don't know what you're
talking about. You saw me with a dead rabbit, that's all. It means
nothing."

A dead rabbit frozen in the middle of a warm room by deadly water magic. That certainly meant *something* to Cleo. In fact, it
meant *everything* to her.

The pursuit of magic and the power it promised had become
the central purpose of her life.

"I said I wouldn't tell anyone and I haven't. We're sisters now,
Lucia."

"Sisters." Finally Lucia turned to face Cleo, her eyes flashing.
"Why? Because you're married to Magnus? You can barely look
at each other. You loathe him and he you—I don't care what you
would have others believe."

Venom rose in Cleo's throat at these poisonous words, no matter how true they were. She wanted to strike back with her own
poison, repeat the rumors she'd heard of Lucia and Magnus's in-
cestuous feelings for each other.

But she swallowed it all down instead.

She put on a mask of deep concern. "Is your magic troubling you again today?"

An edge of desperation flitted across Lucia's eyes.

"I feel . . ." Lucia's voice broke and she turned toward the rose-bush. "I hate this. I hate being here. I hate these flowers and these trees and all I want is to go home to Limeros."

But she wouldn't be of any use at all to Cleo in Limeros.

"Because you felt more under control there?" she asked.

"Hardly. But it—it's home." Lucia let out a nervous laugh that sounded more like a hiccup. But the lightness vanished as soon as it arrived, and she once again looked harshly at Cleo, a frown creasing her brow. "What do you want from me?"

"I want to be your friend."

"Why?"

Because I need your magic to destroy your father, she thought.

"Because in you I see someone who understands my world," she said. "You're the daughter of a king. Like me, you've had responsibilities and expectations thrust upon you your entire life. Very few understand how that feels. You do. And the other day I knew you needed me as much as I need you."

"You need to forget what you saw," Lucia whispered. "It's too dangerous."

A shiver coursed down Cleo's spine. This sounded much more like a pained warning than a threat. "Dangerous for you? Or for me?"

"For both of us." Something beyond Cleo caught Lucia's gaze, and her expression soured.

Cleo turned to see Princess Amara approaching along the winding cobblestone pathway as two Kraeshian guards in dark green uniforms hung back near the castle entrance.

Cleo couldn't be more annoyed. This uninvited guest was interrupting her precious private moment with Lucia. She'd only met Amara briefly at the banquet, but the girl hadn't made a good impression. She was too eager, too familiar in her greeting, and Cleo had instinctively recoiled from the girl.

Her brother Ashur had made a similar first impression on Cleo. Were they friends or foes?

"I've been looking everywhere for you two," Amara said brightly. "If I didn't know better, I'd say you were avoiding me."

"Certainly not," Lucia replied. The faint uncertainty in her tone had been replaced by a confident crispness. "It's a pleasure to see you again. Where is your brother?"

"Out exploring the area around the villa King Gaius is preparing for us." Amara sighed and glanced at the flowers. "Ashur loves exploring the countryside. Alone, no less. He refuses the company of guards."

"That sounds dangerous," Cleo said.

"It does, doesn't it? That's my brother. An adventure seeker at any cost. Cleo, we barely had the chance to speak last night before you disappeared. Were you unwell?"

"Yes," Cleo lied, happy to agree with this ready-made excuse. "My stomach couldn't handle another bite of food."

Amara raised her brow. "Are you with child?"

Cleo opened her mouth to immediately deny any possibility of this. Since, thankfully, it was absolutely *not* possible she was pregnant. She and Magnus had not . . .

Well, they *had not*. Nor would they ever. She shivered with disgust at the memory of standing so close to him on the balcony the previous night.

Loathing, as Lucia had said earlier, was a pale word to represent her feelings toward the prince. Every time she thought she might see something more in him, something pained and vulnerable that pulled at her, she had to stop and remind herself of the unspeakable things he'd done and why she would hate him forever.

"If I am with child," Cleo said as she brushed a hand over the folds of the pale blue gown that hid her flat belly, "it would be a very welcome surprise."

Amara's gaze grew sharper, as if she was assessing every inch of Cleo with much more scrutiny than she had last night.

"It's so wonderful that you're visiting," Cleo said, changing the subject. "My father extended an invitation to your family years ago."

"Auranos is very beautiful, but Father always believed that such beauty held no true value. I, however, completely disagree."

Cleo exchanged a glance with Lucia, who seemed mildly alarmed by Amara's candor. Cleo kept her mouth shut, the corners of her lips turned up into what she hoped was a pleasant expression.

"You must find life here so different from Limeros, Lucia," Amara said, reaching out to touch a rose, carefully avoiding its thorns.

"It couldn't be more different," Lucia agreed.

"All that ice and snow, all those jagged cliffs. It's much more pleasant here, isn't it? If I spent more than a half-day in frozen Limeros I might throw myself into the sea so I could drown and be free from such unthinkable conditions." She laughed, then realized that both Cleo and Lucia were gaping at her in shock. "Apologies. Kraeshians are known to speak their minds without hesitation. Don't hate me for being blunt."

"Of course not." Lucia offered a smile. "No apologies necessary. Such bluntness is . . . refreshing. Isn't it, Cleo?"

"Oh, yes," Cleo agreed. "So refreshing."

Amara considered Cleo closely. "I have to say, I'm surprised to see how well you've adjusted to your new life. I half-expected you to be confined to your chambers, allowed out only for meals. That the Damoras seem to trust you, their former enemy's daughter, fascinates me."

Amara might use the word *blunt*. Others would say *rude*.

Cleo struggled to find an appropriate reply. "My father was defeated because he wouldn't bow down and surrender to King Gaius. Such conflicts are common over the world, in many kingdoms. I can only be grateful that King Gaius didn't punish me for my father's choices, and that he's given me a home here with his family."

The words tasted rancid in her mouth.

"And you've accepted it? Accepted your new family?"

Family. The word made her soul cringe. "As best as I can."

"Cleo is a welcome addition. She's like a sister to me now," Lucia said.

While Cleo's throat burned from having to speak such lies, her heart was lightened to hear Lucia call her *sister*. The fact that Lucia was willing to come to her defense after all but ignoring her just minutes before proved that Princess Amara's admitted lack of tact might have the power to make friends of enemies.

"What a lovely sentiment, Lucia," Amara said, her gaze moving down to Cleo's hand. "What a lovely ring, Cleo. Wherever did you get it?"

Cleo resisted the urge to cover up the amethyst. "Thank you. It belonged to my mother."

"It's very beautiful." Amara's accented voice was even. "It's almost magical how beautiful it is, really. You've very lucky to have it."

Cleo's stomach began to tie itself in knots.

She'd been wearing the ring every day now, hidden in plain sight where it couldn't be lost. It didn't appear to be any more special than her turquoise necklace or golden bracelet, and yet Amara had noticed it specifically, calling it magical.

Prince Ashur had questioned Cleo once before about the legend of the Kindred. And now Amara was here, telling her that this kingdom had more value than her father had ever believed . . .

"If you'll excuse us, Princess Amara," Lucia said, linking her arm with Cleo's, "I'm afraid we're rather late for our next class. Our tutor will be very upset with us."

"You attend classes here together?" Amara said with raised brow.

"Oh, yes." Cleo was quick to back up Lucia's lie. "Today is embroidery. A very useful skill, but our tutor's surprisingly strict."

Cleo hadn't taken a class in any subject since before the palace was attacked. Back then, she thought her education nothing more than a waste of her time that could have been better spent with her friends, but now the thought of her old classes filled her with bittersweet memories of a happier time.

When all of this was over, once she'd finally reclaimed her throne, she would take many classes and learn everything about every subject possible.

Except, perhaps, embroidery.

"Then you'd better hurry. Farewell," Amara said. "I'll see you again soon."

"Yes. Very soon, I hope," Cleo said and smiled sweetly.

"I find her deeply unpleasant," Lucia said once they were out of earshot. "She's lucky I didn't set her hair on fire."

"You could do that?" Cleo said, alarmed and intrigued by Lucia's frankness.

"If I wanted to." Lucia glanced at her with the hint of a smile. "It's so strange to me . . ."

"What is?"

"Being near you is so calming. I thought it was only an illusion the other day, but now I know it's real."

"Don't you see?" Cleo squeezed Lucia's arm. "We were meant to be friends. Despite the difficulties we've had, this is right. Trust in that. Trust in me. I can help you with your magic."

"Perhaps," Lucia allowed, a light frown creasing her forehead.

Cleo's ring had taken on a slight glow from being so close to the sorceress. She repressed a smile.

Perhaps was a firm step in the right direction.

CHAPTER 5

MAGNUS

AURANOS

At the king's request, Magnus and a select group of guards had set out to escort the prince and princess of Kraeshia to a large villa an hour's journey northeast of the palace.

Rather than argue, he had instead grasped hold of the chance to leave the city and clear his head. The trip had been uneventful, surrounded as they were by a swarm of guards both Kraeshian and Limerian, including Cronus, the captain of the palace guard, who rarely strayed far from the king's side. That Cronus had been assigned to join the party today was proof that the king took at least some interest in Magnus's safety when he traveled beyond the city walls.

At last, they reached the villa.

"It's beautiful," Princess Amara said as she and her brother emerged from their carriage.

"Yes," Prince Ashur agreed, sweeping his gaze across the lush green hills the expansive villa was nestled within. "More than ad-equate. It was very generous of the king to give us such a beautiful place to stay."

Magnus nodded. "He'll be pleased that you like it."

His father disliked the Kraeshians, but so far Magnus had found them to be nothing more than an inconvenience, akin to persistent vermin that were immune to swatting. And his father refused to do anything more than swat at these pests, for fear that they'd alert their father and bring war down upon him.

It was unusual for King Gaius to fear anything. Yet ever since the royal wedding, where he'd nearly been killed by the earthquake, the king seemed to be increasingly fearful of his own mortality.

He should be.

Magnus dismounted from his black stallion and approached the large villa.

The front door swung open and a boy no older than five or six ran out along the pathway. Reaching Magnus, he staggered to a halt and looked up at the prince with wide eyes.

"You're Prince Magnus, aren't you?"

"I am."

"My mama has nightmares about you." His little fists were clenched at his sides. "I won't let you hurt her!"

Cronus stepped forward, but Magnus held up his hand to stop him.

"I assure you, young man," he said, crouching down in front of the boy so they were at eye level, "I mean your mother no harm. But I'm very pleased to see she's protected by such a fierce warrior."

A woman with a large belly hurried toward them and gathered the boy into her arms. Her face was pale and drawn—qualities that were now more common than ever since the king's victory.

"Apologies, your highness," the woman said nervously. "My son, he . . . he speaks without thinking. He meant no disrespect."

"None was taken." The child's words held no threat, only a mild sting that Magnus tried to ignore. The front door swung open again, and now a man exited the villa and joined the woman and boy. "And who are you?" Magnus asked.

The man put his arm around the woman and regarded Magnus warily. "I am Lord Landus. Apologies, Prince Magnus. We know we should have already departed, but we were delayed. My wife is with child and her mornings are currently wracked with ill-ness. I assure you, we're leaving now to make way for your"—his gaze moved to the Kraeshians and his jaw grew tense—"honored guests. Just as your father requested."

"This is your home?" Magnus was taken aback; he had thought this was an abandoned property. Now he realized that his father had simply cast out its residents, surely with threats of imprison-ment or worse. Why did this surprise him? The king had never ruled his people with the weight of a feather when a stone would suffice.

The man smiled, but it gave off anything but warmth. "It be-longs to King Gaius now. And to you."

"Then be on your way and don't waste anymore of the prince's time," Cronus said, approaching like a hulking shadow at Magnus's side.

"Of course." Fear flickered in the lord's eyes. "Farewell, your highness."

Magnus watched the three go on foot down the forest road. The little boy looked back at him over his mother's shoulder with confusion. He didn't understand why he had to leave his home, with no idea when, or if, he might be able to return.

They're Auranian, Magnus reminded himself when he found he couldn't turn away. *What do you care of their fate?*

"Hopefully they've remembered all their personal belongings and won't have to disturb us again," Princess Amara said as she stepped inside the foyer. She looked up at the stained-glass ceiling and chiseled, winding staircase with a growing smile. "Yes, this is quite acceptable. The king knows how to treat his valued guests. I'm going to explore."

Prince Ashur stopped and stood in the doorway. "You do that, sister."

Amara disappeared up the stairway, followed by her handmaiden.

"Apologies for my sister's rudeness," Prince Ashur said. "I'm not sure she understands what just happened."

"What's to understand?" Magnus asked, feigning friendliness. "You needed a place to stay, and this is that place."

"We would have been just fine at the palace. We don't want to be any trouble."

No, of course you don't want that.

Magnus turned to Cronus, who still stood at his side. "You'll wait outside with the others until I'm ready to leave. I won't be long."

Cronus bowed his head. "Yes, your highness."

Magnus and Ashur stepped into the foyer and closed the door behind them. Ashur barely spared a glance for the fine architecture, rich tapestries draped on the walls, and colorful mosaic tiled floor.

"Not to your liking?" Magnus asked.

"It's fine, of course," Ashur said, his attention obviously elsewhere. "I must say, I'm pleased we're finally getting a chance to speak privately."

"Are you?"

Ashur nodded. "I'm curious to learn more about Mytica. Given your recent travels, I knew you were the one I should speak with."

Small talk about geography? How incredibly dull. "What do you want to know?"

"I want you to tell me about the Kindred," he replied without hesitation.

The word landed like a blow. Magnus fought to appear impassive and give no sign that his heart had begun to beat rapidly. "My, that is a rather large subject to cover. But, unfortunately, it's also not a worthwhile one. Why would you be interested in the stuff of legends and storybooks?"

"Because I don't believe it's just a legend. I believe the Kindred do exist." Ashur looked at Magnus like a book he was trying to read.

This was what the king feared—outsiders going after his treasure.

Magnus's treasure.

"Is that why you're here?" Magnus asked. "To seek more information about the Kindred?"

"Yes," Ashur replied simply.

Kraeshians had no history of magic in their kingdom, nor did they typically have any cultural interest in such subjects. They were famous for preferring hard facts and common truths, and that the prince defied this trend proved he was either a bored royal with too much time on his hands . . . or a legitimate threat, just as the king suspected.

Magnus forced a smile. "Most . . . *intelligent* people think the story of the Watchers and their eternal search for the Kindred is one that's simply told to keep children well behaved and fearful that magical hawks are witnessing and judging their every naughty act."

"There's also the prophecy of a sorceress reborn whose magic will light the path to this source of ultimate power."

So, Lucia's prophecy was known beyond Mytican shores. Magnus's stomach sank at the thought, but he ignored the unpleasant sensation as best he could and held the prince's gaze without flinching. "I've also heard this rumor. In fact, there are a handful of accused witches in the dungeon as we speak. Perhaps you'd like to ask *them* if they're sorceresses?" He forced another smile. "Don't waste your time on such silly ideas, Prince Ashur. There are plenty of other attractions for you to explore before you set sail back to your home. I'd be happy to suggest several you might wish to see."

The steady, unwavering sharpness in the prince's gray-blue eyes unnerved Magnus more than he'd like to admit.

"Have you heard about the being of fire?" Ashur asked.

Magnus frowned at the sudden change the subject. "I'm not sure what you mean."

Ashur casually ran his hand along the base of the marble banister. "There was a young man seen summoning fire magic in the forest where the recent rebel battle took place. I believe there was a rather large wildfire during that attack, yes?"

"There was." Magnus felt no need to lie; Ashur could have learned this information from many different sources. "The fire killed many. I don't know how it started."

Ashur crossed his arms over his chest and leaned against the wall. "By all reports the flames were supernatural in origin—*elemental*, in fact. A touch of this fire could turn a man's flesh to crystal that could shatter with a single touch."

Magnus's gut twisted as he remembered the strange fire that had licked at his ankles as he emerged from the tent after Jonas

Agallon's escape. He'd seen its effects. He'd been having night-mares about it for days.

"How odd." Magnus shook his head. "But it sounds like all you've heard are peasants' rumors. The same goes for this . . . what did you call him? A *being* of fire?"

Ashur turned his attention to a mahogany table across the foyer carved with a fine pattern of flower petals. On top of it was a vase filled with fresh flowers, which Ashur now studied with a botanist's interest. "This person murdered a guard whose associate says they first thought the young man was an escaped slave. But then he noticed that the fire symbol had been burned into his hand, and that his eyes turned from amber to blue with a strange light. With a mere glance, he burned his victim to death with the crystallizing flame."

Magnus realized he'd stopped breathing. Amber was the crystal commonly associated with the fire Kindred. "What are you saying?"

Ashur spread his hands. "I'm not sure, really. I wanted your take. I thought you might know something." Ashur studied Magnus from head to toe, seemingly unimpressed. "I see I was wrong. Pity."

Magnus's hackles rose. "I would caution you not to take rumors or gossip as truth. Especially rumors and gossip repeated by someone as unreliable as a guard or a servant."

"I'm not surprised you say that, given a few other rumors I've heard around the palace." Ashur smiled, an exact replica of sincerity, which made Magnus envy his ability to pour on charm while speaking such unpleasant words. It reminded him of his father.

"Other rumors?" Magnus asked. "Such as?"

"Nothing worth mentioning."

Just then Amara descended the stairs, thankfully interrupting them. "Are you two going to stay down here all day? Or will you explore with me?"

"Exploring sounds like an excellent idea," Magnus said, offering her his arm as she reached the last step. He felt the irresistible need to put an end to his conversation with the prince. "Let's take a look at the gardens. I've been told they rival the beauty of the palace's."

"Yes, let's. Ashur?"

The prince waved. "Go on ahead. I'll join you shortly."

With Princess Amara's handmaiden trailing a discreet distance behind them, Magnus and Amara went outside to the gardens, which were as beautiful as rumor had promised.

It was obvious that this was not merely a grand home that had been built for nobles. This was a home filled with love—love that had been lavished on every inch, every piece of furniture, every colorful tile or marble surface. The private gardens were vast, ending at a stone wall two hundred paces from the villa. Every color of the rainbow was accounted for in the roses, violets, hydrangeas; the apple, pear, and olive trees. It smelled like life itself out here— sweet and vibrant.

After a moment, however, the sweetness faded and was replaced by a more unpleasant scent. Not yet offensive, but somewhat . . . wrong. Perhaps it was only Magnus's imagination.

But he thought he smelled the acrid scent of something stolen. Much like everything the king claimed as his.

"Oh, it's beautiful," Amara gushed. "I only wish that it was closer to the palace."

As stunning as the villa was, the king didn't choose it for its beauty. He wanted to keep the Kraeshians at a safe distance.

"Transportation will be provided for you and your guards so you can visit as often as you wish. You and your brother are welcome at any time."

Amara was much more welcome than Ashur, in Magnus's opinion. Despite his father's suspicions about the prince's motives, Ashur's questions had blindsided Magnus. They had pulled him back to that deadly battle against the rebels and Jonas Agallon himself. He remembered the strange fire, and the beautiful Watcher who'd perished in a flash of light at Xanthus's hands, but not before she'd told Magnus how to help Lucia:

"There is a ring that was forged in the Sanctuary from the purest magic to help the original sorceress control the Kindred and her own elementia. *This ring is closer that you might expect."*

Perhaps she had only been playing with him, distracting him to allow Jonas the chance to escape.

And now to hear rumors of a being of fire roaming the countryside . . .

"Your grace." Amara touched his arm. "Are you still with me?"

Magnus tried to push the cobwebs from his head and focus on the girl before him. "Apologies. I don't mean to be rude. I was just thinking of your brother. He's very curious about local legends."

She groaned. "He's going on about the Kindred again, isn't he? It's been a hobby of his for years, learning all about magic. I've always thought it was a waste of valuable time." She raised an eyebrow. "Unless, of course, it turns out to be true."

"I hope he's not too disappointed when his quest turns up nothing but rocks and dirt."

"As most quests do." She laughed, gently placing her hand on his arm as they strolled. "I find you very interesting. I see why Cleo is so taken with you."

He stopped in his tracks. "You think she is?"

"Of course. To be married to such a strong and handsome prince . . ." She cast a sidelong look at him through her thick black lashes. "I can't help but envy her."

Magnus wasn't accustomed to the way Amara flirted. He'd found that some girls showed interest by keeping their distance, giggling with their friends as he passed by in the palace halls. He'd encountered a handful of others who had been bold and fearless in their approaches, hoping to gain his attention. But most girls would simply cast fearful glances at him, assuming he was as cruel and cold as his father.

He couldn't help but be slightly intrigued by the sly look in Amara's eyes. She played at being coy, but she was just the opposite.

"Are you not betrothed yet?" he asked as they continued along a garden path flanked by flowers and manicured foliage. A brown rabbit hopped across in front of them, seemingly unconcerned by their presence.

"No. I've asked to wait until I find someone to my liking. No one in my family has ever waited as long as I have to wed. Well, no one except Ashur."

"He's not been betrothed?"

"He has. Three times. Each engagement ended for the same reason: He eventually decided he wasn't interested enough in any of the girls to spend the rest of his life with them." She shook her head, clearly amused by her brother's romantic antics. "He is the youngest son, so my father has allowed him the kind of freedom he never would have allowed my older brothers."

As firstborn and heir, Magnus never expected to be given such freedom, even if he'd been born to a different father. It was impossible even to imagine what it would be like to lead such an unsupervised life. "Perhaps it's best to wait for the right person rather than agree to an arranged marriage, if one has the choice."

"Do you really believe that?"

"I believe only in duty and loyalty to the throne." And that throne would be his one day soon.

Amara turned to him, boldly placing her hand flat upon his chest. He looked down with surprise but didn't step away. "Do you believe in the idea that two people could feel such instant attraction the moment they first meet that it's impossible to ignore? That something intangible happens that binds them together— like they're soul mates?"

Most girls liked to muse about such silly, irrelevant things as love at first sight and hearts ablaze with passion. Quite honestly, Magnus could not think of a single subject he was less interested in exploring, even with a girl as beautiful as Amara.

"I suppose it's possible," he lied. "But I don't—"

Before he could finish, Amara pulled his face to hers and kissed him. It happened so quickly that if she'd had a knife, she could have slain him right where he stood without a fight.

Her lips were soft yet demanding, and she smelled of jasmine and peach blossoms.

Finally, she drew back from him, her gaze now fixed on the ground. "Apologies. I couldn't help myself."

He grappled for a response. "Don't apologize."

"I'd hate for Cleo to find out." She furrowed her brow slightly. "I'd hoped she and I could become good friends. The last thing I'd want to do is to make her jealous."

As if that were even possible. "Let's not speak of it again."

"Not unless you *want* to speak of this again." She paused. "I must admit, I would welcome that conversation."

She was surprising in so many ways, the bold and unexpected

kiss being only the most recent. He wasn't sure what to make of her—was she a princess out for fun and scandal, or was she more ambitious and strategic? Whichever it was, it did feel as if a game had begun between them, and Amara had made the first move.

Amara turned to her handmaiden. "Let's go back inside and ensure the trunks are being placed in the correct rooms, shall we?"

The handmaiden curtsyed. "Yes, princess."

Magnus watched the two girls walk back to the villa. Just before they passed the threshold, out came Prince Ashur, making his way down the garden pathway with a smug look on his face.

"My sister is quite a handful, isn't she?" he said.

That was an understatement, but Magnus was accustomed to dealing with complicated princesses. "She certainly strikes me as a girl who likes to forge her own path."

"Indeed."

"It's time for me to return to the palace. I hope that you have everything you need here."

"Everything except the answers I seek," Ashur said. "Perhaps you can be more accommodating to me another day."

"Perhaps." Magnus turned to go, but stopped himself. "I almost forgot something."

"What's that?"

He reached into the inner pocket of his jacket, pulled out a tightly wrapped package, then unfolded the cloth to reveal a small golden dagger.

Ashur blinked.

"Princess Cleiona offers much gratitude for your wedding gift of this Kraeshian bridal dagger, but she has asked me to return it at my earliest convenience. It's such a pretty present, but it could easily injure someone by accident. We wouldn't want that, would we?"

Ashur took the blade and dared to meet Magnus's gaze. "No, we wouldn't."

"I'll see you again soon," Magnus said, turning away for good now. "I hope you continue to enjoy your stay in my father's little kingdom."

The Kraeshians weren't the only ones capable of playing games.

CHAPTER 6

LUCIA

AURANOS

The walls were closing in on her.

For far too long, Lucia had been cooped up inside the palace. Her father's concern over her health had kept her from being able to freely roam around outside. She'd tolerated the king's overprotective nature, knowing he kept her confined only because he loved her, but as the weeks passed, her desire for freedom had grown.

It was now too strong to ignore. She had to make a stand today, to demand permission to seek fresh air beyond the palace courtyard, to explore the kingdom she had helped to conquer. And she wouldn't allow anyone—not even the king—to control her.

She prayed to the goddess Valoria for the strength and wisdom she needed, then left her chambers, confident in her quest.

Just the thought of breaking free breathed new life into her as she made her way to the throne room, where a council meeting was just letting out. She stood and waited as members of her father's trusted circle brushed past her at the entryway.

"So pleased you're feeling better, princess," one bald, squat man said with a curt nod in her direction.

"Thank you," she murmured.

Magnus was there among the councilmen, but he offered her no greeting, friendly or otherwise, as he slipped from the room like a shadow. Aside from the pleasantries they muttered during formal gatherings to keep up appearances, all of their interactions had been just as cold recently.

It wasn't his fault that their relationship had soured—not entirely. The thought of their broken bond made her heart ache.

Once the last of the councilmen had departed, her father greeted her. "Lucia. It's wonderful to see you, my dear."

She'd practiced the words on her way through the still-unfamiliar corridors. Now all she had to do was say them.

"I'd like permission to leave the palace today," she said, rushing to speak before she had the chance to doubt herself.

He raised his dark brow. "Would you, now."

"I know you don't think it's safe, but I disagree. The city is walled and well secured. I'll take several guards with me. But I—I can't tell you how much I need to get out of here and breathe some fresh air. To see something new. Even the courtyard and gardens are oppressive to me now. I feel like a prisoner here."

"Of course you're not a prisoner, Lucia." The king drew closer, his expression one of genuine concern. "You think I'd deny you this request?"

"I don't know. I know you worry about my safety."

He touched her cheek, a smile playing over the thin line of his mouth. "I've seen what you can do. I have no doubt you would be able to protect yourself if you were ever threatened."

Her heart leapt. "Then you're giving your permission."

"And if I say no?"

A spark of anger ignited within her. "But why would you? I've done everything you've asked of me. Everything! You yourself said I can protect myself. And I can! I ask for one little thing in all these months and you would deny me—"

"Lucia," he said, cutting her off. "I was merely asking rhetorically to see if you'd be willing to fight for what you want. I see now that you are, and that you came here knowing you would accept only one response from me. Good. I like to see that fire in you, that strength. If ever anyone tries to deny you something you want, then you just take it, no matter who they are. Is that clear?"

Lucia relaxed. The king was only imparting a lesson, one that she received happily. "Yes, Father."

"However, I do suggest you consult a knowledgeable guide so as not to waste your valuable time on mediocre sites."

She nodded eagerly, her heart thudding with anticipation. "I will."

"Good." He went to the long council table, glancing at the parchment and letters and formal documents still strewn on its surface from the meeting, then returned his attention back to Lucia. "Tell me, though—how is your magic coming along? Your control?"

The king asked her the same questions every day. He knew how much her abilities had troubled her in the past and had tried to find tutors to help her—so far to no avail. Her magic was more powerful than anything her tutors had encountered before. "Better, I think. I work on it every day." *On trying to repress it, to keep it from killing anyone else*, she thought. "I try my best."

"Of course. I expect no less. One day, very soon I hope, I will need to call upon your gift again to help me." He nodded. "Now. Go enjoy your day in the city and the sun on your face. I will see you back for dinner."

"Thank you, Father."

Just when she had written him off as strict and cruel and oppressive, he showed that he could be the opposite. The way he had just looked at her, the same way he had ever since her first show of *elementia*, with pride and admiration and love . . .

It started to thaw the ice that had begun to settle in her heart.

The king had been unquestionably harsh with Magnus over the years, to ensure his son would grow up a strong and worthy heir. But he'd been nothing but kind and patient with Lucia.

She wanted so desperately to believe he loved her as if she were of his blood.

But you're not, a small voice reminded her. *He stole you from your true mother because of the prophecy. Because he wanted your magic for himself and no one else.*

Despite that constant reminder in the back of her head, the king was her most constant supporter. Even in her most challenging moments, when she'd had no one else to turn to, he'd always assured her that she was a good person, that her powers weren't evil or malicious or dark or hateful. They were good.

She was Princess Lucia Eva Damora, daughter of King Gaius, in every way that counted.

And today she had his permission to leave the palace.

The king had told her to consult a guide who was familiar with the city. But he never specified who this guide should be.

"Apologies, Princess Lucia, but *she* is not allowed past the palace gates without the king's permission."

Lucia looked from the guard to Cleo, who stood next to her, exasperated.

"It's all right," Cleo said. "I'll stay here. I don't want any trouble."

Lucia was still uncertain about Cleo, but if there was anyone who knew this city well, it was her. And if there was anyone besides Lucia who knew what it felt to be trapped inside the palace all day and night, it was Cleo as well.

She turned now to the guard with what she hoped was her iciest glare. "I have my father's permission to leave the palace and I'm taking my brother's wife with me. Let us pass, or I won't be pleased."

"But, princess—"

She raised her hand, silencing him. "You do know how much my father adores me?"

"Of course, your highness. But I have my orders. You must understand."

"I understand perfectly. You see Princess Cleiona as the daughter of the former king. But in fact she is my sister-in-law and she will be your future queen when my brother takes the throne. Therefore, you will treat her with respect. And you will step aside and let us pass while I still have some patience intact."

As the king said, if someone denies her something, then she should just take it, no matter who they are.

She couldn't agree more.

Lucia watched the guard's face scrunch up as he fought an inner battle. Finally, he bowed. "As you command, your highness."

The guards opened the gates, letting Lucia and Cleo—and the four guards attending them—into the City of Gold. Lucia took a deep breath, relishing the moment.

It was like entering a dream.

The day was hot, the sky blue and cloudless. The sun shone bright upon their faces as it transformed the road before them into a glittering ribbon of gold that weaved throughout the city. Only the most privileged and important citizens in Auranos had the honor of calling this area home. The villas were mostly found south of the palace; the shops and industrial center to the north. Encircling it all like an enormous jeweled crown was a tall golden wall monitored day and night by sentinels.

There was no palace city like this in Limeros. There, the royal castle was perched upon the edge of an icy cliff, private and se-cluded. Dotting the landscape were villas owned by nobles and small villages. The Temple of Valoria and the capital city of Raven-crest were each a half day's journey away.

Nothing in Limeros was as convenient as it was here in the south. Anything an Auranian could ever want was readily avail-able within a short stroll of the palace.

"It's so strange," said Cleo as she hurried to keep pace with Lucia's longer strides.

"What?"

"The city has barely changed. I don't know why I expected it to look different—I did see glimpses of it as I left for the wedding tour—but it appears to be exactly the same as it ever was."

Lucia considered this. A new king in power, vastly different from the one he replaced, and yet, through the eyes of a lifelong citizen, daily life appeared to be unchanged. She was surprised that her father hadn't made more adjustments to this frivolous and he-donistic place. The excess of it all seemed distasteful to her—gold and silver and glittering jewels on the throats of seemingly every citizen, gold in the streets themselves, shining under the sunlight.

Limeros wasn't poor like Paelsia was, but Limerians thought it unacceptable to flaunt their wealth as Auranians did. She found the culture here vaguely sickening, but after all she'd heard of this place, it wasn't completely unexpected.

"True change will take time," Lucia finally replied.

"Of course, you're right," Cleo said quietly.

Perhaps that wasn't the comforting response Cleo had sought.

They walked on, drawing the attention of the people they passed. Some pointed and whispered, seeming pleased and even elated, unable to keep their eyes off of Cleo, who returned their waves and smiles without hesitation.

Yet their expressions changed upon seeing Lucia. Many didn't recognize her, but the few who did knew she was the daughter of the king. These were the faces that shifted from happiness to wariness and caution. To fear.

Or perhaps that was only Lucia's imagination.

Everywhere they roamed there was something new and beautiful to feast their eyes upon, and Cleo kept up rapid and entertaining commentary on everything they passed—taverns, shops, parks, gardens. One particular garden reminded Lucia of the labyrinth back in Limeros that a lord had commissioned for her one year as a birthday present. Only this garden was green and lush, not white and icy like her maze. Birds of all colors flew through the air, perching in gigantic fruit trees and dramatic weeping willows. Butterflies flitted on the breeze.

It was all so beautiful.

But it wasn't home.

"Cleo!" a voice cried. Lucia turned to see three unfamiliar girls running toward them. The guards stiffened, but Lucia cautioned them to stand down. As the girls came closer, Lucia regarded the girls with curiosity.

One, a blonde with a foxlike face, embraced Cleo immediately. "I never thought I'd ever be close enough to hug you again! You look wonderful!"

"Thank you," Cleo said, smiling at the trio.

"Your sister . . ." said a dark-haired girl wearing round-rimmed glasses, her eyes welling with tears. "I'm so sorry about Emilia. And your father . . . oh, Cleo. It's all so horrible!"

The third girl, who had dark brown hair and a face full of freckles, stepped in front of her friend. "Yes, it is horrible. I didn't think they'd ever let you out of that castle, you poor thing! There are rumors that the prince keeps you in a tower under lock and key!"

"Oh, how absurd. I'm fine. All is well." But there was something catching at Cleo's voice. "And much gratitude, Maria, for your condolences. I miss my family more than I can ever express." She smiled tightly and hooked her arm through Lucia's. "Girls, I'd like you to meet Princess Lucia Damora. Lucia, this is Dana, Ada, and Maria, three of my oldest friends."

The girls eyed one another with alarm before curtsying.

Lucia made sure not to show it, but this made her feel exceedingly uncomfortable. She was an outsider, an uninvited guest who ruined the party for the inner circle.

Well, that was just too bad, wasn't it? Her father owned this city now. This entire kingdom, in fact. And everyone in it.

They should learn to be more respectful.

"It's an honor, your highness," Ada, the freckled one, said, curtsying again. "I hope we haven't offended you."

"Not at all," Lucia replied.

That was a lie, of course. No matter how much her father believed he had these people under his thumb, she knew they wouldn't easily forget what had happened. And it was not known by many, but Lucia had played a crucial role in the takeover. She had used her *elementia* to break through the magical warding on the palace doors she and Cleo had just walked through.

That moment had changed everything.

Would she have done as her father asked if she could have predicted the results?

If she hadn't, her father would surely have been defeated. He and Magnus would undoubtedly have been killed. She would have lost so much.

Yes, she thought. She would do it again if she had to, if it meant saving the people she loved.

And, frankly, girls such as Cleo's friends were lucky to be alive. They should be thanking her.

"It was wonderful seeing you all," Cleo said hurriedly, clearly just as eager as Lucia was to end this little gathering. "Hopefully I'll see you again soon."

The girls murmured farewells as Cleo and Lucia walked past them. Lucia kept her proud stare on their wary glances until they each looked away, lowering their eyes to the ground.

That's better.

"Apologies if they seemed rude," Cleo said. "They're just a small part of the group I used to socialize with. Perhaps they're confused and hurt because they haven't received an invitation to the palace in so long."

Nor will they ever again, Lucia thought. "Are you very close with them?"

"Can we ever really have friends outside the palace we can truly trust?"

No. They couldn't. Lucia hadn't had many female friends in Limeros, as her father had kept her sheltered from petty socializing. Instead, she formed bonds with her tutors, as well as a few potential suitors from noble families she'd met at banquets and formal events. And, of course, Magnus.

A lump formed in Lucia's throat. She used to consider Magnus not only her older brother, but her dearest friend. The cold way he treated her now pained her deeply.

But she couldn't love him the way he wanted her to. And everything she'd done or said since his confession had only damaged their relationship more.

"Lucia?" Cleo squeezed her arm. "It feels like you're a thousand miles away. Are you feeling all right?"

Somehow the princess's touch helped chase the darkness away. "I'm fine. The heat, though. It's rather oppressive, isn't it?"

"It is quite warm today. Let's stop for a while." Cleo smiled. "I know the perfect place to rest."

She led the way down a narrow cobblestone street filled with shops, then turned along an alley. It led them away from the business area and toward a tree-lined clearing. The grassy field was the size of the palace courtyard, at least a hundred paces in diameter, around which were arranged benches shaded by tall, leafy trees.

"My friends and I used to come here often," Cleo explained. "Quite excellent entertainment, I must say."

All around the clearing, at least two dozen handsome young men practiced swordsmanship with wooden blades. Roped off to the side was another area where they wrestled hand to hand. Most were laughing, their faces dirty, as they flexed their muscles and darted around one another.

"They're not wearing shirts," Lucia observed with surprise.

Cleo grinned at her. "No, they aren't."

Lucia didn't know of anything like this in Limeros.

"Should we be watching this?" she asked.

"Why not? Trust me, they like to be watched. It'll make them fight harder."

Around the circumference of the field small crowds looked on with great interest.

"Guard! Fetch us something cool to drink," Cleo said. "There's a tavern at the end of the lane that stocks the strawberry wine I like."

The guard looked to Lucia, who nodded with approval. Strawberry wine sounded like an excellent idea. "Go ahead."

"Yes, your highness," the guard said, then hurried off.

"So, what do you think?" Cleo asked.

Lucia followed Cleo's lead and took a seat at the edge of the field beneath a tall oak tree and took in the activities before her. The thought of her father's disapproval of all of this amused her. This was an unnecessary display, nothing more than an excuse to show off, and Limerians had always frowned upon vanity. "They seem rather good."

Cleo nodded. "I'm happy to see this practice has continued on. It used to be that off-duty Auranian guards would teach local boys these skills. Now it seems as if the boys are teaching themselves."

"Auranian boys learning battle skills. For what purpose?" Lucia asked, skeptical. "To mount a rebellion against my father?"

Cleo laughed lightly and Lucia eyed her, uncertain what had been so funny. "No, believe me, this is just for fun. I've known boys like these all my life. Beyond little tournaments to draw the attentions of pretty girls, they aren't interested in battle. Besides, if the king saw this as a threat, I have no doubt he'd put a stop to it."

This was true. And Lucia had to admit, the display before her was certainly . . . entertaining.

Still, even now, amidst the sunshine and greenery and handsome young men, Lucia felt the darkness of her magic stirring within her. It was always with her, ever present, but when she was with Cleo it didn't torment her as much as it did when she was alone.

Elemental magic should be natural and beautiful, like life itself. But whenever Lucia let it take over, it seemed to lead only to pain and death.

And part of her, a very small part, didn't mind this at all.

The thought made her tremble.

Cleo reached over and squeezed her hand, the warmth of her skin sinking into Lucia's cool flesh. Immediately, her dark thoughts vanished, as if by magic itself.

She glanced up at the sky, shielding her eyes. A golden hawk flew high above, and her heart jumped at the sight. She'd seen many hawks over the last few weeks. Every one of them gave her a gift of hope, which would then slip away through her fingers like sand.

"You seem so sad today," Cleo said. "Tell me what's troubling you."

Lucia laughed quietly at Cleo's continued attempts to be friends with her. "You wouldn't believe me if I told you."

"Try me."

"Do you think Magnus would approve of you coming here to look at these shirtless boys?" Lucia asked wryly, attempting to change the subject and regain control.

A shadow passed behind Cleo's blue-green eyes. "You'd have to ask Magnus."

That would require Lucia to track him down and talk to him, something he would likely avoid at all costs.

"Do you feel anything at all for him?" Lucia asked.

Cleo paused. "It was an arranged marriage, Lucia. I didn't choose him, nor did he choose me."

"If I were you, I'd hate him." Her words came out more bluntly, and were more truthful, than she'd wanted them to be. Perhaps it was a sign she'd grown more comfortable around Cleo after all. "I'd hate all of us. My hate would burn brighter every day I was forced to sit next to my enemies." Her throat felt tight and strained. "You must understand why I'm guarded around you. I have no real reason to trust that your intentions are for friendship rather than revenge."

"You're absolutely right. You don't." Cleo's eyes glistened and she squeezed them shut. "But what choice do I have but to accept what's happened and try to make the best of it?"

That felt honest to Lucia. Cleo hadn't tried to deny her suspicions, but did Lucia blame her for feeling and acting this way? Did she really think Cleo was anything other than a lost girl searching for some kind of connection, even with those who'd stolen so much from her?

The question was, could she be a friend? A *true* friend Lucia could trust with her deepest, darkest secrets?

Lucia bit her bottom lip and focused on the boys in front of her, but eventually her gaze drifted back up to the hawk circling in the sky.

"Have you ever been in love?" she asked.

"Yes," Cleo said after a moment, softly.

"Where is he now?"

"Dead."

Dozens of questions rose up inside Lucia. *Dead?* How? An accident? In battle? Was it Lord Aron she spoke of, or someone else?

She waited for the heart-wrenching story to come pouring

out, but Cleo said nothing further about it. In the silence, Lucia felt the overwhelming urge to share her own loss with someone who might understand.

"In my life, I've only truly loved one boy." Lucia shook her head, nearly amused. *Boy* seemed such a trivial description for him. "Do you . . . believe in Watchers?"

"Yes."

So many people would scoff at such things, but Cleo's quick, definitive answer and calm expression held the same gravity that Lucia felt in her heart.

She'd told no one this before. No one.

And now the words surged forth before she could stop them.

"When I was trapped in sleep, a Watcher named Alexius visited my dreams. He was the most beautiful boy I'd ever seen. He promised to visit me again after I woke, but I haven't seen him since. And now . . . now I'm not sure if he was ever real to begin with."

It wasn't until she felt the dampness on her cheeks that she realized she was crying. As she remembered the last time she'd seen him, the kiss they'd shared, pain wrenched through her heart, and the heavy darkness within her grew.

Just then, lightning crackled above the field as dark storm clouds gathered, blocking the sun. Thunder rolled, and the rain began to pour. The boys looked up with surprise, their hair and clothes drenched in seconds.

"Princess, we must go now," a guard urged.

Lucia looked up at the clouds with surprise. Auranos rarely experienced anything but perfect, temperate weather.

"Did you do that?" Cleo whispered.

"I don't know." Her *elementia* gave her the power to do so many incredible things—both wonderful and fearsome—but to control weather itself . . .

The thought was just as frightening as it was exciting.

Cleo linked her arm with Lucia's as they stood up together. "I know what it's like to love someone different from you. Someone others might look down upon or deny you. It causes more pain than happiness, especially if the one you love is stolen from you too soon."

"Yes," Lucia whispered.

"Before my father died, he told me to believe in magic. And that's what I do. I believe in things other people think are impossible, and it makes me strong enough to face whatever comes next. I believe that your Alexius is real and that right this moment he's thinking about how much he misses you."

Lucia couldn't deny it. Cleo was getting to her, breaking through that dark wall that surrounded her.

Believe in magic. Believe in the impossible.

Believe, tentatively, in this fragile new friendship with Cleo.

And believe that one day she'd see Alexius again.

CHAPTER 7

ALEXIUS

THE SANCTUARY

In the two thousand years Alexius had existed, he'd never wanted anything as much as this.

He lay back in the grass of his favorite meadow with his eyes closed and reached out through the darkness, searching for her.

Where are you?

No answer. He tried until his head ached, until his body felt weak. Until he was so frustrated he could scream. But once again it didn't work.

The princess was lost to him—out somewhere in the mortal world, alone with no one to guide or protect her.

The thought made him laugh, and the sound rumbled deep in his chest.

Protect her.

"Alexius."

He jumped to his feet at the sound of Timotheus's voice.

"Greetings," he managed to say through his hoarse throat. He hadn't spoken aloud all day.

Timotheus, Alexius's friend and mentor, as well as one of the Three that made up the council of elders, regarded Alexius with his arms crossed and patience in his golden eyes. "Am I interrupting your daily meditation? Or were you attempting to dreamwalk?"

"Neither," he lied. "I was only resting." To admit he was trying to visit the dreams of a mortal would only spark additional questions. Questions he couldn't answer.

"There's something different about you," Timotheus said, walking a slow circle around Alexius as he studied his tall, lean frame. "I've noticed for many months now, ever since you began spending so much time with Melenia."

"I don't know what you mean."

"Be wary of her."

A bolt of worry struck Alexius, and he fought to hide it from his face. "I'm wary of everyone here in the Sanctuary."

"That makes you wise."

"Are you just out for a stroll? Or did you come here looking for me?"

"Neither. I'm looking for Phaedra. She's still missing."

To hear the name of his dearest friend was an unexpected blow. "I know."

"Do you know where she disappeared to?"

"No."

Timotheus didn't break eye contact. Despite their centuries of friendship, despite all the guidance and knowledge the elder had shared, Alexius still had secrets he needed to keep from him.

Horrible secrets.

"I believe Melenia has something to do with her disappearance," Timotheus said. "You might ask her about it the next time you see her, which I presume will be today?"

Alexius chose not to confirm this. "I'll be sure to ask her the next time I see her."

Rumors had begun to spread across the Crystal City that he was their fair leader's newest lover, a designation that drew stares of envy and jealousy from his fellow immortals everywhere he went.

But that rumor couldn't be further from the truth.

"I should be leaving now." Alexius tensed up as Timotheus clasped his shoulder, concern clouding his eternally youthful face.

"Alexius, you can trust me with any secret. Just as you always have. I hope you know that. If there is anything you need to tell me, don't hesitate."

Alexius smiled and nodded, wishing it were that simple.

He needed to know what had happened to Phaedra. The question ate away at him anew as he journeyed to the top of the crystal palace to meet Melenia. The beautiful Watcher greeted him with a smile, opening her golden doors wide to allow him entry into her chambers, which were full of light and the beautiful flowers that were picked daily by her obedient minions.

"You're early," she said, kissing him on both cheeks before she closed the doors. Her long, flowing, flaxen hair smelled like warm saffron and reflected the light from the floor-to-ceiling window that looked out on the rest of the city where the immortals made their home.

He hadn't taken more than a step inside the room before he brought up the troubling subject. "I need to know about Phaedra."

"She has disappeared."

"I know that much. Is she still alive?"

Melenia blinked once. "My goodness, Alexius. What is the

meaning of this? You don't think I had something to do with her disappearance, do you?"

He summoned all the courage he could. "Yes. As a matter of fact, I do. I know you thought she was a problem, that she knew too much and was dangerously close to learning more."

"And for this offense you think I . . . what? Murdered her?" She smiled sweetly. "I assure you, I haven't touched a single hair on her head."

"But you know what happened to her."

"Come and sit. We have much to discuss today. Unfortunately, it will have to wait until I finish with my other visitor."

"Other visitor?"

There was a knock at the door. "Yes. Danaus desperately wanted to speak with me today."

Danaus, the final member of the Three, was a vastly unpleasant immortal whom Alexius habitually avoided. "Don't let him in."

"Don't be silly. Actually, I need him today."

With a clenched jaw, Alexius watched as Melenia practically floated across the silver floor inlaid with sparkling jewels. Her diamond-beaded gown was made from fabric that seemed spun from platinum, and her long, wavy hair shone in different shades of gold. She was the most beautiful Watcher of all.

How Alexius had come to hate her.

She opened the door to Danaus. "Oh," his voice boomed. "I see you're not alone."

"No." She held the door open wider and gestured him inside. "But come in. Please, I insist."

Danaus might have been every bit as beautiful as any of their kind, but his eternally sour expression made him ugly to Alexius. Danaus regarded him now with clear disdain. "Alexius isn't one of us," he said.

"Of course he is. Don't be rude, Danaus. It doesn't become you. Please say what you came here to say. It's clear that it troubles you deeply."

"Very well." He hissed out a breath of impatience. "I've received word from a scout that one of our exiles has been using his magic to help the mortal king build a road. I believe Xanthus was one of your most devoted minions, wasn't he?"

Alexius nearly flinched at the name of Phaedra's brother, gone from the Sanctuary for twenty years. He'd once been Melenia's lover, and her most favored and gifted protégé. She'd coached him in ways unlike she had anyone else in the Sanctuary, which had caused everyone, Alexius included, to suspect and envy him.

Now he knew better than to envy anyone this immortal singled out. Now he pitied those she hand-selected. Including himself.

"The pretty spider in her silvery web, spinning tales to wind around us all."

It was a warning from Phaedra that he'd ignored. She had been smarter than anyone had suspected.

Melenia nodded. "I remember Xanthus very well."

Danaus pursed his lips, clearly annoyed that this news did not incense her. "I believe someone here in the Sanctuary is visiting him in his dreams, guiding his actions."

Her brows arched. "Really. Who?"

"I don't know yet."

Despite Danaus's ancient age and vast wealth of knowledge, he really was deeply stupid. But perhaps Alexius was dismissing him too soon. Like Timotheus, he was an elder. If only Alexius could find a way to meet with them privately, to tell them what Melenia planned behind their backs, that would be two against one . . .

The rebellious thought caused a sudden, intense pain to blossom in the center of his chest. Unlike the vague pang of guilt or regret, this was a literal pain, brought on by the obedience spell Melenia had placed on him to ensure his loyalty. He'd been fighting it for weeks now, but had recently found that it was unbreakable. He groaned audibly, relenting to it.

"Everything all right with you, boy?" Danaus asked, eyeing him warily.

"Of course," he replied, steeling himself until the pain began to fade.

"Ignore him, Danaus, and let me tell you exactly who is guiding Xanthus," Melenia said, her voice calm and even. "I'm already well aware of what's been going on, and I know who accesses his dreams."

His expression filled with wonder. "Who?"

"Me." She smiled. A hint of wickedness flashed in her sapphire-blue eyes.

Alexius was beyond shocked. Why would Melenia share such a valuable secret with the immortal she'd professed to trust the least?

"What?" Danaus stepped forward, leaving little space between himself and Melenia. "That's impossible. We elders can't dream-walk."

"*You* can't. But I can," she said. "I visit the dreams of both Xanthus and the mortal King Gaius. They are both part of my carefully crafted plan. The king wants the Kindred for himself, so much that he's willing to do anything, say anything, *be* anything to get them in his greedy hands. And it's because of this greed that, out of anyone I've ever come across, he's been the easiest to manipulate. Even now, he eagerly awaits my next instructions in another dream."

Danaus's eyes flashed with envy. "How is such a thing possible? You must tell me. To escape this place if only through someone else's mind . . . I crave it."

Of course Danaus would jump on any opportunity, no matter how immoral, that might benefit him. He didn't even seem to care that Melenia had been keeping this secret from him until now.

"You really want to know?" she asked coyly.

"Yes. You must show me!"

A warning rose up inside Alexius and his throat tightened. He wanted to speak, but he couldn't.

"All right." Melenia took Danaus's face in her hands. "Look deeply into my eyes."

Don't. Don't do what she asks.

But Danaus's lust for this skill transformed the justice-seeker who'd entered the room into someone just as blind and greedy as King Gaius.

"I'm surprised you never figured this out on your own," Melenia said. "Then again, it was only an accident that I discovered it for myself."

"Discovered what?" Danaus demanded.

"That Watchers are capable of pulling magic from each other to become more powerful. Power that lets us do all sorts of interesting things—including dreamwalking."

Alexius's heart began to thud, but the tearing pain in his chest kept him still and silent.

Danaus's eyes lit up. "Show me how."

"If you insist."

Melenia locked into his gaze, and her hands began to glow.

"I feel it," Danaus whispered. "I feel the power leaving me and entering you. Incredible. All this time . . . how could I not have known?"

"There is a catch, of course. There's always a catch. If one takes more than just a taste, a mark is left upon the donor."

Danaus winced. Alexius could see that he was beginning to

feel the pain as his magic flowed into Melenia, weakening him and strengthening her. "Enough. Stop."

"But, you see, that's impossible. I've already taken too much," she whispered loud enough for Alexius to hear. "I don't want to leave you to suffer and fade. I am doing you a favor today, my friend."

Alexius's fingers dug into the soft padding of his chair as he watched Danaus begin to glow, his face convulsing.

"Stop!" Danaus cried, the pain most likely excruciating. "Please, stop!"

"I'm grateful for your sacrifice, Danaus. The magic I've stolen from other immortals is meager—but you, an elder, an original like me—you have so much more to give. I'll use this magic well when I'm finally free from this prison."

He screamed as his body was swallowed up by blue-white flames, and, finally, Melena stepped back from him, watching as he disappeared in a flash of light that turned Alexius's vision stark white.

Danaus had existed for millennia, and here he was gone—forever—in mere moments.

"That was incredibly satisfying," Melenia said, sliding her hands through her shimmering hair.

This wasn't right. Melenia had to feel at least a sliver of remorse, and if she didn't, she was even more of a monster than Alexius suspected.

It wasn't too late. Alexius would find a way to get to Timotheus and tell him what had happened here. He and Melenia were the only original elders left.

She had to be stopped.

Pain wrenched through him at the thought.

"Now, where were we?" She fixed her gaze upon him as he sat

stiffly on her chaise. "Ah, yes. Phaedra. You believe I murdered her because she knew too much?"

Her eyes blazed so brightly that he thought they might overflow in a sea of sapphire power.

She was more dangerous than he'd ever seen her, and he couldn't help feeling fear.

He bowed his head. "Apologies, my queen, I never should have suggested such a thing."

"No, you shouldn't have." She sat next to him, so close he could feel the crackle of the magic that now coated her golden skin. "Show me what we worked on the other day."

For the briefest of moments, he hesitated. But the pain rose up again, forcing him to obey. He loosened the ties of his shirt and bared his chest to her. The golden swirl over his heart had dimmed since she'd begun to consume his magic, just as she'd done with Danaus, but less severely. She took a small taste every day, just enough to keep him from visiting Lucia in her dreams or watching over her in the mortal world in hawk form.

He, too, was now a prisoner here, in every way.

"I know I've been harsh with you," she said softly. "But I have no other choice. I can't risk anything going wrong."

"And nothing will, my queen."

He could only blame himself for the position he found himself in. He'd wholeheartedly agreed to collaborate with her, thinking that he could help save his world—help save *all* worlds. He'd understood from the beginning that certain sacrifices would have to be made for the greater good, but his intentions had always been pure.

He hadn't known the whole truth then.

Melenia inspected the symbols she'd carved on his chest with a golden blade infused with her magic. As she traced the wounds with her fingertip, she infused even more of her obedience spell into his very being. The four designs—the symbols for each element—were so simple, yet so powerful, especially when etched so deeply into the flesh of an immortal.

And even when the scars finally faded from sight completely, they would still control him.

She would control him.

"Do you think you're ready?" she asked.

The words bubbled up and escaped before he could stop them. "I exist only to serve you, my queen."

She slid her hands up his chest and throat, then over his cheeks. She held his face between her hands, as she had with Danaus. He had no choice but to meet her gaze, unsure whether she would let him live or kill him now and be done with it.

No, she wouldn't do that. She'd spent far too long preparing him for what was to come. She needed him.

"You will carry out my orders without hesitation. I shall give you a gift in return for all you've done and will do for me, my beautiful boy. Do you understand and agree to this?"

He could feel her scrutinizing him for signs of dissent. If he flinched, she would strengthen her spell even more. More pain, more torture. He would lose that much more of himself. Already the need to obey her was a snake wrapped around his throat, squeezing until he could barely breathe.

He held on to an image of a beautiful girl with raven-colored hair and sky-blue eyes, the girl he'd once pledged to protect with his very life. He believed in her. She would give him the strength to survive this.

"Yes, my queen. I understand completely."

CHAPTER 8

NIC

AURANOS

Cleaning up after King Gaius's vicious wolfhounds was not the duty of a palace guard. But it was Nic's duty. He didn't think it was a coincidence.

A nasty pair of guards named Burrus and Milo laughed as one of the leashed dogs dragged Nic, quite literally, toward the stables in her search for the best place to relieve herself.

"Having fun?" Burrus asked.

"So much fun," Nic replied without hesitation.

"Be thankful this is the worst the king's asked of you this week. He seems to be in a foul mood."

Was the king ever in a *good* mood? One that wasn't just for show?

"Don't worry, though," Milo said with a sneer. "I'm sure he's nearly done with you. Looking after his mutts will seem like a luxury compared to what your future holds."

"Auranians," Burrus mumbled. "Good for nothing."

"Except wiping the arses of the king's hounds."

They both burst into gales of laughter over their own incredible wits.

Ignoring his fellow guards had become easier in the weeks since Nic had been promoted from stable boy to palace guard (although *promoted* was arguable given his current duties). It didn't take long for Nic to decide that, though he shared living, sleeping, and eating space with the other guards, he had no desire to become their friend.

He'd only gotten into one fight this week, which had earned him a black eye from Burrus that had yet to fade completely.

Limerians. He spat to the side.

He hated every last one of them.

He usually tried to be quick with a quip or a joke or a story, anything to distract the enemies that wore the same uniform as he.

He'd come to despise the color red.

Milo and Burrus finally wandered off. "You done?" he said to the wolfhound. She looked over her shoulder and growled at him, baring the same sharp teeth that had torn apart a fat rabbit mere minutes earlier. "No, no, that's fine. Go at your leisure, madam. I have all the time in the world."

She squatted. He waited.

So this was it. This was how he would survive in this new age of the conquered Auranos.

Why am I still here?

"Shouldn't be," he answered himself.

His family was dead. His sister, Mira, had been murdered by the king himself for allegedly eavesdropping on his conversation with the loathsome Prince Magnus.

He'd failed Mira. He should have been there to protect her, but he wasn't. The thought tortured him day and night. He wanted vengeance, but instead he took orders. He was a coward trying to survive, lost in a sea of his enemies.

With a heavy heart, Nic turned to guide the hounds back toward the castle and felt his left boot sink into a pile of dung.

"Fantastic." His voice trembled as the last of his strength left him and he felt on the verge of tears.

Why did he stay here? Why didn't he slip out of the gates, get on a ship, and sail away across the sea to start a new life somewhere far away from here?

He was a palace guard, not the palace jester. Perhaps he should start acting like it.

Nic couldn't leave without saying farewell to Cleo. It would be the first time he'd spoken to her since he'd stormed off after she'd rejected both his romantic intentions and his offer to take her away from this horrible place full of ghosts. That had only been two weeks ago, but it felt as if a year had passed.

She likely hadn't realized it, but Nic had been keeping an eye on her from afar in recent days. Even though she despised him now, he'd still promised to keep her safe.

And how is leaving her behind keeping her safe? he asked himself.

She didn't need his help anymore. Maybe the idea that she ever had needed him had only been an illusion he'd cast forth himself to make him feel worthy.

He found the princess in the courtyard, reading, on a shady bench beneath a large oak tree. The princess was *always* in the courtyard reading—a behavior so different from the Cleo he'd grown up with, the one who only touched a book when her tutors insisted. And sometimes, not even then.

Today's book featured a hawk on the cover, dark bronze against the pale tan leather, and appeared to be about the legends surrounding the immortal Watchers and their mystical Sanctuary. Piled next to her were more books, including a sketchbook he'd occasionally seen her draw in to help pass the time. Art was one class Cleo had seemed to enjoy.

"Cleo," he said softly.

She looked up at him, shielding her eyes from the bright sun. "Nic!"

"Apologies for disturbing you, but I wanted to come here and—"

She leapt to her feet and threw herself into his arms. "Oh, Nic! I've missed you so much! Please, don't be angry with me. I'm sorry I was so cruel to you. I didn't mean it."

A thick knot swiftly formed in his throat and his eyes began to sting. Then a smile took hold of his face and the heaviness that had been seated upon his heart shifted to the side just a little.

She took his face between her hands, staring at him with a worried expression. "You hate me," she said.

"What? Of course I don't hate you, Cleo. I thought that you . . . well, I thought *you* hated *me*."

She gasped. "That's ridiculous. I could never hate you, Nic. Never!"

He felt as close to joyful as he had in recent memory. The message of farewell he'd come to deliver died on his tongue. "I need to ask your forgiveness for what I said to you."

She shook her head. "No forgiveness is necessary. Please, sit with me for a while."

"I don't think I can." He glanced toward the other guards standing against the far wall. Between them, in the center of the courtyard, was a beautiful garden of flowers and fruit trees, but the guard's view of the princess was clear enough.

"Forget them. They won't bother us. And they can't hear us speaking from all the way over there."

She took his hand in hers. He sat next to her on the bench and looked down at her amethyst ring.

"Have you learned more about your ring?" he whispered.

"I have. But I confess I'm not sure what to do now." Then she quietly and quickly launched into the most bizarre story Nic had ever heard—of magic, prophecies, and princess sorceresses.

By the time Cleo finished, Nic was dizzy.

"Unbelievable," he managed to say.

"But it's all true," she said, squeezing his hand. "You're the only one I trust in the world right now." She inhaled shakily. "Lucia's magic is associated with the Watchers. This ring belonged to the original sorceress—they say it helped to control her magic and kept it from corrupting her. With this ring, with Lucia, I'll be able to find the Watchers' greatest treasure . . . the Kindred itself."

This was dangerous information, but Cleo was not wrong to trust him. He would never say a single word to put her life at risk, not even under torture. And not even if he were promised a boat-load of gold in return.

With Mira gone, Cleo was now the closest thing Nic had to a sister. She was his family now—but then again, she always had been.

He hadn't realized until now how heavily the secrets he'd been keeping had been weighing on him. He needed to unburden him-self, to trust her as she trusted him.

He should have done so days ago.

Despite Cleo's assurance that they were out of earshot, Nic

scanned the area before deeming it was safe to continue to speak in complete privacy.

"Prince Ashur asked me about your ring," he began. "He knows what it is, Cleo, and he's very keen on finding the Kindred for himself."

Her face went pale. "When did he speak to you?"

"After our argument. He followed me to a tavern, hoping to squeeze information out of a drunk palace guard busy feeling sorry for himself. I told him nothing. Not that I knew very much then."

Cleo looked stricken. "What else did he say?"

"He believes great magic exists in Mytica and that King Gaius is also after it. And he thinks your ring is a key factor in all of it."

Nic hadn't had a drop to drink since that night. He'd stayed sober, vigilant, waiting for the prince to approach him again with more questions.

But he hadn't. Even at the banquet after Princess Amara had arrived, Nic had been stationed by the doors, and Ashur hadn't even glanced in his direction once.

She twisted her hands in her lap. "What do we do, Nic?"

"This might sound crazy, but I think he could be an ally," Nic said softly. "The Kraeshains are powerful. With their father's vast army at their backs, much more powerful than King Gaius. An alliance might help you win your throne back."

"What would make you believe they might align with us?"

"A gut feeling."

She searched his face. "What else did he say to you to give you such an impression?"

What else did he *say*? Nothing. It was more about what else he *did*.

He wanted to tell her everything, but he still hesitated. Some recent details of his life were difficult for him to put into words.

"Nic . . ." Cleo squeezed his hand. "What is it? You look so distressed."

"Distressed? No. No, everything's fine. Well, as fine as it can be."

"What aren't you telling me?"

He thought back to later that night, when Ashur had followed him out of the tavern and onto the streets.

"It's just . . . something else happened that night that I'm not sure how to interpret. Then again," he chewed his bottom lip, "I was *really* drunk that night."

"Tell me. It obviously troubles you, whatever it is."

That was a rather grand understatement. "He did something."

"Did what?"

The princess trusted him with her deepest and darkest truths. He knew he had to give that trust in return, even about this. "He . . . kissed me."

Cleo blinked. "He *what*?"

The words came faster now. "At first I was certain I'd misinterpreted it, maybe imagined the whole thing. But it happened, Cleo."

She stared at him, bewildered. "You're saying that Prince Ashur Cortas, the most infamous and sought-after bachelor in all of the Kraeshian Empire, *kissed* you."

"I know!" He shot up from the bench and began pacing back and forth, raking his hands through his messy red hair. "I know!"

She considered this. "I suppose that explains why he hasn't taken a wife yet. He prefers—"

"What?" Nic spun around to face her and then lowered his voice so as not to draw the guards' attention. "Seventeen-year-old palace guards who shovel the shit of the king's dogs?" He grimaced. "Pardon my language. No—no, he must have been trying to mess with my head, have me tell him secrets. Maybe he thinks I like boys instead of girls. Maybe he was trying to manipulate me. Kraeshians are very sneaky, you know!"

"Calm yourself." Cleo stood up and took Nic's hands in hers to make him stop moving. "I see that this bothers you. But it shouldn't. It's fine."

"*Fine*? How is this fine?" He'd lost sleep over it, trying to figure out how and why it had happened and why he hadn't done a single thing to stop it.

"The prince approached *you*, Nic . . . you in particular out of everyone in the palace."

"Because he knows I'm your friend."

"Perhaps that wasn't the only reason." She twirled a long lock of her pale golden hair around her fingers. "You have a connection with the prince now. You need to find out if Prince Ashur and Princess Amara could possibly be our allies, as you suspect. I can't afford to turn my back on any possibility at this point."

His heart thudded loudly in his ears. "I don't know."

"Nic, please. You have to be brave. For me. For Mira. For everyone we've lost. I empathize with your misgivings, but this is more important than a kiss. You need to go to Prince Ashur and find out if he can help us."

Damn. He couldn't refuse Cleo this request, not if it might mean all the difference in the world in getting her throne back.

"I don't know when I can get away from the palace to pay a visit to the Cortas's villa," Nic said. "My leash is nearly as tight as the king's hounds'. And, to be honest, Cleo, I'm not totally convinced we would be wise to align with them so soon."

"You'll have to be subtle." Cleo's expression was haunted with worry. "But Ashur approached you personally. He won't consider it strange if you speak with him in private again. Our futures are on the line, Nic. The future of Auranos and all of its citizens is at stake."

"That's a lot of responsibility."

"Yes, it is." She looked up at him, her eyes filling with hope. "So will you do this for me? For *us*?"

A thousand thoughts surged through his mind, half rooting for and half ruling against this request. But in the end, only one thought remained.

"Of course I will, Cleo."

CHAPTER 9

JONAS

AURANOS

It was only last night that Jonas received the news from Nerissa, a former seamstress and currently an invaluable rebel aid. She had managed to coax the names of the imprisoned rebels from the lips of a palace guard, and, had written them down on a note she'd left for him at a tavern in a nearby town, their established meeting place.

When Jonas read the names, he'd nearly shouted for joy

Cato, Fabius, Tarus . . . and Lysandra. All confirmed as prisoners in the palace dungeon.

But he'd sobered quickly.

To be alive and held prisoner at the whim of the vicious Limerian guards and the bloodthirsty king could be a fate worse than death.

He would do anything—*anything*—it took to free Lysandra and the others. And he hoped tonight's journey to the city would be another step toward that goal.

"Far be it for me to question you," Felix said, "but in the event that this plan doesn't work, do you happen to have another one?"

"Nerissa will continue to help us whenever and however she can."

"I'm still surprised your key rebel is a girl."

"My key rebel *is* a girl, but she's not Nerissa. Still, I don't know what I'd have done without her."

Felix shrugged. "To me, girls are meant to be pretty companions, not rebel comrades. They're good for washing our clothes and preparing meals after a long day." He flashed Jonas a grin. "And, of course, they're excellent for warming beds."

Jonas eyed him with an edge of amusement. "You might want to keep that opinion to yourself when you meet Lysandra."

"She's not pretty?"

"Oh, she is. Extremely pretty, in fact. But she'll hand your arse to you on a rusty platter if you ever ask her to cook your meals or wash your clothes. And especially if you invite her to warm your bed."

"If she's as pretty as you say I might try to change her mind."

Jonas's grin widened. "Good luck with that. I'll be sure to bring flowers to your grave."

Felix laughed. "So, do you think your contact will show?" he asked as they entered the City of Gold. After going on a couple of scouting missions and further confirmation from Nerissa, they learned that security had been ramped up to the highest level ever. Sneaking into the palace would be impossible.

Sneaking into the city, however, was another matter.

"We'll soon find out," Jonas replied. To be cautious, they both wore long, hooded cloaks, but, despite the heavy presence of guards—at the gates, stationed in the towers around the city walls, patrolling the streets by foot or on horseback—no one paid much attention to them.

Finally, they reached their destination, and Felix swept his gaze over to the well-traveled cobblestone road. "I'll patrol out here. If anything feels wrong, I'll signal you."

"How are you going to signal me?"

"Trust me, you'll know."

Trust me.

So much about Felix reminded Jonas of Brion that trusting him was a gut instinct. It was so easy to pour his soul out over their campfires each night, telling Felix about what had gone wrong, and how Jonas wished he could fix it so everything would turn out the way it was supposed to. Right back to that fateful day when he and his brother, Tomas, had returned to their father's wine stall to find a lord and a princess from a neighboring kingdom making a purchase.

Life had been hard but wonderfully simple before that day. It wasn't as if Jonas was fighting to turn back time. No, he didn't want that. What Paelsians needed the most was truth and freedom. With those two prizes they might be able to find a way to rule themselves. No throne required.

"Hey." Felix clasped Jonas's shoulder. "Don't fret. It'll be fine."

"I'm not fretting."

"If your contact doesn't arrive soon, though, we'll have to leave. It's too dangerous to be this close to the palace, especially with your pretty face plastered up all over the place."

Jonas had to agree with him there.

He left Felix outside and slipped into the small temple wedged between two populated taverns. A ten-foot-tall marble statue of the goddess Cleiona stood near the entrance. She had long flowing hair, a peaceful yet haughty expression, and the symbols for fire and air—the elements she embodied—etched into her upraised palms. Her robes, despite being carved from marble, were thin and diaphanous and left very little to the imagination.

Those breasts alone are worth worshipping, Jonas thought as he passed the statue.

He pulled the hood of his dark cloak closer around his face as he entered the grand altar room. There were only three other people inside, sitting in pews with their eyes closed.

He took a seat near the back and waited.

There were no temples in Paelsia. No official religion, no deities. However, during his brief visits to Paelsia in recent days, he'd begun to see small clay idols in the deceased Chief Basilius's likeness. It sickened him, knowing that the chief had been a liar and a thief, selfishly living high and mighty in his compound while his people starved.

Jonas didn't mourn his loss, not for a single moment.

He waited in the quiet temple, the rhythm of his heartbeat his only way to know much time had passed. Finally, he heard the creak of the main doors opening, followed by footsteps.

"Wait outside," the new worshipper said firmly to the guard at her side. "I need to be alone with my prayers."

"Yes, princess."

Jonas pulled farther back into the shadows and watched Princess Cleo walk up the aisle and across the row of benches facing a large mosaic of the goddess, making her way toward the back of the temple through an archway. He slipped off the bench and, glancing at the entrance to make sure that the guard had left, followed her down a passageway about twenty paces long that led to a smaller room. Hundreds of candles blazed with light on narrow shelves, celebrating and acknowledging the goddess's fire magic.

Cleo lit a candle and carefully placed it next to the others.

He waited in silence.

"I received your message," she said without turning around.

"I'm glad."

"Are you?"

"Yes. It's good to see you again." After all the hardships he'd faced, seeing the princess in person lightened his heart. "Are you going to look at me?"

"I haven't decided yet."

"Come on. Didn't we part as friends?"

"Did we? I seem to recall the last time we met you were horribly injured and all of your friends were dead."

He flinched at the reminder of that terrible day. "I wanted you to come with me."

"And what? Live in the trees with a group of Paelsians who despise me simply for being who I am?"

He let himself imagine a future just like that—he and Cleo living together in a tree house surrounded by birds and squirrels, far above the rest of the world.

The ludicrous thought almost made him laugh.

No, his life was much more earthbound and practical than that—and so was hers.

"Perhaps not," he allowed. "Palaces with large comfortable beds to share with your new husband are much more to your liking, I'm sure."

She spun around, her eyes blazing, and slapped him. Or, at least, she tried to—Jonas caught her wrist before the blow landed.

So quick to resort to violence—so unlike most Auranians,

who were much more likely to drink and eat and stare adoringly at their own reflections than to fight for themselves. "Easy, your highness. A clandestine meeting with a wanted criminal isn't the best time to make a scene. There are potential witnesses snoozing not so far away."

"You were silent for so long I thought you were dead."

"I didn't know you cared."

She let out a grunt of frustration. "Someone secretly tucked your message into my sketchbook. I was lucky to have found it in time to make my excuses to come here."

"Didn't know you were an artist, either."

Cleo glared at him, her arms crossed over the bodice of her violet gown. Her dress was not nearly as revealing as what the goddess out front wore, but Jonas certainly wasn't complaining.

"Clearly," she said slowly, unpleasantly, "you're alive and well and ready to make light of everything I say."

She was every bit as forthright as he remembered—it was one of his favorite qualities about her. She didn't bother with proper royal etiquette in his presence, which was fine by him. Frankly, he hadn't realized how much he'd missed her until this very moment. "Hardly, your highness. Much gratitude for meeting with me."

"You're being hunted like a wild boar. It was foolish of you to enter this city."

"And yet, here I am."

"I've already heard about your victory at the road camp."

He frowned. "That was no victory."

"Perhaps not overall, but you finally got your revenge on Aron, didn't you?" She wrung her hands, making her large amethyst ring glint in the candlelight. "I'm not saying that he didn't deserve it, of course. He did. And I hate that I feel any grief for him at all. But he's just one more piece of my previous life that's now been taken from this world."

Jonas frowned. "Who told you I killed him?"

"I assumed . . ." A shadow of confusion crossed her expression. "It wasn't you?"

"No." He couldn't lay claim to slaying the murderer of his brother and his friend. "I arrived too late to do the deed myself. But I would have, if your new husband hadn't stolen the opportunity from me."

She stared at him. "You're saying . . . that *Magnus* killed Aron. But why?"

Apparently, this wasn't common knowledge at the palace. "Because Aron Lagaris killed Prince Magnus's mother."

"What?" She grappled for words, a rush of nameless emotions playing on her face. "But . . . but they're still saying *you're* responsible for the queen's murder."

Of course they were. Otherwise, his wanted posters would have been nothing more than fuel for a campfire. "Did you think I was guilty?"

"No, not for a moment. You don't kill women indiscriminately—even one married to the king. You hold yourself to a higher standard than that."

It pleased him to know she knew this about him, even if everyone else seemed ready to jump to the worst conclusion. "Sadly, Lord Aron didn't hold himself to the same standard."

"Magnus killed Aron because Aron killed his mother," she repeated under her breath shakily.

A stab of jealousy pierced through him at the sound of Cleo so casually mentioning the prince's name, but he tried to ignore it.

He didn't have time for such petty emotions. It was time to get to the point of this meeting.

"Not long ago I asked if you'd become my spy inside the palace," he said. "I'm asking you again."

"What do you need me to do?"

Her answer came so swiftly that he needed to take a silent second to compose himself. "I need to know the king's next steps. Conquering Paelsia and Auranos were only the first. I have reason to believe there are ulterior motives behind his Imperial Road."

Motives that called for an exiled Watcher to head the construction. And if the king had a Watcher building his road, then it was more than a way to link the three kingdoms—it was a means to get to magic.

Cleo looked at him with impatience. "Do you think that the king brings me in on his council meetings and asks for my opinion? I know nothing of his plans."

"You're married to the prince."

"So? You think that gives me special privileges?"

"Of course it does. That you're here at all shows me that you're not locked in your chambers as you were before your wedding."

Her expression darkened. "Some things have changed, but others have stayed exactly the same. I can now leave the palace, but I'm still not permitted beyond the city walls. And I'm always surrounded by guards."

"Except for now."

She raised her chin. "Yes, you're absolutely right. I'm completely defenseless. If you decide I'm not as useful as you'd hoped, you could slit my throat and leave me behind as a message to the king."

He was more amused than insulted by her absurd statement. "I could. But I think we've already established that I don't kill women."

"Lucky me."

He'd expected resistance, but now that he knew she was willing to listen to him, he considered his options. "Leaving aside the king and his road for a moment, there's something else I need to speak with you about. Several of my friends are currently being held in the palace dungeon."

"Let me guess—you want to rescue them."

He held her gaze. "I damn well want to try. Anything you hear about them, you must let me know."

She stared at him for a moment in stunned silence. "You're going to get yourself killed."

"Without a doubt."

"And you're going to get me killed, too." She wrung her hands, moving closer to the candlelight so it flickered softly against her golden hair. "As if I don't already have enough trouble as it is."

Her fiery temperament had faded to mere embers in moments. Suddenly he felt compelled to ask her something that had been on his mind since her wedding day. "Does he abuse you?"

"The king?"

"No, the prince. Does he . . . hurt you?"

If she said yes, Jonas would find Magnus and kill him, no matter what the consequences. He would tear him apart and leave him in the Wildlands in small, bloody, twitching pieces for the beasts who lived there to consume.

She hesitated, a frown drawing her brows together. "No. Actually, he never speaks to me if he can help it."

Jonas couldn't repress his sigh of relief. "Good."

"Oh, yes, it's lovely to be completely shut out by those who control your destiny."

Again, her outrage sparked a smile from him. "You control your destiny, princess. No one else."

She studied him with bemusement in her eyes. "You are the most frustrating boy I've ever met."

This made him laugh aloud. "I'm sure it's a close race with the prince."

"You seem rather obsessed with Magnus. Perhaps next time I should try to arrange a meeting between the two of you instead."

"You're already thinking ahead to the next time we meet. I like that."

Color rushed into her cheeks. "Don't be so self-assured, rebel."

He tried to repress his grin. "I've told you what I need from you. Now tell me what *your* plan is, princess."

"My plan?" She touched her chest. "Why do you think I even have one? Perhaps I'm simply grateful to still be alive."

Jonas knew that if she didn't feel there was still a chance to reclaim her throne, she would have escaped long ago. With Jonas, with her friend Nic, with someone who could help her escape the Damoras forever.

"You won't be alive for long if you continue to stay in the midst of your enemies," Jonas said. "Do you think I'm wrong?"

Cleo looked unflinchingly into his eyes. "No, you're not wrong."

She trusted about as easily as he did. He'd managed to gain a lot of that trust, but there was still some ground to rebuild between them after so long without contact.

"Is there anything I can do to help you?" he asked.

"You would help me?"

"I have no personal interest in Auranos, but I don't want the King of Blood to hold it under his thumb a day longer than he has to. More land gives him more power. If I can't do it myself, I'll help anyone who has the means to destroy him. Could that person be you?"

She gave him that look that was half distrustful, half endlessly hopeful. "It could be."

"Then consider me at your service, your highness." They didn't have much more time. He'd already stayed too long and Felix would be wondering where he was. "You can send word to me through Nerissa."

Cleo's brow shot up. "The seamstress from Hawk's Brow?"

He nodded. "She's working at the palace as a servant. If you hear any information, no matter how minor it might seem to you, get a message to Nerissa and she'll deliver it to me."

"You're still aligned with her? And you trust her?"

He nodded. "She's proven herself, time and time again."

Her gaze grew more scrutinizing. "Yes, I'm sure she has."

What was that he saw in her eyes? Mistrust? Or jealousy? Certainly not the latter, although the thought was intriguing.

Cleo's serious expression then gave way to a smile so bright and beautiful it could stop the cruelest killer in his tracks. "Once my enemy, Jonas Agallon now wishes to be my shining hero. How times can change."

Not so long ago, he'd despised Cleo, who had stood by Lord Aron while his brother bled to death. He'd blamed her every bit as much as the coward who'd held the blade.

But as far as she'd fallen, as much as she'd had to endure, she was still a pampered princess who had no idea what a life such as Jonas's had been like.

And he had no desire to be anyone's personal hero.

Cleo could potentially help him, and he her. That was all that would ever be between them.

The thought made everything so much simpler.

"Do you have anything else to say to me?" she asked after silence stretched between them.

"Only this." He grabbed her, pressed her up against the wall, and kissed her hard and deep. He let her go, pulled his cloak up over his head, and slipped out of the temple.

Perhaps things weren't that simple after all.

CHAPTER 10

CLEO

AURANOS

Cleo walked away from her secret meeting with Jonas filled with new purpose, which had very little to do with the rebel's stolen kiss.

Not that it hadn't been a rather intriguing way to end their conversation.

She might not be a fighter, wielding a sword for the rebel cause, but she had eyes and ears. Information was power, and the king had gotten a bit lazy with the private conversations he held in corridors and dark corners.

Cleo already knew of a certain alcove in the heart of the palace where a hidden observer could overhear many interesting secrets.

She used to frequent this hiding spot to spy on her sister and her friends, until Emilia caught Cleo being nosy and told their father, who had scolded Cleo about minding her own business.

But minding one's own business wasn't very interesting. Or useful.

The day after meeting Jonas, she came upon Magnus and the

king talking in this very alcove. She quickly drew back around the corner and hid in the crevice between two columns where she could peer out, unseen, for a clear view of the area just outside of the throne room. Hanging on the white marble wall behind father and son was a gigantic tapestry of the Limerian coat of arms—a cobra before a pair of crossed swords.

She pressed her hands against the cool marble and strained to hear them.

"Gregor, the rebel boy, knows something," the king said. "He's denied what he told you in Limeros over and over, but I know he's lying."

"Don't be so sure," Magnus replied. "He attacked me in clear view of a dozen guards while raving about Watchers. He could simply be insane."

Cleo's breath caught. She immediately knew whom they were speaking of—the moment had been branded into her memory. Gregor was the boy who'd attacked them during their wedding tour, claiming that a Watcher guided him in his dreams.

He had nearly killed her—and perhaps would have succeeded if Magnus hadn't shoved her out of the way.

But instead of having him executed on the spot, Magnus had ordered him delivered here to the palace dungeon.

It seemed now that he was still alive.

Interesting.

"He can't be mad," the king said. "I need him to be sane. He has a clue, a connection to the Sanctuary. I have sent word to Xanthus that I want more information, but I've heard nothing from him."

"There's no way for you to contact Melenia yourself?" Magnus asked.

"Don't you think I already would have if I knew how?" There

was a hard edge to the king's response. "I've done everything she's asked of me. The road is finished. Yet now . . . nothing. A silence stretches out with no information, no guidance. Nothing but a boy with ties to Melenia's world. And he will answer me, I swear on the heart of Valoria he will."

"Of course he will, Father."

"I will question Gregor again later today one last time and I want you there by my side." The king grasped Magnus's shoulder and gazed at him fiercely. "The Kindred will be mine."

The Kindred.

So what Prince Ashur told Nic was true, Cleo thought. The king sought the very same magic that she did.

Her chest tight, Cleo started to hurry away, but as soon as she turned, she stopped.

Cronus stood a few feet behind her, a mountain of a man with his arms crossed over his broad chest. She couldn't speak, couldn't summon the ability to say something witty or disarming.

Cronus grabbed her by her upper arm and dragged her down the hallway, his grip bruisingly tight. They'd gone twenty paces before she finally found her voice.

"Where are you taking me?" she managed, fighting to free herself to no avail.

"Be quiet."

"How dare you! Unhand me this instant." She tried with all her might to sound authoritative, royal. Like someone a mere guard— even a captain—should obey.

She knew she didn't fool him.

Deadly silent, he engaged her with neither conversation nor threats. He came to a door, opened it, and thrust her inside. He slammed the door behind her, plunging her into darkness.

When Cleo was eight years old, she'd had a particularly cruel nanny who, when she hadn't been as well behaved as Emilia, would lock her in dark rooms, promising that demons from the darklands would come in and punish her.

When her father learned of this, he'd relieved the woman of her duties and cast her out of his palace, forbidding her to return. The king had released Cleo from the darkness himself and gathered her into his arms, promising her that she was safe, that no demons would ever harm her.

The darkness frightened her to this day.

"Be brave," she whispered to herself, pacing back and forth in the small space. "Be strong."

After what seemed like hours, she pushed aside the tears streaking her cheeks and stood quietly, waiting in silence for her destiny to claim her.

Finally, the door creaked open. She raised her chin, put her fisted hands at her sides, and tried to remain calm in the face of the king's wrath.

But it was not the king at the door. It was Magnus. With Cronus right behind him.

The prince peered around. "It's too dark in here."

Cronus unshuttered a small window, letting in some sunshine, and used a torch to light three lanterns set into the walls.

"Leave us," Magnus said.

"Yes, your highness."

The door clicked shut behind the guard.

Cleo didn't know why she was surprised not to see the king. After all, why would the king come to deal with her himself? Of course he would send his heir, his most loyal minion.

Her husband.

She couldn't breathe.

"Overhear any interesting conversations lately?" Magnus asked.

"I don't know what you mean." She tried to look haughty, though she felt anything but. "That brute dragged me in here and locked me up like some common prisoner. I demand he be punished!"

"You *demand*, do you?" Magnus crossed his arms and leaned against the wall by the door, his face half-masked by shadows. "What you should be doing is thanking Cronus for alerting me, rather than my father, about your indiscretion."

She would never admit to spying. To do so would be to sign her own death warrant. "I've done nothing wrong."

"I'm sure you don't really believe that."

Unfortunately for this situation, Cleo could always count on Magnus not to dismiss her as a silly young princess who meant no harm, as many others would. "I heard nothing of interest."

"It really doesn't matter what you may or may not have heard. If my father knew you were listening to us, he would ensure those pretty ears of yours would never hear anything else ever again."

Her stomach clenched up. She didn't doubt that the merciless king would dole out such a punishment, and she didn't overvalue herself in his eyes, especially now that the wedding tour was over. "And what would you prefer? A simple beating, perhaps?"

"It's so helpful of you to offer suggestions."

Cleo had to get out of that dark room of despair any way she could. One person blocked her way to freedom—to hope and possibility—and was studying her with more curiosity than accusation.

Perhaps she could try to use that curiosity to get out of here unharmed.

"I can't help it if your father chooses to speak so openly," she said. "It wasn't as if I was crouched in a cupboard in a private room.

You were in the hallway. I happened along and knew if I showed my face while you were in the midst of such an intense discussion, it would anger the king."

"Of course. What were you to do but stand in the shadows and listen?"

She couldn't give in to her fear. She was no ordinary sixteen-year-old girl. She was a princess. A rebel. And she could take charge of this situation. Not all was lost.

She needed to push Magnus off the solid ground he currently stood upon. And she believed she knew what to say to make him lose that careful balance.

"I didn't know you believed in magic," she said.

Magnus blinked. "What makes you think that?"

"Talk of legends doesn't normally transpire between those who think they're too civilized to follow such trivial subjects."

Magnus sighed and leaned against the wall, perhaps to try to appear bored and unaffected. "You have a talent for talking in riddles. I prefer plainer words."

"You'll have to see Princess Amara for that. She prides herself on her bluntness."

"Our Kraeshian visitors are irrelevant to this discussion." He cocked his head and intensified his gaze, as if it would help him to unravel her mysteries. "What do you know of the Kindred, princess?"

The word never failed to make her heart skip a beat. "Nothing at all."

"My, you answered quickly. Far too quickly. Which makes me think you actually know a great deal, especially considering the books I've seen you reading lately. Books about magic and witches and Watchers."

"And sorceresses," she added, watching him carefully for a reaction and seeing only the slightest flicker in his dark eyes.

"Allow me to give you a small piece of advice, princess," Magnus began. "Whatever interests my father, move far away from it. He obsesses over legends and searches for treasures that may or may not exist. And he doesn't like to share."

The confirmation sent a shiver down her spine. "I'd never expect him to."

"Good."

And with that his expression went blank. She knew wouldn't be getting any more information out of him today. But this was enough for now.

"May I leave now?" she asked quietly.

"Not yet." He studied her for an uncomfortable stretch before speaking again. "I have one more question."

"Yes?" said Cleo, fearing what would come next.

"Why do you pursue a friendship with my sister?"

"Because I like her," she blurted, blindsided by the question.

"You're lying."

Anger rose inside of her. "I'm not lying."

"I don't believe it's possible for you to like Lucia. She's a Damora, and therefore your enemy."

"She's different."

His gaze raked over her, as if searching her for weapons and expecting to find another Kraeshian bridal dagger hidden behind her back. "You hate me, you hate my father, you hate anything to do with Limeros. Lucia is part of all of that. Do I believe you're like any other girl who wants to have friends and go to banquets and giggle with her friends? Perhaps you were once, not so long ago, but not anymore. Everything you do, everything you say, is aimed toward your goal to destroy us."

He was far more perceptive than she'd like him to be. He was causing her to lose her composure, her sense of control. Conflicting emotions welled up in her chest too quickly to hold down. "You don't know anything about me."

"Wrong. I know *everything* about you. Your hate fuels you, it gives you purpose. I see it in your eyes at this very moment." He fell quiet for a spell. "Don't get me wrong, I understand why you hate me so much."

The last thing she wanted to talk about was this, again, with *him*, but still her words poured forth; the bottomless pain in her heart had to go somewhere because it was killing her to try to keep it inside.

"You killed Theon."

His expression tightened. "I can never change that fact."

"You also stood by while the king, your *father*, murdered Mira. She was innocent. Harmless. You could have stopped him." This time she made him flinch.

He was ashamed. She saw it in his eyes.

"Anyone else you wish to name, princess? Get it out. It's healthy to unleash pain on the one who caused it. I can take it."

"You killed Aron. More proof that you destroy everyone in your path, whether they deserve it or not." Her words were quiet, but filled with hatred.

"What did you just say?" His voice was equally soft, but there was now danger in his tone.

She suddenly realized her mistake.

There was no one other than Jonas who could have told her about Aron's death, and Magnus could *not* know she'd seen or spoken to him. She had to pull herself together. Overhearing a conversation was one thing, but meeting secretly with a rebel was another altogether.

"Well . . . you may as well have killed him. Aron was inexperienced. You knew how inexperienced he was. The king thrust him into a position of grandeur. He was vain and stupid and didn't realize he didn't stand a chance on the battlefield. I'm not saying you *personally* killed him . . ."

Magnus stepped closer to her, pressing her back against the wall, his gaze alone sharp enough to pin her there.

He drew so near that she could smell the sweet wine on his breath.

To her knowledge, Magnus had never drunk before. He hadn't had a sip during their entire wedding tour. But ever since he'd returned from the battle in the mountains, his habits seemed to have changed.

"No, princess," he said. "That's exactly what you're saying."

"You're paranoid."

"You think I killed Aron? That's quite an accusation. Why would I waste my time killing a pompous little peacock like your former betrothed? He was nothing more to me than dirt under my fingernails."

"He was meaningless," she agreed.

"Entirely. He was a pathetic excuse for an Auranian, not that I think highly of any Auranian. But I'd assumed that most wouldn't fall on their knees to lick the boots of their conqueror. At least, not nearly as quickly as the former kingsliege did. Taking every order, all with a smug smile on his face. Following through, no matter who got hurt, who got killed."

A muscle in Magnus's cheek twitched and he wrenched his gaze from Cleo's, but not before she saw the bolt of raw pain pulse behind his eyes.

It was moments such as this when she found the prince to be

the most confusing. It was so unexpected to see pain in a boy so cold, a boy responsible for all the monstrous deeds she hated him for. But a true monster shouldn't be capable of feeling pain like that.

And then there was Aron. According to Jonas, Aron had killed the queen. But why would he have done such an unexpected and heinous thing?

Could it . . . have been on the king's orders?

The thought made her gasp inwardly. But why would the king want his wife, his queen, murdered?

It made no sense. None at all. And yet, this piece somehow seemed to fit this horribly confusing puzzle.

Although a hundred questions burned on her tongue, Cleo remained silent. She was not fool enough to put such dangerous suspicions into words. Not now. Not here. And not with the unpredictable, intimidating boy who stood before her.

Acting like a cornered victim would do her no justice. She would not tremble before this boy, not ever. She would not beg. She had been a rebel since the day Gaius stole her kingdom and killed her father. Every thought, every goal, every need screamed rebellion.

"Enough of this," she hissed. "You've had your say. You've bullied me to your heart's content. Now, either alert the king to my alleged crimes or release me this instant."

Magnus studied her intently, his expression stony and unreadable despite the storm raging in his dark eyes. "Very well, princess. But let me leave you with this warning. If you're caught eavesdropping again, Cronus will take you directly to the king. And I'll let him. Happily."

He exited the room and closed the door, leaving her there

alone. Heart in her throat, she waited for Cronus to return to extoll further punishment.

But he never came.

Finally, she tried the door to find it unlocked. She slipped out into the halls and navigated the corridors until she found a servant, whom she asked to find Nerissa and send her to her chambers.

Shortly after Cleo was safe inside her chambers, Nerissa arrived.

"Your highness, you wished to speak with me?"

Cleo stood and regarded the girl in the simple gray servant's dress standing by the door. The last time she'd seen Nerissa, her hair had been long and shiny. Now it was cropped short and blunt, making her look different, much plainer than the seamstress who'd led her directly into Jonas's trap. Still, there was no denying how pretty she was, her features holding an exotic beauty that hinted at an ancestry from a faraway land.

Nerissa's face held no fear, but her expression grew tighter as Cleo came closer. Cleo wondered how well Jonas knew this girl and how grateful he might be to one willing to put herself in danger to help him.

She expected to feel jealous, but instead felt only curiosity about what it would be like to be Nerissa, a servant only because of her allegiance to the rebel cause.

But Cleo didn't have time to muse on Nerissa any longer. "You're the one who tucked Jonas's message into my sketchbook."

"Yes, your highness." Nerissa didn't seem the least bit surprised to be confronted.

"And I've been told you can deliver messages to him. Is this true?"

"It is, your highness." She met Cleo's gaze directly.

Cleo studied the girl's face, searching for any sign of deception.

"What are you willing to do to help the rebellion? To bring down the king?"

"Anything." Nerissa didn't hesitate. "And you?"

"The very same." She'd never spoken truer words in her life. They felt right to say, especially to one she had quickly come to believe was a trusted ally.

"Whenever you need me—as a messenger or for anything else—know that I'll be here." Nerissa reached forward and squeezed Cleo's hands, giving her an unexpected smile. "You will have your throne one day very soon, your highness. I swear to the goddess you will."

And then she was gone. Cleo went to her window and looked outside toward the city walls and the green land that stretched out beyond it.

Her beloved home, stolen from her by her enemies.

She swore she would soon steal it back.

CHAPTER 11

MAGNUS

AURANOS

Magnus found Lucia in the courtyard with an alarmingly chilly expression on her face.

"Well, this is quite a surprise," she said. "Did you lose your way?"

"I wanted to speak with you privately."

"You've been back for well over a week. This is the first effort you've made to speak with me at all."

It was true. He'd been avoiding her. They'd both changed so much; a wedge had formed between them, invisible, but strong enough to do lasting damage.

"Come now," he said. "I know you've been busy with your new friend. Wouldn't want to interrupt that, would I?"

He didn't look directly at her, choosing instead to focus on the flowers Lucia tended to. Some of the roses—red, yellow, pink, white—flourished large and plump, while others were brown and withered, as if winter's deadly touch had made its mark in this land of eternal summer.

He didn't have to ask if she'd been practicing her *elementia*. Here were the two sides of it on display—life and death.

"My new friend?" she asked. "I don't know who you mean."

He had no patience for games today. "Don't be coy. You know I mean Cleo."

She shrugged. "Does it bother you that I've learned that the girl you were forced to marry isn't a horrible beast with sharp teeth and claws?"

"Teeth and claws can be easily hidden." He finally looked at her. "Strange, I always thought you were smarter than this."

A smile touched Lucia's lips. "Depends on the day, really."

He'd amused her. He hadn't been trying to amuse her.

"So right now you are merely a good brother looking out for his naïve little sister who might be taken in by one who means her harm?" she asked. "Is that what you believe? Is that why you're here? To warn me?"

"I was concerned."

"Concerned." She spoke as if the word tasted rotten. "Believe me, I'm well aware that Cleo likely harbors deep resentment toward me. Although, it would be difficult for her to hold more resentment for anyone than she does for you."

Such harsh words might have made him flinch if he wasn't already well aware of the truth in them. "This conversation is not nearly as cordial as I'd intended. Why so hostile today, Lucia?"

Her expression was a bit pinched, but Magnus wasn't sure if it was entirely directed at him.

"You avoid me for days, like I'm carrying a disease, and you think *I'm* being hostile?"

"Apologies, *sister*," he hissed the word, "but I was under the impression you wanted to make me forget . . . how did you put it? My *unwelcome thoughts*?"

Her expression stiffened. "You weren't meant to hear that."

His wedding day held more bad memories than a rebel attack, an earthquake, and bridal daggers combined. That day had also confirmed Lucia's continued disgust with his unbrotherly feelings toward her.

Magnus willed himself to stay calm. His confrontation with Cleo had disturbed him more than he wanted to admit to himself.

The rose Lucia held had turned brown and brittle in seconds. Was that earth magic? Or was it the slow, dry heat of fire that had so quickly stolen its beauty?

Perhaps he wasn't the only one trying to stay calm.

Only a year ago, Lucia had come running to Magnus, her arms laden with storybooks. Such fantastical, entertaining reading material wasn't usually permitted in the Limerian library, which was meant to contain only educational texts, essays, and facts.

They'd spent an afternoon poring over the books and had found a tale about a secret magical gateway in northern Limeros, which allowed access to worlds apart from this one, but only if the traveler prepared for the possibility they might never return.

"*Would you want to go through the gateway?*" she'd asked him.

"*I don't know.*" He had considered it carefully before answering. "*Go somewhere far from here where everything's fresh and new and full of possibility? I might. As long as you came with me.*"

"*I could never leave my home,*" she'd replied with a laugh. "*What a silly thought!*"

She didn't realize it, but her words had wounded him deeply. When the day was over he'd taken the book with him, torn out the pages that contained the story about the gateway, and burned each one, watching the parchment curl and blacken before his eyes.

Torn, burned, and forgotten—this was what should always be done with useless fantasies.

"All I wanted to say to you today is . . . be careful with Cleo," Magnus said. "She's very deceptive."

"Aren't we all when we need to be?" Lucia said with a slight smile. "If there's nothing else, Magnus, I have other things to do."

A voice nearby caught Magnus's attention before he could respond. Not that he knew what else to say to her. "Your highness." It was Cronus. "The king summons you."

Clearly Lucia didn't want his guidance—or company—anymore. She wished only for him to leave her alone.

Very well. Wish granted.

"Good day, Lucia." Magnus turned on his heels and followed Cronus along the path back to the palace. On the way, he passed Cleo, heading toward the flower garden.

"My sister is waiting for you," he said.

"Glad to hear it," she replied.

She sounded so lighthearted and carefree; it was as if they'd never had their discussion earlier. Was she really so certain he wouldn't tell his father everything she'd said? Everything she'd overheard? "Be careful, princess."

"I always am."

"Always? Or starting today?"

The glare she sent him over her shoulder was so fierce it very nearly amused him.

Magnus left the sunlight of the garden. When his eyes had adjusted to the darker interior of the palace, he realized that Cronus was closely scrutinizing him, surely wondering why Magnus had let Cleo go with no more than a warning.

"Your comment is not required," Magnus muttered.

"I wouldn't dare offer it, your highness," Cronus replied.

"What does Father want from me today?"

"He requests your presence when he questions the rebel."

He didn't see what help he could offer, but he didn't protest. He would do as his father commanded, even though just being in the same room as the king made his blood boil.

He thought again about Cleo. He hadn't admitted a thing, but he wondered what she would say if he told her the whole truth about Aron, about his mother, about the king.

Would she tell anyone about her suspicions that Magnus killed Aron? And would it even matter if she did? She had no allies within these walls, apart from the useless and inconsequential Nic.

And, of course, her new best friend, Lucia.

Before he could meaningfully consider any of this, they'd arrived at their destination—a place that struck him with surprise.

"He's questioning the rebel in the throne room?" Magnus asked.

"Yes, your highness."

Fancy. Perhaps the king didn't wish to soil his fine clothes or dirty his boots by descending into the dungeon today. Several guards were stationed outside the doors, and four more stood inside. Gregor, the rebel who'd attacked Magnus in Limeros, kneeled at the bottom of the stairs that led up to the large golden throne, where the king calmly sat.

"Finally," the king said to Magnus. Then he addressed the guards. "We're waiting for one more guest. In the meantime, the rest of you can leave. Cronus, you stay."

Cronus bowed. The other guards turned and marched out of the room, closing the tall, heavy doors behind them.

"Who are we waiting for?" Magnus asked.

"Something vital I feel has been missing until now." The king fixed his gaze on Gregor. "I believe you two are already acquainted."

Gregor didn't look up, and Magnus regarded him with disdain. This boy had made him bleed. And he would have killed him, had Magnus not been so alert.

Magnus walked a slow circle around Gregor, who was much thinner than he last saw him a month ago. His dark hair was matted and dirty; his left hand was bandaged with dirty rags crusted with dried blood. His face showed fading bruises. His lip was split.

And he smelled rancid.

"Gregor has the answers I need." The king's tone was surprisingly calm, almost friendly. "And he's going to tell us everything."

"I've already told you all I know." Gregor finally spoke, his voice hoarse.

"I want you to tell me more about Phaedra, the Watcher who visited your dreams."

The name took Magnus by complete surprise.

"Phaedra," he said aloud. "Her name is *Phaedra*?"

"Perhaps," Gregor said, shrugging.

Magnus reeled around and grabbed the boy by his throat. "The proper answer is either *yes* or *no*, rebel scum."

"Yes," Gregor hissed. Magnus released him. "Her name is Phaedra."

It was the name of the Watcher Magnus had seen, the one who'd saved Jonas's life before Xanthus snuffed out hers.

It couldn't be a coincidence.

"You haven't dreamed of her lately, have you?" Magnus said.

"No."

"This," the king said, "I find hard to believe. Gregor, tell me what Phaedra told you about the Kindred. I want to know if she instructed you how to find it."

Gregor's cheek twitched. "I don't know anything about the Kindred."

The king offered him a grimace of a smile. "You see, I, too, have been contacted by a Watcher. Although not this Phaedra; I've never heard of her before. But perhaps lowly peasants dream of lowly Watchers. Still, that she chose you . . . it gives me pause."

The king did enjoy the sound of his own voice. Magnus wished very much he'd get on with it. He needed answers, and long-winded speeches weren't getting him any closer.

"What I know," the king continued, "is that the Kindred exist. And after many years, it can finally be found. I only need to know precisely how."

"Perhaps you should ask your own Watcher, because I can't help you," Gregor said, his voice shaking with naked contempt.

Magnus glanced at the king to see a cold smile twisting his lips.

"So you don't know," the king said.

"No. And you know what?" With the simple raising of his chin, Magnus could see Gregor had made the fateful decision to choose defiance over obedience. "Even if I did, I wouldn't tell you in a million years."

The king nodded, his neutral expression unchanged. "Exactly as I figured."

Just then the throne room doors swung open.

"Ah," the king said. "Very good. This should help."

Magnus watched Gregor's face go ashen as a girl, flanked by guards, her hands tied behind her back, entered. She had long, curly black hair and flashing light brown eyes. She wore a dirty canvas tunic over dark brown trousers, the clothing of a boy.

She looked ready to kill.

"I've come to believe this girl is your sister," the king said. "She is, yes?"

Gregor hadn't taken his eyes off the girl for a second. "Release her."

"Not so fast. Here's how this will go. You will tell me what I need to know. We will discuss the matter man-to-man without any need for violence. After that, you and your sister—Lysandra, correct?—you and Lysandra will be prepared for public execution. Apart from having to endure the presence of the crowd, your deaths will be quick and virtually painless. However, if you refuse to tell me what I need to know, I will have your sister tortured to death in front of a much smaller audience, which will include you. Should I go into detail about what will be done to her?"

The calm demeanor with which the king delivered this news sent a chill racing down Magnus's spine.

He wasn't bluffing.

Why did the threat of torture set Magnus's stomach churning? He hated his father, but he *was* a Damora. This threat shouldn't sicken him; it should energize him.

Lysandra had gone quiet, had stopped struggling, but the hatred in her eyes still burned bright. "Tell him nothing, Gregor. One way or the other, he's going to kill us both."

Gregor was visibly shaking now.

"Lysandra, forgive me," Gregor said, causing the king to break out in the slightest of smiles. Lysandra's face quickly became etched with worry, clearly fearful of what he'd say next. "Death is one thing. But torture. . . . no. I can't let that happen to you." He turned to the king, his face a mask of hatred as he began to speak. "Phaedra told me that the Kindred were ready to be *awakened*. That's the word she used. Interpret it however you wish. But she warned me that they should remain unfound, even if it means the fading of both her world and ours."

"Nonsense. How could that be?" the king prompted.

"Because mortals can't control power like that," Gregor snarled. "And anyone who thinks they can control it is a damn fool."

This boy has courage, Magnus thought, mildly impressed.

"What else?" King Gaius hissed, ignoring Gregor's insult.

"She believes that when the Kindred finally awaken, the world will burn."

"Burn," the king repeated. "What does she mean, *burn*? Surely she doesn't mean the world will literally burn?"

"I don't know. I was sure she'd return to tell me more, to tell me how to help her, but it's been weeks since I last dreamt of her. I swear on my parents' souls I'm speaking the truth. I don't give a damn about the Kindred. For all I care you can have it!"

The king pressed his fingertips together as he studied Gregor. "What do you know of a young man in Paelsia who can harness the power of fire?"

Magnus's back stiffened. Ashur had shared this rumor with him, but this was the first time he'd heard his father mention it.

"I've never heard of such a man," Gregor said, shaking his head.

"No matter, I suppose." The king leaned forward. "How do I find the Kindred, Gregor?"

Magnus felt a sudden sense of relief. For the king to dismiss such a fantastical notion so easily likely meant he'd found no truth in it.

"You're so sure that I know, but you're mistaken." Gregor's harsh tone turned wistful. "I'm certain Phaedra means to contact me again—she wouldn't just leave me. She was good and kind and wanted the best for the world . . . but she had enemies. She feared something . . . or—or *someone*."

"Perhaps she's dead," Magnus murmured.

"Yes," King Gaius agreed. "Perhaps this Watcher of yours is dead, and if so, she's no use to anyone, is she?"

"But Watchers are immortal." Gregor's gaze flickered uncertainly between father and son, his chest heaving with labored breath. Then he seemed to summon his courage again. "You need me. I've had direct contact with a Watcher who chose me above any other mortal. I am her proxy in this world. That makes me special, valuable. I promise to work for you, your majesty. I ask only that you spare my life and the life of my sister."

"Gregor, no!" Lysandra cried out, her voice breaking up with horror and disgust.

"Shut up, Lys," he growled. "Do you want to die?"

"I'd rather die a rebel than kneel before this royal sack of shit."

A guard backhanded Lysandra across her face so hard that she cried out.

Gregor jumped to his feet, but Cronus pushed him back down. "Forgive my sister," Gregor managed. "She's always been hotheaded, but not me. I can see opportunity when it presents itself. You need me, your majesty. When Phaedra contacts me again, I will tell you everything, without hesitation. I'm not lying!"

"No, you're not lying." The king reclined back in his throne, his hands grasping its golden arms. "You would do this, I can see that. You love your sister. That kind of loyalty is very important to me. Family is the most precious thing in this world. Family is the only way for us mortals to guarantee our own immortality. I respect the love you have for your family."

Gregor let out a slow, shaky sigh. "Good."

Father might really show lenience to this boy, Magnus thought. Despite his initial resistance, Gregor was ready to turn his back on his rebel leanings and pledge his allegiance to King Gaius in order to save his sister's life.

The king regarded Gregor in silence. "The problem is, I think your Watcher is either finished with you or she's dead. And she told you next to nothing to begin with. She sounds worthless to me, unlike Melenia, who has made me great promises that I know she'll keep. And to me, this makes you just as worthless."

"No, your majesty. That's not true!"

Lysandra struggled against the guard holding her in place, her gaze darting everywhere as if searching for a means of escape.

King Gaius didn't so much as glance in her direction. "Much gratitude, Gregor, for teaching me a very important lesson today," he said. "Sometimes I allow myself to be led by impatience and anger. But I've waited a lifetime for the Kindred, and I can continue to wait until the time is right. After all, I already possess the key to unlock this mystery. I simply need to learn the proper way to use it."

Panic dashed through Gregor's eyes. "I *can* help you. I can be invaluable to you!"

The king smiled, baring his straight white teeth. "Don't worry. You did prove to me that you weren't lying. That's a good thing. It means you can keep your tongue. And your sister will escape any overt unpleasantness. I'm not a monster who'd torture a young girl solely for his own amusement."

"So we will still be executed together?" Gregor said, his voice dull with defeat.

"Not quite." The king glanced at Lysandra. "Clean her up and make her beautiful—or as beautiful as a Paelsian can possibly be.

I haven't yet been able to present a female rebel to the people as an example of how I don't make exceptions when punishing those who would oppose me."

"What about my brother?" Lysandra spat. A trickle of blood slid down from the corner of her mouth where she'd been struck.

"Don't worry. Your brother will still be there to watch you die," the king said. "Cronus, bring me the boy's head. I'll make sure it's put on a spike with the very best view of the palace square."

A pained shriek escaped from Lysandra's throat. "No!"

Cronus didn't hesitate. He drew his sword as two guards grabbed Gregor's arms and held him in place.

Words of protest died in Magnus's throat. There was only one way this could end; Magnus knew his opinion was worthless now that the king had made his decision. Speaking up now would only make it worse.

Lysandra screamed and Magnus turned to her as she fought and clawed to free herself from the guards.

But there would be no stopping this.

"I'm sorry I failed you. Fight, little Lys. Fight till the very end!" Then the sword fell in one clean, heavy stroke.

Lysandra's horrified screams wedged themselves deeply into Magnus's chest, and he knew their echoes would haunt him from this moment forward.

There was no fight left in Lysandra after it was done. The guards effortlessly dragged her from the throne room to take her back to the dungeon.

Gregor's body was removed as well, and his head was placed on a silver platter.

"Well done, Cronus." The king nodded, and flicked his hand. "Now take it away."

"Yes, your majesty." Cronus's expression was ice cold and emotionless—just as it always was after carrying out executions. It was the face of a man of stone rather than flesh and blood.

Cronus left father and son alone, with only a bloodstain where Gregor had been kneeling as evidence of what had happened only moments before.

Magnus was silent. His mind had gone black, no thoughts, just a dark, heavy cloud.

"It had to be done," the king said.

"Did it?" His reply came out sharper than he'd meant it to. "A private execution of a rebel you'd previously found useful? No, I don't think it *had* to be done."

The king shot Magnus a look of surprise.

"You did that because you wanted to relish in the look on that girl's face as you murdered her brother right in front of her," Magnus went on. "You enjoyed it. You wanted to break the spirit you saw in her so she would accept her own fate without a fight. So her fiery spirit, which lingers despite having been locked up in your dungeon, doesn't rile up the execution crowd, which I know you'll pad with your most loyal minions. Well, let me be the first to congratulate you, Father, because you succeeded."

The king narrowed his eyes. "What is wrong with you, boy? Why must you oppose everything I ever do?"

Magnus found it difficult to breathe as every bit of frustration, doubt, and anger directed at his father, feelings he'd tried so very hard to repress, surged to the forefront. "Because not everything you do is right!"

"I only do what I must to maintain my power here in this era of transition, so that one day you won't have as much to struggle with. This is a dangerous time for us, son. There is no room for dissent."

"Is that why you ordered a piece of shit like Aron Lagaris to murder Mother? To lessen my struggle?"

The words were out before he could stop them, and they earned him a satisfying look of shock from the king. Why stop now?

"Funny, I thought you knew everything that happened in your kingdom, thanks to all your spies and informants," Magnus continued. "But you didn't know this tidbit. You didn't know that Aron confessed to me, confessed that you had him take a knife to my mother in the dead of night, ending her life so you could blame it on Jonas Agallon."

The king's expression of shock leveled out to neutral. "You're the one who killed Aron."

His secret was out. Now he had nothing to lose. "I'd planned to bring him back here to answer for his crime, but he tried to kill me. Obviously, he failed. Seeing the life leave his eyes wasn't as satisfying as I'd hoped. But he wasn't the real criminal. He was only the weapon. *You* killed my mother and—"

"And now I assume you want me dead as well." The king cut him off and rose from his throne, descending the steps so he stood face-to-face with Magnus. "Of course you do. Here." He placed a silver dagger in Magnus's hand. "I will give you this one chance to end my life, if that's what you really want. Here and now. Do it."

Magnus's hand trembled. "This is a trick."

The king kept his gaze fixed on his son. "Althea was working against me. She opposed my quest to find the Kindred—she always did. She hated me and wanted to keep me from any power that might strengthen my reign. She wanted Lucia dead and I believe that she meant to kill you as well, to prevent me from having a true heir. She had to die, Magnus."

Magnus's very bones shook. The hilt of the dagger felt like ice against his skin. "That was not your only option."

"Yes, it was. I know some of my decisions have been harsh, but they've all been necessary."

Lucia had told Magnus that their mother wanted her dead because she feared her magic, that she'd been giving Lucia a potion to keep her asleep for so long . . . but Magnus didn't believe that was reason enough for the king to murder her. Punish, yes. Banish, perhaps. But death? It didn't make sense to him and it never would.

"But Mother—" he began.

"Althea wasn't your real mother."

The blunt statement hit Magnus like a fist to his gut. "What?"

The king gazed at him steadily. "She lost the baby she believed was you and went mad with grief. Shortly before this, another child had been born of my seed, and I gave that child—*you*—to her. You brought her back from the brink of insanity. She believed she was your mother up until her last breath, but she was never of your blood."

Magnus stared at him, his mind reeling. "You're lying."

"Your true mother was Sabina."

He felt gut-punched again, and he staggered back from the king in horror. Sabina, his father's mistress, an evil, power-hungry witch. Dead now, killed by Lucia's magic. "Another lie! Sabina tried to kill me—she tried to kill me after she tried to *seduce* me."

The king lowered his brow. "She was a complicated woman, I'll admit that much. Her passions sometimes went beyond what even I could understand. But it doesn't change the truth. You're mine and Sabina's only son. She hid her pregnancy from everyone. Only Sabina, I, and the midwife who helped you into this world ever knew what really happened."

"No." Bile rose in Magnus's throat. The world had shifted on its axis; the ground was now unsteady beneath his feet.

The king gripped Magnus's shoulders so tightly he winced. "You have the blood of both a witch and a king running through your veins. Every witch has ancestral ties to the Watchers. *You* have that. That is why I've always seen something special in you, something superior."

Magnus couldn't accept this. All his life he'd known Sabina as his father's mistress and advisor, but to Magnus she'd never been more than another irrelevant presence he'd had to tolerate. He hadn't mourned her death for a moment. He'd hated her.

She would *never* be his mother.

Magnus's stomach was in knots, his heart a dark, heavy weight in his chest.

He wanted to drink. To allow that pleasant fog to spread through his mind until it obliterated all thoughts. "Why haven't you told me this before?"

A shadow of reverie crossed the king's face, making him appear older than his years. "I should have. I'm sorry I didn't. But now you see that Althea had no true claim over you. You are free of any lasting allegiance to her. She was a cruel and heartless woman. She always was."

No, she wasn't, Magnus thought. *Not always.*

"So often I saw how starved you were for the love of a mother who wouldn't give affection to you. Her mind was faulty, her sanity shaky, especially these last eighteen years. All of this led her to make the mistakes that sealed her fate. She was standing in my way. In *your* way. You must accept these truths if we have any chance of moving forward. You are my son. My heir. We are one and the same."

To be like the king—strong, ruthless, dominant, relentless in pursuit of his goals. This was what he'd always wanted.

And Sabina had been the same in so many ways.

"Everything I do is for you, Magnus. *Everything*. Please forgive me for withholding this truth from you and for anything I've done that has hurt you in the past. My only goal was to make you stronger. I love you, my son."

The king pulled Magnus close in a tight embrace. Magnus stood like a statue, stony and silent, his mind trapped in turmoil.

He let the dagger fall from his grip and clatter to the floor.

His father had never embraced him like this before.

And for just a moment before he pulled away to leave the throne room, Magnus let him.

CHAPTER 12

JONAS

AURANOS

Jonas's mood was as black as the night sky.

That evening he was in a village called Viridy, a half-day's journey northeast of the City of Gold. It wasn't his first visit; he had begun to use a tavern there as a central meeting place. He'd sent Felix on ahead to meet him there tonight, while he had spent the last day and a half following a whispered rumor about some rebels and a group of Paelsian slaves who'd escaped from the road camp alive. But that rumor had proven to be false.

Even though King Gaius's rule brought out a palpable edge of uneasiness amongst the people, affluence still glittered in Viridy like gold, much like every other Auranian town Jonas had visited. The streets were paved not in dirt and rock, but sparkling cobblestones. The storefronts were made not of clay, but of sturdy stone and wood.

This was the home of thousands of citizens who paid high taxes to whichever king sat his royal arse on the throne, but still they lived well. No one starved, wandering the streets in rags searching for their next meal. No one froze in alleys because they were denied warmth or shelter during a cold winter's night, as they did in Paelsia.

But unlike someone who'd actually experienced pain and squalor, the people here didn't appreciate what they had. That they took it all for granted put a sour taste in Jonas's mouth. He had no doubt they'd collectively crumple if their easy lifestyles were ever stolen from them.

On the whole, Paelsians—for all their struggles and naïve beliefs in unavoidable destiny—were a hardier breed than Auranians. They were survivors. It's what Jonas loved most about his people.

Walking along the side of the street, he felt a hand grip the sleeve of his hooded cloak, stopping him in his tracks outside an inn.

"You—" An ugly face cocked to the side as a man peered at Jonas through the shadows. "I know you."

Jonas regarded the man warily. "Doubt that. Let go of me."

"Yeah, I do know you." A slow smile crept onto his face. "You're that rebel I've seen on the posters."

Jonas's stomach sank. He'd prefer not to be recognized tonight if he could help it. "I've no idea what you're talking about."

"Don't worry, kid. I'm impressed." His slurred words were enough to prove he had been drinking heavily. It was a special day in Auranos, the Day of Flames, which honored one half of the goddess Cleiona's legendary magic. The holiday gave its citizens a reason to drink more wine than usual and dress in orange and yellow to represent the eternal fire of their deity. "I've been thinking I'd make a good rebel myself. Like to kick the arse of the King of Blood right out of the world of the living."

"I think you have me confused with someone else," Jonas said evenly.

He wasn't in a mood to recruit ordinary citizens. His meeting tonight was with representatives from an Auranian group of rebels whom he hoped could help him free Lysandra and the others.

Suddenly, a loud cracking sound made him jump and reel in the direction of a burst of sparkling yellow light. Somebody screamed, and a blond boy about sixteen years old raced down the street, his tunic ablaze. He launched himself face-first into a barrel of water.

"Not again," the drunk mumbled. "Petros, you're a damn fool!" he shouted. "You're going to get yourself killed playing with fire like that!"

The boy pulled himself out of the barrel and cast a dark look at the drunk. "Mind your own business, old man."

"You burn down our home and it's my business. I'll drown you in that barrel if you don't do as I say!"

The boy didn't offer anything more than a rude gesture in the drunk's general direction and a dour glare at Jonas before he jogged away.

"What was that all about?" Jonas asked.

"My idiot fire-obsessed son," the man replied. "He likes to experiment with ridiculous concoctions that do little more than burn his eyebrows off. Tonight his excuse is that he is honoring the fire goddess by causing his trouble throughout the village with these works of fire. Foolish boy."

Jonas had no time for chitchat with drunken locals about their troublesome sons. He needed to join Felix at the tavern in time for their meeting.

With a mumbled farewell and a word of good luck, he successfully slipped away from the man. Before he reached the tavern, he sensed someone else following him.

Two someone elses, to be exact, one of whom stepped out of the shadows and blocked his way.

"You look like that rebel the king's after." The man was a half-foot taller than Jonas and had a long, crooked nose.

"I might look like him, but it's not me," he said.

The second man had blond, greasy hair and a thin, rodentlike face. He yanked Jonas's hood right off his head to get a better look at him.

"Yeah, you're the one who stuck a dagger in the bitch queen. Don't be shy about it. We applaud you for a job well done."

All the more reason to avoid them if they were the types to celebrate the death of a woman.

"Let me pass," Jonas hissed.

"C'mon. It's a night of celebration. Try to be friendly."

"Let me pass," he said again, "or we're going to have a problem."

The bald man laughed and elbowed his friend. "Not very friendly, is he? And here I thought you might be able to help us out."

Jonas glared at them. "Really? And how did you think I might help you out?"

"The reward on the posters . . . it's a hefty one. While I appreciate anyone working to send the king back to his land of ice—to be buried in it, preferably—I could use that gold."

Only more proof that the vast majority of Auranians were greedy and selfish.

Jonas didn't hesitate to fight his way out of the situation. He slammed his fist into the bald man's jaw, sending him staggering back to fall in a grunting heap on his backside. The blond one grabbed him from behind, and Jonas immediately felt the sharp, cold edge of steel at his throat. He stopped struggling. The bald man wiped the blood off his bottom lip with the back of his hand and pushed himself up off the ground.

They were alone in the street. It was dark, and the tavern was still a few streets away.

The bald man crossed his arms and grinned at Jonas through the darkness. The other one didn't move, his dagger still digging into Jonas's throat. "Yes, the king'll pay good coin to get his hands on you. It's your choice now, dead or alive. I really couldn't care less which."

Before the bald one could signal his friend to cut Jonas's throat, Felix's voice sliced through the night, stopping them.

"Again? I leave you on your own for mere moments and you find yourself in yet another tight spot?"

"Afraid so. A little help, please?"

The bald man spun around and eyed Jonas's sizable friend with alarm.

"The reward is large enough to split three ways," he said.

Felix crossed his arms. "Reward, huh? How much?"

Jonas stopped breathing. When all was said and done, he'd only known Felix for a couple of weeks. Did he have any true assurance that he wouldn't switch allegiances the moment it suited his purposes?

"Ten thousand Auranian centimos."

"That's steep. A third of that could set me up in a nice villa for the next few years. Problem is, I've never liked to share. Sorry."

Felix grabbed the bald man and pressed his knife to his throat, then shot a nasty look at the blond. "Release my friend. Now."

Relief washed through Jonas. Why had he doubted him?

"We don't want any trouble," the blond said.

Felix shrugged. "Could have fooled me."

"He's a wanted criminal," the bald man sputtered.

"The wine is flowing like water tonight, and by the smell you two have been swimming in it. This kid isn't who you think. Not even close. We're just a couple of farmer's sons out for a night of drinking in the name of the goddess. Nobody special. You should be thanking me for stopping you before you lost your own heads for bothering the king's guards."

Finally, an edge of uncertainty crept onto their faces.

"Let him go," the bald man growled. "Do it."

Reluctantly, the blond released Jonas.

Felix shoved the bald man but didn't sheath his knife just yet. "Do we still have a problem here?"

"No problem."

"Good. Now be off with you."

Without another word, they scurried away.

Jonas knew he was having an off night when it came to watching his guard. On a normal day, he could have handled the two of them on his own without intervention.

It was embarrassing, really.

"Do me a favor?" Felix said, finally putting his weapon away.

"Sure."

"Keep that hood up over that famous face of yours. It'll make things much simpler for us if you don't get recognized again. Got it?"

Jonas nodded with a jerk of his head. "Got it."

The Silver Toad was owned by a rebel sympathizer who had readily agreed to let Jonas to use the tavern and inn when needed. Tonight the tavern was packed wall to wall with people celebrating the Day of Flames, spending all they had on wine, their coins glittering beneath the lanterns hanging from the rafters. Before he'd entered the tavern, Jonas had caught another glimpse of Petros nearby.

The boy continued to celebrate the goddess with his dangerous fire displays outside, causing patrons to jump up with surprise at the occasional explosions.

Jonas tried to ignore the distractions and focus on the task at hand as he waited for the Auranian rebels to show.

"How long are we going to wait?" Felix asked.

"As long as it takes."

"They're not coming. This is their answer, Jonas. They're not going to help."

"They promised they'd be here."

"You sent a message requesting them to risk their necks to save a few of your friends—"

"I didn't put it like that."

There was strength in numbers, and Jonas knew there were others who shared his goals to end King Gaius's reign and to help to free the Paelsians that had been enslaved to work on the Blood Road.

Despite his distaste for those who called this kingdom home, these were his allies. Auranians or Paelsians, they were united in their hatred of the king.

"They have their own plans," Felix said. "They won't help us with ours."

Jonas blinked hard, knowing Felix spoke the truth. Nobody was coming. He was a joke—the rebel leader who led his people to their deaths time and again. "Why are *you* still here if I'm so damn pathetic? Why haven't you taken off yet? Stick with me and you'll end up dead."

"Promises, promises." Felix regarded him patiently, his arms crossed over his chest. Then he went to the bar, returning quickly to Jonas's table with two large tankards of dark ale that splashed onto the wooden surface as he set them down.

"Drink up," Felix said.

Jonas stared at the liquid offering. To their left, a band had started to play a song about the goddess's beauty. People were singing and stomping their feet on the floor in a drunken dance.

"Ale won't solve my problems," Jonas said.

"But I doubt it'll make them any worse."

Jonas took a long swig of the strong drink, and the liquid burned going down his throat. "I have to save her."

"If what you've told me about Lysandra is true, she knows the risk you'd be taking. She won't want you to lose your head over her."

Lysandra wasn't the type to want to be rescued by a boy. She'd probably be furious that Jonas had continued to obsess over her rather than focusing on bringing down the king.

She knew that, more than anything, Jonas wanted to be the one who dealt the fatal blow.

"Well, what do we have here?" Felix said. "There's a cute little thing looking right at you, friend. Please tell me you're willing to share."

Jonas frowned and glanced over his shoulder at a girl who stood about a dozen paces away, eyeing him through the crowd. She pushed back the hood of the dark cloak she was wrapped in to reveal her short hair and dark brown eyes. She caught his eye, then made her way over to sit down at the table.

"Nerissa," Jonas said, his mood immediately lightening. "It's good to see you."

She flashed him a grin. "You, too."

Seeing Felix eye the pretty girl with interest, Jonas flicked him a glance. "Nerissa Florens, this is Felix Gaebras."

She assessed Felix with guarded interest. "Where'd you meet him, Jonas?"

"Traveling."

"You trust him?"

"Yes." And that trust had been proven yet again tonight—money wasn't as important as loyalty to Felix.

Her expression grew pinched. "I'm sure you'll forgive me if I hold back my enthusiasm. He looks like a hired thug."

"Such charming words." Felix shifted to the seat next to her, his smile widening. "And from such a charming mouth. Can it do anything besides talk?"

She held his gaze boldly. "It can bite."

"Good to know." The warning only seemed to intrigue Felix more.

He'd better be careful, Jonas thought with amusement. Nerissa wasn't joking.

"I have news," Nerissa said. "And a message. Which do you want first?"

His lightened mood vanished as quickly as it had arrived.

"The news," Jonas said.

"The executions are set for the day after tomorrow. Midday in the palace square. The king's arranged for a large group of his most ardent supporters to surround the execution stage to ensure their cheers will be the loudest."

The world slowed and darkened around Jonas. "It's too soon. I can't—I don't have enough time to do anything." He swore under his breath, damning the Auranian rebels for not even hearing him out tonight. "How am I supposed to stop the execution of four rebels?"

"*Two* rebels, I'm afraid." Nerissa's expression was grim. "Two have already died in the dungeons."

A fist slammed through his chest and clutched his heart. "Who still lives?"

"Tarus and Lysandra. Cato and Fabius were both killed trying to escape."

He drained the rest of his ale. The thought that he'd lost any-one at all was painful, but he couldn't help being silently relieved that Lys and Tarus had survived.

Only to fall beneath the executioner's ax in less than two days.

Felix clasped his shoulder. "I'm sorry."

He'd failed Tomas. He'd failed Brion. He'd failed his rebels as he marched them to their doom.

Everything he touched turned to ash.

"What's the message?" Jonas asked, his throat tight.

Nerissa pushed a folded piece of parchment across the table to-ward him. He broke the wax seal and unfolded it, holding it closer to the candlelight.

J—

> *The king seeks the Kindred. He believes the crystals exist, but he doesn't yet know where or how to recover them.*

> *We must find them first. They cannot fall into his hands, or else he will be unstoppable.*

> *I will send another message when I know more. Tell no one about this.*

> *—C*

Jonas's heart beat louder and faster with every word. He read Cleo's note twice before holding it over the candle and burning it.

The Kindred. Once he would have scoffed at the idea of magic, but no more. He didn't doubt the truth of the princess's message for a moment.

"What did it say?" Felix asked.

He would honor Cleo's request to tell no one, especially since there was nothing in the message that could help them—only a hint of more information to come. "The king refuses to leave the palace, fearful of a rebel attack."

Felix snorted. "What a coward."

Bang!

Jonas started and Nerissa shrieked, gripping the edges of the table. The tavern fell silent and the patrons turned with alarm in the direction of the noise outside.

"Young Petros, always making trouble," one woman grumbled. "He's going to kill this entire village if he's not careful."

Peals of laughter rang out, and then the patrons returned to regular conversation.

Jonas was silent, lost in the thoughts now swirling around his mind like a tornado.

"I can save them."

"What?" Felix studied him.

"Lys and Tarus. I can save them."

"You sure about that?"

"I wasn't before, but . . ." Jonas stood up, his dark mood fading away as a plan solidified in his mind. "I need help . . . and I think I know who can help me."

"Help *us*, you mean." Felix stood, his chair squeaking loudly against the wooden floor. "What do you have in mind?"

"Jonas," Nerissa protested. "I hate to muddy the waters of your conviction, but this is far too dangerous. Trying to stop those executions with less than two days to plan is going to get you killed as well."

"Perhaps." A smile slowly stretched across his face from ear to ear. "But I can think of far worse ways to die."

CHAPTER 13

NIC

AURANOS

His journey to see Prince Ashur had started off so well.

Yet now Nic lay in a shallow pool of his own blood, having been beaten nearly senseless. He gazed up into the bright summer sunlight at the faces of his two attackers.

Burrus pressed the point of his sword firmly against Nic's chest. "Thought you could be like us? You're nothing like us. You're worthless."

"Just kill him and get it over with," Milo said, bored. His knuckles were red and raw from the pounding he'd given Nic after yanking him off his horse.

"What do you have to say for yourself, maggot?" Burrus was the more playful of the two, like a cat who enjoyed batting mice around for hours before finally gnawing off their furry little heads.

He wanted Nic to beg, that was clear enough. To show them how pathetic and weak he was. But even if he begged, Nic knew they'd kill him anyway.

All he could do was glare up at them and hope his eyes showed no fear.

He'd finally found a good enough excuse to leave the palace and travel to the Cortas's villa to learn more about Ashur and Amara's potential to be allies to the princess. But then he'd been interrupted by these two.

"You've been lucky so far," Burrus continued. "Prince Magnus's blond bitch of a wife calls you her friend—I can't think of any other reason for the king to have kept you alive this long. You're the most worthless guard I've ever seen."

"That little sister of yours was pretty sweet, though," Milo said. "Would have liked to get her on her back. Too bad she's dead."

His vision turning red with fury, Nic used every last ounce of his strength to push himself up from the ground. But the pressure of the sword and the pain as it pierced his skin drove him back down.

"Do not mention my sister again," he snarled, ready to fight. Ready to kill.

Burrus smiled cruelly. "Must make you so angry to have to bow down before her killer every day."

Burrus was right. Being forced to serve his sister's murderer made Nic so angry he couldn't see straight. The need for vengeance on those who had destroyed his life and his family consumed his waking hours and haunted his dreams.

Helping Cleo destroy the king and his family was Nic's sole interest now.

Suddenly, the two thugs froze and glanced warily at each other as a carriage approached, stopping right in front of them. The door creaked open and Princess Amara craned her head out and gazed back at them.

"Good day," the princess said sweetly.

"Good day, your grace," the two replied, straightening their shoulders.

Nic raised his hand from his crumpled position on the ground and gave a small, silent wave.

"Your friend looks like he's had a difficult day," Amara said.

"Don't mind him," Milo replied. "He ran into some thieves, nearly lost his life. Too weak to fight them off. Lucky for him we arrived before they killed him."

"Help him into our carriage. I'll have my maids tend to his wounds back at the villa."

Milo and Burrus hesitated. To deny royalty a request, even from a foreign princess, would be a very unfortunate misstep.

"Yes, your grace."

The two got Nic to his feet and roughly shoved him into the carriage.

Burrus gave him a tight smile. "We'll continue our conversation later."

The carriage door closed and Nic suddenly realized that the princess wasn't alone in the carriage. Her brother, Ashur, sat next to her.

Nic's mouth went dry. "Your grace."

"It's good to see you again, Nicolo," Prince Ashur said, frowning as he assessed Nic's condition. "Will you be all right?"

Nic hunched over in his seat, sure that at least two of his ribs were broken. He had a series of shallow stab wounds peppering his entire body, but the blood didn't show against the red of his uniform. His face felt as if it had been through a meat grinder; his right cheek throbbed with every beat of his heart.

"I think so," he managed. "Much gratitude to you both for your assistance."

"You're Cleo's friend, aren't you?" Amara asked.

"I . . . I am." He spared a glance at Ashur, who studied him curiously.

"Friends since childhood," the princess continued.

"Yes, that's right."

Had the prince shared with his sister their discussion from that fateful night? Did she know Ashur sought the Kindred, or was that his secret? It would be only one of many secrets the prince kept behind those gray-blue eyes.

They arrived at the luxurious villa which looked down upon a lush green meadow. The princess had two male servants assist Nic out of the carriage, helping him into the expansive home. After two handmaidens cleaned and bandaged his wounds, he was escorted to the villa's courtyard, where he sat down gingerly on the patio. A servant handed him a goblet filled with peach juice, which he drank with enthusiasm.

The princess sat opposite Nic, and suddenly the gravity of the situation lay heavily on his shoulders. Being pampered by the princess herself had certainly helped get him closer to the royals than any other guard would get without great effort. If his body didn't feel so broken and bruised, he might have actually thanked Burrus and Milo for facilitating this opportunity.

"Now, let's get one thing straight," Princess Amara said, breaking the silence. "I don't believe for one moment you were set upon by thieves. Those two brutes did this to you—two against one. Would they have killed you had we not shown up when we did?"

"I believe that was their plan," Nic admitted. "I'm very grateful that you intervened. I owe you my life."

"Why would they want to hurt you?"

"Because they don't like me."

Amara laughed lightly at his honesty. "Yes, I believe their sentiment is now written all over your face."

Ashur walked out and joined them, sitting in a chair next to Nic while Amara rose to receive a flower arrangement a servant brought into the courtyard.

"From King Gaius, who hopes you're enjoying this villa," the servant said. Amara nodded and waved her away.

"King Gaius," Amara repeated the name as she brushed her hand over the beautiful orchids. "How kind of him, don't you think, brother?"

"Very kind," Ashur said dryly.

"He banishes us to a forgettable location outside the palace walls, then sends flowers as a sign of friendship. Does he think we'll be wooed by this paltry offering?"

"I'm not quite sure what that man is thinking." Ashur paused. "Perhaps our friend Nicolo might know."

Nic straightened his back, which only made his ribs hurt more. "Believe me, I'm just a lowly palace guard. You might want to talk to Cronus if you want some inside information. He's quite chatty."

His description of the silently intimidating captain of the guards earned him a smile from the prince and a quizzical look from the princess. Perhaps she didn't understand his sarcasm.

Nic wanted to speak with Ashur alone, but Amara was making that impossible.

Ashur leaned closer. "How are you feeling? Did they do any permanent damage?"

Being near the prince, remembering what had happened in that alleyway, was much more difficult than he'd anticipated. "I'll heal."

"You look very pale."

"That's how I always look."

"You look fine to me, otherwise," Ashur said, raising an eyebrow. "Happily, bruises fade and I'm sure you'll be good as new before too long."

Nic shifted uncomfortably in his seat. "I hope you're right."

"I know you're already well acquainted with my brother," Amara said.

Nic wasn't sure how he should respond to her statement. "We've spoken before."

She studied him with open interest. "Ashur believes your relationship with Princess Cleiona makes you quite valuable."

"Oh?"

"She sent you here today to speak with us, didn't she?"

He gaped at her. "Excuse me?"

"It's an educated guess. Please correct me if I'm mistaken. There's no other reason for you to venture all this way, is there?"

He cleared his throat and sipped some peach juice to compose himself. "If that's what you believe, what reason would she have for sending me?"

"So you can assess whether we're friend or foe," Amara said simply. "And she chose you because she trusts no one else."

Nic glanced at Ashur.

The prince's lips quirked up at Nic's stunned expression. "My sister's educated guesses are legendary in Kraeshia. She's almost always right."

"The princess should know that we *are* worthy of her trust," Amara continued, as if she hadn't just directly stated what Nic had been trying to be extremely delicate about. "We are happy to offer our friendship to Cleo, but she needs to be willing to help us in return."

Nic drained the rest of his drink in a single gulp. No reason to deny anything. Now he had to gather as much information as he could. "What do you want?"

"What we want," Ashur said, "is the Kindred. My father has finally accepted there might be a treasure here worth claiming for Kraeshia. But he's a man of brute force rather than delicate finesse. Many will die if he and his armada come here to challenge King Gaius. I'd rather prevent all of that, if possible."

From Ashur's description, Emperor Cortas was every bit as fearsome as his public reputation, and every bit as ruthless as King Gaius. A shiver shot down Nic's spine. "You think Cleo knows how to find the Kindred?"

"Yes," Amara said, smiling.

Nic fell silent, eyeing the two with doubt and suspicion. They were too eager to state their intentions, too ready to align. Was all of this just part of the simple Kraeshian candidness, or should Nic be heeding this as a warning?

His first priority was to protect Cleo. He couldn't tell them everything they wanted to know. Not until he trusted them completely.

And he was far from that point.

Ashur laughed. "I think we've scared him. Too much too soon, perhaps."

Amara slid her hand over her shiny black hair, patting a few loose strands back into place. "And here I thought you had him wrapped around your little finger. Has your infamous charm finally failed you, brother?"

Nic felt what color he had left drain from his face.

"Don't be upset. You're certainly not the first creature to be caught in my brother's pretty net." Amara leaned forward and patted Nic on his knee. "My goodness, you look like you're ready to throw yourself off the nearest cliff."

Wrapped around his little finger? Pretty net? What exactly did Amara think she knew?

Nic was not wrapped around *anyone's* little finger. Except Cleo's, perhaps, and that was entirely his choice. Cleo was family—the only family he had left. Ashur was nobody to Nic except a potential threat who already knew far too much.

Amara voice took on a gentle tone. "Tell Cleo that we're willing to share the treasure with her. We'll take two crystals, and she can keep the other two. Once all is said and done, my father will invade and claim Paelsia and Limeros for Kraeshia. Auranos will remain under Cleo's control. There will be no reason for further bloodshed if she complies with the emperor's wishes."

Wishes? These sounded more like demands.

No, this didn't feel right at all. Coming here was a mistake.

Ashur rose from his chair and walked toward the edge of the seating area, his face in shadow as he regarded Nic. "In addition, you will inform us about the king's shifting plans. I'm positive that he also searches for the Kindred."

To even *speak* about this was to commit treason. If Nic were found out, the punishment he'd receive at the king's command would make the beating he took from Milo and Burrus look like a gentle hug. He'd be joining the accused rebels tomorrow at their public execution, and not to watch, but to lose his head as well.

He had to get out of there. He had to get back to Cleo and tell her everything, that he didn't trust the Kraeshians—not yet. Only time would tell if they would be true to their word.

"I'll share your offer with the princess," Nic said.

"Kindly ask her to be swift about her response," Amara said. "We can't be expected to wait forever, can we?"

"I will be sure to convey the message," Nic said, his throat tight.

He made excuses to leave, and Ashur walked him out to a waiting carriage bound for the palace.

"Excuse my sister," Ashur said. The sun shone more brightly on this side of the villa, turning his eyes more intensely blue than gray. "Sometimes she is a little too . . . enthusiastic. And impatient. She meant no offense."

"None was taken," Nic said tightly.

"She constantly underestimates me. I'm the youngest son, the brother with the least responsibility. She may be the baby of the family, but she goes after what she wants with every weapon in her arsenal."

This didn't surprise Nic in the least. "And you?" he asked.

Ashur smirked slightly. "I'm rarely interested in the same thing for more than a day or two unless I consider it of true importance. Often that which I find the most special is of little interest or value to others. But it doesn't matter to me what anyone else thinks about my choices. What about you?"

The deep tone of the prince's accented voice was nearly hypnotic. "I don't know what you mean."

"Do you care what others think of you?"

Nic shied away from his gaze. "I'm a lowly palace guard, considered worthless by my peers. This was proven to you today on the roadside. When it comes to my destiny, your grace, I have no control over it or what others think of me."

The prince shook his head. "You're dead wrong about two things."

"Really?" He turned away and crossed his arms over his aching rib cage, fighting not to roll his eyes. "What's the first?"

"No one controls your destiny but you."

"If you say so." Nic hissed out a long breath. "And the second?"

"That, to me, you are the very opposite of worthless."

Nic looked at the prince with surprise, but Ashur just turned and began to walk away.

"May you have a safe trip back to the palace," the prince said without turning around.

The guards assigned to escort Nic home unceremoniously shoved him out of the carriage five miles outside of the city walls.

"You can walk from here," one sneered.

"Excellent," Nic said. "Thanks so much for the ride." As the carriage rode off, he added, "You rancid piles of horse dung."

Injured, bruised, exhausted, and humiliated, he began the walk across the green fields and forest land that would, further east, intersect with the king's shiny new Imperial Road.

He had no idea how to explain his day to Cleo. Everything about it felt so surreal that, if it weren't for his aching rib cage and a back tooth that now felt a little loose, he would have believed it was all a dream.

He thought he might save some time by taking a shortcut through a thatch of forest. Just as he started to praise himself for his first good idea of the day, a shadow swiftly approached him from either side. Before he knew it, Nic was on his back again, his breath knocked out of him.

"We meet again," said an oddly familiar voice.

Nic blinked until his vision cleared enough for him to see Jonas Agallon crouching over him, pressing his jeweled dagger against his throat. It was the second time that Jonas had held that very dagger to Nic's flesh.

"You—" he began.

"Don't talk," Jonas said. "Not yet. I'm going to explain something to you quickly before you speak. Understood?"

The rebel's face was cast in the shadows of the canopy of lush trees overhead. Insects buzzed a constant symphony all around. The heat, combined with all the blood he'd lost earlier that day, made Nic feel close to losing consciousness.

He shot a glance at Jonas's companion: a tall, tanned, and dangerous-looking boy standing with his arms crossed over his broad chest. Finally, Nic's gaze returned to Jonas and he gave a small nod of agreement.

"We've had our differences in the past," Jonas said. "And seeing you in that red uniform, I'm not sure this conversation isn't going to be a huge waste of my breath, but here it goes. I have friends who are scheduled to be executed tomorrow at midday. I need to save their arses, but I'm running out of options. Despite that uniform, I believe you to be loyal to Cleo. If you're loyal to Cleo, you're not loyal to the Damoras. In fact, I'm going to bet you hate them. Yes or no?"

Nic managed to speak through gritted teeth. "Yes."

Jonas nodded once, his expression grim. "I want them dead. But first I need to help my friends. And to help my friends, I need assistance from someone trustworthy inside those walls, someone who wears your uniform. I know what's being said about me and what I'm accused of. If I'm recognized, I'll be killed on the spot and my murderer will get a nice fat reward."

"We gotta get out of here, Jonas," his companion growled. "Let's speed this up, all right?"

Jonas didn't take his eyes off Nic. "I'll need your help tomorrow. You should know, saying yes may end up getting you killed, but I promise it'll be a damn glorious death. If you say no, I won't kill you. You can go back to your new life at the king's knee. It's got to be your choice. Your answer can seal your destiny, Nic—right here and right now. Are you with me? Or are you against me?"

After this day of beatings and abuse and being made to feel worthless, Nic was finally being given a choice. By someone he'd hated since the moment he'd first learned his name.

A Paelsian savage driven by vengeance.

A rebel leader who'd failed many more times than he'd succeeded.

The alleged murderer of Queen Althea.

The kidnapper of Cleo.

Jonas Agallon was about as trustworthy as a slimy sea snake.

And no decision in his life had ever been easier.

CHAPTER 14

LYSANDRA

AURANOS

She remembered when the boys in her village would pick on her when she was six, maybe seven years old. Once, one particularly mean boy had tripped her on her way back from the forest, her arms weighed down with the wood she'd been sent to gather.

She hadn't seen his foot. And she hadn't noticed the mud puddle beneath her until she landed face-first in it, the firewood flying out of her grip and falling into the muddy water after her. Ruined.

"Lysandra's a crybaby," another boy had taunted as her tears began to flow. His friends joined in his laughter. "Boo hoo! Cry, Lysandra! Cry harder!"

They'd run away when Gregor approached, but she could barely see him through her tears. The firewood was spoiled and it had taken her forever to gather enough dry twigs and branches. Without it, there would be no dinner. No warmth.

She didn't try to get up. She sat there, her skirts soiled, and she cried.

"Stop it," Gregor had said.

But she couldn't. She couldn't stop crying, no matter how much she'd wanted to.

"Stop it," he said again, grabbing her wrists and pulling her roughly to her feet. "Stop crying!"

"That boy—he pushed me. He's so mean!"

"And you're surprised? He's mean to everyone who lets him. C'mon, little Lys. I thought you were better than this."

His words surprised her. "Better?"

"Maybe you *are* a crybaby."

"I am *not*!"

He shoved her until she staggered back and dropped into the puddle again. She stared up at him with shock.

"You're going to let me do that?" he demanded.

"Wh-what?"

"Get up!"

Shock gave way to anger as she got to her feet. She glared at him, her small fists clenched at her sides, her tears forgotten.

"That's better," he said. "You don't cry when someone pushes you down. You get up. You get up and you fight back. And pretty soon nobody's going to shove you anymore because they'll see it's not worth it. You won't let anyone push you around and make you cry. Got it?"

At the time, Lysandra didn't understand what he'd been trying to teach her. All she knew was that her skirts were muddy and her mother would be angry that she'd spent so long gathering nothing but dirt.

Get up. Again and again. There are those who would push you down into the mud and laugh at you. They wanted to see tears. They wanted to see defeat because it made them feel better about their own sad little lives.

But sometimes it was hard to rise back up. Sometimes the mud grew so solid and so thick around you that there was no escape. And the taunting laughter never stopped.

Suddenly, the sting of a slap made her gasp, and Lysandra was pulled out of her memories to find herself staring into the freckled face of Tarus.

"Come on, Lys!" He had her by her shoulders, his fingers biting into her flesh. "The guards are coming. I need you."

"Good," she whispered. "It's finally time to end this."

He shook her. "No! You can't give up. It's only us, you know that? Cato and Fabius are dead—they were killed trying to escape. We're the only ones left!"

The news was yet another blow, but she wasn't surprised. Cato and Fabius would have preferred to die fighting, rather than as a spectacle before a crowd.

Safe travels to the ever after, my friends, she thought, her heart heavy.

She glanced over to the corner where her brother had once slept. Where he'd searched and searched his dreams for his Watcher, hoping she held the answers he'd desperately needed to survive.

A sharp pain now twisted in her chest. Already the memory of his death had settled into her mind like the roots of a dark, malevolent tree, twisting and writhing, choking away all the life, all the hope, until nothing but darkness remained.

They'd killed Gregor in front of her and all she could do was scream.

"Lys, please." Tarus grabbed her face as she began to tremble. "You've *always* been so strong. Please be strong today."

"And what will strength accomplish now? We're going to die."

Now that she'd accepted her fate, a feeling of calm spread

through her, numbing her senses. Her heart did not mirror the panic on Tarus's face.

Soon it would be over. All the pain. All the misery. All the misplaced hope.

Soon there would only be silence.

Tarus smacked her again. "Lys! Stay with me!"

How she wished she could share this newfound serenity with him and take away his fear.

The guards entered their cell. They bound their hands behind their backs with rough ropes and led them out of the dungeon. Earlier, the prisoners had been allowed to wash the dirt from their skin and faces and had been given clean clothes for their presentation to the crowd. In her daze Lysandra could vaguely hear the taunts and heckles of the other prisoners they passed, along with a few blessings from those who hadn't yet lost their souls to this cesspit.

The good and the bad—it was easy to ignore every last one of them.

"No fight left," one guard said to his colleague. "This one had fire in her eyes mere days ago, but it's died out now."

"Wouldn't help her anyway," said the other.

They were right. Before, she was made of pure fire and fury. She'd been a girl no one dared push into mud puddles.

It seemed that the King of Blood had killed that girl before her own execution.

They passed the cell holding the nameless girl Lysandra had been forced to fight. Her grimy hands were curled around the iron bars and her expression was vacant.

Lysandra wondered if there had also once been fire in that girl, whose spirit had also clearly been doused forever.

They exited the dungeon and walked straight into the open air. After two weeks of being imprisoned in near darkness, the brightness of the day blinded her. For a moment, all Lys could see was white light, making her squint. She heard the crowd cheer, their chant of "Death to the rebels!" waking her from her daze and chilling her to the core.

As her eyes grew more accustomed to the sunlight, she saw just how many people had gathered in the palace square. There were a countless number of faces and bodies milling about. Conversation buzzed like insects, whispers and murmurs thick in the warm air. Curious stares followed Lysandra and Tarus as they were led to their place of death.

A crowd surrounded the execution stage, cheering louder than anyone else in attendance. Behind them, Lysandra could sense that the larger crowd was beginning to lose its enthusiasm, looking on more quietly and solemnly than those closest to the stage.

At least that was something to hold on to. Perhaps there was still some hope after all, some tiny shred that showed Lysandra that not all of these people were as lost as she'd thought they were.

Limerian guards in crimson uniforms patrolled the crowd, swiftly gathering up and arresting protestors the moment they raised their voices against the king, dragging them away from the spectacle before they could provoke others to do the same.

Lysandra's vision narrowed and she stumbled, causing the guard to hold her more firmly.

"One foot in front of the other, girl," he muttered. "Make a good show for the crowd and the king."

The king.

The crowd quieted as the king and his heir approached a raised dais next to the execution stage to witness the proceedings up close.

Something stirred within her, deep down under layer upon layer of grief and defeat. She found she couldn't look away from the monster who'd ordered her brother's death, or from the prince who'd just stood there studying her reaction as Gregor was decapitated.

Trailing close behind King Gaius and Prince Magnus were the two princesses. One was dark haired with a serene expression, and Lys knew her immediately as Princess Lucia Damora, the king's daughter.

The other was blond and familiar.

Lysandra had met Princess Cleo before, when Jonas had foolishly insisted on kidnapping her, believing her to be an asset the king would bargain to retrieve. But plans—especially those made by Jonas—never seemed to work out as expected.

Jonas had been infatuated with this shallow, insipid princess, his head turned by her golden beauty.

Lysandra was sickened to have the princess amongst rebel ranks. And, she had to admit, the way Jonas had looked at Cleo during that week had spiked jealousy in her like nothing ever had before.

But such petty things no longer mattered.

Lysandra looked upward to the balcony to see King Gaius gazing down upon the square. To his right stood Prince Magnus.

She was forced up five steps, the wooden slats creaking beneath her feet, to where the hooded executioner waited. Tarus stood at her side, trembling.

She didn't care what happened to her anymore. But Tarus . . .

He was only fourteen.

Her throat grew tight at the thought of Tarus dying by her side without having been given the barest chance to live a full life.

She looked down at the people who chanted so enthusiastically for her death. There were a hundred of them, maybe, among the thousands here. She studied one fanatical face after another, finding that they looked much the same as anyone else. Yet these were the people who'd chosen to celebrate, rather than somberly observe, this day. Did they really believe this execution to be a just punishment for their crimes? Did they truly think Gaius Damora was a good, honest king who could do no wrong?

Or were they simply cowards, afraid that the same fate could befall them if they stopped chanting and shouting in support of his decisions?

Something heavy and wet hit Lysandra's chest and she staggered back a step. A ripe tomato. She looked down at the messy splatter with surprise and dismay.

"Die, rebel!" yelled the man who'd thrown it.

She stared back at him blankly. *What a waste of a perfectly good tomato.*

The king began to address the crowd, the sound of his voice raking against Lysandra's skin, each word a tiny dagger dipped in poison

"The two rebels before us are responsible for the deaths of many Auranians and Limerians alike. Do not feel pity as you gaze upon their young faces. They are dangerous insurgents. They are savages, through and through. They must be held accountable for their actions. May their deaths be a reminder that the laws of the land are there for peace. For prosperity. For a bright future, lived out hand in hand with our neighbors."

Lysandra yearned for that sweet ease of nothingness she'd felt all day, but the king's words affected her. Her muscles tensed up with hatred and the desire to wrap her hands around his throat and squeeze until the life left his eyes. She'd wanted to kill him ever since he'd torched her village and killed her parents, ever since he'd enslaved the survivors and forced them to build his precious road.

Such lies he spoke. Yet, looking beyond the fanatics in front, a sweep of the faces in the crowd revealed apathy and distaste. Perhaps these people were no longer willing to swallow the king's words like wine that would lull them into a false sense of security.

She looked back to the king. How laughable that this monster was once again making her feel a spark of life just moments before he was to order it over.

She tore her gaze from the king and his hateful family to Tarus, whose tearful eyes met her steady ones.

"I'm not afraid," he said.

"Of course you're not afraid," she whispered back. "You're the bravest kid I've ever known."

He smiled, just as a tear splashed down his cheek. But the smile disappeared at once as a guard curled his mitt of a hand around Lysandra's arm and jerked her to the side.

He dragged her up the four steps to the stage and forced her down to her knees, shoving her cheek down against a hard wooden block.

"Don't watch," she told Tarus, her voice hoarse as the guard yanked her hair to the side to bare her neck. "Please look away."

But he didn't. He kept his gaze locked with hers to show he was trying to be strong. For her.

She tried to focus on the dais and on the king who stood watching the proceedings, his expression smug and satisfied. She saw Prince Magnus's scarred cheek twitch, but otherwise he appeared impassive. Princess Lucia stood still behind him, her beautiful face calm and cold.

Princess Cleo, on the other hand, looked frantic, her gaze darting from Lysandra to Tarus to the crowd as if she were a nervous hummingbird searching for shelter.

As the executioner hoisted his heavy ax above his head, Lysandra finally squeezed her eyes shut to block out the sight of the king's followers, who continued to cheer her impending death loud enough to drown out any protests from the back. There was one thing about which the king had been truthful: This wouldn't be a torturous death. It would be over swiftly.

She had no deity to pray to and no faith in the goddesses of other lands, so she thought of her parents and of Gregor and, lastly, of Jonas.

I love you all.

Just as she exhaled one long, last breath, an explosion rocked the stage. Lysandra's eyes snapped back open and she saw a plume of orange flame rise up before her. A dagger flew through the air and caught the executioner in his throat, forcing him to stagger backward and drop hard to the floor. Beneath his hooded mask, Lysandra saw that his dead eyes were still open and filled with shock.

Another explosion bloomed to the left, crashing directly in the center of King Gaius's supporters. Bodies and debris flew through the air, catching fire, the carnage extending into the rest of the audience, who began to scatter in all directions. Now they screamed for their own lives instead of Lysandra's head.

Stunned, Gregor's warning echoed in Lysandra's ears: *"When the sorceress's blood is spilled, they will finally rise. And the world will burn."*

If Lysandra wasn't mistaken, the world was burning right now.

"Lys! Help!" Tarus yelled. A guard was hauling the boy backward toward the dungeon, away from the sudden chaos.

She didn't hesitate. She lunged toward the fallen executioner and turned to slice through her bindings with his discarded ax. Out of the corner of her eye, she saw the royals being ushered away toward the safety of the palace by a flank of red-uniformed guards who stepped over bodies strewn on the ground below the dais.

Lysandra jumped down from the stage, shoving and punching anyone in her path as she tried to get to Tarus.

An iron bar of an arm came around her throat from behind. She clawed at it, fighting and kicking. A man had fallen to the ground nearby, screaming, his body ablaze.

"Let go of me!" she shouted.

"Why? Do you have somewhere else you need to be?"

She froze. The firm arm was clad in the hateful red uniform, but as soon as she heard him speak, she stopped fighting.

Her captor loosened his hold just enough for her to spin around and confirm his identity.

"Jonas!" The word was nothing more than a throaty rasp.

He didn't greet her with a smile, not even a smug, self-satisfied one. He didn't even look at her; his gaze was fixed on the crowd, his expression deadly serious.

"That explosion hit closer to you than I wanted," he growled. "Idiot doesn't know how to follow orders. He killed too many people today. And he came damn close to killing you, too."

Jonas wasn't remotely gentle as he began yanking her along with him, following Tarus and the other guard through the melee. Thousands of spectators fled the explosions, and the detonations kept coming. One after another after another.

Two guards raced past them without giving them a second glance. A third slowed his steps and cast Lysandra a sour look.

"Where are you going with the prisoners?" he demanded of Jonas and the other guard—another disguised rebel, Lysandra had figured out—who had Tarus by his shirt.

"I was told to take them back to the dungeon until this area is secure," Jonas said. "Unless you want to take them?"

"No. Carry on. And make haste." The guard continued on his way.

"Oh, I'll make haste," Jonas spat past his gritted teeth.

"Are you trying to get yourself killed?" Lysandra growled. "Because you're doing a great job so far."

"Good to see you, too. Oh, and you're welcome for saving your arse. Now shut up."

Jonas moved so swiftly that Lysandra nearly tripped over her own feet. She was weak from dehydration and hunger, from grief and fear. What did he think he was doing? He and this other boy had just risked their own necks to rescue her and Tarus. Idiots!

"You don't think anyone will recognize you dressed like that?" she hissed. "It's not like that uniform covers your face."

"What part of *shut up* don't you understand?"

"Who's that with Tarus?" She eyed the boy now ten paces ahead of them.

"A friend. Now do me a big favor and please act like a prisoner so we don't draw more attention."

Lysandra shut up.

The four of them reached the guarded opening in the eastern wall that allowed the river to flow through the heart of the city, providing it with its main water supply. The frightened crowd was trying to squeeze through the exit as fast as they could.

A guard stepped in front of them. "Where do you think you're going?"

"We're leaving," Jonas replied.

"You're leaving the city with the prisoners?"

"Yes, that was the plan."

The guard looked closely at Jonas's face, and Lysandra's heart sank. "You—I know you. You're Jon—"

The hilt of a sword struck the guard suddenly in the head. He fell to reveal another guard standing behind him, one whose carrot-colored hair stuck out at all angles and clashed with the crimson shade of his uniform.

Jonas flashed him a smile. "Good to see you, Nic."

The redheaded guard grinned back at him. "It's good to be seen."

"When your friends wake up, please thank them for lending us their uniforms. They were very useful."

"*If* they wake up they'll be blamed for letting a couple rebels get the better of them. Nice display back there. I'm almost impressed." Nic slapped Jonas on his back. "Now get out of here and don't look back."

Without another moment's delay, the four of them fled the city. Jonas and his friend discarded their stolen uniforms in a nearby forest where they'd hidden their regular clothes, as well as some food and water for Lysandra and Tarus. They made them drink and eat as they walked, putting as much distance between them and the city as possible.

Finally, once they were several miles away, Jonas stopped when Lysandra stumbled. Her legs were weak.

He regarded her with alarm. "I'm going too fast for you."

"No, it's fine. I'm just clumsy." *And exhausted*, she thought. *And in shock.*

"You didn't look injured back in the city. . . ." He checked her skin, pulling her hair away from her shoulders.

She pushed his hand away. "I'm not."

He didn't look convinced, he looked worried. "Did those bastards hurt you?"

She was still in a daze, uncertain if this was real or a dream. "They were about to chop off my head."

"They kept us in a dark cell and barely fed us," Tarus said, his voice quavering. "But they didn't beat us. They beat up Gregor, badly, when he wouldn't talk."

"Gregor," Jonas repeated, his eyes flicking to Lys's. "Your brother's in the dungeon too?"

All she could do was nod until she found her voice. "He was. The king killed him. He made me watch."

Jonas clenched his jaw and he swore under his breath. "Lys . . . I'm so sorry."

"Me too." She let out a shuddery breath, weary from her grief. She wished so much that Gregor were here, too. Then she remembered their new companion. The older, dark-haired boy peered at her with silent curiosity, his arms crossed over his chest. "Who're you?" she said.

"Sorry, I should have already made the introductions," Jonas said. "Lysandra, Tarus, this is Felix Gaebras. Not only do you owe him your lives, but so do I. Without him, none of this could have happened."

"Pleasure," Felix said.

Lys's first instinct was to demand more answers, but words vanished before she could speak.

Jonas was right. If it weren't for Felix, and for Jonas, she'd be dead. She decided to reserve judgment on this boy until she got to know him better.

She nodded toward Felix. "Are you responsible for the explosions?"

"Nope," Felix said. "That would be Jonas's other new friend."
"*Friend* might be overstating matters after what happened back there," Jonas growled. "Petros likes to watch things burn too much. He's got no control. He could have killed Lys and Tarus."

Felix shrugged. "They're fine. Anyone standing there ready to watch your friends lose their heads deserved what they got. Nothing to feel guilty about."

Jonas hissed out a long breath. "I suppose you're right."

Lysandra was still stunned. "Why?" she choked out.

"Why what?" Jonas asked.

"You risked your life—both of your lives—to save us." She reached for Tarus's hand and squeezed it.

"And?"

"And . . ." She shook her head. "And it doesn't make sense. There are more important things for you to be doing right now."

"Really, Lys?" Jonas shot her an impatient look. "And what if it were me in that dungeon? Would you have let me rot there until they hacked me into little pieces so you could go on doing more important things? Or would you have been busting your arse trying to save me?" He barked out a laugh. "Forget I asked. Of course you'd have been much more practical than that. The life of one rebel wouldn't be worth the risk, right?"

There was no questioning what she would have done if the tables had been turned. She would have risked anything to save Jonas.

"I did it because Brion would have wanted me to, that's why," Jonas said, turning away. "End of story."

Brion. Another boy taken before his time because he stood up to those who oppressed him. Brion, who had loved her in spite of—or because of—her fierce, argumentative nature.

"Understood," she said softly.

"Now come on. Let's move. They'll be searching for the two of you as soon as they realize you're gone."

"Where are we going?" Tarus asked.

"Paelsia. I'm taking you back to your family, kid."

"But, Jonas—"

"No buts. You're too young for all of this. You get another year stronger and then you can join me again if you want."

"But I—" Any further protest died on Tarus's tongue, and Lysandra saw a whisper of relief slide through his eyes. "Fine. If that's your official order, I'll do as you say."

"It is."

Lysandra's mind relaxed for the first time in what felt like ages. The thought of Tarus with a chance to be relatively safe was a huge relief.

"What about me?" Lysandra asked. "I don't have a family to go home to anymore."

"Yeah . . . you. You're more of a problem." Jonas exchanged a look with Felix. "So I guess what you do now is your choice, Lys."

Mere hours ago, she was as good as dead. Now her whole future was ahead of her.

"What's your plan?" she asked. "If it's still to kill the king, he was out in the open today. You could have taken a shot."

"He wasn't my priority today. I couldn't lose focus for anything. But now that you're free, my old plan is new again. I won't rest until the king has lost his throne and his power is taken away forever. Until he has taken his last breath. Until all Paelsians are free to control their own destinies."

Lysandra and Jonas locked eyes. "Then we have the same goal."

He nodded once. "Then I guess you're staying with us."

"I guess so."

Just when she'd been ready to accept her death, her fire had returned. It had been trampled, but it had never been fully extinguished.

Lysandra was alive. Her spirit was renewed.

And she was ready to fight again.

CHAPTER 15

LUCIA

AURANOS

How fascinating, to study the face of someone who knew she was moments from death.

Lucia hadn't been present for the last set of executions, but there had been plenty of them in Limeros during King Gaius's reign. In the past she'd always found it an unpleasant necessity, but she'd never felt sorry for the criminals. After all, those who lost their heads had chosen to commit crimes. They'd known the punishment but had acted unjustly anyway.

Her father had also put many accused witches to death over the years—all cruel women who'd used their magic to hurt others. After her *elementia* had awakened, he'd explained to Lucia how her magic was different from theirs.

The witches' magic was evil, strengthened by blood sacrifice and dark deceit.

Her magic was pure, prophesized. It was good.

"Barbaric," Cleo said under her breath as the two rebels were brought to the stage.

"Didn't your father have executions?" Lucia asked Cleo. A boy with bright blond hair darted through the audience and caught her eye. He was one of few who didn't stand with the crowd, transfixed by the king's speech. In fact, he moved in the opposite direction with a lit torch in his hand, drawing annoyed looks from those he brushed past.

"Of course he did," Cleo replied. "But they weren't public spectacles like this."

Was it cruel of Lucia not to care about the fate of these two rebels? She searched her heart, trying to find some sense of unease about their impending deaths, but found she had no sympathy for them at all. They'd chosen their path, and this is where it had led. They had no one to blame but themselves.

Out of nowhere, just as the girl rebel—a savage little thing with a wild mass of black curls and a demonic look on her face— was about to die beneath the ax, a thunderous boom sounded out.

"What was that?" Lucia exclaimed, but before anyone could answer, the dais was rocked by another explosion that knocked her off her feet. She lost her balance and fell off the platform, straight into the crowd. The world spun in circles as she got to her feet, disoriented.

"Father!" she called out, but she couldn't see him, nor could she see Magnus or Cleo or any guards. Down on the ground, she was surrounded by unfamiliar faces wracked with panic and fear. No one paid her any attention as people ran for their lives, fleeing the fire.

To her left was a man ablaze, twitching on the ground . . . reaching for her, his mouth contorted as he screamed . . .

She thought back to that fateful day when the king had her break down the palace entrance with her magic. It seemed so simple a request.

But magic met with more magic, and a fiery beast had risen up and crashed down, destroying the palace entrance and killing everyone in its path.

She scrambled out the burning man's way before he could grab her skirts and set her on fire as well.

"Magnus!" she cried. She took hold of the edge of the dais, trying to climb onto it again, but the flow of the massive crowd swept her along with it and more panic swelled within her.

She hadn't been out among commoners like this without protection in . . . well, she had never been left unattended in her entire life. But no one looked in her direction, as they were all busy searching for safety and escape.

The crowd pushed Lucia along until she was out of the palace square. Finding herself on a city street, she craned her neck in search of a clear path back to the castle.

"Are you lost, princess?" A man's large hand curled around her wrist. "Allow me to assist you."

She spun to face him, fear taking hold inside of her. "Let go of me."

He frowned. "If you'll just—"

Any of these strangers could mean her harm, and she didn't want to be manhandled by any of them. And this man knew who she was and could take her hostage as leverage against the king.

"I said," she hissed, *"let go of me."*

With barely a thought she summoned fire magic to heat up her skin. Instantly, the man released her with a yelp, his hand now blackened and burnt, his eyes wide with pain and confusion. She turned and ran away from him as fast as she could, her skirts swishing around her legs.

Her heartbeat thundered in her chest, but she felt a swell of pride over what she'd done. Instead of allowing fear to rule her, she'd protected herself. Anyone who wanted to hurt her would be wise to keep their distance.

She gasped as she spotted a familiar face in the crowd. It was Princess Amara, in a burgundy gown, her long ebony hair loose and flowing past her shoulders. Amara's eyes widened as the girls locked gazes.

"Lucia!" Amara closed the distance between them and grasped hold of her hands, wincing as people ran past them without a second glance. "I'm so thankful I found you. I decided to visit the palace today, but wanted to wait until the king returned from the execution before my attendants announced me. And then . . . the explosions. I—I lost track of my guards."

"Thank the goddess we found each other." Lucia linked arms with Amara and guided her into an alcove where they found shelter. They watched the swarms of people scatter in all directions as they escaped from the palace square.

Rebels were responsible for this, no question. They'd meant to cause a distraction and rescue their compatriots.

The thought infuriated Lucia.

A boy ran against the crowd, eyeing his surroundings with distaste and suspicion before disappearing into a bakery. Lucia immediately recognized him from the moments just before the blasts—the blond boy with the lit torch, which he still held in his grip like a weapon.

"That boy, he's the one," she whispered.

"The one?" Amara repeated. "What do you mean? *Who* do you mean?"

"The one responsible for the explosions. He must be." It was a gut instinct more than anything else, but one worth pursuing. She knew it. The boy couldn't be allowed to escape. He was a murderer and had come very close to killing her family.

Lucia scanned the area for a guard to alert, but there were none close by.

"Come on," she urged, pulling Amara by her arm. "We can't let him get away."

Amara didn't protest as Lucia led her into the bakery. The place smelled of cinnamon and vanilla; several trays of sugar cookies and pecan tarts had been left, untouched, on the countertop. Lucia scanned the room until her gaze fell upon the boy in the far corner. The light from his torch flickered, illuminating his widening eyes in the dark interior of the shop.

"This is all your fault, isn't it?" Lucia said sternly.

He met her gaze directly without even a flinch. "You shouldn't be in here, girl. You'd be smart to leave me alone or you might get burned."

He didn't seem the least bit ashamed, nor was he trying to deny her accusation. "Why would you want to hurt so many people?"

He snorted. "Why do you care? You look just fine to me. Not a bit of dirt on your pretty gown. Be gone, both of you. Or else."

It seemed he didn't know who she was.

"I care because I don't like it when innocent people are blown apart simply for being in the wrong place at the wrong time." She stole a quick glance at Amara to make sure she hadn't frightened her, then drew closer to the boy. "You helped the rebels escape."

His eyes narrowed, glittering in the firelight. "Leave. Me. Alone."

Even now that the horror was over, he didn't seem to want to let go of his torch for a moment.

"Bringing fire into a building like this is dangerous," Lucia said.

"Then I suggest you stay away from me."

"He's rather rude," Amara observed, crossing her arms over her chest. "You should use your magic on him."

Lucia's gaze snapped to her with surprise. "What did you say?"

Amara fixed her with a patient look. "I've heard the rumors. There are so many of them about you. My father has heard them as well. In fact, you're one of the reasons he asked me to come here. You're King Gaius's secret weapon, a girl of prophecy and magic."

Lucia's first impulse was to lie, to deny Amara's rumors. But why should she constantly have to deny what she was and what she could do? She knew her father considered the Kraeshians to be his enemies, but that he took solace in the fact that Emperor Cortas would have Lucia's magic to contend with if he ever chose to attack Mytica.

The king expected so much of her—almost as much as she expected of herself.

"Enough of this nonsense," the boy said, rolling his eyes. "I have other places to be." He attempted to dodge and slip between the two princesses, brandishing his torch to show he'd burn them if they got too close.

Casting a dark look at him, Lucia summoned air magic. Suddenly, the boy was slammed backward against the wall and pinned in place, his torch extinguished.

Once again, the magic required barely a thought. Some days it was so very easy for her.

Lucia then extended her hand and summoned a dancing flame into her palm.

"What—?" he managed. "What *are* you?"

A smile had crept onto Amara's face. "I knew it. You have magic at your fingertips. It's incredible."

Lucia raised an eyebrow, pleased by the stunned reactions such a simple trick could garner. "It certainly can be." She drew closer to the boy, allowing the hatred she felt toward him to flicker through her and brighten her fire. "Tell me your name."

He couldn't take his eyes off the flame in her palm. "Petros."

"You're a rebel."

"Not usually. But today I was, I guess." His eyes reflected her fire. "You're absolutely amazing. You're like a goddess—a beautiful goddess."

His praise pleased her for the briefest of moments. The way he regarded her, as if she was something he should worship. "Am I?"

"Like the goddess Cleiona. The perfect embodiment of fire and air."

And with the utterance of that name, her pleasure vanished. "Cleiona murdered Valoria, my goddess, trying to steal her magic. How dare you compare me to an evil creature like that?"

He blanched. "Apologies. Please forgive me. I meant no disrespect."

"Are you going to question him?" Amara said. "Or let him stare adoringly at you all day?"

"A fair point," she agreed.

Amara looked at her not with awe or fear at her very real magic. Rather, she seemed pleased and impressed.

It was a nice change from the terrified reactions her *elementia* usually received.

"All I want to know is *why*," Lucia said to the boy. "Why would you assist the rebels today? Do you wish to defeat my father for reasons of your own?"

"Your father . . ." Petros's brows drew together before recognition dawned. "You're Princess Lucia."

"Give the boy a prize," Amara said with a smirk.

"I am," Lucia said to him. "Now answer me."

"They asked me to help."

"*Who* asked you to help?"

"Jonas Agallon. He wanted to rescue his friends. He saw my fire displays and thought I could help. For me, any chance to work with fire—to watch it rise up and destroy anything in its path. . . . It's what I love the most. And I can tell you like it too, princess."

Jonas. That name had been coming up an awful lot lately. Jonas Agallon, the rebel leader accused of murdering the queen. Which was all fine with Lucia. It had saved her from having to do the deed herself.

Such dark thoughts, a voice said inside her. *To use your magic is to summon malevolence. Be careful or it might consume you.*

"I need to leave," Lucia said, her voice small and uncertain as doubt descended.

She lost her focus for a moment, and Petros managed to break free of her air magic. He pushed off from the wall, shoving her out of the way in his haste to get to the door. But Amara was there, blocking his way.

He glared at her. "Get out of my way or I'll kill you."

"I doubt that." She reached into the folds of her gown, pulled out a dagger, and sank it into his chest.

The boy looked down with shock. He touched the hilt with trembling fingers, then fell hard to his knees and crumpled fully to the ground. A pool of blood began to seep out and surround him.

Lucia's eyes widened. "I wasn't expecting that."

Amara reached down and yanked the dagger from the boy's body, wiping off the blade with a clean white handkerchief. "I'm sure he wasn't, either. No loss to the world, I'd say. Kraeshians like to deal with criminals swiftly and with finality. We don't tend to waste much time on incarceration and public executions." She glanced over at Lucia. "I hope this isn't a problem for you. He was going to get away . . . and he knew your secret."

Lucia had thought Amara merely a spoiled princess from another land. But she was much more than that.

Lucia eyed her now with wariness.

"If you're worried I'll tell anyone what I saw here"—Amara tucked her weapon away and moved closer to Lucia—"don't be. I can be very discreet."

"What do you want from me?" Fire magic crackled down Lucia's arms, ready for summoning if Amara said the wrong thing.

Amara wasn't the only one willing to end a life today if there was no other choice. She would protect herself—and her family—at any cost.

Confidence flickered on the foreign princess's face. "I want to be your friend, Lucia. That's all I've wanted since I arrived in Auranos. I hope you'll give me that chance." She smiled. "The crowd must have dissipated by now. It's time to make our way back to the palace."

"You go without me," Lucia said. "I need time to think."

Amara didn't argue. "Very well. Be safe, Lucia. I'll see you again soon."

She turned and stepped over Petros's body, not looking back at Lucia on her way out of the bakery.

Lucia let her go but stood at the doorway and watched the princess until she disappeared from view. Amara knew what Lucia was capable of. She would be wise to keep such knowledge to herself.

Lucia glanced down at the dead boy's face, feeling nothing in her heart but relief. Finally, she left the shop. By now, the streets had cleared and she found herself nearly alone in the city.

In the distance she saw the golden spires of the palace, and she turned down one crooked lane after another in an attempt to head toward it. The city was a maze—much like the halls of the palace itself. One could easily get hopelessly off course if one wasn't careful.

And even though she could see her destination, she knew she was lost and alone here. No one understood her. She couldn't trust anyone—not even her family.

A sob caught in her chest as an unexpected, overwhelming wave of sadness swept over her. She was on the verge of tears when she turned the next corner.

And there he was. Standing in the middle of the cobblestoned road, as if he'd been waiting for her to arrive.

"You're a dream," she whispered. "I'm dreaming right now."

Alexius's silver eyes met hers and he smiled. "Not this time."

But it had to be. This couldn't be real. "You're not here."

"I'm not?" He looked down at himself, holding out his hands and inspecting them back and front. "Are you sure about that?"

The road lined with lush green trees, the sparkling stones that paved the walkways, the storefronts glittering under the sun . . . they all fell away and Lucia saw nothing—nothing but him. Only Alexius.

He approached, and she took one shaky step backward.

His brows drew together and he raked a hand through his bronze-colored hair. "I thought you'd be happy to see me."

"But . . . how is this possible?" The words piled one on top of one another in their hurry to get out. "I'd all but convinced myself that you were a figment of my imagination. But you said we'd see each other again. That you'd find me."

"And here I am." He took her by her arms and drew her close.

She was so dumbstruck by the sight of him that it didn't occur to her for a moment to summon her magic, which had quickly become a natural instinct when she was startled or afraid. "I'm sorry it took so long, but I came as soon as I could."

But this didn't make any sense! "Watchers can't take mortal form in Mytica. You should be a hawk. I've been searching for hawks all this time!"

Alexius grew serious. "We can take mortal form here if we exile ourselves."

She actually stopped breathing for a moment.

He nodded, registering her shock. "I've left the Sanctuary permanently. That's what took me so long. It's rare to leave that realm voluntarily, believe me. One must be very certain that he wants to embrace the life of a mortal."

He'd given up his immortality, could never return to his true home. "But why would you do such a thing?"

"You really don't know?"

She shook her head.

He leaned closer and whispered to her, "Because I'm in love with you." He grinned in response to her stunned expression. "Yes, princess. I'm here because there's no other place I want to be than by your side. Now, shall we make our way to the palace?"

All she could do was stare. The explosions, the rebel escape, the confrontation between Amara and the arsonist, and now . . . now Alexius was confessing his love for her.

It was barely midday!

"The palace . . ." She grappled to find words. "Oh, yes, let's march into the palace and introduce you to my father as my new suitor—an exiled Watcher from the Sanctuary who visited my dreams when I was asleep for months." She nervously scanned the clear sky, her gaze drawn toward the slightest glimpse of the golden spire. "He'll begin planning the wedding immediately. No, more likely he'll have you thrown into the dungeon!"

The smile remained fixed on Alexius's handsome face. "Let me handle your father, princess."

That smile quickly eased its way into her heart.

This was real.

Only yesterday everything had been bleak and unpleasant. Now Alexius was here, and hope once again bloomed all around Lucia.

CHAPTER 16

ALEXIUS

THE SANCTUARY

He'd been gone from the Sanctuary a whole week before he found Lucia.

"Alexius!" Timotheus had called out to him as he was leaving the Crystal City for the last time.

Alexius tried very hard to ignore him.

But he had stopped when Timotheus laid his familiar hand on his arm. He turned to face his mentor, who looked at him with a drawn brow. "I've been told you plan to exile yourself today."

"You were told correctly."

Timotheus shook his head. "Don't do this. We can talk. We can work this out. I know Melenia's filled your head with all sorts of plans and promises, but—"

"This has nothing to do with her." Alexius's throat hurt from all the lies he'd had to tell since aligning with Melenia. Abandoning the only home he'd ever known was difficult enough, no matter if it was as much a prison as it was a paradise. But having someone who cared enough to try to stop him made everything worse. "I can't stay here. I've fallen in love with a mortal. My place is by her side."

Timotheus's fingertips bit into his shoulder. "There's another answer."

"I've thought long and hard, and this is the only way."

"You can never return. You won't be able to take hawk form once you leave here. You will forfeit your immortality. If you die out there, it's the end for you. You're giving up everything."

He looked into Timotheus's eyes. This was his friend, the one he knew he could tell all his secrets to without being judged. They had so much history together, but Melenia had forced an immovable wedge between them.

The merest thought of defying her command caused Alexius so much pain he couldn't function, couldn't think. Melenia's obedience spell had sunk its claws deep into his throat and wouldn't let go.

"I'm sorry." Alexius embraced him for the briefest of moments, ignoring the sting of tears in his eyes. "Farewell, my friend."

Timotheus didn't say another word. With his eyes on the elder, who watched him now with a bleak and solemn expression, Alexius shifted to hawk form one last time. He flapped his wings and took flight, heading toward the ancient stone portal that would grant him entrance into the mortal world.

Before Alexius could find the princess, he first had to take care of a task in Paelsia.

The Imperial Road stretching from Auranos to Limeros was now complete, but Xanthus had remained behind at the last deserted work camp to ensure that the magic in the stones would hold.

This was where Alexius had found the exiled Watcher, crouched at the side of his road, the Forbidden Mountains looming like unfriendly giants behind him.

Alexius approached, unsteady on his newly mortal legs. He knew they were the same legs he'd always had, but now—walking on Mytican soil and knowing he, too, was mortal—they felt different. Weak.

"Alexius," Xanthus said, a grin lifting the corner of his mouth. "Melenia told me to expect you. It's good to see you again after all this time."

"Hard to believe it's been twenty years." Alexius scanned the tall man from head to foot. Once eternally youthful, Xanthus had aged during his time here, but his bronze colored hair and copper-colored eyes were still as bright as they ever were.

"Yes." Xanthus reached for his hand and shook it firmly. "Though it doesn't feel that long. Welcome to your new home. You'll like the mortal world. Come, I'll prepare something for us to eat." He turned to go, motioning to Alexius to follow, but the younger Watcher didn't budge.

"I know what you did to Phaedra."

Xanthus stopped in his tracks.

"She loved you. She missed you all this time. She thought you were lost to her forever. I can only imagine how betrayed she must have felt."

Xanthus turned with hard eyes to meet Alexius's. "It had to be done."

"Because Melenia ordered it."

"Phaedra was a complication."

"She was my friend. And your sister."

Xanthus's brows drew together. "I had no choice. Melenia commanded it, and I obeyed. But I promise you, she didn't suffer."

"Perhaps she didn't." Alexius drew out the dagger he had hidden beneath his cloak. "But you will."

As her gift to him, Melenia had told Alexius what Xanthus had done, and had allowed him this brief opportunity for vengeance.

"You don't need to do this!" Xanthus ducked and dodged the blade.

"Wrong. I do. Now that the road is complete, you too are a complication. This is also an order from Melenia, but it's a punishment you deserve."

Xanthus fought back and managed to slice Alexius's leg with a sharp piece of wood, which succeeded in slowing him down.

But not enough to stop him.

Soon Alexius's dagger found its mark, and he watched the life drain from the eyes of Phaedra's brother and murderer. In all of his two thousand years, Xanthus was the first person he'd ever killed. The thought chilled him, taking away any warmth he had left in his heart. But it also filled him with resolve.

"She commands," Alexius said, "and I obey. Just like you did."

"Then may your fate be the same as mine," Xanthus hissed with his last breath.

Alexius walked away and didn't look back.

Phaedra's death had been avenged. He'd completed his journey to the City of Gold. And he'd found his princess. As if she were a beacon calling out to him, it had taken barely any time at all to locate her in a city scrambling for safety in the wake of a rebel uprising.

Suddenly there she was, every bit as beautiful as he remembered.

Seeing Lucia again brought him more joy than he'd thought possible, which helped to balance the pain a little, but not nearly enough. He could never tell her the truth. No matter how much he wanted to, he could never warn her to stay away from him. It was impossible.

After recovering from her surprise, the princess took him to the palace.

Upon their arrival, a herd of guards immediately ushered Alexius and Lucia into the throne room, where both the king and Prince Magnus were waiting. The two turned to look at them as they entered.

Magnus was in front of Lucia in an instant, his expression one of anguish as he took hold of her arms.

"What happened?" he demanded. "One moment you were right there next to me, and the next you were gone. I thought you were dead!"

"By the looks of it," the king said, "she's very much alive. Not a scratch. I told you she could protect herself. I don't know why you always refuse to believe me."

Magnus kept his eyes on his sister. "Are you all right?"

She nodded. "I got lost in the crowd for a while, but I'm fine. All is well, brother."

Finally he let go of her, his expression turning icy. "You should be more careful. You were standing too close to the edge of the platform. Anyone could have grabbed you." His dark eyes shifted to the boy who stood silently at Lucia's side. "And who are you?"

Lucia had told Alexius plenty about the prince in the time they'd spent together in her dreams. She'd felt comfortable enough with him to unburden her soul and tell him everything about her life, her family, her hopes and dreams. Her disappointments. Her problems. Her fears. *Everything*.

"Yes, Lucia," the king said. He drew closer to them and waved his guards away for privacy. "Who is this boy?"

Alexius knew that Lucia was uncertain of what to say about him. She might be a powerful sorceress, but she was tentative when it came to her family.

"My name is Alexius," he said, seeing that Lucia wouldn't be providing introductions.

Magnus frowned, studying Alexius's face as if it held the answer to a particularly difficult riddle. "I know this name. Why do I know this name?"

Alexius regarded the prince patiently. This boy was full of bluster, full of doubt and fear and pain. So sad to know that he'd imagined himself in love with Lucia, simply because she'd shown him the kindness that he didn't receive anywhere else in his cold, lonely life.

He held no jealousy toward Lucia's adopted brother, nor did he feel that Magnus was a challenge for Lucia's affections. In fact, he pitied the prince.

And Magnus would be wise to stay out of his way.

"Alexius is important to me," Lucia said, boldly hooking her arm through his.

Perhaps she wasn't that tentative after all—at least not when it came to him. Melenia would be pleased to know that Alexius was already working his way back into the princess's good graces after such a long absence.

"Important, is he?" the king echoed. "How so?"

Alexius couldn't read King Gaius's expression, but he knew enough not to underestimate him. The king would never allow Alexius anywhere near his daughter if he believed him to be nothing more than a suitor visiting from another land.

"Melenia sent me," he said, pleased to see the king's eyes immediately widen at mention of her name.

"Melenia?" Something sharp and dangerous then slid through his gaze, something that could easily intimidate someone less determined than Alexius. "What do you know of Melenia?"

Alexius loosened the ties on his shirt and bared his chest, showing the royal family his golden mark, the evidence of his heritage. And of his magic. The scars from Melenia's spell had already healed and vanished, but they were still branded on his soul. "She sent me here because she has been unable to contact you. She apologizes for any confusion she may have caused you, but wants you to know that she holds true to her promises and, going forward, I am to be her representative in the mortal world."

Magnus stared at him as if he were a six-legged, horned beast that had just walked into the room. "You're a *Watcher*."

"I was." A flicker of pain distracted him—emotional, not physical, this time. Two thousand years he'd spent in the Sanctuary . . . and now the rest of his days were reduced to the lifespan of a regular mortal. He could no longer soar as a hawk. He could no longer dreamwalk, save for when Melenia called upon him.

If only it had been his choice to come here, rather than one made for him.

But it was done, and there was no turning back now.

"He's telling the truth," Lucia said. "When I was asleep for so long, he visited me in my dreams. He showed me his home."

Magnus frowned at her. "You never told me this."

"And when would I have told you?" she asked sharply. "You've been avoiding me like I have some horrible disease."

"With something this important, I would have thought you'd seek me out."

"I didn't know for sure it was real. That *he* was real."

"And yet, here he is," Magnus said, eyeing him with distaste.

"In the flesh. And now what are we to do with him? Put him up here at the palace? Feed and clothe him? All so he can sit there and look pretty and relate orders from the Sanctuary?"

Alexius gave the insolent prince a tight smile. "I can certainly do more to earn my keep. Melenia has suggested that I become Lucia's *elementia* tutor. I'm certain that I'm much more knowledgeable than any of her other tutors."

"This was Melenia's idea?" The king's skeptical expression remained fixed.

This could all go very wrong. The king was unpredictable. He seemed furious, so disappointed in Melenia for ignoring him for so long that he might have Alexius thrown in the dungeon to keep him from Lucia's side.

He could certainly try, but he wouldn't like the consequences.

There was only one outcome to this story, and it had been scored into his flesh with Melenia's magic.

"It's an excellent plan." Lucia nodded enthusiastically. "Alexius would make a wonderful tutor."

"I don't like this," Magnus said. "Any of it."

"What *do* you like? Ever?" Lucia's eyes flashed. "Can't you, just once in your life, try to think beyond what *you* like? What *you* want?"

He flinched as if she'd struck him. Then coldness spread across his features. "Apologies, sister. I'm only trying to look out for you."

"Don't bother," she replied.

Oh, yes. They certainly had a complicated relationship.

The king assessed each of them in turn, his gaze finally falling upon Alexius's swirl of magic once again. "We will talk, you and I. I want more information about Melenia. About all of this."

"Of course, your majesty."

"But can he stay?" Lucia asked, her voice filled with hope.

There was a long stretch of silence in which the king scrutinized Alexius even more closely. "Yes. And I agree wholeheartedly with Melenia's plan. Alexius will make an excellent tutor. If I'm not mistaken, I think he and I have the same goals for your magic."

The king believed that he and the Watchers were collectively after the Kindred, and that he would be the one to possess and control their magic, making him a god.

If only he knew the truth.

"We do indeed have the same goals, your majesty," Alexius said.

The king nodded. "Then go. You will begin your lessons first thing tomorrow once Lucia has a chance to rest. Welcome to my kingdom, Alexius."

CHAPTER 17

MAGNUS

AURANOS

The Beast.

The name of the tavern was humorous to start with, but after Magnus had finished his second bottle of wine, he found it downright hilarious.

"Another bottle," he barked. "Now."

The server placed a third bottle of Paelsian wine in front of him.

"Silas Agallon Vineyards," Magnus read aloud from the etching on the green glass bottle.

He was drinking wine made by Jonas Agallon's family.

Even more hilarity.

Despite his distaste for the kingdom itself, Magnus had quickly come to prefer Paelsian wine. Still, the place was a dry wasteland at best. And at worst, it was the site of bad memories and poor choices, of humiliation, defeat, and regret.

He drank straight from the bottle now, ignoring his goblet. How stupid that his father had forbidden such pleasures in Limeros all those years, citing religious reasons. Valoria had taught that to keep a clear mind was to keep a pure heart, and her people had obeyed. Magnus had always subscribed to this credo, believing that he truly preferred a clear mind to this . . . this . . .

Yes. *This* was better.

Drunk was much better than sober.

He cast a dark glance around the shadowy tavern. What few patrons remaining at this late hour had moved to tables in the back. The only people near Magnus were a couple of his guards.

He'd told them to leave him alone, but they'd ignored him. They were there "for his protection."

Impudent bastards.

He raised the bottle. "To my sister and her shiny new tutor," he said, tipping the wine toward the server before taking a long drink. "And to my father. Family—so important. So valuable. May they all rot together in the darklands one day."

His own words amused him deeply, as did the server's horrified response to his toast.

Magnus was halfway through the third bottle when he felt a hand clamp down on his shoulder.

"Your highness," Cronus said. "It's time to leave."

Magnus flicked the guard's hand away. "But I'm not nearly finished."

"It wouldn't please the king to see you like this."

"Oh, no! The king wouldn't be pleased. But I absolutely, positively want to please the king at all times. Don't I?" He took another swig.

"You've had enough to drink."

"Did you wake up this morning and suddenly decide to become my wet nurse, Cronus? Apologies, but I have no desire to suckle at your nipple tonight."

"I could carry you back to the palace, but I'd prefer to give you the chance to walk."

The prince responded to the guard's rudeness with only a wry look. If anyone else spoke to him with such disrespect, Magnus would wish them dead. But having been the king's most loyal and trusted guard for too many years to count, Cronus had gotten used to speaking his mind when necessary without fear of repercussion. He'd established his place in any palace the Damoras should ever occupy. And one day he would be loyal and obedient to Magnus's every command.

But, unfortunately for Magnus, that day wasn't today.

"How kind of you. Walking is one thing I'm sure my father agrees that I do rather well."

Cronus fixed him with an impassive expression. "The king himself sent me here to retrieve you."

"And, of course, you obeyed without hesitation."

"He knows that you've developed a fondness for wine."

Magnus cast the guard a curious look. "Does he? And what does he think of that?"

"He's remarkably understanding. He knows what you've been through and forgives you your missteps. But he'd rather you drink inside the palace from now on, instead of at questionable establishments such as this, where one's words or actions could be used against him, no matter who he might be."

"How thoughtful of him." The lightness that the wine had infused into Magnus's head now began to darken at the edges. He stood up from his stool and faced the patrons at the back of the tavern. "My father forgives me for all of my missteps! He allows me to drink myself into a stupor as it will help me accept my destiny! I am the Prince of Blood, my father's heir—and the path to my future is set in stone. Do you fear me as you do him, you worthless peons?"

Cronus pushed firmly against his right shoulder. "Enough. This is no place for the crown prince to be, especially after yesterday's chaos. It's not safe here."

"Don't touch me." Magnus whacked the guard's hand away, but this time he was not so gentle.

Cronus remained patient as ever. "I'd prefer for you to leave this place of your own free will, but my orders from the king are clear. I'm to return you to the palace, and if need be, your highness, I will render you unconscious and drag you back."

Cronus was fifteen years Magnus's senior and more skilled and experienced by far. He had no doubt that the guard could and would follow through with his threat.

Magnus might have been drunk, but he wasn't stupid.

"Fine," he spat out. "I'm finished here anyway."

The other guards glanced at each other warily as Magnus strode out of the tavern with Cronus directly behind him. The early evening air was warm and sweetly scented with roses—both the official flower and the official stench of Auranos.

Limeros smelled of ice. Paelsia of dirt. But Auranos smelled of roses.

Magnus hated roses. What other purpose did they serve besides looking pretty?

Though he stumbled as he walked along the narrow cobblestone road, he kept up a quick pace, and didn't once glance over his shoulder to see if the others were keeping up with him. He didn't care.

His steps finally slowed as he turned a corner to find six guards standing outside of a grand building with a façade of white marble flanked by pillars, sandwiched between two ordinary stone taverns.

"What is this place?" he asked.

"It's a temple of the goddess Cleiona," Cronus said.

"Such places should be torn down," Magnus muttered. Then, louder, "Why are there guards here? Have they abandoned Valoria to worship at another goddess's feet? Father wouldn't be too pleased about that, would he?"

Cronus went to consult one of the guards and returned a moment later.

"It seems that Princess Cleiona is inside. She's been given permission to worship here several times a week."

This was the last thing Magnus expected to hear. To his knowledge, the princess hadn't been allowed to leave the palace since the wedding tour. "Why didn't I know about this?"

Cronus spread his hands. "It was the king's decision."

"Was it." Magnus's gaze was fixed on the temple doors. He should have been consulted about this. Why should she be given such privileges? "It wasn't the king's decision to make. He's not the one who was forced to marry her."

"*All* decisions are the king's to make."

This was completely unacceptable.

"Wait out here," he commanded. "I want to inform the princess this is the last time she will be allowed to come here."

He expected Cronus to protest, but the guard just nodded patiently. "Very well, your highness. Do what you must."

Magnus pushed through the temple doors, leaving the guards to wait outside. The space looked like a miniature version of the grand Temple of Cleiona, where he and Cleo had been married, which had been big enough to hold thousands. That was, before the earthquake that had reduced it to a pile of rubble, making it unsafe for anyone to venture inside.

Though this temple was much smaller, it was still ornate and beautiful. White marble floors. Carved benches. A statue of the goddess peering at Magnus with what looked like disdain. The symbols of fire and air were etched into her upraised palms.

"You're not welcome here, Limerian," she seemed to sneer at him. Too bad.

The temple was empty apart from the blond girl seated in the front pew. She gazed up at a gigantic mosaic depicting the goddess with the green valleys of Auranos behind her. On her left was a wildfire, burning with flames both orange and blue; to the right, a tornado.

Cleo gave Magnus a sidelong glance as he approached and sat down across the aisle from her, his attention fixed on the mosaic.

"Have you come here to worship?" she asked.

He repressed a laugh. "Hardly."

"So you're here only to interrupt my prayers."

"As if you're actually praying."

She looked at him with narrowed eyes.

"Spare me such accusatory glares," he said, rolling his eyes. "I've seen no sign that you're devout in your religious beliefs. You're the same as anyone in this hedonistic, self-centered king-dom. Your religion is nothing more than a series of pretty marble statues adorning gaudily ornate spaces."

"You are entitled to your opinion."

Her dismissive attitude would do nothing to help her cause tonight. "You come here to escape the palace even if it means you must be accompanied by a half-dozen guards. This is where you can think in private, perhaps about how best to destroy us."

Cleo crossed her arms over the bodice of her gown. "Oh, so now you're a mind reader, are you? It's incredible that you have the talent to know exactly what's in my thoughts at all times."

"You'd be surprised what I know about your thoughts, princess."

She assessed him with a single sweep of her eyes. "You're drunk."

"Am I?"

"You're slurring your words."

He wasn't slurring anything. She likely said this only to wound him—a constant goal of hers. "Apologies for not making myself clear. I came in here to tell you this will be the last time you will be allowed here."

She didn't seem overly concerned by his proclamation. "The king told me I could come whenever I wanted."

"I don't care what the king told you."

The princess raised her chin. "What right do you have to prevent me from doing something that has already been approved by your father?"

How obtuse she was being! He barked out a laugh. "What *right*? I'm your *husband*, princess. That gives me the right to stop you from doing anything that displeases me."

She sighed. But Magnus could tell it was one of weariness rather than defeat. "By morning," she said, "you'll have forgotten all about this conversation. Tell me, how much did you drink? A gallon? Did you fall face-first into your wine and swim around for a while?"

"I see you're attempting to change the subject."

"I find that those who drink to excess wish to forget their troubles."

"Oh, really? Is that what *you* do?"

She paused, seemingly undeterred by the jab. "I drink far less than I used to. I found it never led me to the places I wanted to be."

"Oh, that's right. It led you into Aron Lagaris's bed, isn't that right?"

Her expression soured. "How kind of you to remind me."

"But alas, you won't be finding yourself in his bed ever again. It would be a rather cold place to be now."

He could tell she was fighting to keep her emotions in check, but her cheeks had gone very red. "You want me to leave, yet you don't seem in any hurry to leave yourself. What's out there you're trying so hard to avoid?"

"Everything." He said it without thinking, without meaning to.

She studied him carefully. "I think you're drinking to forget about what happened to your mother."

His chest tightened. "Shut your mouth."

She swept her glance across the temple, which was empty but for the two of them. "You won't believe me, but I understand the pain you feel. Your need for vengeance."

Their conversations rarely got as personal as this. "I feel nothing of the sort."

"I don't believe you."

"I don't really care what you believe, princess. And I'm not looking for a friend."

"Perhaps you should be. From what I've seen, you've no other friends to speak of."

That she seemed to know him so well unnerved him. "I don't need friends."

She studied him for a silent, uncomfortable while, her brows drawing together. "You try so hard to be horrible, to be cruel, to remain detached from anything that might cause you pain. But I saw the look on your face as they dragged you away from the executions yesterday. You were frantic when Lucia went missing in the crowd. You thought she'd been hurt."

The fact that she'd so easily noticed this weakness made him wince on the inside. "My sister can take care of herself, believe me. She was fine, only temporarily lost. And she returned to the palace not only unhurt but with a handsome new tutor in tow. How delightful for everyone."

Cleo stood up and sat right next to Magnus. The gesture surprised him, but he didn't let it show.

"I find you . . . deeply confusing," Cleo said. "More so with every day that passes."

"Some girls are easily confused."

"Time and time again you prove yourself to be vile and disgusting and hateful."

This coaxed a fresh laugh from him. They'd finally returned to more familiar ground. "Your opinion is irrelevant to me, princess."

"You are all of those things." She nodded, as if agreeing with herself. "But the more I think about you, the more of an enigma you become to me. Yesterday was only another example. Before that, you could have exposed me to your father as an eavesdropper, but you didn't. You could have let that boy stab me in Limeros, but you stopped him. You defended me when Aron exposed my loss of chastity. The king would have cast me out otherwise. And you didn't tell your father about the bridal dagger Prince Ashur gave me."

She made it sound as though he'd done these things deliberately, to help her. "You're imagining kindnesses that were anything but."

"You're the one who chooses to call them *kindnesses*. Are you sure that's not what they were?" She searched his face, making him feel naked and exposed, as if the masks he'd spent so many years building up were crumbling down all around him like sand castles in the wind.

"You know nothing about me," he growled. For the first time tonight, he cursed the fact that he'd drank to excess. He needed his mind to be clear in the face of his enemies.

Why had he bothered to come inside? Was it simply to exert his force of will upon this girl? To remind her that she had no power? To bully her in an attempt to regain his strength?

It had only made him weaker than he'd been before.

"All I can do anymore is think," Cleo said after a long silence. "All day, all night. I think about everything that's happened and I replay it over and over in my mind. And do you know what I think, Magnus?"

Why did he remain here and continue to listen to her? He needed to leave this place. "I don't care what you think."

"I think that you hate your father. You hate him almost as much as I do."

It took him a moment to realize he'd stopped breathing. "And what difference would it make if you're right?" he finally managed.

"All the difference in the world."

She was brave this evening, saying things to his drunken self that she'd never say to the sober one.

He hadn't given her a direct answer, but he hadn't denied it, either.

"You're not like the king," she said softly, when he said nothing in reply.

He turned away. "You're wrong. I'm *exactly* like the king. I aspire to be as great a man as my father. It's all I've ever wanted."

She touched his arm and he flinched. "You aspire to be like a man who would slice open a child's cheek as punishment for some meaningless offense?"

He glared at her as he brought up his hand and touched his scar. He never should have told her that bit about his past. He had exposed yet another weakness, and now she was using it against him. "What do you think you're doing here, saying these things to me?"

She bit her bottom lip before replying. "I'm simply trying to have a civil conversation with you."

Enough of this. "Then this civil conversation has happily reached its end." Magnus stood up and began walking away. But suddenly she was up and standing there, blocking his path.

"I'm not done," she said.

"Oh, you're done."

"No. I'm not."

He was through with this. He grabbed her arms, turned her around, and pushed her backward until she touched the mosaic. The goddess rose up above her, a fearsome, omnipotent guardian watching over the Auranian princess.

"There is no goodness inside of me, princess, so please don't waste time fantasizing that there might be."

"Lucia is your sister and she's not bad," Cleo said.

"You want truth, princess? Lucia was adopted. We share no blood, not that it makes any difference to her. I'm sure you've heard the rumor—a brother who lusts after his own sister. It's all true. But don't worry. She didn't sully herself with the notion that we could ever be together. That was my fantasy alone, not hers. I disgust her every bit as much as I disgust you. That's one thing you have in common with this girl you're attempting to blossom a friendship with."

Cleo looked stricken with shock. He knew that these admissions were spilling from his lips like wine from an overturned cask, but he didn't really care anymore.

"I must admit, she doesn't torture me as much as she used to, by day and by night," he went on. "Lately my more troubling dreams have shifted from ones of my dark-haired sister to ones of a princess with hair of pale gold." He took up a lock of Cleo's waist-length hair and twisted it around his index finger. He stared at it, transfixed. "Dreams of the one I was bound to against my wishes."

Her cerulean eyes widened. "You dream about me?"

His gaze snapped back to hers. "Nightmares only."

He wished they were only nightmares.

Magnus tried to pull back from her, but she grabbed hold of his shirt.

"Rather than always fighting ," she whispered, "we could find a way to help each other. It's possible we have similar goals."

Such words were more than enough to sign her death warrant. Was she so stupid as to say these things to the son of the king?

Or did she really know him so well that she felt confident being so bold?

Cleo wanted her throne back. There was no doubt about it. She wanted her kingdom returned to her family name, and she wanted his father dead so he would never again hurt anyone she loved. She fought quietly but fiercely for this with every day that passed, every word she spoke.

And in this moment, he thought she was the bravest and most beautiful girl he'd ever known.

The effects of the wine still swirled through his mind and body, the world sparkling all around him. But one thought was crystal clear.

This princess, who looked at him tonight with hope rather

than hate shining in her eyes . . . if he let her, she could destroy him.

Magnus slid his hands down her silk gown and circled her narrow waist. He could feel the rapid beat of her heart he pressed himself against her.

She drew in a shaky breath as his mouth brushed the curve of her ear.

"Tell me, princess," he whispered. "What would Theon say if he could know you'd allow me to get this close to you?"

Cleo gasped and shoved him back. Her eyes were wide and already glossy with tears at the harsh reminder of her lost love.

She slapped Magnus across his face and the sting of it im-pressed him. She was much stronger than she appeared.

"How dare you even speak his name!" she hissed, tears splashing to her cheeks.

This was the reaction he'd hoped for, the one that could put an end to this dangerous confrontation. "It took no effort at all to shove that sword through his back and send him to the ever after." He forced himself to smirk. "And yet now you suggest an alliance with me. How soon you have forgotten who your true enemies are, princess. It makes me question your intelligence."

Cleo's cheeks flamed. "I hate you."

"Good. You should never forget your place in this palace. You continue to live only because my father doesn't yet want you dead. You have no power here. And, most especially, you have no power over me."

He watched her reel with emotion, and then her gaze became flat and dead, the bright rosiness of her anger fading from her cheeks. Her guard was back up—not a surprise when it came to him.

"Much gratitude for the reminder," she said.

"Good evening, princess." With that, Magnus left the temple, not even glancing at Cronus, who still waited outside.

"The princess?" Cronus asked.

He flicked his hand. "Let her worship to her heart's content. I don't care what she does."

"Your opinions have changed much in the short time you were inside."

"Nothing has changed. I just remembered how apathetic I am about that deceitful creature."

"Apathetic, are you?"

Magnus shot a sharp glare at Cronus. "Yes."

"If you say so."

He did. And he returned to the palace by way of the darkening city streets without taking any more detours into dangerous places.

Once inside the palace walls, he went straight to the courtyard to be alone with his dark thoughts. His mind was still in a drunken fog, but he knew the morning would bring regrets about speaking so many secret truths.

The truth about Lucia's adoption and his feelings for her.

And the truth about Cleo.

What truth about Cleo? There was no truth. She was merely a girl he'd been forced to marry. But if he felt nothing for her, why did he continue to protect her? He hadn't even realized that's what he'd been doing until she'd brought it to his attention, but she was right. Time and again, he'd chosen to keep her safe.

Magnus remembered all too clearly his encounter with Theon Ranus. It had been his first kill. At the time, he hadn't known that Theon was protecting Cleo not only because he was a palace guard sent to retrieve the princess from a dangerous land but because he loved her. And she loved him.

It wasn't just his father's orders that had seen Magnus there that day. It was fate. Back then, he'd just been a boy with no experience in battle.

He'd slain the guard to save his own life. He regretted nothing about it now . . . except for the look of pure hatred in Cleo's eyes after the deed had been done.

But she was the daughter of Limeros's enemy. His father had conquered Cleo's kingdom and she should be grateful that they'd allowed her to live another day.

That he even spared her a single thought when there were so many more important things to think about was beyond ridiculous.

Pacing the courtyard, he told himself that she was nothing more to him than an inconvenience.

"My goodness, Prince Magnus, you look rather upset. Is everything all right?"

He spun on his heels to see Princess Amara seated in the shadows on a nearby bench. The moonlight glinted against her dark hair and the jewels she wore at her throat.

"Apologies. I didn't notice you there," he said.

In the wake of the attack, the king had insisted that Amara stay at the palace for a couple of days, thinking there might still be some rebels nearby. It was a courtesy the king had extended only because he felt he had no other choice—potential enemy or not, it wouldn't look good for him to throw this royal girl to the wolves.

"I'm glad for the chance to speak with you alone." Amara stood up from the bench. "I wanted to apologize for what happened at the villa."

Magnus tried his best to be as cordial to her as possible, despite his current mood. "What do you mean?"

"When I kissed you." She looked up at him without a hint of shyness. "I feel I may have offended you."

"Not at all." If only stolen kisses from beautiful visiting princesses were his only problem.

Amara drew closer to him. "You and I have so much in common, don't we? Our fathers are both important men with the insatiable desire to grow their power."

"True enough."

Amara was so vastly different from Cleo. She was just as intriguing and beautiful, certainly, but Magnus wasn't drawn to Amara like a moth to a flame. She didn't have the power to burn him to the ground with a look, with a touch.

She studied him through the darkness. "Sometimes it's nice to find a kindred spirit, even if the situation is not entirely ideal. It's good to find solace with someone like that, to perhaps indulge in a night of pleasure with an understanding friend when, by day, the world is full of enemies. Don't you agree?"

He didn't have to search too far to understand her meaning.

"I agree completely," he said.

He pulled her to him and crushed his mouth against hers, breathing her in, letting her command his senses.

Yes. She was exactly what he needed tonight.

CHAPTER 18

CLEO

AURANOS

It didn't seem to matter whether the previous day had been good or bad; the sun would always rise the next morning. And for the briefest moment, as warm rays streamed through Cleo's window and touched her face, it seemed as if everything was back to the way it had been before. Her father and sister were alive and well. Her friends were preparing for parties and outings. The palace was filled with happiness and life.

But the daydream was over as soon as it had arrived, and she remembered that those visions were now only the ghosts of a past that continued to haunt her.

But she accepted this new reality. She had no choice here, only determination. And patience.

Nerissa arrived at her chambers to help her with her hair. The ex-seamstress had been assigned as her new handmaiden only yesterday, replacing two horrible Limerian girls. Seemingly capable of manipulating her way into any position at the palace, she had sought out the reassignment herself. This was an enviable skill, to say the least, and Cleo was grateful to have someone to talk to who knew the same secrets she did. Already Cleo had trusted the girl to deliver a message to Jonas about the king's confirmed interest in the Kindred. She hoped to have more information to aid the rebels soon.

"Did you find out how many were killed?" Cleo asked now.

"Twenty-seven," Nerissa said, meeting her gaze in the mirror.

"So many." Cleo had already known of the plan to rescue Lysandra and the other rebel. Nic had told her of his agreement to assist Jonas at the palace by disguising him and his associate in Limerian uniforms and ushering them safely from the city. Her fear for Nic's safety had almost trumped her trust in Jonas's abilities, and she had been very close to insisting that Nic bow out of the deal. But Nic had insisted it was the right thing to do. It was an act of rebellion that the king couldn't ignore.

And the fact that Nic's bullies Milo and Burrus had been blamed for the explosions and now sat in the dungeon awaiting their fates didn't cause her heart any unrest.

But those twenty-seven people who had been killed in the process unsettled her deeply. So much damage, so much suffering. Had Jonas felt that this much loss of life was warranted?

"I wish there'd been another way," Cleo said.

"I know, princess. But don't lose faith. Jonas only wants the best for all of us."

Cleo twisted her amethyst ring, trying to take strength from it. "So, basically, he's the very opposite of Prince Magnus."

"I like to think so."

Memories of last night replayed in her mind. She'd gone to the temple on a whim, to pray and be silent with her thoughts. But then *he'd* shown up.

To think that for even a second she'd been so close to . . . what? Trusting him? Believing he was something more than a cruel boy who took pleasure in torturing her?

She was such a fool.

"I hate him," she spat. "I hate him so much I can barely see straight."

Nerissa wove Cleo's long pale locks into a thick plait, which she then wound into a loose bun at the nape of her neck before pinning it securely into place. "Yes, that's definitely your problem."

Was that judgment in her voice?

Cleo blinked with surprise. "Excuse me?"

"Hatred is like fire. It burns the one who harnesses it. It's also extremely hard to see more helpful truths through its flames."

Nerissa was wise beyond her eighteen years.

"You're absolutely right," Cleo said, her brow furrowed as she remembered her conversation with the prince. She pushed past the blinding flames of her hatred toward the boy who'd thrown Theon's death back in her face, making her deeply regret thinking she might be able to trust him.

But she wasn't the only one who shared dark truths last night. Magnus had told her that Lucia was adopted—a revelation more shocking than his confirmation of his feelings toward her.

Perhaps Magnus had realized he was opening himself up too much, peeling back the hateful layers that concealed his true self. He knew he needed to push her away before he revealed too much of himself . . . and of what he had in common with Cleo.

He'd succeeded, at the time.

But today was a new day.

Cleo had allowed herself to be manipulated by the memory of

Theon's death, and Magnus had managed to push her away when she'd gotten too close.

Nerissa was correct. Fire burned. Fire blinded.

Clever, Magnus, she thought. *Very clever.*

But not clever enough.

With every step she took toward Magnus's chambers, Cleo wavered between having confidence and doubting what she was about to attempt.

Magnus's natural demeanor was acidic, his manners unpleasant at best. But he'd also saved her. Helped her. Kept her secrets.

There had to be more to him.

When she reached his door, she allowed herself a moment of hesitation.

I can do this, she told herself. *I need to be strong.*

She raised her hand to knock, but before she could make contact, the door swung open and she found herself face-to-face with Princess Amara.

Amara smiled brightly. "Good morning, Cleo."

Stunned, Cleo merely stood there and blinked. "Amara, I—I didn't expect to see you, here." Her gaze then fell to the partially unfastened ties on the girl's dress.

Amara's brows drew together. "Oh, dear. This isn't a problem, is it? I'd assumed, based on what I'd heard, that such affairs were unimportant to you."

Cleo glanced past Amara to see Magnus approaching the doorway. His dark hair was messy and his shirt was missing, revealing more bare skin than she'd ever seen on him before.

The realization that these two had spent the night together hit her like a lead weight.

"To what do I owe this unexpected visit, princess?" Magnus leaned against the door frame, showing no sign he was having difficulty recovering from all the alcohol he'd consumed last night. Apparently good Paelsian wine caused no ill effects other than loose tongues, spilled secrets, and the inability to care who shared one's bed.

Cleo grappled to find words to fill the silence. "After our harsh words last night I thought we should speak again. But I see you're otherwise occupied."

"I was just leaving." Amara cast a worried look at Magnus through her thick eyelashes. "Have I crossed the line?"

"No line I didn't want you to cross." He put his arm around her waist, drew her back against him, and kissed her. "I'll see you again soon."

"Good day, Cleo." Amara gave her a tight smile, then slipped past her and down the hallway. Cleo watched her go until she disappeared around a corner.

She'd heard all about the conversation Nic had had with the Cortases at their villa a few days ago, and it had made her head spin with both possibility and doubt. She knew she would have a great deal to consider before making any decisions or allegiances, no matter how powerful they were.

From what she'd seen this morning, however, it seemed as if Princess Amara was offering up alliances to everyone.

"She really is stunningly beautiful, isn't she?" Magnus said. "Her beauty makes me wonder why I've never thought to visit Kraeshia before. I'll have to make a point to go there soon. Now, you said you wanted to speak with me? I can't imagine what we have to discuss."

She cast him a dark look. "What will the servants say?"

"About?"

"Don't you care about the rumors they'll spread? There are already so many about you and Lucia . . . but now they'll start talking about you and I not sharing the same bed!"

He studied her with flatness in his dark eyes. "Apologies, princess, but I'm sure they're already well aware of that. Besides, the servants can say whatever they want, it doesn't bother me. Our marriage is meaningless. We share nothing but an unfortunate arrangement neither of us chose. That you're the least bit surprised that I'd choose to share my bed with someone else is laughable at best." She gave him a look that was livid enough to make him laugh. "Do I deserve another slap? Don't try it, or this time you might get slapped in return."

Why had she come here? It was pointless to try to reason with this loathsome creature. "I wouldn't waste my energy."

"Excellent. Now say what you have to say and be done with it. I need to get dressed."

Another unnecessary reminder that he was currently half-naked.

"It was nothing," she bit out. "A mistake."

"Oh? Or perhaps seeing Amara temporarily removed any other thoughts from your mind. Did it bother you to find her here?" He smiled, looking like a predator baring its teeth. "Don't tell me you're jealous, because I won't believe it."

Her cheeks burned at the very suggestion. "Not jealous, Magnus. Appalled. Disgusted. Embarrassed."

"That is quite a litany of emotions. So many, princess, all directed at me and whom I choose to sleep with. Interesting."

The fire of her hatred *was* blinding. Cleo could barely see past the flames, but a sharp burst of laughter escaped her lips. "Believe me, Prince Magnus, I don't care who you sleep with. Servant, courtesan, or . . . or *goat*. It's less than meaningless to me."

"I highly doubt I'd ever choose a goat."

"Doesn't seem that way to me."

He curled up his lips as he leaned closer. "Your tongue is sharp for so early an hour. Amara's was much less sharp. I should know; I got to know it very well last night."

She'd had enough of this nonsense. Cleo turned away, clenching her hands into fists to stop them from trembling.

"Are you sure you've changed your mind about wanting to chat?" he called after her.

She kept walking and didn't dignify Magnus's words with a reply.

Cleo searched the palace for a friendly face to help her see clearly again.

She found Nic stationed near the throne room and gestured for him to meet her around the corner where they could speak in privacy. After what she'd just witnessed, she now doubted everything.

"What's wrong?" he asked, having snuck away successfully.

Cleo let out a long, shaky breath and tried to release the hatred that continued to burn inside her. She looked up at Nic, wincing at the bruises on his face.

She gently touched his cheek. "That looks like it hurts a lot."

"Less every day. I'm fine, really. But it seems that you're experiencing a flurry of angst today."

"More like disappointment. Our potential ally seems to have found herself in bed with the enemy." She told him about her recent encounter.

"Wow." Nic's brows shot up. "Although, now that you mention it, I have heard Kraeshian girls are known to be rather . . . *friendly*. Looks like Amara represents her empire well, even if her taste is questionable."

She grimaced. "It makes me wonder what she's really after, and if she and her brother have different goals after all."

Nic appeared to consider this new information. "Perhaps she assumes Magnus can lead her to the Kindred. Does she think he has it buried under his blankets?"

She glared at him. "It's not funny."

"I would never dare make light of something like this." But his lips were twitching slightly.

Nic had once been jealous of how she had behaved toward Magnus during the wedding tour. But he had to understand that it had been necessary for her to feign a certain level of affection. Still, he'd accused her of falling in love with the prince.

What a truly ridiculous notion *that* had been.

She was still insatiably curious about Nic's dealings with Prince Ashur. Apart from his confession of their kiss, he hadn't been inclined to divulge much. Cleo tried to be patient. He'd confided so much in her already, and she was certain he'd tell her more if there were more to tell.

"I don't trust them, Nic. I can't align with anyone I don't trust. So what do I do now?"

"I wish I knew."

She felt her life and goals spiral out of her control, spinning like a top. "I need a sign. Something to tell me what to do next. Some sign to tell me there's still hope for us."

Just then, the throne room doors swung open and voices boomed down the hallway. Cleo peered around the corner to see the king emerge, followed by the handsome boy that had been assigned as Lucia's new tutor. Lucia had spent all day yesterday locked in her chambers with the boy as they began their private lessons.

What constituted these lessons had not been disclosed to anyone, but many servants had begun to whisper that they involved Princess Lucia's secret and dangerous talent for *elementia*.

Whatever the truth might be, Cleo could see why Lucia seemed so eager to devote herself to her new studies. Her tutor was tall and lean and devastatingly attractive. His features looked as if they'd been forged from precious metals—bronze hair and silver eyes. His skin glowed with an ethereal golden tan as if lit from within.

"Do you know anything about him?" Cleo asked Nic.

"Not much. Apparently Lucia crossed paths with him in the city after the rebel escape. She brought him back and the king accepted him with open arms. Very unlike him." Nic eyed the pair with disdain. "Knowing his majesty, I give Alexius a week, maybe two, before he's dead."

Alexius. She'd heard his name in passing, but with her mind so set on a multitude of other problems, she couldn't quite place it.

But suddenly, the name resounded deep within her.

Cleo's breath caught and held as she remembered what Lucia had confessed the day they toured the city together.

"A Watcher named Alexius visited my dreams. He promised to visit me again after I woke, but I haven't seen him since."

"Cleo?" Nic touched her arm. "You've gone pale. What is it?"

She met his concerned gaze and a smile slowly spread across her face. "That sign I wanted? To give me hope? I think it just walked through those doors."

CHAPTER 19

LUCIA

AURANOS

The king had readily agreed to make Alexius Lucia's *elementia* tutor.

Yet somehow, Lucia hadn't realized that this decision would result in *actual lessons*, having considered it merely an excuse for Alexius to stay at the palace.

Initially, back in Limeros, Magnus had tried to help her with her magic—encouraging her to use air magic to lift objects heavier than flowers, to summon fire magic that would do something more powerful than light a candle. For all her recent difficulties with her brother, he'd been the first to encourage her, to help her accept her burgeoning powers rather than think of them as evil, as it was with witches who were executed for their crimes. For this, she'd always be grateful to him.

Much more recently, the king had released an accused witch from the dungeons, in the hope she might help his daughter learn how to further control her abilities.

But the witch had been an inadequate tutor. She'd been offensively weak and easily intimidated by the far superior magic Lucia displayed with barely any effort. And that had been the end of her.

Alexius was quite different. After all, as an immortal, he was *created* from magic. Even in his mortal form, he embodied it. Although he readily admitted that the magic he could summon paled in the light of Lucia's prophesied *elementia*, he had full confidence he could be an asset to her. And to her father.

He and Lucia had shared one full day of lessons, from sunrise to sunset, locked in Lucia's chambers with the furniture and rugs pushed to the edges of the room to create plenty of space for them to move about freely on the smooth marble floor.

Similarly to Magnus's teaching style, Alexius had Lucia lift objects with air magic, and use fire to light small blazes. She used water magic to create ice, and earth magic to nurse dying plants back to life.

"I can heal your leg," she said to him, having noticed his slight limp as soon as he arrived. "Shall I try?"

Alexius brushed his fingers against the fabric of his trousers. "That'll be impossible, I'm afraid. This cut will have to heal the same way a mortal's would. Earth magic—healing magic, either mine or another's—won't work on me anymore." He offered her the edge of a smile at her look of dismay. "It's all right. There are many penalties for choosing to leave the Sanctuary. This is but one of them. I'll be fine, I promise."

"I don't accept that. I still want to try," she insisted.

"Very well, my stubborn sorceress. Try." He pulled up his pant leg and unwound the gauze bandages. Lucia winced upon seeing the gash on his otherwise flawless golden skin. She shrugged off her surprise and focused, channeling as much earth magic as she could into the wound—just as she'd done when she'd healed Magnus after he'd been horribly injured during the siege to take this kingdom.

But where she'd succeeded with Magnus, she failed with Alexius. Still, she continued to try until she felt weary from the effort.

"Enough, princess." He finally grasped her wrist. "Our final lesson of the day is this: You can't win every battle."

More than anything, she was annoyed by her failure. And she hated that Alexius was hurt and she couldn't help ease his pain. That had been the end of yesterday's lessons; she had become so exhausted, her mind so filled with the darkness that naturally came from using her magic, that her body ached. She wanted to sleep for a week.

Still, her head swam and she marveled at the reality of having Alexius here in the flesh. So much so that, as she lay in bed that night looking up at the silk canopy above her head, she realized she'd barely asked Alexius anything about . . . well, *anything*. They'd talked of nothing beyond her lessons and her promises to show him the city. She swore to rectify that the following day.

He arrived shortly after her light breakfast of tea and yogurt with sliced peaches. The servant who'd brought the tray to her chambers eyed both her and Alexius with curiosity, so Lucia quickly sent her away and locked the door for privacy.

He brushed his gaze over her face. "You look . . . rather determined today."

"I am," she agreed. "Did you meet with Father last night?"

The king had insisted that the exiled Watcher give him updates at the end of each daily session. He would probably enjoy personally monitoring their lessons as well, but Lucia wouldn't agree to that. Luckily, he hadn't yet suggested it.

"Yes, and I told him his daughter is doing quite well, and that he should be very proud." He walked around the large room, his gaze landing on the canopied bed, the vanity table, the reading and study area through an archway to the left, and the open balcony doors that let in fresh air and sunlight. "We'll work in here again today, but tomorrow I think we should take your lessons outdoors to be closer to nature. Closer to the elements."

"What about Melenia?" Lucia asked.

He grew still and glanced at her, his brow raised. "What about her?"

"Has she contacted you?"

"Actually, yes. She visited my dreams last night for the first time since I left the Sanctuary. She was very pleased to know I've arrived and made contact with the king. And, of course, with you."

When she'd found Alexius in the city, he didn't mention that he was a messenger for another beautiful immortal with mysterious ties to her father. Alexius had said only that he'd exiled himself to be with her. Because he loved her. When he'd admitted the true purpose behind his arrival to the king in the throne room, she'd been blindsided and uncertain how to feel about it.

She knew that she was missing many pieces to the puzzle of Alexius's true purpose for being there. She wanted—no, she *needed*—to gather them all as quickly as possible.

"What does she want?" she asked, attempting to lighten her words with a smile. "And how often does this beautiful immortal woman plan to visit you in this rather *intimate* way?"

Alexius drew closer. His silvery eyes met hers, and she saw that they were filled now with an unexpected whisper of humor. "You're not jealous, are you?"

She bristled. "Of course not."

"Melenia is my elder and my leader, even now that I've left. She cares for my well-being, especially in my first few days as a mortal. Try not to concern yourself with her or your father's interest in the ways of Watchers. Instead, focus on what's important: getting stronger, gaining control, and growing your power."

"Does that translate to 'don't be a silly girl who asks silly questions'?"

"Hardly." The amusement in his eyes did not wane. "We should begin today's lessons. We'll burn off some of this paranoia you've woken up with this morning."

Perhaps he was right. "Fine. Then let's begin."

This second day of lessons turned out to be much different than the first. Alexius began by forming a flame in the palm of his right hand, which reminded her of the one she'd conjured to both impress and frighten the boy responsible for the explosions during the rebel escape. A memory she'd just as soon forget. She'd heard that Amara had been staying at the palace the last couple of days, but Lucia hadn't wanted to speak with her. Knowing Amara would have questions about her magic that Lucia wasn't prepared to answer, she wanted to avoid the other princess for as long as she possibly could.

She'd deal with her another day.

"Here's what I want you to do," Alexius said, his face lit up by the flickering flame. "Concentrate on this fire I've created with my own magic—concentrate on it with every part of your mind. Without using any fire magic of your own, I want you to take this flame away from me."

It took her a moment to understand. "You want me to *steal* your magic."

"That's right," he said. "This is quite different from what we did yesterday, which was just simple elemental manifestation."

"Yes, so simple." She raised an eyebrow.

His lips curved upward. "For you, it seems to be. However, I guarantee that this will be more of a challenge. Think of your magic as an invisible muscle that, when strengthened, will increase your control. You can conjure fire yourself, or you can take someone else's."

"All right. My magic is a muscle." She studied the flame dancing on the palm of his hand. She concentrated with all her might, until the world closed in around that small tuft of fire. She could feel the warmth of both the flame and Alexius.

Not her magic. *His* magic.

She focused as much as she could, until beads of perspiration formed on her forehead. "This is difficult," she managed.

"Yes, it is," was his rather infuriating reply.

She refused to give up. It took several minutes, but, finally, with great effort, the flame disappeared from Alexius's hand and reappeared in hers.

She inhaled sharply, then laughed with relief. "I did it!"

"You did. Well done, princess." He nodded, his expression pleased. Then he waved his hand and extinguished her flame. He held out his palm and a second flame appeared. "Now, do it again."

Her laughter faded. "Again?"

"That's right."

She placed her hands on her hips. "Did Eva have to do these sorts of lessons?"

Now Alexius was the one to laugh. "Well, Eva was an immortal, born of magic and power. The original sorceress was not a mortal girl whose *elementia* didn't awaken until the age of sixteen. So, no. Eva didn't have to do these sorts of lessons."

Lucia knew she could complain and today's lessons would end

immediately, but that wouldn't get her anywhere. Controlling her *elementia* was her sole purpose, and Alexius could help her. Plus, she couldn't say that spending hours upon hours with the boy of her dreams was that much of a hardship, even if she'd already found him to be a harsh taskmaster.

She focused on the flame, her brow furrowed with concentration. This time, it took her half as long to steal his magic. She held the fire in her hand and grinned at Alexius.

"Good," he said. Once more, with a wave of his hand, the fire disappeared and reappeared in his palm. "Again."

Her smile fell.

And so it went, the same lesson again and again—ten, twenty, thirty, forty times—until she could do it with ease. As they neared midday, Alexius finally called for a break and went to the balcony to gaze out at the landscape beyond the palace walls.

She stared at the flame, entranced by its beauty before she squeezed her hand into a fist to extinguish it. "You know, I've come to learn that this palace's library has many more books about your people than the Limerian library does."

"*My* people?" Alexius glanced over his shoulder from where he stood at the banister. "You mean Watchers?"

"It's funny to me that you call yourselves Watchers."

"Most of us don't. Only those who have had contact with the mortals, who coined that title for us. Really, a more appropriate moniker would be *Guardians*."

"Because your kind was created to guard the Kindred."

He eyed her with curiosity. "You have been reading some interesting books, haven't you?"

"Some. But there are many legends that have been passed down through generations. Generations that existed before the age of books." Lucia once had a nanny who would tell her bedtime stories that the king or queen wouldn't have approved of, had they known . . . stories of beautiful immortals that could turn into hawks.

"My people," he said, "were originally created to be guardians to this entire world, to help keep it safe. To protect it from anything or anyone who might wish to harm it. But some plans don't work out the way they're intended." Lucia joined him on the balcony, enjoying the feel of the warm sun on her face. "Originally, six immortals were created to be these guardians. They are the elders of our kind, and they existed for centuries before the rest of us came into being."

She was pleased that he seemed willing to share new information with her today. "Melenia is one of the six elders?"

He nodded. "Eva was one, too."

"I read she was the youngest, and the most naïve."

"That's not true," he said quickly. "Actually, Eva was the first immortal created, which is why her magic was the most powerful. All who were created after her were somewhat . . . *less*. She drew a lot of envy because of this."

Lucia frowned. This was not what she'd believed all this time, and it was a revelation. Eva was the first? "That isn't a well-known detail of the legend. It's not in any book I've ever read."

"No, it wouldn't be. There are some who prefer to keep such truths locked away to serve their own agendas." He winced, and began to rub his chest as if it pained him to speak.

"Are you all right?" she asked.

"Yes, I'm fine." A grin spread across his handsome features. "I guess you wore me out with our morning of lessons."

That made one of them. Lucia felt energized, ready for more.

Looking down at her hands, she said, "So . . . my magic is the same magic Eva possessed. It's as if it's a separate entity entirely, which can be passed from one person to the next. Much like what we did with the flame."

Alexius shook his head. "It's not nearly that easy. Your magic is a part of you, but it is powerful enough to survive beyond death."

She struggled to understand all of this and her place in it. "Why me? Why was *I* the one chosen to receive Eva's magic after all these years? Why not some other girl?"

He looked around the room as if searching for answers, and his gaze caught on the silhouette of a golden hawk soaring past the balcony in the distance. His expression grew wistful. "It was meant to be you, princess. It's your destiny, no one else's. But I'll admit I can give you no tangible reason as to *why* you in particular. It simply . . . *is*."

"Lucky me." She paused for a silent moment. "In the dreams we shared, you told me that my magic can save you—save everyone—from destruction. You said I can stop magic from fading from the world."

Alexius turned to face her, his eyes filled with admiration. "You can. And you will."

"How?"

"When the time is right, we will talk of this again. This is your destiny, princess. You are stronger than you think."

She raised her chin, frustrated that he refused to tell her everything right here and right now. "I never said I wasn't strong."

"But if you ever start to doubt yourself, don't. You are a mortal girl, that's true, and Eva was an immortal. But it doesn't matter. You were meant to hold this power within you. I believe that with all my heart."

His words warmed her, chasing away her doubt. "Thank you."

"However, this doesn't mean I'm going to go easy on you this afternoon. We are going to work very hard. You might just hate me by the end of the day."

"Impossible," she told him, finally smiling again. She glanced at the soaring hawk against the blue sky. "Why hawks?"

"What do you mean?"

"Immortals—Watchers, guardians, what have you—can take the form of hawks. Why not eagles? Or sparrows? Or lizards, even?"

"It's said that when the maker of the universe created Eva, a hawk flew past at the precise moment the elemental magic was forming her body. The hawk's spirit was fused with her soul, and with the soul of every immortal created afterward." He searched her eyes for a reaction, smiling slightly. "What can I say? Even my people tell legends to each other."

"But in other words, you don't know for sure."

"No. Not entirely. However, the feeling of taking the form of a hawk and flying high into the sky to keep an eye on all of you mortals is like no other feeling in the world."

"I'm sure you're right." She couldn't even imagine how incredible it would be to fly high up in the sky, away from all earthly troubles. "I'm sorry you've had to give that up."

The barest edge of a shadow crossed his expression. "Don't be. There's no other place I need to be than here, now, with you. Believe that, princess, for it's the absolute truth." He took her hand in his and squeezed it. Her heart skipped a beat as their gazes locked. "Now, shall we resume our lessons?"

Before she could reply, there was a knock at her door. Annoyed, she asked, "Who is that?"

"Only one way to find out," Alexius said.

"The servants know not to disturb us." Reluctantly, she left Alexius's side and walked across the room to unlock and open the door.

"*You*," Cleo said without waiting for Lucia to welcome her. "I'm very cross with you."

Lucia raised her brow in surprise at this unexpected greeting. "Oh?"

"I haven't seen you in *two days*! Not a word since the chaos at the executions. I had to hear from servants that you had returned to the palace, alive and well. I couldn't wait a moment longer to see it for myself, so I came here. And now, I see that you look just fine. Actually, you look particularly lovely today. I can't tell you how relieved I am." She gave Lucia a bright smile.

Lucia had come around to find Cleo disarmingly exuberant and friendly. Yet she continued to feel guarded toward her. Still, she couldn't deny that, after a long morning of lessons, Cleo was a pleasant sight, even if she had interrupted her private time with Alexius.

"All is well," Lucia said. "Thank you for stopping by to check on me."

Part of her had wanted to visit Cleo yesterday after Alexius had bid her good night, in the hopes that she might ease the sensation of darkness rising within her from using so much more magic than she was used to. She knew that a mere moment with the princess had the potential to chase it away.

Instead of going to her, she'd waited, having decided it was still too early to fully trust the other princess. The darkness had faded on its own eventually, allowing sleep to claim her.

"I hear you have a handsome new tutor," Cleo said, glancing past Lucia. "And here he is."

Lucia looked over her shoulder at Alexius, who stood silently in the center of the room. "Yes, here he is."

"His name is Alexius," Cleo said.

"That's right."

"That's the same name as the Watcher you told me about." Lucia spun back around, and Cleo held her gaze unflinchingly. Lucia's heart began to pound, hard and fast. "It appears that he's real, and not just a dream," Cleo finished.

Lucia grabbed Cleo's arm and pulled her into the room. She'd entrusted Cleo with that secret in a moment of weakness, never thinking that Alexius would actually appear. "I shouldn't have told you about him."

"Don't worry." Cleo's smile was calm as she reached down to take Lucia's hand. Immediately, a sense of serenity spread through her. "I won't tell anyone else. I swear it."

Lucia searched Cleo's face and found only sincerity. "Good."

Alexius now approached the two girls. "Will you introduce us?" he asked Lucia.

"Of course." Lucia hastened to find her manners. "Alexius, this is Princess Cleiona—*Cleo*—my brother's wife. Cleo, this is Alexius."

Cleo gave him a sweet smile and extended her hand. "It's lovely to meet you."

"And you as well." Alexius took Cleo's hand and frowned down at it.

It charmed Lucia to see this, an ancient boy seemingly uncertain of how he should greet an unfamiliar princess.

"Is everything all right?" Cleo asked after a moment, when Alexius didn't release his grasp.

His frown only deepened. "It's just . . . your ring." His quizzical gaze snapped up to hers.

Cleo yanked her hand away and tucked it behind her back. "I should go. I didn't mean to bother you."

Lucia watched the pair with confusion. "Her ring? What are you talking about?"

Alexius continued to stare at Cleo. "How did you get that? Where did you find it?"

"I don't know what you're talking about. This is my mother's ring, passed down through generations. It's a family heirloom."

"Of course," Alexius murmured, as if speaking to himself. "It's all a matter of destiny, isn't it? You're here. Lucia is here. Melenia had to have known this already, I'm sure of it. But *I* didn't."

"Anyway," Cleo interrupted, a cool smile on her lips. "I must be going. Have a lovely day."

She turned for the door and opened it slightly, but Alexius darted in front of her to block her way. He shut the door and flipped the lock. "Not so fast, princess," he said.

"Explain yourself right now, Alexius," Lucia demanded, shocked by his unexpected rudeness. "What about Cleo's ring has you acting so strangely all of a sudden?"

His gaze shot to hers and he took a deep breath as he rubbed his chest again, as if the golden mark on his flesh caused him deep discomfort. Slowly, he gained authority over his expression.

"Eva once possessed a ring that helped control her overabundance of magic. The ring is said to have been created from pure *elementia*, drawn from the Kindred themselves. As such, it allowed her direct contact with the Kindred without any ill effects. But after her death, the ring was lost." He glanced at Cleo, who still had her hands tucked behind her back. "And yet, here it is now. Resting on the hand of your brother's wife."

CHAPTER 20

CLEO

AURANOS

Cleo was reminded of how she'd felt when she'd stood up on the dais next to the execution stage as the detonations went off, causing bright, fiery plumes to rise up before her eyes.

Her world was exploding all around her.

She fought with every last ounce of strength to remain impassive in the face of the Watcher's revelations.

He *knew*. There would be no denying this, no way to get out of this situation unscathed. She'd reached the end of the road.

She'd been such a fool to think she could wear this ring without anyone ever knowing what it was, that it might be safer on her finger than hidden behind a stone in the wall of her private chambers.

But she couldn't despair, or all would be lost. She couldn't let on that she'd known the secret of the ring all along, had even seen an illustration of it in a very old book about the original sorceress. Cleo had torn that drawing out and burned it, so no one else would ever see it, even though it had pained her to think of how appalled Emilia would have been to know that she had destroyed even a small piece of the palace's rare tomes. Her sister had loved books.

And Cleo had loved Emilia.

She held on to that love now and let it strengthen her in this moment of despair.

Lucia stayed silent for a while, regarding Cleo with shock and confusion. "Did you know this?" she finally asked.

Remain calm, Cleo commanded herself. *Do not lose everything you've worked so hard to gain.*

She looked down at her amethyst ring, forcing a frown. Then she raised her brow as she directly met the gaze of the other princess. "Did I know that the ring my father gave me moments before he died in my arms once belonged to a legendary sorceress? I can't say that I did." She turned to face the Watcher and boldly held out her hand toward him. "You truly believe this—my mother's ring—is the same ring you speak of?"

She saw confusion on his face as well, which helped lessen her fear by a fraction. If she were to be exposed as a liar and a manipulator in her attempts to befriend Lucia, it would be the end of everything.

An irony, really, as she'd honestly come to care for Lucia, despite her horrible family.

Not her real family, she thought, remembering Magnus's drunken confession. *She's a Damora only by name, not by birth.*

"It *is* the ring," Alexius said with certainty. "I can feel its power. This ring—along with your magic, princess," he spoke to Lucia now, "can awaken the Kindred."

Lucia spun toward him, her eyes wide. "You can't be serious."

Cleo had never seen a boy look more serious than Alexius did now.

"You said you want to know about Melenia: what she tells me and what she's discussed with the king. I wanted to wait, but now . . . this is part of your prophecy. The king knows your magic is the key to what he desires most: possessing the Kindred, which he believes will give him endless power over this world. Melenia has guided him in many ways, but she has a secret that he doesn't know. That he *can't* know."

Cleo went as quiet as a corpse. Alexius continued to speak as if she were not in the room, as if he didn't care if she overheard any of this.

Perhaps he didn't see her as a threat, only a clueless girl in possession of a ring with a long and magical history.

Good.

"What is it?" Lucia reached down to take his hand, gazing up into his tense face. She, too, seemed unconcerned that Cleo was present for these revelations.

Cleo barely breathed as she waited for his answer.

"The king cannot claim the Kindred for himself," Alexius said. "It can't be allowed. I told you that Watchers are guardians. We've searched for the lost crystals for a millennium, to no avail, all with the goal to return the four Kindred to the Sanctuary where they belong, where their magic will be safe and protected. Their absence all these years has resulted in a slow fading of the worlds— both yours and mine. Magic—life itself—has drained away. You see this in Limeros's transformation to ice, in the wasting away of Paelsia's farmlands while its people starve. And here in Auranos, the temperatures have been steadily rising. It may not seem so drastic now, but before long the heat will become unbearable. After that, this fading will stretch beyond Mytican shores to lands— and worlds—beyond. A thousand years of this fading magic and the only solution has been for the Kindred to return to its rightful home. All this time, the missing piece has been you, princess. Your magic will light the way. And this ring will help you."

Cleo's head spun. She wasn't sure she believed Alexius's little speech, though his prediction of Auranos's future was beyond disturbing. The Kindred were meant to be hers, to give her the magic it would take to reclaim her kingdom.

But if what he said was true, she had much to consider.

"Without the ring, I could still find the crystals?" Lucia said after a ponderous silence.

"*Finding* is perhaps the wrong word. But, yes, your magic is sufficient. However, since this magic is so new to you, it would take months of hard work and practice to build up the necessary skill. But now . . . everything has changed." Alexius rubbed his chest and began to pace back and forth in short lines, his forehead deeply furrowed. Finally he glanced at Cleo, his expression more curious than accusatory. "Did you know anything about this?"

The attention again on her, she raised her chin and pretended to consider this, wondering how transparent she should be. How good were Watchers at sensing lies?

"I know about the Kindred, of course, through legends and stories. I even met an exiled Watcher a few months ago in Paelsia, when I was there searching for a cure for my sister's illness." It was best to have a layer of truth to help cover any deceit. Still, to relate this memory caused her heart to ache. "She told me a story, a truly fantastical tale . . ."

"About what?" Alexius asked after she trailed off, uncertain of how much she wanted to say.

She licked her dry lips and forced into her voice a confidence she didn't feel. "About Eva and the mortal hunter she loved, of the child born to them who was lost after her death. And the goddesses and how they weren't really goddesses at all, but immortals who had stolen the Kindred and murdered Eva. When, years later, they destroyed each other in a battle for power, the hunter took the crystals and hid them all over Mytica, where no one has been able to locate them since." She tried to smile. "I'm not sure how much of it to believe."

"Some of it," Alexius said. "But certainly not all. I'm not surprised. Very few of my kind know the whole truth apart from the legend we tell ourselves, even after all this time."

"What's the truth?" Lucia asked. "And why hasn't anyone been able to find the crystals?"

"Because in the thousand years since Cleiona and Valoria ceased to exist, the Kindred have not been *physically here.* Not buried, not hidden, not anywhere in this world. But now they can be summoned back. Melenia has worked so hard to lay the groundwork for this quest. No one is more dedicated to it than she is."

Cleo recognized the name *Melenia* from the conversation she'd overheard between the king and Magnus. She must also be a Watcher. Cleo desperately wanted to ask for clarification, but she held her tongue.

"I'm ready, Alexius," Lucia said brightly, as if this strange conversation had energized her. "If this is really my destiny, I'm ready to do whatever it takes. It's all so hard to wrap my mind around, but I want to help you, and Melenia. My magic can be used for good, like you said. To help save the world from destruction. This, precisely, is what you meant, isn't it?"

"Yes." Alexius's expression remained rigid, pained even. "Perhaps tomorrow . . ."

"No, *today.* Our morning lessons haven't exhausted me. I'm ready. If we're going to do something, let's do it now. Why wait a day longer than necessary when you've waited so long already?" She smiled, her sky-blue eyes lighting up with excitement. "Show me what to do. You're my tutor. Tutor me."

"Very well." His jaw was tight. "Do you want her to stay?"

Lucia glanced at Cleo for a long, heavy moment. "That depends," she said. "After all you've heard here, do you even *want* to stay?"

Was that a trick question? To gauge how strong Cleo's interest was in this subject?

No reason for her to falter now.

"Yes," Cleo said firmly. "It's all so incredibly fascinating. I want to stay, if you'll let me."

Lucia didn't speak for a moment, her attention sharp and unwavering in its assessment of her. "Yes, you can stay," she finally said. "After all, it's your ring that seems to be the important piece here." She held out her hand. "May I have it?"

"Of course." Cleo didn't hesitate to pull it off her finger and give it to Lucia, who looked down at it with awe.

"It's beautiful," she said.

It was. And it wrenched Cleo's heart out of her chest to see it in someone else's possession.

Breathe, she told herself. *Just breathe. This could still work.*

Alexius pulled the shutters over the windows and closed the balcony doors, casting the room into shadow. He lit several candles and placed them in a cluster in the middle of the floor.

"Melenia went over this spell with me in detail, which will channel all four parts of your *elementia*," he said. "Please, sit, both of you."

Cleo sat on the floor, about five feet away from Lucia. Alexius sat down in front of them, creating a triangle with the candles at the center.

"I will warn you, princess," Alexius said to Lucia, "that this will drain both your magic and your energy. I don't yet know how much. But if I find it's harming you, I will put a stop to it."

Lucia nodded. "Understood. I'm not afraid. How do we begin?"

"Melenia has been working with your father to construct the Imperial Road," he said. Cleo gasped as Alexius motioned with his hand, sending light spreading out across the floor between them. Finally, the light morphed into a shimmering map, which Cleo recognized immediately as Mytica. Mountain ranges, forestland, beaches, cities, towns, villages, lakes, and rivers—all rendered in exquisite detail on this magical landscape. It was like something from a dream.

Alexius studied the map. Then a new line of light appeared, etching itself into the landscape.

"It's the road," Lucia said, her eyes wide. "I recognize it from the maps my father studies every day."

"The road is important," Alexius explained. "It was engineered by an exiled Watcher, like myself. The road is infused with his magic, specifically as Melenia has instructed.

"There are four points along this road, four locations that Melenia determined to be powerful places that hold a more concentrated level of elemental magic than anywhere else in Mytica. She has used the road to join these places of power, threading them together like pearls on a necklace. Three of these locations have been the setting of fateful moments of blood magic. Blood that was spilled on or near the road then triggered elemental disasters, which confirmed them as ideal locations."

Cleo stared at Alexius now, barely breathing. Elemental disasters—she'd experienced one herself. A massive earthquake on the day of her wedding right after the slaughter of Jonas's group of rebels.

Blood magic. Could it be true?

"Sounds complicated," Cleo said.

He nodded. "The recovery of the Kindred is a complicated, lay-ered process. Nothing this important is ever easy."

She had to agree with him on that.

"So where are they?" Lucia asked. "These places of power?"

"I can't reveal that. You must be able to see them for yourself, using your own magic. When you do see them, you will then be able to awaken the crystals and draw them to these magical loca-tions. Your magic is as pure as the magic possessed by the Kindred themselves, and it is only through that spark of magic that they can be physically claimed, piece by piece." He glanced at Cleo. "The claiming is slightly less complicated than the awakening."

"How are they claimed?" she ventured, needing to know every-thing she possibly could.

"Through blood magic. To make the crystals appear, the sym-bols for each Kindred must be drawn in blood at the locations."

Incredible. It was all too much, yet she wanted more. "I've heard it said that the power of a crystal is so great, it can corrupt one who touches it," she said. One of Cleo's beliefs about her ring was that wearing it would protect her from corruption.

"That warning that applies to Watchers," Alexius said, his ex-pression distant in the flickering light of the map and the candles. "A warning which has often gone unheeded in the past, I'm afraid."

So the crystals wouldn't corrupt a mortal. Was it true? Could she trust anything this boy said?

He could be lying. She had no way of knowing for sure what was true and what was false.

"How do I do it?" Lucia asked, now frowning as she stared at the map. "How do I awaken the crystals?"

"This will help you. Watch." Alexius leaned over and took the ring from Lucia, then balanced it on its edge before her, flicking it to set it spinning. "As long as you concentrate on it, it will keep spinning. Clear your mind of everything else. Think only of the ring and the magic it contains. Its power will enhance what you already have."

"You learned all of this from Melenia?" she whispered.

"Yes," he replied simply.

"She sounds amazing. So wise."

"The ring, princess," he urged. "Don't let it stop spinning or we'll have to start over. I'll guide you."

"All right." The excitement in Lucia's eyes had dissipated and was now replaced by steely determination. Cleo was impressed by her willingness to embrace this unexpected turn of events so eas-ily. Then again, it *was* her destiny.

Our destiny, Cleo corrected herself.

Lucia concentrated and the ring spun around and around. The amethyst cast its own light upon the map, turning it violet and sending a cascade of sparkling light onto their faces and the stone walls.

"Good, princess," Alexius said. "It's working."

"What do I do now?" Lucia asked, her voice growing strained.

"Think of the Kindred. Four crystals containing the purest es-sence of elemental magic. Amber for fire, moonstone for air, aqua-marine for water, and obsidian for earth. Picture them in your mind. See them."

"I can see them," Lucia whispered.

"Now you should be able to feel where each belongs—the cho-sen place of power in Mytica where the element is meant to be awakened."

"I don't understand."

Cleo watched them both tensely, her gaze moving back and forth between sorceress and tutor.

"Trust your magic, princess. It is ancient, as ancient as the Kindred itself. It knows what to do. Let it guide you." He hesitated. "And if you can't, then we know it's not yet time. We can wait a day, a week—"

"I can do it," Lucia insisted. She kept her gaze on the spinning ring. "I can see it. I can see the earth crystal . . . where it will be awakened . . ."

And so could Cleo. The spinning ring moved across the map of Mytica. The light then transformed before Cleo's eyes, giving the image more dimension and depth. She suddenly had the sensation that they were hawks, flying high above the land, looking down at the surface. The spinning ring moved along the line of the Imperial Road until it stopped at a point near its origin in Auranos. Cleo recognized it immediately.

"There," Lucia whispered. "The Temple of Cleiona . . . it's the chosen place of power for earth."

The earthquake. Earth magic.

"I awaken the earth Kindred," Lucia said softly, but with the weight of a command.

Amazed, Cleo watched the display before her, which now showed the outline of the temple itself. Then a symbol appeared, burning, as if it had just been physically branded onto the magical landscape.

A circle within a circle.

Alexius inhaled sharply, his gaze snapping to Lucia. "You did it, princess. You've awakened the earth Kindred."

Lucia's mouth stretched into a shaky smile. "That felt natural. Hardly any effort at all."

Cleo could tell she was lying. Whatever she'd just done, it had taken a lot out of her. The sorceress trembled, her forehead damp with perspiration.

Cleo couldn't help but be amazed.

"So all it will take," Cleo ventured, "is to do what you mentioned—draw the corresponding symbol in blood at the actual site—to claim the crystal."

"Yes," Alexius said, but his attention was fully on Lucia. "Can you continue, princess, or do you want to stop?"

"I can go on." Lucia didn't blink, her attention still fixed on the spinning ring. Cleo realized with sudden shock that Lucia's eyes had turned amethyst—the color of the gemstone, and they were bright with light.

The map shifted to another location along the road, one in central Paelsia. It looked like a small village enclosed by a wall.

"The former compound of Chief Basilius," Lucia said.

"You know this place?" Cleo asked with surprise. Her own knowledge of geography was not nearly as vast.

"I didn't before." Lucia smiled shakily. "And yet, now I do. I know it with such clarity . . . Cleo, I can't even explain it."

"You don't have to. This is amazing, Lucia."

"Yes . . ." Lucia's brow furrowed and her eyes brightened. "The air crystal shall be awakened here, in the wake of a tornado that swept across this location. Air, hear me. I awaken you."

The air symbol—a spiral—branded itself upon the location.

Earth and air, Cleo thought. For so long she'd waited, and now everything was happening so quickly.

"Princess," Alexius said, watching Lucia with concern. "Be careful. You are expending more magic than I thought you would need to, and it could hurt you. Let's stop for today."

"No. This is my destiny." Lucia's eyes blazed with light. "I can do this. I *am* doing it. We shall find the Kindred. All four crystals will be returned to the Sanctuary, and my prophecy will be fulfilled. And all of this struggle will be over. I will be free. Please, let me continue."

She didn't wait for permission. The map shifted again as the spinning ring moved along the bright line of the road, east into Paelsia, near the Forbidden Mountains.

"This," she began, her voice becoming hoarse, "is where Magnus fought against the rebels. A road camp . . . where there was a massive fire. Fire is the Kindred that can be awakened here . . ." She frowned as she trailed off. "Wait. It's so odd. . . ."

Cleo studied the map, which had closed in on a section of land that looked to be smoldering and smoking. A symbol had already been etched into the map's light. A triangle.

Fire.

"It's different here. I feel that this crystal has already been awakened." Lucia shook her head. "But that's impossible, isn't it?"

"Of course it's impossible." Alexius studied the map with a concerned expression. "Princess, this could be a sign that your magic is growing weak—"

"Fire," Lucia said, ignoring him. "I awaken you. I awaken the fire Kindred here in this chosen place of power."

Three crystals. Cleo couldn't believe it. But it was true: Three crystals had been awakened, ready to be claimed.

"One more," Lucia whispered, her voice weaker now, though her eyes were as bright as tiny suns. "I can do this."

"Lucia." Alexius reached for her and grasped her wrist. "This is too much for you."

"You're wrong." She tried to pull away, but failed. "I'm strong enough!"

"Yes, you're strong. But this is enough for now. I insist."

Cleo watched as Alexius's hand began to glow. Lucia drew in a ragged breath, finally breaking her concentration. The purple light in her eyes faded as she turned a furious look upon Alexius. But then, the next moment, she collapsed in his arms, unconscious.

The ring stopped spinning and its magical light went out.

The map disappeared as if it had never been there in the first place.

"You did that," Cleo said, her voice hushed. "You stopped her."

Alexius glanced at her. "She was harming herself, pushing herself too far. I couldn't let that happen."

Lucia began to rouse. She blinked and looked up at Alexius, who cradled her in his arms. "How long was I asleep?"

"Only moments. And before you ask: *No*, we will not be trying again today."

"But we were so close! The water crystal—"

"Can wait until I deem it's time to do this spell again," he said, more sternly than any tutor Cleo had ever had.

Cleo leaned over and picked up her ring. She held it tightly as they all rose to their feet, Alexius assisting Lucia. She wanted to pinch herself, to know for sure that this had really happened, that it hadn't only been a dream.

Earth, air, fire. She knew where they were and how to claim them.

Three out of four wasn't bad at all.

But she knew she had to do something that couldn't be post-poned a moment longer.

"Lucia," Cleo said, moving toward the princess. "I've seen for myself that what Alexius said is true. I don't know how this ring came into my family, but now that I know what it really is, what it can do . . . I want you to wear it."

She pressed the ring into Lucia's hand. The other princess looked down at it with amazement.

Lucia could have taken this from Cleo easily, but it was best to give it up of her own free will before the sorceress had the chance.

It was the hardest thing she'd ever had to do.

Lucia looked at her, her blue eyes filled with genuine gratitude. "This ring is proof that we were meant to meet. It was fate that our paths crossed the way they did. You've proven yourself to be a true and loyal friend today. Thank you."

Oh, it was definitely fate. Of that, Cleo had no doubt. "I ask only one thing in return," she said.

"What?"

Cleo forced confidence, bravery. She would not show any weakness.

"That when you go to claim the first crystal," she said, "you'll let me join you."

Lucia slipped the ring onto the middle finger of her right hand and stared down at it, transfixed.

Then she grasped Cleo's hands in hers before pulling Cleo into a tight hug. "Of course. You'll be with us, I swear it."

CHAPTER 21

JONAS

AURANOS

Tarus's parents, still in mourning for their younger son who had died after being forced to fight in the battle for the Auranian palace, received him with tears in their eyes and words of gratitude toward Jonas and his friends.

After a full week of travel to and from Paelsia, Jonas, Felix, and Lysandra returned to the village of Viridy, and they went immediately to the Silver Toad. After several nights of sleeping outside under the stars and braving the elements, Jonas decided they'd stay at the inn for the night.

"This is because of me, isn't it?" Lysandra said outside her room. "I don't need a soft bed and a roof over my head. I don't need to be pampered."

Jonas disagreed. Although she'd been making a valiant effort, he knew it would take her much more time to move past her ordeal in the dungeon.

"Speak for yourself," he said. "You might not feel like a little pampering, but I do. So we're staying, no more argument. Just try to get some sleep. I'll check on you later."

He closed the door and descended the staircase to the tavern, which was currently deserted. The owner, a man named Galyn, wasn't here tonight, but his white-haired father, Bruno, was behind the bar, rubbing it vigorously with a cloth.

Felix sat at the same table they'd occupied back on the Day of Flames, when they'd recruited Petros to their cause. Jonas wasn't sure what had become of the boy after the attack, but he hoped never to cross paths with him again. Irresponsible fool.

"Sleeping beauty's doing well?" Felix asked, his hand curled around a tankard of ale.

Jonas nodded. "As well as can be expected."

"Good. Sit down, we need to talk."

Jonas sat down in a hard chair facing his traveling companion and braced himself for the conversation he had been dreading for some time. "What is it?"

"You know what it is. Her. She's a liability."

And there it was. What had remained unspoken between them for their week with Tarus had finally risen like the stench of a rotten potato. "You're wrong."

Felix took on a grim expression. "Look, I know she's important to you. But she's broken, Jonas. Whatever happened to her in those dungeons . . . she's no good to us."

Jonas's insides tightened. "The king forced her to watch as her older brother's head was hacked off. Do you know anyone who could recover immediately from something so horrific? She's grieving, even if she refuses to admit it. She needs more time to heal and recover."

"And just how long do you plan to give her?"

Jonas knew Felix was impatient, but he had to understand that Lysandra wasn't just any rebel. She was his friend. And she was an asset, she just hadn't been given a chance to show it yet. "As long as it takes."

Bruno approached their table, gripping tankards in both hands. "Brought these over for you, boys. On the house! My son admires everything you've done for the rebels, and that's worth some free ale in my opinion. Anyone who's devoted his life to killing the king is aces in my book!"

Jonas looked up at him, slightly alarmed. "Thanks?"

The smiling barkeep set the tankards on the table and slapped Jonas's back. "Any time, son. Any time!"

He retreated to the bar without another word.

"Do you think he would have said all that if we weren't the only ones in here?" Felix asked.

"I would hope not."

"That makes two of us. But back to the subject at hand." His paused. "The night we met. Remember it?"

Jonas nodded. "Vividly."

"I never told you, but I made a major decision in my life that night. A major shift in my goals. I thought to myself, *I have the chance to help the infamous Jonas Agallon kick arse and change the world.* Change the *world*, Jonas. But so far, what have we done other than rescue a couple of rebels and walk a great deal?"

"We've done much more than that." Jonas took a gulp from his glass, trying to swallow down his annoyance along with the strong, bitter ale. What was Felix getting at, bringing up his past for the first time since they'd met?

"And now it seems that your big plan is to wait around for the king to stroll out of his palace and offer you his neck. Genius."

Jonas's eyes narrowed. "Thanks so much for reminding me of my shortcomings. You don't think I already feel like a failure after everything that's happened?"

"I don't know what you're thinking."

"I have eyes and ears at the palace—three willing spies in place, all happy to tell me anything I need to know to ensure victory over that Limerian bastard and free my people from a future at the mercy of that monster. I will get to him, don't ever doubt it. My plan to abduct Prince Magnus could still be a sound one—or perhaps Princess Lucia. The king would venture out of his safe little kingdom to save her neck if he thought it was at risk, don't you think?"

"Kidnapping. Right. You've tried that before, haven't you? Snagged Princess Cleo herself. How'd that work out?" Before Jonas could respond to his snide comment, possibly with a fist to his jaw, Felix's gaze shifted away from him. "Well, well. The sleeping beauty awakens. Welcome, sweetheart."

Jonas turned to see Lysandra standing behind him. He opened his mouth to speak, but she held up her hand to stop him.

"I couldn't sleep," she said.

"I don't think you were trying very hard," Jonas replied.

"Perhaps I thought it would be smarter to stay awake so I could come down here and listen in on what you two say behind my back."

"The more the merrier, I say. Come join us." Felix patted his knee. "Why don't you sit right here?"

She regarded him with a bored look on her face. "Why don't you kiss my arse?"

"Bring it over here and I'd be happy to consider it."

"Over my dead body."

"That can be arranged, too, if you ask real nice." Luckily for Felix, he said this with a jovial grin rather than an edge of menace.

Jonas groaned inwardly. These two had been squabbling all week, and it was nearly impossible to be around them once they got going. He thought he knew the real reason Felix didn't want Lysandra around; it had very little to do with the speed at which she was recovering from being the king's prisoner, and a lot to do with him disliking being challenged by a girl.

Lysandra pulled up a chair and glared at Jonas. "Why do you put up with him?"

Yet again, he had to be the intermediary, a job he'd never asked for. "Felix is an arse, but, like you, he's an asset and a friend."

"I agree with you on the arse part." She regarded Felix, scrutinizing him from head to toe. "But do you really know anything about him?"

"I know enough," Jonas replied, although silently he had to be more honest. He knew next to nothing about the boy sitting across the table.

"What can I say? I'm a private guy. But if you have concerns, Lys," Felix said, "I'm happy to answer any questions you have. Or you can continue to talk about me like I'm not even here."

Lysandra pursed her lips, giving him a sour look. "Fine. To start, where do you come from?"

Felix smirked. "Everywhere and nowhere, sweetheart."

"See?" She shot a glance at Jonas. "He's cagey and dodgy. Smarmy, too."

Felix's smirk vanished. "Smarmy?"

"He saved my life," Jonas countered. "And yours as well."

"Fine. But we have no idea where he came from or what really motivated him to join you."

"Hey," Felix said. "Still sitting right here."

"Well, what's your story, Felix?" Even though Felix had proven himself trustworthy to Jonas time and again, he had to admit he was curious to know more about him. "Seriously. Share a little of it tonight."

"My story? Extremely handsome. Renowned troublemaker. Entertaining and delightful to be around. Apparently, a bit smarmy. What more do you need to know?"

Just then Bruno appeared with a drink for Lysandra. "Here you go, honey. Some nice wine for a nice young girl."

Lysandra stared into her glass with distaste. "You two boys get ale and I get wine. I don't even like wine."

Jonas was still looking at Felix, who studied him back just as intently. The subject had been raised, and Felix had given vague answers to direct questions. Now he wanted more than ever to know everything

"I need to know your story, Felix," Jonas said. "Tell me something real. You're not much older than I am. How did you get into this kind of life? Where is your family? Friends?"

"Honestly? You want to know where my friends are?" The last glimmer of humor had faded from Felix's eyes. "They're at this very table right now. Every last one of them." He swallowed a mouthful of ale before continuing. "Pathetic, I know. But I've never had friends. Wasn't raised that way."

Lysandra frowned. "And what about your family?"

"Dead," he said, not looking at her. "My parents and brothers were killed by a pack of thieves and assassins employed by a very important, very dangerous man. They broke into our villa when I was six. On a whim, they spared my life. Raised me as one of their own. Taught me how to steal, fight, kill, and how to use those skills to make money for the man in charge." He paused and gave Jonas a tense look. "And they taught me how to collect reward money for capturing Paelsian rebel leaders and alleged murderers."

Jonas's mouth went dry. "So that's how you found me."

He nodded. "I'm a great tracker. I could find anybody, anywhere. But no, I never planned to collect that reward. If I had, you'd be dead by now."

It clearly caused Felix great pain to relate all this. These were the kinds of memories most people chose to repress.

"So where are the people who raised you now?" Jonas asked. "And this employer of yours?"

"Your guess is as good as mine. I ran away last year. Been on my own ever since, looking for work. Looking for trouble." Finally his smile returned, curling up the edge of his mouth. "I have a talent for finding it without searching too hard."

"I don't doubt it for a moment," Lysandra said, her careful eyes still on him.

"Was that enough information for one night?" Felix asked. "Did you enjoy that walk down my own personal memory lane?"

Lysandra was quiet a moment. "It's enough for now."

"Good."

"I still don't like you."

"Alas, the feeling's not *entirely* mutual." Felix's grin widened. "You're a bit too cute to earn my total dislike, despite you being a pain in my arse. But don't worry, I won't try anything. I know Jonas wants you all for himself."

Jonas choked and sputtered halfway through a sip of his drink. "What?"

Felix shrugged. "You're in love with her."

In love with Lys? He glanced at her out of the corner of his eye. "No, I'm not."

"We nearly killed ourselves busting her out of that palace

square. You were just upstairs tucking her into bed and singing her lullabies. And you've defended her to your last breath to keep her in this trio. Please. I'm not blind, friend."

Lysandra laughed, a low chuckle in the back of her throat. "Sorry to break it to you, Felix, but Jonas isn't in love with me. He's too busy being in love with Princess Cleo."

Felix blinked. "As in, her royal *highness*, Princess Cleo, wife of Prince Magnus? She whom you met in that temple cloaked by shadows and mystery? The princess you kidnapped—what was it, *three* times?"

"Twice." Jonas glared at Lysandra for even bringing up the subject.

She looked at him innocently. "Problem?"

"I'm not in love with the princess."

"Why not?" Felix laughed, then drained the rest of his ale. "Half of Auranos is. Why wouldn't you want to kneel before the golden princess's skirts and beg for her attention like the rest of us?"

"I'm not sure I can picture Jonas *kneeling*," Lysandra said, raising an eyebrow.

Jonas couldn't keep the grin off his face at this sudden, and rather unwelcome, change of subject. "For the right girl I just might. However, there's nothing to discuss when it comes to Princess Cleo. She's a princess, and I'm a . . . whatever I am."

Lysandra scrunched up her nose. "She's a royal. That'll never change."

"And she's married," Felix added.

"Thanks for the reminder." Jonas thought back to the note he'd received from the princess. He felt it was time to share its contents.

"Do either of you believe in legends?" Jonas asked after a silence had fallen between them.

"What kinds of legends?" Felix signaled to the barkeep for another round of drinks. Lysandra peered into her wine glass, finally taking a tentative sip.

"Of magic—the magic that is said to have history here in Myt-ica," Jonas said. "And . . . of Watchers. And the Kindred."

Lysandra drew in a shaky breath. "What about Watchers?"

"That they really exist." Lysandra trembled at his response and, alarmed, Jonas reached across the table to squeeze her hand. "What is it? What's wrong?"

She took a long sip of wine. "I didn't say anything to you about this before, because I've tried to block it all out. But Gregor claimed that a Watcher used to visit him in his dreams—it's why the king kept him alive so long. So he could question him. The king believed his story; I saw it in his eyes. He believes in magic, and he's greedy for it. When Gregor couldn't give him the answers he wanted to hear, the king had him killed."

Jonas stared at her, shocked. The king *was* after magic—just as Cleo had informed him.

Felix watched them both in silence.

"When Phaedra stopped visiting his dreams, it broke his heart," Lysandra whispered.

Hearing that name felt like a hand gripping Jonas's throat.

"At the time," Lysandra continued, "I thought he'd gone mad, but maybe it was true. Maybe she was real."

"Did you say . . . Phaedra?" Jonas asked.

"Yes. Why?"

Phaedra. The name of the Watcher who had healed Jonas at the brink of death. "This is impossible."

Felix leaned back in his chair and pushed his hands through his short dark hair. "Wow. We definitely need more drinks. Barkeep! More drinks for my friend here, please. He needs one very badly."

Bruno hobbled over, his permanent smile still plastered to his face. However, instead of drinks, he held just a folded piece of paper sealed with wax. "I almost forgot all about this! Your lovely lady friend Nerissa delivered this message a few days ago. She worried you wouldn't be back for weeks! Oh, she'll be so pleased you were here to receive it. She said it's quite urgent. What wonderful timing you have."

Lysandra watched the man warily as he slapped the message down on the table and then wandered away without another word. "He's delightful, isn't he?"

"Very," Felix agreed. "But look here. Another message, with the same seal as the last one. A perfumed love letter from the princess, you think?"

Glancing at Lysandra, Jonas picked up the message.

"Open it," she urged.

He nodded, then broke the seal and unfolded the paper.

"What is it?" Felix asked. "What does it say?"

Jonas's eyes lit up with every word he read. "It's a request."

"A request from her royal highness," Lysandra said, and, for the first time when speaking of Cleo, her voice held no palpable animosity. "And are you planning to grant her request?"

There was a time he would have thrown the note away and laughed about such a ridiculous appeal.

He wasn't laughing now.

"Oh, yes," he said. "All three of us are. At first light tomorrow, we're setting out to do exactly what her royal highness wants."

CHAPTER 22

MAGNUS

AURANOS

A lexius. The name Lucia had whispered like a prayer as she'd slept for weeks.

Alexius. The Watcher who'd preyed upon Lucia in her dreams when she'd been unconscious and defenseless.

Alexius. Now here with the king's full permission, and officially appointed as Lucia's private tutor. They'd barely left Lucia's chambers since he'd arrived here a week ago.

The boy was a problem and a threat. But no one seemed to believe this except Magnus. He'd taken it upon himself to keep an eye on the Watcher and make sure he behaved himself.

Today, the king had given permission for Alexius, Lucia, and her new friend Cleo to leave the palace on a journey to a festival in a nearby village.

Magnus was not surprised that he hadn't been invited to join them. But that didn't stop him from going anyway, following them on horseback at a discreet distance.

It was no secret that he didn't trust Alexius—or Cleo, for that matter. Lucia was a fool to trust either of them, even in the company of guards.

He followed their carriage for hours, until finally it came to a stop. Magnus directed his horse into the shelter of the forest line so he could watch unseen as the three stepped out into the sunshine. Lucia said something to a guard, and then headed off with the Watcher and the other princess into the forest. The guards didn't follow.

How odd.

Magnus waited until they'd disappeared before he approached the guard Lucia had consulted, who stiffened at the sight of him.

"Your highness," he said, his voice strained.

"What's this?" Magnus asked. "Where are they going?"

"Princess Lucia requested that we stop here, then asked us to stay behind and wait as they go for a—a stroll."

"A stroll."

"Yes, your highness. She was adamant that we give them privacy and said they'd return when they were done—"

"Strolling," Magnus finished. "Yes, of course."

"If you want us to go after them . . ."

"No, don't bother. I'll go. Stay right where you are."

He left his horse with the guards and strode into the forest, following a trail of trampled grass and broken twigs. With every step he took he became more suspicious of the nature of his sister's day trip. Especially when accompanied by the likes of Alexius and Cleo, both of whom had dubious motives for spending time with the young sorceress.

He hastened his pursuit. He needed to learn the truth.

It didn't take long for him to draw in on Lucia's party. They were conversing, but the words were indistinct, so he decided to get closer. Then, suddenly, all fell silent.

Curiously silent.

What exactly is going on here?

He stopped and listened carefully.

"You! Come out!" It was Lucia. "Whoever you are, you're fearless enough to follow us, so show your face and prove you're no coward."

His adopted sister sounded particularly fierce today. Perhaps this was the influence of the company she'd begun to keep.

Magnus was no coward. He was ready to confront them about where they were strolling off to in the middle of nowhere, so far away from their supposed destination.

Magnus emerged from the trees and stood on the pathway. They all regarded him with varying expressions of surprise.

"I was never told about a day trip," he said, sliding his gaze from Cleo to Lucia, whose clenched fist blazed with fire magic. Her new and irritatingly attractive tutor stood tall next to her. "You can douse the fire, sister. Don't worry your pretty little head. I mean you no harm."

It took a moment, but she finally tamped out the flame. She watched him with both caution and suspicion.

"What are you doing here?" she demanded.

"Following you. Obviously." Steadily, he regarded each of them in turn. "I hear you're going to a festival. I hate to break it to you, but it's a bit of a walk to any village from here."

Lucia exchanged a glance with Alexius. "We're not going to a festival."

"I'm shocked. Perhaps the three of you have journeyed out here to commune with nature. Is that it?"

He felt Cleo glaring at him, but didn't spare her a glance.

Their silence spoke volumes. What were they trying to hide?

"And you." He turned to Alexius. "What are your intentions today, luring two young girls out into the middle of nowhere, away from their assigned protection? Should I guess? Or should I go ahead and kill you where you stand?"

"Magnus!" Lucia cried.

"Am I being rude? So sorry, sister. But I'm sure you'll forgive me for showing the caution you seem to lack. What exactly do you know about this boy other than that he claims to come from the Sanctuary as Melenia's representative?"

She raised her chin. "I know enough."

"But I don't." Magnus regarded Alexius, who stood passively, his expression relaxed. "You're not easily intimidated, are you?"

"No," Alexius replied, having the audacity to look bored by Magnus's barely restrained ire. "Why? Is that what you're attempting to do? Intimidate me?"

He smirked. "I've been able to coax at least a trickle of perspiration from Lucia's previous suitors. That's what you are, isn't it? In addition to being her so-called tutor? I see how you look at her and I don't like it. I don't trust you like she does."

"You don't know me."

"I know enough." Magnus walked a circle around Alexius. He could see no reason to mince words. "Why have you come here today? There's nothing around for miles besides the Temple of Cleiona."

The three exchanged a look, confirming to Magnus all the more that they were up to something.

Finally, Lucia broke the silence. "We need to tell him."

"Lucia," Cleo protested.

"He may be a bit brash and rude, but I trust him—I trust him every bit as much as I trust the two of you." Lucia turned to Magnus. She searched his face and took a deep breath. "We're here today to claim a part of the Kindred."

Every ounce of his bravado and composure Magnus walked into this situation with washed away in an instant. All he could do was stare at her, wondering if he'd heard her wrong.

"Are you certain of what you're saying?" he said with a rasp in his voice.

"It's true." She nodded. "Father wants it for himself, but he can't have it, Magnus. That's why I had to lie today. He doesn't know the truth."

His throat was tight, his mouth dry. He suddenly realized how warm it was today and felt as if his heavy black coat was trying to choke him.

"What truth?" he asked.

"That the Kindred must be found and immediately returned to the Sanctuary. If they're not, the world will . . . it will . . ."

"What?" He forced himself to regain his composure. "Will life as we know it end? Is that what your new tutor told you?"

"Essentially," Alexius said.

Of course. How better to manipulate Lucia than to convince her the world would end without her assistance?

Magnus glanced at Cleo. She held her arms across the bodice of her rose-colored gown, which was far fancier than anything typically worn on a walk through a thick forest on a hot day. She regarded him with a silent, sour expression—not a new look for her by any means.

"And why are *you* here?" he asked her.

"I want to help," she replied.

"Oh, yes. So helpful." If Lucia honestly believed this duplicitous creature was a true friend to her, she was a fool. For all her rigid upbringing and the lack of love and guidance from her cold and calculating mother, Lucia could be so unforgivably naïve. "How convenient it is that you're along for the ride today. With your interest in the Kindred and all."

"Of course I'm interested in the Kindred," Cleo replied quickly. "I live in Mytica and have heard the legends and stories all my life. However, I didn't know it was all true until just the other day."

She said it with such confidence, even Magnus almost believed her.

Almost.

Magnus looked at Lucia. "You should have told me about this." He didn't mean to sound so harsh. But they used to share so much, it pained him that she hadn't trusted him.

"I'm sorry. I should have told you. But I know how close you've become with Father lately. You two are practically inseparable."

"That is vastly overstating matters."

"Magnus is right," Cleo said. "He doesn't spend all his time with the king. Some of his time—or at least some of his nights— are spent with Princess Amara."

Lucia looked at him, shocked. "You and Amara?"

He'd spent only the one night with the Kraeshian princess. She hadn't made contact with him since returning to her villa and it hadn't bothered him one bit. She'd been a pleasant distraction, nothing more than that. But no one had to know that but him.

"I couldn't help myself," Magnus said. "Amara is irresistible. We do have so much in common. That girl is full of possibilities."

He half expected a retort from Cleo, but she stayed silent.

"If you say so." A new frown creased Lucia's brow. She turned to Alexius. "I want Magnus to be a part of this. I trust him not to say anything to Father."

Lucia's words tugged at Magnus's heart. She still cared about him, trusted him, even though he couldn't think of many reasons why she should.

Alexius said nothing, keeping his gaze fixed on Magnus. There was something in the Watcher's eyes that seemed far more ancient than his otherwise youthful appearance. "As you wish," he said at last.

Lucia nodded and turned her attention to Magnus. "Father can't know. Promise me, Magnus. He can't know about this."

"Oh, I promise," Magnus replied. "Father will never possess even one crystal now that I know they have much more important purposes."

Although, not the important purposes Lucia believed in.

But first he needed to see it, to prove to himself it was real. Then he'd figure out what to do next. If this journey led to nothing, he could use this as a means to get rid of Alexius, to soil the Watcher's reputation in the eyes of the king. Just another useless boy with his goals set on the king's daughter.

He knew that Alexius and Lucia could be extremely dangerous if provoked or betrayed. And Cleo . . . well, he didn't underestimate her, either.

"Let's keep moving," Alexius said. "We're almost there."

Alexius and Lucia walked ahead and Magnus trailed behind them with Cleo, who walked slowly, as if treading on broken glass.

"Trouble with your shoes? Are they too tight for the long walk?" he asked, eyeing the fine golden sandals that peeked out from beneath her skirts.

Her jaw clenched. "Not at all."

"Good. I'd hate to think you were in constant pain due to your poor choices."

They continued on in silence. Magnus tried to ignore the uncomfortable heat and resisted the urge to remove his jacket. And, frankly, his boots were rather uncomfortable as well.

It was an unpleasant day, but one made infinitely tolerable because it might lead to triumph.

They were so close, and now the king would never lay his hands on what he wanted most. That single thought gave Magnus more pleasure than he'd felt in months—or even years.

Finally, they arrived. The Temple of Cleiona had been a massive structure of white marble, thick pillars, and stone carved with artistic precision. It had been the grandest and most impressive structure that Magnus had ever seen in his life. When he'd come here for the first time, it had actually taken his breath away.

Now it lay in ruins. The large statue of the goddess out front had crashed to the ground during the earthquake and in pieces. A massive crack split the marble floor down the center. The ceiling was mostly caved in.

The site of his marriage to Cleo had been abandoned. Where once many had come to pray, there was now but the four of them.

"You're certain a crystal is here?" Magnus said, still finding it hard to believe that they could be so close.

"I'm certain." Lucia held out her hand, and Magnus noticed that she wore a familiar ring—the ring he'd often seen Cleo wearing. "I used this ring to help awaken it in this place of power. And now we can claim it through a ritual."

The ring.

Magnus fought to keep his expression neutral. Phaedra, the

Watcher in Paelsia, told him about a ring that could help Lucia control her magic.

This was it. His heart pounded at the realization. She'd found it, it had simply dropped into her lap, when he'd had no idea where to even begin looking.

Magnus cast a dark, quizzical look at the blond princess, and Lucia caught his eye. "Cleo gave it to me," she said. "To help me. To help us all."

All this time, Cleo had had the ring. It couldn't be a coincidence. "Did she now?"

"I like to help when I can," Cleo said evenly.

He forced a smile and said, "If you'll excuse us for a moment, I'd like a quick word with my *wife*."

Lucia regarded him with uncertainty. "Of course."

She then took Alexius's hand and drew him away, closer to the temple's entrance, to give the pair their privacy.

Magnus studied the ruins before him, remembering, with a churning sensation in his gut, the last time they'd been here. Cleo stood nearby, just as quiet and still as the crumbling statue of her namesake goddess.

"I know what you're trying to do," Magnus said to her finally. "And you can't have it."

"Can't have what?"

He wrestled with frustration. Cleo had a way of testing his carefully crafted composure that was unlike anyone else he'd ever met. "The Kindred belongs to my family, not to you."

"That's strange. Didn't you just hear Lucia say that the Kindred belong to the Sanctuary? And I thought I heard you agree with her."

"As if I believe you'd willingly let it go."

"To do my part to save the world? Why wouldn't I?"

"Mark my words." He leaned closer. "If you try to steal the crystal, we will have a very serious problem, you and I."

She sighed with impatience. "Well, I wouldn't want that, especially since we've gotten along so well up until now."

"Tread carefully, princess, or this will end very badly for you."

Her gaze turned to ice. "How ashamed I am that I could have ever thought for one tiny moment that you were anything more than what you appear to be."

"And what's that?"

"A hateful, selfish monster with no kindness in his heart."

He repressed a wince, despising the fact that sharp words from this particular girl could succeed in wounding him. "Hear me well, princess. I'll say this only once. Keep your hands off any treasure we find today or I swear I'll reduce you to nothing but ashes to scatter on the wind."

Before he could hear Cleo's rebuttal, he walked off toward Lucia and Alexius, who waited at the temple's entrance. He'd expected something cutting and sarcastic, but she said nothing.

He supposed this was his way. When someone pushed him, he responded by crushing them.

"We need to go inside," Alexius said.

Magnus eyed the shattered rooftop and the crumbling beams waiting for them at the top of the stairs. "So it can collapse on our heads?"

"Magnus," Lucia said sternly. "We'll do as Alexius says."

Lucia's decision to defend the Watcher without hesitation annoyed him deeply. "Fine. Then please show us the way, Alexius."

The Watcher led them up the broken stairs to the grand entrance. Sunlight shone through the damaged roof. Cleo peered around with a pinched expression on her beautiful face.

"So this ritual. What does it involve?" Magnus asked.

Alexius pulled out a dagger. "It's a blood ritual."

Magnus almost laughed aloud. "Isn't it always."

Without hesitation, Alexius pressed the blade against his palm, letting crimson blood drip to the floor.

Watchers bled the same shade of red as mortals. Interesting.

Alexius knelt on the ground and used his blood to make a mark on the temple floor. A circle within a circle.

It was the symbol of earth, the element associated with Goddess Valoria's magic. Magnus recognized it well.

When Alexius completed the symbol, Lucia bound his hand with a handkerchief.

"Now what?" Magnus asked.

"We wait." Alexius frowned as he turned around, scanning his surroundings.

"We wait for what?" Magnus prompted, but the others were silent.

They waited. Nearby, a skull-sized chunk of marble dislodged from a pillar and crashed to the ground—Magnus noticed it had been ornately carved into the shape of a rose. A glance confirmed these rose sculptures adorned many spots in the temple. Strangely, he hadn't noticed that detail until now, when it was all toppling down.

Magnus looked up warily at the roof. "How long must we wait?" he growled.

"I don't know," Alexius said.

"I'd think a wise and magical Watcher like you would know these things."

"And yet, I don't know everything." Alexius looked impatient, perhaps a little bit desperate, as if he'd expected things to go differently.

Then something caught Magnus's eye. A mark on a clear patch of floor behind Cleo.

"What is *that*?" The sinking sensation in his gut was enough to tell him he already knew the answer to his own question.

"It can't be," Alexius said under his breath. "It *can't*. How could they know?"

Drawn on the pristine surface was another symbol identical to Alexius's. The blood was still red and fresh.

Someone else had gotten there first.

CHAPTER 23

JONAS

AURANOS

*I can only hope this message finds you in time. You must
go the Temple of Cleiona, as quickly as you can. There you will
use your blood to draw the symbol of earth on the floor. This
will reveal the earth Kindred. However difficult you find this to
believe, you must trust me and do what I say.*

Claim the crystal and keep it safe until we meet again.

Jonas, Lysandra, and Felix had set off for the temple the very next
morning. Jonas nearly stumbled at the crumbling site of the first
rebel battle, which had gone so horribly wrong. Of the two dozen
rebels who'd volunteered to stand with him that day, he alone had
walked away. Crawled away, really.

Lysandra touched his shoulder. "Jonas, are you all right?"

"Perfectly fine."

"Why don't I believe that?"

Her concerned gaze made him grin weakly. "It's funny . . ."

"What?"

"You never used to look at me the way you are now. You used to look at me like you wanted to kill me."

"I did want to kill you. Still do, sometimes." She offered him a smile.

"Come on, you two," Felix urged, marching ten paces ahead of them. "Let's go find some treasure."

Lysandra grabbed Jonas's arm. "Are you absolutely sure you trust him?"

"I'm sure. Despite any admissions of his past from last night, he's earned my trust, Lys. Again and again."

She nodded. "All right. If you trust him, then I will too. Your golden princess, on the other hand . . ."

He began to climb the temple steps behind Lysandra. "I know you don't like Cleo, but that she wanted me to do this for her . . . is it stupid that I consider that an honor?"

"No, it's not stupid." She glanced at him over her shoulder and her light brown eyes met his. "So what happens if we find it?"

A month ago he believed in neither Watchers nor the Kindred, but now they could mean all the difference in the world. All because of some magic rocks.

"Honestly? I have no idea." He grinned. "I try not to plan too far ahead."

As they entered the temple, Jonas's grin fell away. A rush of memories pressed at him from every side, making it hard to breathe.

He'd been so blind that day, and so incredibly cocky. For a brief, shining moment, assassinating King Gaius and Prince Magnus and liberating his people had seemed like a true possibility. There had seemed to be so few guards there to protect the royals, but really the guards had been disguised as wedding guests, waiting to crush a rebel attack.

The blood from that day was still there, dried to reddish brown stains on the pale marble floor. The temple was in a shambles and each step they took brought more creaks, more crumbling, as if one wrong move might destroy it completely. Its majesty had been tarnished. What was once a sacred place to worship the Auranian goddess was now a dangerous beast waiting to consume intruders.

"Let's make this quick," Felix said. "Or this whole place is going to cave in on our heads."

Jonas found a bare patch of floor and kicked away some ragged shards of stone.

He pulled out his jeweled dagger and cut his hand. The pain was sharp and deep, but he didn't even wince. He squeezed his fist, and blood began to drip to the floor. He crouched and smeared it into a circle with another circle within it.

When he was done, he rose to his feet, his stomach churning nervously.

"Okay, princess," he muttered. "Now what?"

The ground rumbled. Small chunks of marble came crashing down around them.

Lysandra looked up and grimaced. "You must have triggered something. This place is going to fall to pieces any moment."

"Wait." Felix grabbed Jonas's arm, his fingers biting deep enough to cause pain. "Look over there."

Along the aisle sullied by the blood of his fallen rebels, a narrow shaft of light streamed through a hole in the roof, illuminating a small object. Jonas followed the light and stared down at the object with stunned disbelief.

"It worked," Felix said, breathless. "I can't believe it, but it worked."

It was a sphere of obsidian the size of a small plum, and so smooth and polished that it reflected the image of the three of them staring down at it.

Hearing new voices close by, Jonas grew tense. He grabbed the black orb and shoved it into his pocket.

"Let's get out of here," he said. "Now."

"No time," Lysandra whispered harshly. "We need to hide."

The three rebels ducked behind a pillar and peered out to see four people enter.

It was none other than Princess Cleo, Princess Lucia, Prince Magnus, and another boy Jonas didn't recognize—tall and lean, with golden-tan skin and coppery-brown hair.

Jonas and his companions held a collective breath from their hiding spot as the four made their way deeper into the temple.

"What's the ritual?" Magnus said.

The other boy pulled out a dagger. "It's a blood ritual."

"Isn't it always."

As the boy prepared to cut his hand, Jonas indicated to Lysandra and Felix to slip out of the temple while the others were distracted. Following Jonas's lead, they raced down the broken stairs and kept running until they were shielded by the nearby forest.

"Keep going," Jonas said. "We need to put all the distance we can between us."

He only wished he could have seen the look on Magnus's face when he realized the crystal was gone.

"I assume they were not friends of yours," Felix said.

Jonas nearly laughed. "Didn't you recognize his highness, Prince Magnus? And his sister, Princess Lucia?"

"And don't forget Princess Cleo," Lysandra added. "Jonas's beloved."

Felix hacked at the thick foliage with his blade as he led the way. "Every bit as beautiful as I've heard."

Lysandra grunted. "I guess, if you like that type."

"Rich, privileged, and gorgeous? I certainly do like that type."

They stopped to rest in a clearing, which was quiet save for a chorus of chirping birds and buzzing insects. Lysandra took a seat on a fallen tree trunk.

"It just appeared. Like magic," Felix said, shaking his head and grinning. "Which, I suppose, isn't that strange considering it *is* magic. Let's see it."

The crystal was heavy in Jonas's pocket. He ran his hand over its cool, smooth surface before drawing it out. The obsidian orb glittered under the light shining through the thick canopy of trees.

Jonas shook his head, amazed. "I've stolen a lot in my life, but this is the first magic rock I've ever had my hands on."

Lysandra drew closer. "It's beautiful."

"What is *that*?" Felix said, leaning in. "There's something moving inside."

Inside the orb was an even deeper darkness, a wisp of ebony smoke swirling around in an endless loop.

A shiver shot up Jonas's spine. "Just a guess, but . . . perhaps that's the magic?"

"What does it do?" Lysandra asked.

"No damn idea."

"Can I see it?" Felix asked.

Jonas handed it to him and Felix went off to the far side of the clearing, holding the crystal up to the meager light to get a better look.

"It's all so incredible," Lysandra said, reaching to take Jonas's hand and squeezing it. "Isn't it?"

Damn, she was beautiful when she smiled. He found himself distracted for a moment, but then Felix strolled back over, tossing the crystal up and down. He shrugged. "I have no clue how this thing works. Anyone know how to harness the magic?"

"No idea, but you should probably stop playing with it. You might break it." Jonas held out his hand.

Felix placed the black orb in his palm, but continued to eye it. "I don't know if you should just hand that over to your princess. Do you have any idea what something like that could be worth? I know people, Jonas. They're not *nice* people, sure, but they have mighty deep pockets."

"Tempting," Jonas allowed, squeezing the rock and trying to get some sense of its magic, but he couldn't even feel a tingle. "But these crystals have a higher purpose."

"So you do want to give it to your princess."

"Again, she's not *my* princess, but yes. I'm leaning that way."

Lysandra frowned, her arms crossed over her chest. "Did you say *crystals*? As in more than one crystal?"

"I did say crystals, didn't I?"

She gave him a stern look. "Is there something you haven't told us?"

Today felt like a victory already, but this battle had only just begun. Jonas hadn't felt this good in weeks. "The princess's message included more than just *this* location."

"You know where to find more, don't you?" Felix said.

Jonas couldn't fight back his grin. "Actually, I know where to find three out of four."

"Where?" Lysandra asked, breathless.

Jonas tossed the earth crystal up in the air, caught it, and slipped it back into his pocket. "Two of them are back home in Paelsia. A fitting place, I think, to hold the power to crush the king."

CHAPTER 24

LUCIA

AURANOS

If there was one lesson Lucia had learned from her mother, it was this: Anything less than perfection is unacceptable.

The queen had been obsessed with appearances and made it a priority for her adopted daughter to look as lovely as possible at all times. To be a perfect princess. She'd made Lucia do extensive memory work as a child, forcing her to learn long passages from the Books of Valoria by heart in addition to her regular studies. Whenever the Damoras would host important guests and local nobles, Lucia was brought out like a showpiece and made to recite her learnings. If ever Lucia stumbled over a word or struggled to recall the next section, the queen would draw her lips into a thin line, but she'd say nothing.

Not until later.

"Idiot girl," the queen would snarl once the guests had left. "You embarrassed me."

"I'm sorry, Mother. I thought I knew it. I—I didn't mean to forget."

"You need to practice more. Don't give in to laziness. It makes all of us look bad. Tonight you were nothing but a disappointment."

Such belittling words had shrunk Lucia's affection for the woman, and she grew to hate her.

That harsh but important lesson had stuck with her. Perfection was all that mattered, at any cost.

Heart stinging with disappointment over the failure at the temple, Lucia returned to her chambers to be alone with her thoughts. She stood on the balcony and let the warm breeze dance through her hair and across her skin.

The ring on her finger—Cleo's ring—brought her only a modest amount of peace. Perhaps without it she would have already set something on fire to let out her frustrations.

But the day wasn't yet over.

She hadn't been wrong about the temple. The earth crystal had been awakened there—she *knew* it. But they were too late.

Someone had stolen it before they arrived.

But it made no sense. Who else could possess the magic to figure out where to go and what to do?

She'd wanted to go to Paelsia immediately to claim the air and fire crystals, but Alexius had refused and had made her promise not to tell Magnus any more of their secrets. He already knew too much, he'd said. Besides, the king had given permission for a day trip, not for a lengthy journey to dangerous neighboring lands.

Reluctantly, Lucia had agreed to stay put for the time being.

And whoever stole the first crystal will beat you to the next two as well, a nasty, dark voice inside of her said. *How kind of you to give them a head start.*

Alexius had stopped her before she could locate the fourth

crystal. He'd told her to wait, to allow herself to get stronger and continue their lessons without tapping into the deeper magic necessary for the awakening spell.

She'd also agreed to this. That spell had been much more intense than she'd anticipated, but she'd done it. Yet now Alexius made her doubt her abilities. Perhaps he was right—perhaps she wasn't ready.

But, no. She *was* ready.

Was it possible that she could awaken the last crystal on her own?

Practice. Do it again. Don't stop—don't give in to weakness. Don't embarrass me, you idiot girl.

It was her mother's voice, still in her head after all these years.

The queen had thought Lucia's magic was evil, but it wasn't. It was pure. It was life itself. Alexius had insisted on this, and she'd begun to believe it.

And now with Eva's ring on her hand, she finally had a measure of control over it. Lucia was no longer its victim. Her magic was a part of her. Her magic *was* her.

The realization gave her new strength. She shuttered the windows, lit a dozen candles and placed them in the middle of the floor. Feeling bold and rebellious, she sat down, neatening her skirt and crossing her legs. She pulled the amethyst ring off her finger and studied it carefully in silence, then set it spinning in front of her. Just as Alexius had instructed her, she concentrated on it to keep it spinning, never stopping.

Alexius had only been her guide the last time, her tutor. But his presence wasn't necessary. This magic was hers alone to command.

With great focus, she created a map of Mytica out of magic

and light and spread it across the floor before her like a blanket unfurled for a picnic.

Very good.

She homed in on the final piece of the Kindred—the aquamarine water crystal—letting go of any final doubts and fears.

"Where is your location?" she asked aloud.

The spinning ring sped along the Imperial Road, past the temple in Auranos, past the air crystal in southern Paelsia, and further east toward the Forbidden Mountains, where it paused at the location of the fire crystal. The mountain peaks were tall and jagged and frightening, even in this magical representation.

"No, not this. I've seen all of this already," she murmured.

Suddenly, the mountains lit up with a gigantic triangle. It blazed like an ember, then with blue, orange, and white flames, so bright that Lucia nearly lost her concentration.

Fire.

She felt herself especially drawn to this symbol, so close she was certain the flames would burn her.

Then something shoved her backward, sending her spinning swiftly and wildly away from the symbol until she grew dizzy. She struggled to maintain her hold over her magic so she wouldn't lose the map. The ring nearly stopped spinning, but she grasped hold of it with her mind again, just in time.

She refused to accept defeat. She was strong—especially with the ring now in her possession. She could do this.

Her *elementia* washed over her once again, taking hold of her, a dark beast stretching its limbs and sharpening its claws. But this time she chose to embrace it. It was wild and dangerous, but with the ring as her anchor, she knew it would obey her.

The brightness of the map intensified again, so much that her eyes began to sting. The spinning ring sped along the Imperial Road on until it reached its northernmost point.

She recognized the location of the final place of power immediately. The Temple of Valoria in Limeros.

Before coming to Auranos, the temple had been like a second home to Lucia. She had gone there once a week for her entire childhood to worship the goddess.

It pleased her that this was where the final Kindred was kept.

"Water Kindred . . . I awaken you," she whispered.

On the map, the temple was now branded with the symbol of water. Two wavy, parallel lines began to swirl around and around, growing brighter and more brilliant with each movement.

But this felt different than it had with fire. It wasn't right. She couldn't look away; her gaze was fixed upon the symbol burning bright beneath the amethyst ring. Tears streamed down her cheeks.

"Enough," she gasped. "How do I end this?"

Before, Alexius had pulled her free from the spell. How was she to do it on her own? Could she? Or would this blazing light scorch her eyes right out of her head, leaving her blind?

Her heart raced, pounding loudly in her ears. The painful brightness before her eyes continued to grow into a scream building at the back of her throat. . . .

Then everything went black.

There was nothing for her to sense, nothing to feel. Only silence and darkness surrounded her for a small eternity.

Terrified, she blinked rapidly as four human figures took form before her eyes. They couldn't be real; these figures shimmered like the map of Mytica had. Like they were made of light and magic.

What is happening?

One of the figures, a stunningly beautiful young woman with long golden hair and sapphire eyes, spoke. "It's come to this. Give them back to me, Eva. I've won. You've lost. Don't make this any worse than it has to be."

Eva.

Lucia drew in a sharp breath in at the sound of the original sorceress's name.

Eva was just as beautiful as the shimmering, golden creature, but she had dark hair and eyes the color of midnight. She shook her head. "You'll have to take them from me."

"If you insist." The golden one nodded to two girls next to her—one with dark hair, one with light. "Take them."

There was something wrong with Eva; she was pale and shivering. But even though she knelt on the ground before the golden one, she looked up at her with defiance.

The girls came forward and snatched up the objects lying on the ground before Eva—four small crystal orbs.

Lucia watched in stunned silence.

"Such a stupid mistake." Eva shook her head. "You will regret following her orders."

"Shut up, you fool," the dark-haired girl snapped. "You wanted to keep this power all to yourself."

"No. I wanted to protect you from it. But it's too late now."

Each girl held two crystals. They swiftly grew brighter in their grips until they blazed like tiny suns.

"What's happening?" The fair-haired girl gasped, staring down at the spheres of amber and moonstone she was holding.

"Stop this." Panic rose in the golden woman's voice. "No! This *cannot* happen."

"I warned you, Melenia. Over and over." Eva clenched her fists at her sides. "But you ignored me."

Lucia shot her gaze to the golden one, as if seeing her for the first time.

"I—I can't let go!" cried the dark-haired girl, who held aquamarine and obsidian. "It hurts!"

Melenia rushed toward Eva and grasped her throat, digging her fingers in without mercy. "Stop this."

"I can't. It's too late. This was your choice. Always remember that."

"I've stolen your magic. You have nothing left. You should be dead already. This is the end for you."

Eva eyed her with disdain, but didn't attempt to free herself. "Do you honestly think it's that easy? My magic is eternal. My blood on your hands seals your fate."

"I want him back!" Melenia struck Eva across her face, the harsh sound of it making Lucia wince. "He belongs to me!"

Blood trickled from the corner of Eva's mouth. "He doesn't belong to anyone. He never has and he never will. He used you and you allowed him to, Melenia. If I hadn't stopped him in time, he would have destroyed everything."

Melenia trembled with rage, tears streaming down her cheeks. "I love him."

"That is your greatest mistake. The love you felt for him wasn't love at all—it was obsession. Real love means sacrifice, not selfishness."

The two girls started screaming, shrieks of pain that sent ripples of sympathy through Lucia. But Eva looked satisfied, as if their screams were music to her ears.

The screaming finally ceased and Lucia's eyes went wide with shock.

The crystals were gone. What remained were four symbols, burned into the palms of the girls' outstretched hands.

Earth and water.

Fire and air.

Lucia could barely breathe. These girls were the goddesses Valoria and Cleiona. . . .

Suddenly, before she could soak up the realization any longer, her world crashed into darkness again. She fell backward, tumbling around and around, into a bottomless ebony pit.

"Lucia," a voice said from the darkness. "Lucia! Wake up!"

She tried to grasp hold of the voice and use it to pull herself back to the real world. She held on tight, until finally she realized she was actually clutching the soft material of a shirt.

"I'm here. I won't leave you, I promise," the voice said.

Magnus? Magnus had always been there to protect her, had always cheered her when she felt at her lowest, just as she'd always tried to do for him in return.

She forced her eyes open to see it wasn't Magnus who held her. Instead she saw eyes the color of dark silver regarding her with worry.

"Alexius," she managed.

She was still on the floor, the group of candles before her. Alexius held her against him, stroking her hair away from her face.

"You were asleep. Having a nightmare, by the sound of it."

The dream had already begun to recede in her memory, but the realization of what she'd witnessed remained.

"I dreamt of Melenia," she said. "And Eva. And the goddesses."

He furrowed his brow. "All of them? That's quite a dream."

"Melenia was . . ." But the words died on her lips. Melenia was evil, horrible, manipulative. A murderer.

But she was also Alexius's trusted leader, the reason he was here. She wanted to return the Kindred to the Sanctuary for the greater good of the world.

Lucia wasn't ready to admit to Alexius what she'd done. Despite being certain that she'd successfully awakened the water crystal, something bad had happened. She knew how close she'd come to being harmed.

Alexius would be furious to learn that she'd attempt the spell without him.

She would tell him soon, but not today. Today it would be her secret.

"I was worried about you for a moment there," Alexius said after she didn't continue speaking.

The gravity in his voice coaxed a small smile to her lips. "You were worried?"

"Incredibly. I don't want anything bad to happen to you. You're far too important to me, princess." He leaned in to her and brushed his lips against hers.

Her heart swelled and the darkness that had risen within her, all the fear and despair she'd felt, was washed away in the moment of tenderness.

"I love you," he whispered. "No matter what happens, please don't ever doubt that."

When he kissed her again, the horrible memories of the spell and the nightmare swirled away and vanished into smoke.

Two days passed without incident. Lucia kept the secret of her clandestine awakening spell to herself, but she decided she would soon be ready to swallow her pride and share it. She would accept Alexius's anger at her foolhardy decision to forge ahead without his guidance and protection.

Today's lessons included more magic stealing. Alexius had insisted on it, despite her protests.

"We're wasting time," she said. "We need to find an excuse to leave the palace and claim the other crystals. We can't wait any longer. Why don't you seem more concerned? Someone might steal them as well!"

He regarded her with patience. "I *was* concerned, princess. But then, last night, Melenia visited my dreams. I told her of our progress, about what happened at the temple. I suggested that she send hawk scouts to watch over the other locations."

"And what did she say?"

"She said that she already had." At Lucia's gasp, he smiled.

"So hawks have been watching them."

"It's what we Watchers do."

Lucia worked this possibility over in her mind before she spoke again. "Does this mean she knows who has the earth crystal?"

He nodded.

"Who?" she prompted when he didn't readily tell her.

"Jonas Agallon."

Her eyes widened, immediately recognizing the name. "The rebel leader."

Alexius watched her evenly. "You are a sorceress, princess, with vast magic at your fingertips. What has been stolen can and will be stolen back. This is why I'm not overly concerned. And you shouldn't be, either."

"But Jonas could use the crystal—"

"First he'd have to figure out how," he cut her off. "And trust me, princess. It's not that simple."

Trust me.

She did trust him, she had to admit. Despite his horribly annoying tendency to hold back information he thought would upset her, she'd come to trust Alexius with of all her heart and soul.

"But who could have told Jonas where to go and what to do?" she said, half to herself, half to Alexius.

"Is the answer to that question really that difficult?" he replied. "Only three of us were there for the awakening spell, princess."

Before she could reply to this stomach-churning statement, Cronus came to the door to escort Alexius to his daily meeting with the king. He was earlier than usual, but no wonder the king needed him so urgently; the palace was a swarm of activity today as it readied itself for the wedding of a Limerian girl from a noble family. Her father, Lord Gareth—one of the king's most trusted advisors and friends—had requested the honor of King Gaius's presence at the ceremony. Though not normally one to consent to such frivolous requests, the king had decided the wedding would be an excellent excuse to hold a large feast and had issued orders to organize it swiftly.

Ever since moving to Auranos and taking his seat upon his new golden throne, her father seemed to jump at any chance to hold celebrations. She wasn't sure if it was all for show, a way to further intoxicate his new subjects, or if he actually enjoyed such events.

Alexius bid her farewell, leaving Lucia to pace her chambers, her head spinning with everything he'd just told her. Suddenly there was a knock at the door, and she opened it to reveal Cleo.

"Am I interrupting?" Cleo asked.

For a moment, Lucia couldn't find her voice. Cleo now visited her daily, ready to draw her into talks about boys, about life in general. She was only interested in frivolous discussions and long walks in the courtyard and through the palace corridors. For days after Cleo had given her the generous gift of the ring, Lucia had been fully open to this. She was happy and deeply relieved to finally have a close friend she could trust with her secrets.

Now she wasn't sure what to think.

She opened the door wider to invite the princess inside. "Not interrupting. Alexius isn't here."

Cleo entered and walked right past her, sweeping her gaze over the lit candles and hundreds of flowers arranged around the room. "It looks to me as if more romance than *elementia* lessons has been going on in here."

"Trust me, the candles and flowers are for the lessons only."

Cleo raised an eyebrow. "How disappointing."

Lucia watched the other princess carefully. "I'm glad you're here. I've been wanting to talk to you."

"Then I'm also glad I came. What's on your mind?"

"I did the spell again, on my own. I awakened the water Kindred."

Cleo gasped and her gaze snapped to Lucia's. "Where is it?"

Such a fast reply. So eager, so greedy.

Had Lucia been foolish to trust her even for a moment? To think Cleo could be a true friend in a kingdom of enemies?

Alexius's words echoed in her mind. *"You are a sorceress, princess, with vast magic at your fingertips. What has been stolen can and will be stolen back."*

He was right.

"In Limeros," she said. "At the Temple of Valoria."

She wanted to see Cleo's reaction to the truth, to see if she could sense any deception. Was it possible her suspicions were wrong? After all, when could the princess have had contact with a wanted criminal such as Jonas Agallon?

But the fact remained—and Lucia had been raised to value facts and truths above all else—that only two people other than herself had known the location of the earth Kindred before they'd discovered it stolen.

Only two. And one now stood before her—a girl whose kingdom, whose very freedom, had been stolen by Lucia's family.

CHAPTER 25

CLEO

AURANOS

Cleo's plan had worked like a charm.

Her future was looking brighter than ever and, if she could manage it, that future would include Lucia. She'd tried not to—had only planned to put on a show—but she liked her. Genuinely *liked* her and valued her friendship.

Lucia's veins didn't flow with the ice water that was Damora blood, so this surprising outcome was perfectly acceptable to Cleo.

A small part of her cringed when she had to lie to Lucia, but it was a necessary evil.

The Temple of Valoria. The home of the water crystal—the fourth and final Kindred.

Lucia had awakened it, and soon it would belong to Cleo.

She would wait until after she'd heard from Jonas to give Nerissa a message about this news. A thought kept nagging at her. Why hadn't he sent word to her yet about his success at the Temple of Cleiona?

It will take time, she reminded herself. She'd revealed all three locations in her last message to the rebel, and Nic had looked at her with shock when she'd confided to him what she'd done.

"You really trust him," he'd said.

"I do." Trusting Jonas with something as important as this was a risk she was willing to take. It was a leap off a high cliff, and she was hoping very much for a soft landing.

"It's amazing," Cleo now said to Lucia, shaking her head. "Your *elementia* . . . it leaves me in awe."

"Your ring does wonders for my control." Lucia looked down and studied the amethyst, and Cleo felt a deep pang of envy. It wasn't only a force of magic with ties to the Kindred. The ring had belonged to her mother, and her father had given it to her in his last living moments.

Her heart ached for it, but she knew it was now just another loss for her to grieve.

"I'm glad," she said, forcing a smile.

A frown creased Lucia's brow. "You knew what this ring was before Alexius told you."

A heavy moment of silence passed between the two princesses as Cleo struggled to understand exactly what Lucia was suggesting. Her words weren't posed as a question. They were presented as a statement. "Of course I didn't."

"Don't lie, Cleo. It's too much of a coincidence for me to believe."

A swift sensation of alarm whipped through her. "I'm not lying."

"You had this ring for, what? Months? This ring's secret is why you first approached me with offers of friendship. This is how you knew, before you even saw it for yourself, that your presence would give me peace. And you used that knowledge to manipulate me."

While Cleo's stomach tied itself up in knots, her mind worked furiously to find a way out of this, to ease Lucia's worries. The princess was only being paranoid, which was nothing new.

It wasn't time to panic yet.

"Lucia." Cleo offered her a bright smile. "How could I know I possessed a magic ring? It didn't provide *me* with any magic. And, in case you aren't aware, I'm only sixteen. I didn't know Eva personally like your boyfriend did. And, need I remind you that I gave that ring to you freely the moment I knew it could help you? Now stop being silly."

"Silly?" Lucia's expression grew dark. "I assure you, silly is the very last thing I'm being right now."

Perhaps it was nearing the time to panic.

"I should leave you to your studies. It's clear you're in a foul mood today and I don't want to add to it, especially with the wedding to attend this evening." She turned and opened the door.

But it slammed shut before she could leave.

Slowly, she turned to face the sorceress, her heart pounding so hard she could hear it.

"I told you about the water Kindred because I wanted to see your reaction," Lucia said softly. "I thought I might be wrong, but there it is in your eyes. I see how much you want the Kindred for yourself."

"I don't know what you mean. Now let me leave."

"Why? So you can alert Jonas Agallon and direct him to Limeros? I suggest he wear furs. It's very cold there, even in midsummer."

Cleo suddenly forgot how to breathe. She grappled to find her voice or an excuse that would satisfy the girl standing before her with her fists clenched at her sides.

"You accuse me of this, but you don't know anything with certainty," Cleo said, her tone sharp enough to cut glass. "What about your boyfriend? Has no doubt been cast in his direction? Only mine? Perhaps when it comes to him, you're blind. He's ancient, isn't he? Why would he bother with a teenaged girl if not to manipulate her powers to find the Kindred for himself?"

The air around them crackled and shimmered, and the ring on Lucia's finger began to glow with bright violet light.

Cleo had said too much.

"Lucia," she began, holding up her hands. "Don't—"

Lucia thrust her hand out, sending Cleo hurtling backward into the wall. The force knocked the breath from her lungs, and she gasped but couldn't find enough air to breathe. It *was* air itself, pure air magic, that Lucia now used to pin her against the wall, to wrap an invisible hand around her throat to choke her.

Cleo's feet left the ground as the magic pressed her upward.

"I hate liars," Lucia said simply. "And that's all you do. Lie."

The ring was now blazing. It was supposed to help Lucia control her magic, but perhaps this magic *was* under control. The controlled chaos of a sorceress.

"Don't, please!" Cleo managed. "We're friends! I care about you, Lucia. I do!"

Wind swirled violently through the room, sending everything in its path crashing to the floor. Lucia stood before her, her long dark hair flowing.

She was a nightmare come to life—a demon risen from the darklands to destroy everything in its path.

"Magnus was my only true friend in this world," Lucia said. "And now he lies to me too, just like my father. Just like everyone."

"I haven't lied to you! I've done nothing wrong. Nothing!"

Cleo would deny it until her very last breath. Even if Lucia *did* know that it was Jonas who'd claimed the earth crystal, there was no way she could possibly know with any certainty that Cleo had been the one to tell him. This was only a guessing game, and Cleo refused to play along.

But she would play a game of her own, as well.

Whatever was going through Lucia's head right now, whatever idea had sparked this act of violence, it didn't matter. They'd had moments of true friendship, and Cleo knew Lucia's heart was not cold and black like her father's. There was kindness inside of her.

"Your father destroyed my life and tore apart my family, but I offered you my friendship anyway. I gave you my mother's ring and expected nothing in return. You're wrong about me—I was loyal to you and I swear to the goddess I didn't tell anyone what I learned here. But if you want to kill me anyway, then do it and be done with it."

Suddenly the wind vanished and Cleo dropped from the wall like a stone, bruising her knees on the marble floor. She stayed there, crouched in a protective ball, looking up at the sorceress with fear.

There was no pity or understanding on Lucia's face now. Only hatred.

"Get out of here, you lying bitch," Lucia said. Her fists began to blaze with fire. "I never want to see you again."

Cleo ran from the room as fast as she could, stumbling down the hallway in her hurry to flee. She had to find Nic and tell him that they needed to make other plans. She needed to contact Jonas as soon as possible to get the other crystals from him. And in the meantime, she had to hope the Kraeshians were still interested in an alliance.

Cleo wiped away her tears as fast as they fell.

"Is everything all right, princess?" a guard asked. He and another guard had left their stations near Lucia's chambers to flank her as she moved down the long hallway.

"Everything is fine. Just fine." She eyed them warily. "As you were. I don't need any assistance."

"I'm afraid you're wrong about that." The guard took her arm. "You're coming with us."

"What?" She tried to pull away. "Unhand me this instant!"

"It's over, princess." He looked at her coldly. "We won't be taking any orders from you anymore. Not that we ever did."

"Let go of me!" she shrieked. She kicked and pulled, fighting to break away from them. She scanned the corridor for help, but found no one else in sight. "You brute! I'll tell the king about this!"

"The king is the one who sent us."

She stared back in horror, then dove at him, sinking her teeth into his arm until she tasted blood and he let her go with a grunt of pain. She turned and ran, but the other guard grabbed her before she got very far.

"We gave you a chance to come with us without resistance," he said. "Don't say we didn't."

Placing his mitt of a hand over Cleo's face, he slammed her backward against the stone wall and darkness fell over her immediately.

CHAPTER 26

LUCIA

AURANOS

As Cleo ran off, Lucia fell to the ground, bracing herself with her hands on the floor as the coldness inside her departed, leaving only the heat of her fury behind. Even with the ring in her possession, her *elementia* burned inside of her. And the more she resisted, the more it hurt.

You should have killed her, her magic hissed in the voice of her dead mother.

No. She couldn't kill anyone else.

She deserves it. She lied to you. They all lie to you and they use you. They don't care about you. They only want the Kindred. And you're only a means to an end.

The king will take what you give him and throw you away afterward without a thought.

All you are to them—the king, Cleo, Magnus—is a means to possess your magic for themselves.

Each of these terrible thoughts was like a dagger to her heart because she knew they were true.

And the more she realized it, the angrier she became. She stood and looked down at herself, realizing that she was covered in flames from head to foot: a blue fire that somehow left her dress, shoes, hair, and skin undamaged. She stared down at her hands, half fascinated, half horrified.

She went to the window and looked out at the perfect day. She concentrated until dark clouds amassed in the previously blue sky—a marriage of water and air magic. When the skies broke open with a storm, she went to the balcony, squeezed her eyes shut, and let the rain soak her. It doused her flames, but did nothing to chase away the darkness gathering within her.

That darkness that had begun to consume her.

You should kill them all for what they've done to you.

Her eyes snapped open. For a moment, she imagined doing just that: using her magic to destroy the people who had claimed to love her, but who only used her. For a moment, the thought was pleasing.

But then she realized the horror of it.

Her hair and dress now soaking wet, she pushed away from the balcony banister and raced across her chambers, scattering the flowers she'd used in her lessons earlier that day.

In a daze, she left her room and stumbled down the hallway, not bothering to look at who might be around. She was sure she received some strange reactions to her disarray as she dripped water in her wake, but she didn't care.

"Princess," a guard asked as she passed his station, "are you all right?"

"No," she whispered. He started to trail after her offering further assistance, but she summoned air magic to press him against the wall, allowing her to slip away without resistance.

She wasn't sure where she was going until she got to the room in the servants' wing that had been given to Alexius. She'd pro-tested the decision to give him servants' quarters rather than more opulent guest accommodations, but he'd said he didn't mind. He'd understood and said he liked it there just fine.

Lucia pushed the door open and went inside, trembling from both the cold water slick on her skin and the magic that slithered just beneath it.

She waited in the dark room and tried not to lose control, tried not to dip further into her powers for fear of what would happen next.

Finally, a sliver of light from the torches in the hallway bright-ened the room as Alexius opened the door.

"Lucia," he said. "What are you doing here?"

Seeing him didn't give her the relief she'd hoped for; rather, it only intensified the pain she felt over what she'd nearly done. "I don't know what's wrong with me."

The torches on the walls began to blaze, distracting her for a moment. She hadn't done that; Alexius had lit them with his magic.

Suddenly he was taking her in his arms, his handsome face now a mask of concern.

"What happened?"

"I nearly killed her."

"Who?"

"Cleo. She was lying to me, all this time. She betrayed both of us. I actually believed she could be my friend." She inhaled rag-gedly, feeling more heartbroken than she'd thought possible over that deceptive girl. "But I was stupid. So stupid to trust her, even for a moment. I can't trust anyone!"

"Lucia. Look at me. Please try to breathe."

"I wanted her to die. I wanted to make her scream in pain for what she's done. I know that's wrong, that it's horrible. So horrible."

"No," he said, shaking his head. "It's not wrong."

"How can you say that? I'd begun to believe my magic was good, but if it can make me feel this . . . this darkness I can barely control even with this ring . . . then how can it be right?"

"You have to stop doubting yourself. There's darkness in the world, of course, but there's always a balance to it. You're living proof of that balance. To accept the good, you also have to accept the bad. If you keep fighting this truth, it will only tear you apart." His expression grew anguished. "Damn it. I don't want lose you. I don't want to ever lose you. Do you understand?"

"But, Alexius—"

He pulled her closer, his hands on either side of her face, and kissed her deeply. She gasped with surprise against his lips, then sighed with relief. This was what she needed—his touch, his assurance that all was well. His mouth against hers in a kiss that never stopped, only deepened further.

It was a kiss unlike any other they'd shared, comparable only to their first in her dreams, which had shattered her unconscious world to pieces all around her.

This kiss held every bit of passion that that one had, only this one was real, flesh and blood. But it too made her feel as if her entire world were breaking apart, this time leaving behind nothing but Alexius.

"Please," he whispered against her lips, "don't ever doubt yourself. You're perfect to me in every way. I love you, Lucia. I love you so much."

He kissed her again, and she fully returned it this time, opening herself up to the bright glow deep within her that helped chase away what darkness remained in her heart.

It felt so good. She wanted more.

Lucia worked to find the ties of his shirt, pulling them away to reveal the golden swirl on his chest. It was darker today than when she'd first seen it in her dreams and again in the throne room, appearing more as a tattoo than the physical evidence of his Watcher origins. She brushed her lips over it, feeling the rapid pulse of his heartbeat beneath.

He inhaled sharply, his hands gripping her arms, halting her. "Princess . . ."

She looked up at him with sudden doubt. "Do you want me to leave?"

He let out a very light chuckle. "No. I don't want you to leave."

"So you want me to stay."

"Yes."

The single word pleased her greatly. "For how long?"

A shadow crossed his face. "Here in this room, alone with me?"

She nodded.

"If it were up to me, I'd never want you to leave," he whispered. "Ever."

She smiled up at him. His words were a salve for her invisible wounds, healing her and renewing her joy and hope.

"Good," she whispered.

There was confusion and pain in his gaze, so much suffering that she wanted to ease. But alongside the suffering she also saw something deeper and endless, and directed only toward her.

"Are you sure about this?" he asked, his voice hushed as she pulled off his shirt, letting it drop to the floor. "You were so upset a moment ago; I don't want to do anything you're not ready for."

"I'm sure," she told him, more confident now than she'd ever been about anything. "And I am ready."

"You're so young . . ."

"I am my magic, and my magic is as old as the stars." She smiled, unwilling to give up. "And I've waited long enough. I love you. Make love to me, Alexius."

She thought he might hesitate again, give her a look of doubt, or try to argue some more. But his silver eyes just filled with bottomless desire as he cupped her face between his hands.

"As you wish, princess."

When he kissed her this time, there was no restraint. Just as the skies had opened up at her command and brought a storm down onto temperate Auranos, this kiss created a portal into a deeper, more beautifully chaotic corner of her soul.

At her command, Alexius was hers . . . both body and soul.

She couldn't lie about this, not even to herself. She'd imagined being with Alexius before, but her imagination hadn't done him any justice at all.

Her mother had often warned her about what it would be like to share flesh for the first time. She'd warned of the horrible things men liked to take from girls with or without their permission. How one's chastity had to be protected at all costs—most especially the chastity of a princess.

What a tall heap of lies those warnings had been. Love made all the difference—it always did. There was nothing foul or wrong about what she and Alexius shared.

Being with him fully, here, now, in his tiny room, on this small cot with his beautiful golden body covering hers . . . it had been perfection.

A pleasant shiver raced through her as he traced a slow line over her bare shoulder. She lay very close to him, with her hand pressed against his chest. His touch made it impossible to concentrate.

"Run away with me," he whispered.

"And where would we go?" she asked, moving even closer to nuzzle his neck, sliding her lips along the column of his throat.

"Anywhere you want."

Alexius offered such incredible possibilities, an endless and exciting selection of them. "My father would go mad if I ran away from home."

"I have no doubt he would."

"Then again, he'd also go mad if he knew I was here with you now, like this."

His hand settled at the curve of her waist. "His head might explode, actually."

She smiled at the very idea of it. "Cleo was nearly banished for making a similar choice, although she blames her loss of chastity on too much wine. I have no such excuse, do I?"

He stroked her long dark hair, twisting a thick lock around his fingers and studying it as if it fascinated him. But then he frowned and his gaze locked with hers again. "Do you have regrets?"

She pulled him closer, kissing him again. "I only regret that we waited so long. You've been here for nearly two weeks. So much wasted time."

He groaned low in his throat. "You *are* dangerous, princess. But it has little to do with your magic."

She grinned, feeling both wicked and happy. Who knew she could feel both ways at the same time? "I can accept that kind of danger."

A bronze lock of hair fell across his forehead. "I should remind you that I am mortal now. I can be murdered by angry kings who find their innocent daughters in bed with their tutors."

Lucia raised an eyebrow, her grin widening. "We have to make sure he never finds out."

Alexius pushed her onto her back, holding her arms out to either side of her. "Marry me."

Her breath caught in her chest. "What?"

"You heard me. If we ran away and got married, the king wouldn't have much to say other than congratulations."

He had no idea what—and how much—he was asking of her, especially when considering how it would affect her family. "My father might still kill you."

"It's a chance I'm willing to take." He grinned at her stunned expression. "What? You said you loved me. You've just shared yourself with me in the most intimate way possible, wholeheartedly and without regrets."

She shook her head before he could take her look of trepidation the wrong way. "You're right. I love you—I do. I'm just . . . There's so much going on right now. . . ." Her head swam with all of her troubles, all of her doubts. "I can't forget about what happened with Cleo. I—I'm better now, I am. I know I overreacted." A shadow fell over her as he touched her cheek, tracing the line down to her chin. "But I still don't trust any of them. I know they want to use me. They'll never let me go."

A flash of worry crossed his gaze. "I think you're right. There are probably many who would use someone with your abilities, your prophecy. You must be careful."

His confirmation surprised her. "Alexius, I should have told you this already, but I did the spell again, by myself, to awaken the last crystal."

He went very quiet. "What?"

"I know you wanted to be there, but I succeeded on my own. With no problems," she lied.

A shadow crossed his expression. "I asked you to wait, princess."

"I know you did. But everything is fine. The spell worked perfectly. The water Kindred is waiting to be claimed as we speak."

He let out a long breath, his face still set in stern lines. "Very well, it's done. Tell me where you awakened it."

"The Temple of Valoria." She didn't see any flicker of surprise in his eyes, which told her she was right. The temple was without a doubt Melenia's fourth place of power.

It all made sense. On the maps she'd seen her father studying, the Imperial Road terminated close to the temple.

"There's been no disaster there," Alexius said. "No blood has been spilled. And yet you believe this is the place."

"I'm certain it is," she said. But then a shadow of worry clouded over her confidence. "I shared this information with Cleo, to get a reaction. To see in her eyes proof that she'd been the one to betray us."

"And if she does, and her rebel friend, Jonas, claims the crystal?"

"Then I'll steal it back." As soon as she said it, she felt the truth of her conviction. Her doubts disappeared again.

"Good." A smile played at his lips before his gaze grew pensive. "The Temple of Valoria is an excellent place for other important events as well, I think."

"What do you mean?"

"It's the perfect place for us to be married."

She couldn't help but laugh at his persistence. "You're serious, aren't you?"

"Of course I am. Unless you were waiting for an official betrothal to a lord, that is. I'm not sure a lowly tutor could ever compete with that."

She wanted Alexius more than any lord who'd ever existed. "You're impossible."

He took her face in his hands again. "Say it. Say we can run away to Limeros today to be married and claim the last crystal as ours, and no one has to know until we want them to."

Today? She stared at him, a million thoughts racing through her mind. A million doubts, a million questions, all swirling about into a storm of confusion.

But there was one thing she wasn't confused about.

"Yes. Yes, I'll marry you, Alexius."

CHAPTER 27

MAGNUS

AURANOS

"The king summons you."

Cronus stood at the archway of the palace library like the looming shadow of a mountain. Magnus was there to search the shelves for more information about the Kindred and, due to his father's recent claims about his true birth mother, he was also researching quite a bit about witches.

"Does he, now. Immediately, or at my leisure?"

Cronus crossed his arms. "Immediately."

"I was joking, Cronus." Magnus threw the book he'd been flipping through onto a large pile in the center of a long oak table. The librarian—a strange little woman with bright red hair and high arched eyebrows—would put them back where they belonged eventually.

"Of course. Shall we, your highness?"

"Oh, you've been officially assigned to usher me to him today, have you? That must make it extra important."

Cronus eyed him. "You're in a rare mood today."

"You think?" Actually, Magnus was in an apathetic mood. He'd boiled with anger for two full days about getting to the temple, only to find the treasure gone.

Now he was trying to focus on what he could control. He'd sworn to keep an extra vigilant watch over Alexius from that day forward. He knew the exiled Watcher was responsible for the missing crystal—it had to have been him. Who else could it have been?

Perhaps the king still trusted Melenia and the boy she'd sent in her stead, but Magnus didn't. Not for a single, solitary moment.

"Lead the way," Magnus said to the captain of the guard.

Today could turn into a good day, if he could only convince the king to separate Alexius and Lucia until further notice. A good day, at least, until he was required to attend Lord Gareth's daughter's wedding feast with Cleo that evening.

He'd rather forget about that obligation if he could. Another "opportunity" for him to socialize with hundreds of guests who'd likely rather be anywhere else. Well, at least they had that in common.

When the throne was his, he thought, he wouldn't jump at the chance to throw feasts for the daughters of every nobleman who asked nicely. He preferred privacy and solitude, a life in which public speeches were required only rarely and with much advance notice.

It took ten minutes to reach the throne room through the labyrinthine hallways of the palace. Magnus would never tell anyone, but he'd gotten lost in these hallways far too many times before he'd finally taken the time to sketch a map to help him find his way.

Every hallway looked exactly the same. Lit by lanterns, with marble or brightly tiled mosaic floors, and paintings and tapestries adorning the walls.

Magnus focused on his steps, staying silent at Cronus's side as they reached the throne room. The guards stationed outside pushed the doors open to let them in. Magnus approached the dais at a confident clip.

"We need to talk about Lucia's tutor," Magnus said before the king could utter a word.

The guards closed the doors, giving them privacy. Cronus remained in the room after the king gestured for him to stay.

King Gaius regarded him placidly. "Do we?"

"I don't trust him."

The king stood up and walked down the steps to face Magnus. "I'm not surprised you've taken exception to him, given your feelings toward Lucia. He's very handsome and, for all her power, she's still just a beautiful young girl."

Magnus's chest tightened at the mention of his *feelings*. "My concerns have nothing to do with that."

"If you say so. But I don't want to talk about Alexius right now." The king rose from his throne and poured himself a drink. "I've sent a spy to Kraeshia, who has reported back to me that the emperor is currently making plans to launch a fleet of ships set for our shores. He means to conquer us. Conquer *me*."

Magnus's mouth went dry at the thought. Emperor Cortas could crush Mytica with his vast armada in days, as he'd done to countless other lands over the two decades he'd been in power. The Limerian army was skilled and obedient, but they couldn't withstand a massive, organized attack. "Why now?"

"Because he wants what I have, of course." The king sounded ominously calm about this, which didn't ease Magnus's mind at all. "What *we* have."

"How do we defeat him?"

"Lucia will help, but one girl's magic against a force of thousands—tens of thousands?" His knuckles whitened as he clenched his goblet and took a sip from it. "She's mortal. One lucky arrow could end her life. I can't depend on her alone. And my patience regarding news of the Kindred is waning. Alexius assures me that all is going according to plan, but I can't help worrying."

The king had just admitted he was worried. This was turning out to be a truly momentous day.

Magnus wrestled with himself to keep his expression neutral. "So what do we do now?"

"I must make other plans. And those plans must involve more than a reliance on Lucia and the Kindred. I already have something else in mind, and I want your opinion."

"What is it?" While he had his endless criticisms of his father, on this they were united. Magnus would do anything in his power to protect Mytica from invaders.

"There is talk amongst the servants that Princess Amara has shared your bed. Is this true?"

An uncomfortable silence fell between them.

There really were no secrets in this palace. Magnus sent a quick glance at Cronus, whose expression remained blank. "Yes."

There was no judgment in the king's gaze, only consideration. "If I could present a betrothal between you and Princess Amara to the emperor, to convince Amara's father that uniting our kingdoms through marriage would be easier than his taking Mytica by force, it will give me more time to find the Kindred and crush him first."

Magnus stared blankly as his father's proposition took hold. Then he began to laugh, unable to help himself.

The king's gaze turned to ice in an instant. "Is something amusing to you?"

"*Another* betrothal?" Magnus got his laughter under control, but barely. "You can't be serious."

"Do I *look* anything but serious to you?"

Magnus sobered quickly, casting another look over his shoulder at the silent Cronus who stood nearby like a statue, his hands clasped behind his back. "In case you've forgotten, I'm already married to Princess Cleiona. At your command."

"That arrangement can be reversed at my whim."

Magnus hissed out a breath of frustration. "Even so, the emperor would never agree to this."

"His daughter is nearly nineteen and unmarried. You are the son of a king and the heir to my throne. You've already shared flesh with her. I don't see any reason for him to refuse."

As he always did when dealing with this impossible man, Magnus struggled to maintain his composure. "You need to listen to what I'm saying to you, Father. Trust me, if I believed this was a solid plan I'd embrace it. But it's not, so I won't. It is a meager attempt to solve a very large problem. Amara isn't a naïve, simple girl who swoons at the sight of a prince. What we shared wasn't . . . well, believe me, it wasn't the kind of connection that would make her beg her father to make me her husband. If the emperor wants Mytica, he will take it. A wedding—such as the gaudy spectacle you've arranged for Lord Gareth here today— would be meaningless to him. Go ahead and present this plan to the emperor if you're so determined, but don't be surprised if he also responds with laughter."

Anger flashed in the king's eyes and Magnus thought he might strike him for speaking his mind. But King Gaius's fist stayed at his side.

Almost immediately the anger was replaced with a visage of contemplation. Could it be possible that, for the first time, he would actually listen to reason?

"I know there has to be a solution," Magnus said evenly, refusing to give up what little ground he'd gained. "But I don't believe this is it."

The king placed his empty goblet on a table and paced back toward the stairs leading to the throne. "Perhaps you're right."

A small victory. But it was a true surprise.

"Besides," Magnus said, gaining confidence "the people of Auranos would find it strange if you were to annul my marriage to the princess so soon after presenting such a pleasant facade during our wedding tour."

The king searched Magnus's face, making him feel self-conscious, like a child caught behaving naughtily. "Have you developed feelings for Cleiona?"

The question was laughable, especially given his recent and deeply unpleasant altercations with the princess. "She's a means to an end. That's all she's ever been to you or to me."

"She's become a problem."

"When has she *not* been a problem?"

"A former lord of Auranos," the king began, "claiming absolute loyalty to me, came forth earlier today to alert me that he witnessed Princess Cleiona meeting with Jonas Agallon two weeks ago in a local temple. He was at the temple to pray to the goddess when he saw the rebel leader enter the building, followed by the princess. They then spoke in private, he says, for several minutes before leaving separately. If this information weren't so crucial I might have had him executed on the spot for waiting so long to come forward."

A welling sense of unease closed up Magnus's throat. "And you believe this lord?"

"I'm inclined to consider the possibility that your wife has been feeding inside information to rebels in an attempt to destroy us, yes."

"And you have what proof? The word of a man who would wait two weeks to say anything?"

"It's enough to make me doubt her innocence."

Magnus wasn't blind about Cleo in this regard. He was all eyes and ears when it came to that scheming girl.

Jonas Agallon. That name, *always* that name. Magnus should have killed him when he'd had the chance.

"Has she confessed to any of this?" he asked.

"She hasn't been interrogated yet. In fact, I want you to be the one to question her, Magnus. Immediately."

The request was ludicrous and set Magnus's stomach churning. "You're telling me you'd like me to casually stroll by her chambers and bring up the subject of rebels over tea? Or perhaps I should wait until this evening when we're seated for dinner at Lord Gareth's daughter's wedding?"

"She won't be attending the wedding. She's currently being detained in a private cell in the dungeon."

Magnus went quiet. Of course she was. A traitor and a spy, even only a suspected one, wouldn't be allowed to roam about freely.

He wasn't sure why this had taken him by surprise—he'd never trusted the girl himself—but *this*? To think that she'd been in contact with Jonas without Magnus suspecting a thing . . .

Or perhaps his father was just being paranoid, reaching for answers and accepting ones that were lighter than air itself.

The king put his hand upon Magnus's scarred cheek, holding his gaze fiercely. "I want you to show me your strength today—a strength I already know you have. A strength I know we share. We are together in this. Do whatever you must to wrench the answers I need from her lying tongue, but in the end, it really doesn't matter if she chooses to stays silent. Suspicion of rebel leanings is enough to warrant a death sentence. I've ordered Cronus to execute her immediately after you finish your interrogation. We'll finally be free of her."

A heavy silence washed over the room. Magnus struggled to find his voice. "Execute her? Is that completely necessary?"

"Yes, it is. The citizens of Auranos will mourn, but they'll come to understand that when it comes to treason, this is the only decision we can make." He patted Magnus's arm. "Go with Cronus. I have faith in your abilities and your strength, my son. Your future—*all* of our futures—hang in the balance."

And with that, the king left the throne room. Magnus stood there for a moment, reflecting on what had been said, what had been commanded of him.

"Your highness?" Cronus prompted.

The king had issued an order. There was no room to argue. "Let's not delay. We can be finished with this by the time the wedding guests arrive."

Magnus had never interrogated a prisoner before, but he'd seen it done. He'd witnessed the effects of torture. In most instances, it took very little to make prisoners spill every secret. For some, the mere threat of pain was enough for them hand over their own mothers if it would save them from any amount of suffering.

Another guard intercepted them as he and Cronus headed toward the dungeons.

"Captain," he said to Cronus, holding up a piece of parchment. "A servant found this. I thought you should see it immediately."

Cronus took the parchment and scanned the message. "Has anyone else seen this?"

"No, sir. I brought it directly to you."

"Your highness," Cronus said, turning to Magnus. "You need to read this."

Magnus took the parchment from Cronus and began to read.

His heartbeat quickened and his stomach sank further with each word.

Alexius and I are eloping. Please know that I'm fine, but don't try to find me. All is well. Better than well. I'm happier than I've ever been, so please don't be angry with me. I love Alexius more than anything in this world and it was meant to be this way. I promise to return as soon as I can.

—Lucia

Magnus tore the parchment in two, his hands trembling with rage. He'd known there was something going on between them, but to realize it had escalated so quickly to this inconceivable point . . .

"Send as many guards as you can spare. Scour the city and find them," he growled. "And when you do, kindly let me be the first to know, so I can kill the bastard."

"Yes, your highness," Cronus said.

"Keep this information from the king for now. Don't tell him until after his wedding speech. I wouldn't want my sister's foolish decision to upset him before it's absolutely necessary."

Cronus nodded at the other guard, who then scurried off to arrange a search team.

Magnus crushed the parchment into a ball and swore under his breath. "I'd go with them, but I have other important matters to attend to, don't I?"

Cronus's tone sharpened. "About the task at hand. I need you to accept that the king has given his order and I will do as he commands. There's only one way this can end, your highness."

Magnus nodded with a firm shake of his head. "I'd expect no

less from you than to do as the king commands. My father's been very lucky to have such a loyal guard all these years, whether or not he's ever told you so himself. Now, let's not keep the princess waiting."

Magnus had toured the main dungeon before, had gotten a good look at the imprisoned rebels and other thieves, murderers, and vagrants who filled the cells of this stinking pit. But today he was taken to a different part, down a darkened hallway and to a heavy wooden door at the far end. The guard who stood outside nodded at Cronus and the prince, then opened the door to give them entry.

The rest of the dungeon smelled like a cesspit, but this area, which was reserved for upper-class prisoners, smelled only of the dry, woodsy sawdust scattered across the floor.

The circular room was surprisingly large, about twenty paces in diameter. Shackles and other restraints lined the circumference. The stone walls were set with torches and lanterns that cast a flickering, shadowy glow on everything.

And there she was. Directly in the center of the room, her hands raised above her head, her wrists bound by rope and fastened to a hook hanging from the ceiling. Magnus drew closer, and she raised her chin as she watched him approach.

He saw blood at the corner of her mouth, trickling down to her chin and the edge of her turquoise gown. As he walked around her slowly, he noticed with displeasure that her pale hair was also stained with blood.

Someone had struck her very hard.

"Did she give you any trouble when you took her into custody?" Magnus asked the guard at his side.

"Yes, your highness. I have a wound on my arm where she bit me. Her teeth are very sharp."

Magnus wasn't surprised. The girl would be a fighter until the very end of her life. He couldn't help admiring her for it. "I'm sure they are."

Cleo kept her gaze on his, silently watching him wherever he roamed. He forced himself to look at her not as a girl—his *wife*—with blood on her face, but as his enemy. The enemy to his father's throne. To *his* throne.

If she had her way, they'd all have been dead by now.

"So, here we are," he began. "Do you have anything to say for yourself, princess?"

"I would demand immediate release and a thousand apologies," she said curtly, "but I doubt you'd give them to me."

This would normally be the point when a prisoner would begin to beg for mercy. But not Cleo.

"And to think some say you're not smart." He tried to ignore the blood on her face. "Let's get to the point, shall we?"

"That would be lovely."

"Are you working with rebels?"

She glared at him. "Did your father tell you to come here and question me? And did you accept immediately, knowing you'd have the chance to abuse me?"

"I haven't abused you."

"Look at me," she snarled. "You can see for yourself your father's guards have been treating me cruelly for no reason. All I've done since your family stole my father's throne is try to get along with you. I've done what you've asked of me so the Auranian people wouldn't rise up against you, and this is the thanks I get?"

He wondered how she'd be acting right now if it were the king here instead of his son. "I don't believe you answered my question, princess."

"Why even bother with titles, Magnus? Here in this horrible place where you've had them tie me up so I can no longer defend myself, why bother feigning civility anymore?"

"Very well, *Cleo*," he replied. "But you're wrong about your innocent behavior. You've been a problem since the very beginning. My father should have gotten rid of you months ago, and yet you're still here. Your every waking moment has been dedicated to finding a way to destroy my family."

"Not all of you. I considered your sister a friend until earlier today, when she tried to kill me."

The mention of Lucia hit him with the force of a blow. "What do you know about what my sister did today?"

Her eyes flashed. "She's insane. Her magic's driven her mad and paranoid and she's just looking for a reason to be violent with those who care about her."

Amazing. She still continued on with this façade of friendship. "You consider yourself one of those people, do you?"

"I did, until she nearly choked me to death with her magic while her tutor was meeting with the king."

What? Cleo must have been with her just before she ran off with Alexius. The thought that Lucia had run away with that exiled Watcher stirred his fury like nothing else. "What did you say today to push her so fully into his arms?"

Cleo raised her brow. "Alexius's arms? What do you mean?" Then her eyes narrowed, as if coming to a realization. "It torments you that she's in love with him and not with you, doesn't it? How sad."

He clenched his right hand into a fist so tightly his short fingernails bit painfully into his palms. "Let's get back to the subject at hand, shall we? What have you told the rebels?"

"Nothing," she said. "I haven't met with any rebels. I'm a prisoner in this palace and have been for months."

"Wrong. You're allowed access to the temple and that is where you were seen with Jonas Agallon two weeks ago."

Her gaze remained steely and determined, never looking away, never flinching. "Lies. Who saw me? You? The king? A guard?"

"It doesn't matter who saw you."

"Yes, it does. If someone is accusing me of something as serious as this, I deserve to know the name of my accuser."

Cronus and the other guard stood silently, watching as Magnus moved close enough to whisper in her ear, loud enough for only Cleo to hear. "Did you tell him about the earth crystal? Is that why it wasn't there when we arrived?"

"The last time I saw Jonas Agallon was when I escaped from his rebel camp in the Wildlands, where he was holding me as his kidnapped prisoner."

She was very convincing, a skilled liar. He wondered if she'd always been this way, even back before her throne had been taken from her, or if this was a skill she'd only recently developed.

Or perhaps she spoke the truth and the king was the paranoid one, looking for the perfect excuse to get rid of her once and for all.

"You said Lucia tried to kill you today."

"She did."

"Why would she do something like that? Did she suspect you of being more of a traitor than a dear friend?"

"She did it because she can't control her magic with *him* around."

Fresh emotion flashed in her eyes with an intensity that surprised him. "Even with the ring, she struggles with the darkness of her *elementia*. And I see it in his eyes—he likes that struggle. He wants her to go out of control."

"You don't trust Alexius."

"Not for a moment."

"Alexius and Lucia eloped today. I can only assume it was he who convinced her," Magnus said.

Cleo's eyes went wide. "What? No, he doesn't want to *marry* her. He—he's using her to find the rest of the Kindred. You're her brother. You need to help her!"

"I'm not her brother. Not really. And she's made it perfectly clear to me that she wants nothing more to do with me." He glanced over his shoulder at the guards, then returned his attention to the restrained princess. "You and I? I think we're finished here. You'll tell me nothing more I need to know."

"I know where they've gone," she said, raising her chin. "And it's not here in the palace city, or any other township in Auranos. Free me from this place and I promise I'll tell you."

He stood in silence, looking from the sawdust at his feet to the princess before him, considering his options. They were few and far between.

"Are you finished with your interrogation, your highness?" Cronus asked, his sword flashing in the entryway.

Magnus looked to Cleo. Her eyes flashed with fear as she realized how this was to end.

"That's right," he said evenly. "You've been sentenced to death by the king for being under suspicion of aiding a rebel. We will carry out the execution immediately."

She began to tremble. "No, don't do this. You're better than this, Magnus. You're not like your father. You're capable of good, I've seen it in your eyes. I know it in my heart!"

"In your heart?" He laughed, a dry, brittle sound that hurt the back of his throat. "Those are rather flowery words for a time like this, but you should save your breath. It's time for this to end."

As soon as the words were out, Cronus shifted his expression into a battle mask: his eyes cold, serpentine, and free of emotion, just as they'd been the day he slayed Gregor. Even when tasked with executing a helpless sixteen-year-old girl, he didn't flinch.

The futures of Mytica, the king, and of Magnus himself—they all depended on Cleo's death here and now.

She struggled with the rope binding her wrists as Cronus drew closer, as if she had any hope of freeing herself. But even in the face of imminent death, she didn't cry out. She didn't scream, didn't beg.

Cronus raised his sword, preparing to thrust it through the fine silk of her bodice. He would make it a quick death without excessive pain and suffering—over fast, in the blink of an eye with only a moment of pain to endure.

But before Cronus could send the blade through Cleo's heart, he halted for a mere fraction of a second.

Because another blade found his heart first.

Cronus gasped, looking down at the tip of the sword impaling him from behind. He dropped his weapon and fell to his knees on the dungeon cell floor.

Magnus yanked his weapon back, letting Cronus drop fully to the ground as he hissed out his last breath.

The second guard grappled for his weapon, but Magnus got to him first, his bloodied sword nothing but a flash of metal in the flickering torchlight as he struck him. The confused guard dropped soundlessly and was dead before he hit the floor.

Magnus, muscles tense and blood dripping from his blade, studied the body for a moment. Slowly, he turned to look at the princess, who was staring at him with shock etched onto her face. A shriek finally escaped her throat as he raised his sword and hacked through the ropes above her head.

He grabbed her arm and pulled her across the room, kicking the door open.

"What are you—?"

"Shut up," he hissed. "Do not talk."

"You killed them!"

He had had to. There was no other way this could have ended today. He'd run out of options. He'd gone against his father's direct orders and murdered the king's most trusted guard, whom Magnus had known since he was only a child.

Cronus would be missed, but he'd had to die. He wouldn't have obeyed Magnus's command to stand down over the king's order to execute Cleo.

He closed the door behind them to hide the carnage inside and they hurried down the dank and narrow dungeon corridor.

Very few in the palace knew who was being held in that private cell. With the wedding soon to commence and servants and guards scurrying to accommodate the last-minute arrangements, Magnus reasoned that it could take hours before anyone would learn the truth.

He had some time. Not much, but he hoped that it would be enough.

They finally cleared the dungeon and were outside. Magnus turned to Cleo, who was staring up at the brilliant late-afternoon sky as if she'd never expected to see it again.

"You said you know where Lucia and Alexius have gone," he said.

She nodded. "I must confess, it's only a guess. But I'm certain it's the right one."

"Where?" When she didn't answer right away, he took her by her arms and nearly shouted it. *"Where?"*

"Limeros," she finally replied.

Limeros? His homeland was far from here; it would take days to reach by ship. "Why Limeros?"

Instead of gazing at him with gratitude for saving her life, Cleo glared at Magnus with her same old defiance. "Because the water Kindred can be claimed at the Temple of Valoria. Lucia told me this only today, just before the guards took me. If I'm right, and if Alexius wants more from Lucia than her hand in marriage, then that's where I think they're headed. And what better way to lure her away from her family than with the promise of eloping to the home she's missed for months?"

Another crystal uncovered and ready to be claimed. Magnus's gut told him Cleo was right about everything.

"Then that's where we're going," he said firmly. "To Limeros."

She gasped. "We?"

"Yes, princess. *We.*"

CHAPTER 28

NIC

AURANOS

Five hundred invited guests attended the wedding of Lord Gareth's daughter, held at the Auranian palace—those of importance in this kingdom who'd pledged their loyalty to its new king, and those who'd made the journey here from Limeros. An invitation to such an important event could not be ignored.

Even Prince Ashur and Princess Amara were among those gathered for the ceremony of the plain girl in the elaborately beaded and embroidered gown. Her new husband was a thin but handsome young man from northern Limeros whose expression—which Nic couldn't help but note from his position by the entrance of the throne room—was pinched as their vows were exchanged.

The banquet was to be held next in the great hall, a mass movement of the gathered from one large venue to the next, overseen by the palace guards.

Nic edged closer to the prince and princess of Kraeshia when he noticed that they moved against the flow of the crowd, like salmon swimming upstream.

"We've made our appearance for the ceremony," Ashur informed one of his green-uniformed personal guards. "We wish to return to the villa. No need to extend our stay here any longer than absolutely necessary today. Likely, the king won't even notice we've left."

"Yes, your highness."

Without another word, or even a glance in Nic's direction, the Kraeshians quietly left through the nearest exit.

Lucky them.

Nic then went to stand sentry at the entrance of the great hall and wearily watched as the wedding guests ate heaps of food, listened to boring speeches, and toasted a bride and groom he couldn't care less about.

Cleo was nowhere to be seen. At least one of them had managed to avoid what promised to be an endlessly painful evening.

King Gaius made his speech to the bride, orating about how he'd known her since she was a young girl, that she'd been as important to him as a second daughter. When the guests toasted the newlyweds, Nic had felt his bland and hastily eaten dinner churn unpleasantly at the insincerity of it all.

His speech complete, the king descended the dais. Nic watched as a guard approached him, leaning in close enough to speak confidentially.

On the king's face, his perfect smile turned to stone.

He strode out of the hall without another word, the guard following dutifully behind him.

Clearly, he'd been given bad news.

Good, Nic thought darkly.

Shortly after this, Nic noticed several guards leaving their posts. Strange—the wedding would continue on until late that night and the king had insisted on extra protection. He didn't want to risk repeating the death and destruction that had tarnished Cleo and Magnus's wedding. But why was everyone leaving?

Nic soon realized he was one of the few guards who remained in the hall.

"What's going on?" he asked Idas, one of a mere handful of guards who didn't treat him like a pile of dung. Idas didn't treat Nic *well*, either, but compared to Burrus and Milo, who were both currently held in the dungeon on suspicion of assisting the rebels escape, Idas was as a close to a friend as he had here.

"Trouble," Idas replied.

"What kind of trouble?"

"Cronus is dead."

Nic inhaled sharply. "How?"

"His body was found in the dungeon along with another guard's. Both stabbed."

"Who did it?"

"Apparently it was a prisoner who managed to escape. But our job tonight is to keep watch over the wedding. We'll leave the hunt for fugitives to the others."

Cronus? *Killed* by a common prisoner? Cronus had given Nic the impression he was practically immortal—a skilled warrior forged from steel, virtually indestructible.

It seemed that was only an illusion.

"Do me a favor?" Idas asked. "If you happen to spot Prince Magnus among the guests, tell me. The king will want to alert the prince about Cronus the moment he shows his face."

"I'll do that."

Idas then went off to speak in whispers with another guard.

A prisoner had escaped and managed to kill two guards in the process? That just didn't happen. Sure, there were escape attempts every now and then—such as what had happened with Jonas's friends. But, to Nic's knowledge, a prisoner had never successfully escaped the dungeon itself.

Until today.

But who had the prisoner been?

As Nic watched three more guards leave the hall, he found his curiosity was piqued enough to provoke him to leave his station. Not that it would matter. After all, who was monitoring the guards' duties tonight? Certainly not Cronus.

No one paid him any attention as he made his way back toward the throne room. King Gaius stood at the archway, surrounded by more than a dozen guards.

". . . in addition to the main search, which takes precedence," the king said, "you will locate both Prince Ashur and Princess Amara, and, as quietly as possible so as not to disrupt the banquet, arrest them while they're still under this roof. Do you understand me?"

"Yes, your highness." The men echoed one another.

"The emperor will have second thoughts about coming anywhere near my kingdom when he learns his beloved son and daughter are being held at my mercy."

Nic doubted his ears. He'd expected to overhear only the king's reaction to Cronus's death, not a command to arrest the Kraeshians.

It didn't make sense.

And yet . . . if King Gaius believed the Emperor of Kraeshia meant to destroy him, making Mytica the latest in a long list of conquered kingdoms, then this was a smart move. Possibly the king's only move.

However, the king didn't seem to know that the Kraeshians had already left the palace, well over an hour ago.

Nic slipped away without being noticed by the king. Just another guard in the group. Same uniform, same duties.

Different allegiances.

After all, Nic was a rebel now.

He wanted to find Cleo and tell her of his plans, but there was no time.

It wouldn't be long before news reached the king that Ashur and Amara were no longer in the palace. The king would then send guards directly to the villa to make their arrests.

He left the palace without permission, knowing every decision he made now would change his future. For better or worse, he didn't know for sure. All he knew was that he had information, and he potentially had powerful allies who needed it in order to survive.

Then there was the simple yet horrible thought of Ashur, imprisoned in the dark dungeon, at the mercy of the king, never to be free again. . . .

That wouldn't happen. Not if Nic had anything to say about it.

It was an hour's ride to the villa. To his knowledge, he wasn't followed. It was fully dark when he arrived, the moon bright in the evening sky.

He jumped off his horse and approached the entrance of the villa. A green-uniformed guard stepped into his path, his ugly mug showing disdain for this boy in red.

"Has the prince arrived back yet? I must see him immediately," Nic said. "I have a message from the king."

Not a lie—it *was* a message. Although it certainly wasn't one the king would have wanted to arrive ahead of time.

"I can deliver the message," the guard growled, thrusting out his hand. "Give it to me."

"It's too important—too *private*—to be written down." Nic

crossed his arms. He refused to be intimidated by anyone tonight. "I'm the only one who can relate it."

The guard's stern expression quickly turned to boredom, and he relented, allowing Nic inside. A servant showed him out to the same patio in the courtyard where the prince and princess had offered him an alliance, only now the beautiful gardens were in shadows.

Nic began to pace as a thousand thoughts and worries swirled through his mind—thoughts and worries that he hadn't let himself consider on the rebellion-fueled ride.

It wasn't long before Prince Ashur appeared at the edge of the garden with a smile on his lips. "Nic. I was just told you'd arrived. What a pleasant surprise. I would have thought you'd be much too busy tonight at the wedding to visit."

Nic's mouth went dry, his heart pounding hard as a hammer. "I am busy, but I wanted—no, I *needed*—to see you."

"How intriguing." Ashur glanced at a servant waiting in the doorway. "Bring us something to drink."

The servant bowed and departed.

"Please sit." Ashur gestured toward the plush patio seating, the area lit by torches. "The guard told me you have a message from King Gaius?"

"Yes, that's right . . ." But then his words faltered.

Treason against the crown. That was what he was about to commit.

A treasonous tongue would ensure his execution. Would coming here tonight put Cleo in jeopardy? Had he made a horrible mistake?

Ashur watched him carefully, his expression grave. "I sense being near me makes you uncomfortable, which is why I haven't mentioned it since, but what happened between us that night in the alleyway . . . I know it was unwelcome. I want to apologize for being so bold."

Nic didn't want to talk about that now. He wasn't sure if he ever wanted to talk about it. But still, questions rose inside of him, questions that had tormented him since that night that he couldn't hold back now. There was no time for this, but he couldn't help but ask it. "Why me? Why would you—I mean, other than to get me to reveal what I know about Cleo . . . I get that. It's not uncommon around here for someone to do whatever it takes to get somebody to talk. But did I give you the impression that I wanted . . . ?" He winced and found he couldn't continue.

This *really* wasn't why Nic was there tonight.

He had to focus. He had to decide if he was going to tell Ashur the king's plans and hope it was the right decision or make up a meaningless message from the king and get out of there as quickly as he could before someone at the palace noticed his absence.

More guards were probably already on their way.

"I shouldn't have brought this up," Ashur said, his expression strained. "There's no reason for you to feel uncomfortable around me. I mean you no harm."

Nic groaned, his storming emotions in turmoil. "I don't think you want to harm me. And you're wrong. I'm not sorry you kissed me."

"No?"

Damn. Enough of this.

Nic's cheeks had suddenly grown very warm. He was tired of being timid, fearful, and uncertain. He may have been once, but no longer.

He met Ashur's gaze directly. "I overheard the king give orders to arrest you and Princess Amara. He believes you're still at the banquet, but I saw you leave so I came here myself to warn you. He means to detain you in the dungeons indefinitely to prevent your father from launching an armada."

There, he'd said it.

And now he felt as if he were going to be sick.

"I see." Ashur leaned back in his chair, seemingly unfazed by the monumental information Nic had just committed treason in order to tell him. "Why would you tell me this?"

"Because I hate him," he replied simply and truthfully. "Because he killed my sister. Because he destroyed everything I love, and to this day controls the fate of my dearest friend. He is evil. And he needs to be defeated."

Ashur watched him intently for another long moment, then nodded. "You made the right decision."

"You need to flee immediately."

"Kraeshians do not flee." He fixed Nic with a slow smile. "Ever."

"Pardon me for saying, but when his fleet of guards arrive here they will far outnumber yours—and you'll be taken easily. The king will win."

"You underestimate me. And you underestimate my sister. Much gratitude to you, Nic, for following us here with this warn-ing." He reached across the table and placed his hand on top of Nic's. "I appreciate it more than you know."

Nic studied Ashur's hand: dark and flawless against his own pale, freckled skin. "You're welcome."

Ashur glanced toward the entryway as his servant returned with a tray bearing a pitcher of apple cider and two silver goblets. Nic yanked his hand away from Ashur's as she set it down on the table between them. As the servant left, another figure brushed past her.

"We speak of her," Ashur said, "and she appears as if by magic."

As she emerged onto the patio, Amara's gaze fell on Nic. "Has Princess Cleo decided to align with us?"

"That's not why I'm here."

"No, Amara, Nic is here to warn us of the king's plans. They're exactly what we expected. He means to capture us both tonight."

She sighed with annoyance. "How deeply inconvenient."

How could neither sibling seem frightened by the possibility of spending the rest of their life in the dungeon?

Ashur filled the goblets with cider and pushed one toward Nic. "I'd like to make a toast."

"To what?" Nic asked. He raised his glass and found that his hand still shook with anxiety despite the unexpected atmosphere of absolute serenity at the villa.

"I have a suggestion," Amara said. "Let's drink to Princess Lucia, the sorceress reborn. The girl who will lead us to the Kindred."

Nic's stomach flipped upon hearing Amara repeat the same secrets Cleo had entrusted him with. "To Princess Lucia," he whispered.

He took a quick sip of the sweet drink.

"Magnus has been of no use to me at all," Amara said, crossly. "Pity. I had plans for him, but now they'll have to change. He either knows nothing, or he's unwilling to share even a sliver of information."

"That sounds like the prince," Nic admitted.

"Tell us more, Nic. Tell us everything you know about the search for the Kindred." Amara sat down next to him, took his hands in hers, and stared into his eyes. "The king is as much our enemy as he is yours. He fears our father. Join with us and we will offer absolute protection to both you and Cleo."

He'd already come halfway. He may as well continue.

After another healthy sip from the goblet, he took a deep breath and quickly related everything he knew, everything Cleo had told him—about the awakened crystals, about the blood magic ritual needed to claim them. When he was done, he felt purged of darkness.

"So Cleo doesn't have one in her possession yet," Amara said.

"No, not yet."

"I see." She appeared to ponder this as a servant approached and whispered into her ear. "Yes, very good. Go ahead and send him out here."

"Please, your grace," Nic spoke again to Ashur. "I urge you to leave this villa immediately."

"You worry too much," Ashur replied with a smile.

"And it seems as if you don't worry at all."

"I simply choose my worries very carefully."

A flash of red caught Nic's eye. He turned to see who had now emerged onto the patio, and, jumping up to his feet, he knocked over his goblet and spilled the rest of his cider across the tabletop.

Burrus, his enemy, stood before him.

"What are you doing here?" Nic demanded. "You're supposed to be in the dungeon."

"Not anymore," the thug replied.

A thought hit Nic like a sucker punch. "You're the prisoner who escaped, who killed Cronus. Aren't you?"

Burrus snorted. "Hardly. I was freed yesterday. Milo is still inside and he can rot there as far as I'm concerned. Now shut up, maggot. I didn't come here for you." He glanced at the princess. "I have information."

"Very good," she said with a nod. "Tell us."

Nic watched with shock as a slow and unpleasant realization had begun to set in.

The Kraeshians had more than one Limerian guard in their pocket.

"Late this afternoon, Prince Magnus and Princess Cleiona were spotted boarding a ship bound for Limeros, following on the heels of Princess Lucia, who has eloped with her tutor."

"Limeros?" Ashur said.

"Yes. They left in great haste. I know this much: Princess Cleo was charged with treason and imprisoned earlier today. She was to be executed. And yet she's now boarded a ship while being very much alive."

Nic's world ground to a halt. "What do you mean, she was to be executed?"

"Did I stutter? Are you stupid? Oh, wait. I already know you are." Burrus rolled his eyes. "Princess Amara, don't bother trying to coax information out of this useless idiot. I'll tell you everything you need to know. For the right price, of course."

"Of course." Amara smiled at him and reached forward to pat his arm. "And I'm grateful for that. What else do you know?"

"Nothing at this time, princess."

"So all who hunt the Kindred, apart from the king himself, have picked up and left for Limeros. Coincidental, don't you think?" She glanced at Ashur.

"I don't think it's coincidental at all," he replied.

"Apologies," Burrus said, "but did you say 'the Kindred'? As in, the legendary treasure of the Watchers?"

"Guard!" Amara called out. A moment later, the guard from the entrance appeared at the archway.

"Your highness," he said.

"We're done with our friend Burrus here. He knows far too

much; I can't let him leave. Take him away and kill him, as quietly as possible."

Burrus inhaled sharply. "Wh-what? Your grace, I've done everything you've asked of me."

"And you've been very helpful. But now we're done."

Two more guards appeared to help remove Burrus from the patio as Nic looked on, stunned.

He hated Burrus to his last breath, but he never would have expected this.

Nic realized that Amara was studying him as if she were considering painting his portrait. "Tell me, brother," she said. "Has he been of any use to you?"

"Some," Ashur replied. "Although not nearly as much as I'd hoped."

His tone was strangely cold, confusing Nic deeply. "What's going on?" he asked.

Amara stood and squeezed Nic's shoulder. "I know it must be difficult to realize that things aren't always as you believe them to be. And I know my brother can be devastatingly charming. He could make a wild boar fall in love with him if he put his mind to it. You were hardly any challenge for him at all. Was it that first forbidden kiss that sealed your destiny? Did it make you dream of sharing more?" She cast an amused look toward Ashur as Nic just gritted his teeth in silence. "So what now? Shall we kill him, too?"

Nic was about to leap up from the table when he felt the cold pressure of sharp steel at his throat and Amara yanked him back against her.

Cleo would be so disappointed in him. He'd betrayed her in an attempt to save her by sharing information with these two. This was all his fault.

"No. He can still be of use to us." Ashur dragged his chair closer to Nic's. "If you're right about Cleo and the others, we will need something on hand to convince her to help us, won't we?"

"Yes," she said after a moment. "I suppose you have a point."

Ashur reached into the pocket of his surcoat and pulled out a small glass vial. "I happen to have this on hand, just in case."

Amara laughed lightly. "My brother, prepared for anything."

The prince righted Nic's toppled goblet and refilled it with cider, then flicked the stopper off the vial and poured in the contents. "This is a sleeping potion. It's very powerful, but completely tasteless. Drink it now, please."

Nic stared at him, his disbelief at this betrayal rendering him numb. Of course, Prince Ashur had been manipulating him all along. He'd started his game that night in the tavern, planning to slowly plant more seeds over time. Ashur had given him just enough, the smallest taste, proving himself to be an expert at this particular sport.

"Drink, Nic," Ashur said, his tone even. "Or my sister will cut your throat."

Trembling with anger and the ache of disappointment, Nic picked up the goblet, tipped it back, and drained it in three gulps.

I'm so sorry, Cleo.

"Good." Ashur nodded as Nic's world began to dim. "Now, let's proceed, shall we?"

CHAPTER 29

CLEO

LIMEROS

Cleo didn't have enough time to find Nic and tell him what was happening before she fled the palace.

The thought that he'd have no idea whether she was alive or dead pained her. She prayed that he'd stay safe. She had to hold on to her knowledge that Nic was as smart as he was loyal, that he'd find a way to survive until they saw each other again.

Unaccompanied by guards who might notify the king of their unscheduled plans, the prince and princess quickly journeyed to the docks at King's Harbor. After pressing some gold into a dockworker's hand, Magnus learned that Lucia and Alexius had been there hours earlier, and that they'd boarded a ship bound for Limeros.

It was the confirmation they needed.

More gold secured another ship for them, set to sail along the eastern shore toward the northern kingdom of Mytica in pursuit.

The captain of the ship had recognized Magnus immediately. The prince confided in him that he and Cleo were chasing after

Lucia to stop her from eloping with her tutor, and that it had to be kept secret.

Again and again throughout the trip Cleo tried to corner Magnus for a private conversation about what happened in the dungeon, but despite their small ship, he managed to avoid her at every turn.

Days after their departure, the ship finally reached its destination. The captain took the Niveus Seaway, which cut east into Limeros, and finally docked in Ravencrest, the largest city in the kingdom.

Finally. Another day on this cramped ship with only her thoughts to keep her company, and she'd go absolutely mad.

Cleo disembarked and gathered her dark gray cloak closer, pulling its fur-lined hood up to shield her identity. Her breath froze in clouds in front of her.

Everywhere else it was midsummer, but in Limeros, winter seemed to stretch out eternally. While at a glance it was beautiful, so pristine and white, it would be horrible to have to live in a place that stayed so cold all of the time.

It had just started to snow and the ground was slippery beneath the smooth soles of Cleo's shoes, which were meant for walking in much warmer places.

"Let's go," Magnus said. He, too, had his hood up over most of his face. While they did have legitimate cause for being in Limeros, it would be best to avoid recognition as much as possible.

Just as they were about to get on their way, a voice called out, stopping them. "Prince Magnus? Oh my! Could it really be you? Here? How wonderful to see you and your lovely wife again!"

So much for staying incognito.

Magnus groaned, his steps slowing as an older woman covered

head to toe in furs approached them. Cleo recognized her from the wedding tour. They'd met briefly at the Limerian palace before Magnus's speech, but she couldn't recall the woman's name. Remembering the names of nobles had always been her older sister's forte, not hers.

"Lady Sophia," Magnus said, baring his teeth in a reasonable facsimile of a smile. "A pleasure, as always."

Lady Sophia's cheeks were bright from the cold and her smile was stretched, coaxing wrinkles to the corners of her eyes. "I had no idea you were in town."

"We just arrived."

"To stay, I hope? Or have you become so used to Auranos's warmer climes that you've abandoned your true home?" she said with levity, without even an edge of accusation.

"I could never abandon Limeros forever."

He sounded so composed, but he couldn't be. They'd been recognized, which Cleo knew was the last thing he'd wanted.

"Where are you staying tonight? Nightfall is upon us and the snow is thickening. Many believe it will be a very bad storm, I'm afraid."

The darkening skies above looked very grim indeed. If a storm gathered, it would make traveling on foot next to impossible.

Cleo started as Lady Sophia grasped and squeezed her hands in greeting.

"Princess!" she gasped before Cleo could respond. "Your hands are so cold! Your highness, your beautiful wife is freezing to death out here! We must get her somewhere warmer immediately. I'm staying at my city villa tonight after a day of visiting with my sisters. Please, allow me to offer you the hospitality of my home for the night. Unless you have somewhere else in mind?"

Cleo couldn't help but be charmed by Lady Sophia's exuberant and generous offer. And with the oncoming storm, where *did* Magnus propose they sleep? Outside, where they'd turn into blocks of ice?

"That's very generous of you," Cleo said when Magnus stayed silent. This decision would be hers to make. "Yes, of course, we accept your kind offer. Much gratitude to you. However, we'll need to be on our way at first light."

"Certainly." Lady Sophia beamed, then gestured for her servants to draw her carriage up. "Where are your trunks?"

"They'll stay on the ship for now," Magnus said. What little they'd managed to gather before leaving didn't take up much room at all. "I brought my wife here to see the local shops, and to show her that Auranian dressmakers aren't the only ones capable of creating magnificent gowns."

His *wife*. That word, from his lips, always sent a shiver down her spine.

And she had to admit, he was very a good liar—nearly as good as she was.

"Very true." Lady Sophia nodded enthusiastically. "Oh, what fun! I adore having honored guests at my villa!"

Oh, yes. What fun indeed.

Lady Sophia's villa was much grander than Cleo had expected. It was every bit as large as most of the villas in the City of Gold, only the decor was much less elaborate. Whitewashed walls, sparse artwork, smooth unadorned floors. But quite comfortable.

And cozy. She'd forgotten how the cold outside could help one appreciate the warmth inside. It was a thought that never occurred to her in Auranos, where fireplaces were used only for decoration.

Soon they were ushered by servants into the dining room and seated at a long table.

"Hmm. I have missed the taste of *kaana* these last months," Magnus said over dinner, his expression a bit stiff.

"My cook does wonders with it," Lady Sophia said from the other end of the long table. "I'm sure your father would be pleased to know that we continue to include this official Limerian delicacy with most meals. What do you think of it, princess?"

Cleo looked down at the yellowish muck adorning her plate, sitting next to some overcooked chicken and limp asparagus. Limerian delicacy? *Kaana* tasted like slimy, rotting seaweed.

"Delicious," she replied.

"How is your sister, Prince Magnus?" Lady Sophia asked as the servants refilled their goblets with peach nectar.

Magnus dabbed the corner of his mouth with his napkin. "Delightful, as always."

"Still unbetrothed?"

His lips thinned. "You could say that."

True. Elopements did not require a betrothal.

Cleo tried another mouthful of the disgusting *kaana*, forcing herself to swallow it down.

"My son, Bernardo, remains unmarried, believe it or not," she said with a bright smile. "I will never give up on my dream of joining our families through marriage."

"Nor will I, Lady Sophia."

This woman amused Cleo deeply. She seemed completely oblivious to everything and everyone around her, yet entirely genuine in her comments and questions. Cleo needed more Lady Sophias in her life.

The woman's expression then shifted as if a cloud had crossed her inner sunlight. "I want to offer my deepest condolences for your mother's passing, your highness. Queen Althea was a dear friend for many years and, I know, a wonderful and devoted mother to you and Princess Lucia."

Magnus nodded stiffly, focusing entirely on his plate. "Thank you for your kind words. She was certainly a special woman."

Cleo watched him from across the table. Mention of the queen had brought a flicker of grief to his eyes, but it was restrained, just like everything else about him.

She still believed it had to have been the king who'd given Aron the order to kill the queen. Did Magnus believe that too? And, if so, had he confronted his father about this? If he had, nothing had resulted from it. She imagined only more lies had left the king's lips to divert Magnus's suspicions..

The king lied to get what he wanted, to anyone and everyone.

Cleo only lied to protect herself and those she cared about. And she'd continue to do so when needed, without shame or remorse.

Whatever it took to survive this. Her fight wasn't over yet. Far from it.

"I certainly hope it's not too unpleasant," Lady Sophia said as she accompanied Cleo and Magnus to their bedchamber. The woman's finely lined face was finally starting to show signs of worry, and she patted her salt-and-pepper hair nervously at the doorway. "If I'd known you were coming, I could have made much more suitable preparations."

"No, it's perfect." Cleo grasped Lady Sophia's hands and squeezed. "Thank you for your wonderful hospitality."

"Any time, princess. Any time at all!" Lady Sophia beamed brightly. "Good night."

"Good night."

She closed the door, leaving them alone.

"This is absolutely ridiculous," Magnus grumbled. "We shouldn't even be here. We're wasting precious time."

"It's snowing," Cleo reminded him.

He glanced toward the window. "It's always snowing in Limeros."

"We'll find Lucia tomorrow morning. Besides, I'm sure she and Alexius have also taken shelter for the night."

"Yes, much gratitude for the reminder that my sister is somewhere alone with *him*."

Was this jealousy? Or pure concern for her safety? Cleo wasn't entirely sure.

"It's getting late. Wouldn't want to stand in the way of your beauty rest." Magnus swept a glance across the room, stopping at the canopied bed. "The floor is all yours."

She was sure Lady Sophia wouldn't think that deciding who got the bed was something a newly married couple would have to discuss, yet it most certainly would be an issue tonight.

When Cleo didn't reply, Magnus frowned. "No cutting comeback, princess? I'm disappointed."

Squabbling wouldn't do either of them any good right now and it only wasted time. "What happens tomorrow?" she asked.

"It's simple. We find Lucia. We stop her from making the horrible mistake of marrying Alexius or helping him claim the crystal in any way. And then I will kill him."

She stared at him. Was that his solution to every problem? "That's a bit rash, don't you think?"

"Is it? He's using her; he has been all this time. It's one thing we agree on."

"That doesn't mean he deserves to die."

"We'll have to disagree on that. No surprise there."

He was being deeply unpleasant this evening, more so than usual, which was saying a lot. "What about the crystal?"

"I won't be leaving Limeros without it."

"You."

"Yes, me. What?" He cocked his head. "Did you think I'd give it to you as a gift? It's mine. It's always been mine."

"And your father's, you mean."

"No. Not his." Magnus went to the window and peered outside. "It seems that Lady Sophia was mistaken. The clouds are passing, the snow is stopping. And there's a full moon on the rise. That'll help light our way when we head out for the temple tonight. Lady Sophia will have to deal with my rude disregard for her hospitality as best she can."

Suddenly Cleo realized that she and Magnus were finally alone with no one listening in. Total privacy.

It was time to get to the truth of matters.

"Why did you do it?" Cleo asked, her stomach in knots, and not only because of the meal she'd forced down to be polite.

He didn't turn around. "Do what, princess?"

She forced herself to sound confident, keeping her chin high. "I can't figure it out. I've been thinking about it for days now and it still makes no sense. Based on your sullen attitude and the fact that you've barely looked at me since we left Auranos, all I know for sure is that you regret saving my life. Of course, why wouldn't you? It was the stupidest and most irresponsible decision you could have made and I'm sure your father will never forgive you."

Magnus turned to face her directly. On his face was an annoying mask of indifference, as if they were discussing nothing more important than the weather. "My father would forgive me for anything if given enough time. His children are one of his few weaknesses. It's something I've only recently realized."

In Cleo's opinion, Magnus vastly overestimated the king's capacity for forgiveness. "You murdered Cronus. The king valued him more than any other guard."

"I was left with no other choice. He wouldn't have spared you, even on my orders. He'd already been issued a direct command by the king, and Cronus never failed my father. Ever. And the other guard . . . well, he was in the wrong place at the wrong time. That was too bad for him." Magnus shook his head. "I don't want to talk about this."

She didn't care if he wanted to talk about it or not. She needed answers and she wouldn't give up. "As much as it pains me to admit it, your life would be a lot easier if you'd let him kill me. No fake marriage, no worrying about your secrets being exposed, no more threat to your father's stolen throne."

He focused on the sleeve of his coat, brushing off an invisible piece of lint as if it were the most important task in the world. "You knew where I could find both Lucia and the water Kindred. I needed that information. And when I return with both of them, my father will come to appreciate why I did what I did."

"I didn't say anything about the crystal until after."

"Then all I can say is that I have no further explanation that will properly satisfy you."

Cleo groaned. "You are the most frustrating person I've ever known."

"More frustrating than Jonas Agallon?" Magnus frowned. "I've met him, you know, so I find that hard to believe. He's quite frustrating."

He still believed she'd met with Jonas—had aided Jonas and the rebels—despite her adamant denials. She couldn't possibly reveal the truth now; it would serve no purpose at all. Her dealings with the rebel would be her secret . . . and Nerissa's and Nic's.

"You believe I helped a rebel and yet you still spared my life. You must want something—something beyond that crystal. Beyond my help in finding Lucia."

His eyes flashed with sudden anger. "What do you care for Lucia, anyway? You said she tried to kill you."

Back in Lucia's chambers, Cleo had been certain she was going to die. She hadn't been able to breathe or move; she'd been helpless before the sorceress's rage. Still, she couldn't hate Lucia. In fact, she actually welled up with pity for the girl. There was so much magic inside of her, enough to drown her if she wasn't careful. "I care about Lucia. I do. And I don't want anything bad to happen to her. Now, answer me, Magnus. What do you want from me?"

"Nothing at all."

"Then *why*? Give me one good reason why you wouldn't let Cronus kill me."

Contrary to what she'd expected, Magnus didn't storm from the room, nor did he drag her out of it and slam the door in her face. He just stood there, arms at his sides, his attention fixed on something on the wall over her shoulder. His expression was pained, as if he couldn't quite bear to look directly at her.

"You really want to know?" he asked.

"Yes. I really do."

He was silent for so long that she wasn't sure he'd ever speak again.

"My whole life, all I wanted was to be like my father," he began in a monotone voice. "I've wanted to follow in his footsteps, to be strong. Smart. Resourceful. Cunning. Intimidating. Ruthless. To be respected and feared. To have his power and influence. What else is there for someone like me—the heir to his throne? Without that to aspire to, I have nothing. I am nothing."

What a thing to say. He'd been raised as a prince, brought up in privilege—he should have more of a sense of self-worth than this. "You're wrong."

He held up a hand to silence her. "I've always been told I look like him, sound like him . . . I essentially *am* him. But no matter how hard I try, I always fail. Because at my core, where I need to be the strongest, I'm weak."

Cleo kept quiet now, listening carefully. Barely breathing.

"You want to know why I did what I did?" His dark brows drew together as if he were only now allowing himself to consider this question. "It's fairly simple, actually. It's because, without your bravery in the face of all that's happened to you, without your constant scheming behind my back, without that fire of hatred and contempt and *hope* in your eyes when you look at me . . ." He hissed out a breath. "In the shadow my father has cast over my entire life, you are the only light I can see anymore. And, whatever the cost, I refuse to let that light be extinguished."

All she could do was stare at him until he scowled and turned away.

"Satisfied, princess? Now, stop asking me stupid questions."

As soon as her shock began to fade, an uncontrollable rise of laughter escaped her throat. As she laughed, he cast a look at her and a flash of pain crossed his face before he could shutter it off.

"That's right, princess. Laugh at me. It is funny, after all."

She laughed until tears flowed down her cheeks, hysterical now. Gasping for breath. "It's just . . . what Nic said once . . ."

"And what, pray tell, did Nic say?"

Cleo sobered quickly as an invisible hand clutched her throat, squeezing hard, making it nearly impossible to breathe. "That he thought I was falling in love with you."

Magnus stared at her. "What an idiotic thing for him to say."

"I know. Because I'm not. Never. How could I be? I hate you."

And then she was kissing him, and she wasn't even sure who approached whom first. It had happened so quickly, and there was no way to stop it. His lips crushed against hers, her hands twisting into his shirt, sliding over his shoulders, and up to tangle into his hair. He pulled her closer, until there was no space between them at all.

It was desperate, this kiss. Violent, even.

But of course it was. It had been building up between them for such a long time, as the battle about this boy who had destroyed her life had raged inside her. This boy who had saved her life, who was cruel and kind, strong and weak. Who was selfish and selfless all at once.

This boy who had, in a single moment of fear and weakness, taken someone so special from her. She knew she could never forgive him for that. This was the boy she was forced to marry in a destroyed temple, surrounded by dead bodies and an ocean of blood.

This was the boy who now kissed her without reservation, as if he were dying and she was air itself.

A sharp knock at the door made her gasp and pull away from him. She stared up into his eyes as she touched her swollen lips. He looked back at her, no invisible mask in place now to cover his shock.

Finally he turned away and went to the door. He opened it up with such force that she was surprised he didn't tear it from its hinges.

Princess Amara stood at the doorway, a smile on her lips. She glanced past Magnus at Cleo.

"Did I interrupt anything?" she asked. "Apologies, of course. But this couldn't wait."

It took Cleo a moment to fully register the fact that the princess was standing right there in front of her. Here, on the other side of Mytica, in the house of a woman they'd met by chance.

This couldn't be real.

"What are you doing here?" Magnus asked. "How did you find us?"

She shrugged. "I'm very good at negotiations. People spill many secrets for the right amount of gold. And here we are. If both of you could come downstairs with me, that would be lovely."

"What's downstairs?" Cleo asked guardedly, though she knew whatever it was couldn't be good.

She knew that Amara had followed them, just as they'd followed Lucia.

"Come and see."

Cleo didn't like the sound of that, but she had no choice but to do as the princess requested.

Standing in Lady Sophia's central hall were six green-uniformed Kraeshian guards, along with Prince Ashur and . . . *Nic?*

There he was, hunched over, his hands bound behind his back.

"Nic!" Cleo surged forward, but a guard put out an arm to stop her from getting too close. "What have they done to you? Are you all right?"

"Cleo," he managed, casting a hateful look at Ashur and Amara. "I'm alive, so that's a start."

Another guard held a pale and trembling Lady Sophia by the arm. Cleo's heart twisted for the kind woman who hadn't done anything to deserve this rough treatment.

"What is this?" Magnus asked, his tone edged with warning.

"Another of my negotiations." Amara moved toward Ashur. "And one we had to come all the way to Limeros to discuss, which is unfortunate. This is not a place I'd ever choose to come to if I had any say in the matter. But here we are."

"A negotiation about what?"

"We tried to do this the pleasant way. We offered Cleo an alliance, but we couldn't wait forever for a reply, could we? And Magnus—I did what I could to gain your confidence, but I knew your heart wasn't in it. Too bad. I don't waste my time or attention on boys I can't manipulate."

"We're all here in search of the same thing," Ashur said. His gray-blue eyes were steely, and fixed on Cleo in particular. "The Kindred."

The prince was as cold and calculating as his sister, and every bit as greedy. Even if Cleo had agreed to their terms, she wouldn't have been able to trust them. The moment they got what they wanted, they would have betrayed her.

She caught Nic's gaze and searched his face for injury, but saw nothing. Even the bruises and cuts from the guards' horrible beating had faded in the time that had passed.

I'm so sorry, Nic, she told him silently. *This is all my fault.*

The Kraeshians knew how important he was to her. Now they would shamelessly use that knowledge to manipulate her.

"The Kindred?" Magnus said. "Sorry to disappoint, but we're in pursuit of my sister, who has unwisely chosen to elope with her tutor. We want to stop her from doing something she'll regret for the rest of her life."

"Of course. Her tutor." Amara nodded. "First, let's get one thing straight—I know what Lucia is and what she can do. Second, I know about the earth Kindred at the Temple of Cleiona and how you failed to claim it first. So. Let's proceed, shall we?"

"Nic . . ." Magnus said slowly. "You're not so skilled at keeping secrets, are you?"

Nic ignored him. "Let Cleo go. I'll do whatever you want."

"You've served your purpose already," Ashur said, his tone cold. "You've ceased to matter."

"Now," Amara said, her smile returning. "There's no need for argument. We're certain you're here for another crystal that Lucia has located. We want it, and you will lead us to it."

"Nic stays here with the woman," Ashur said, nodding at Lady Sophia. "We'll leave a guard behind to watch over them and make sure they cause no problems."

"Speaking of guards," Magnus said. "I have a few of my own, you know. They should be here any moment."

Cleo eyed him, but stayed silent. He was bluffing. No guards had accompanied them from Auranos. They were on their own with no protection.

"Let them come," Amara said. "I'll offer them so much gold I can guarantee that they'll give me no reason to spill any more blood tonight than necessary."

Magnus's expression grew dark, but he offered no rebuttal.

"Let's move this along." Ashur nodded at a guard.

The guard put the edge of his sword to Nic's throat, and Cleo couldn't hold back a shriek. "Don't! Spare him, please."

"You'll take us to the crystal," Ashur said.

She was about to speak, to tell them everything to save her friend, but Magnus spoke first.

"Very well. We'll go at first light," he said.

"No," Ashur replied. "We'll go now. All we need to know is where."

Magnus gave him a look sharp enough to kill, but said nothing.

Amara nodded at the guard with Nic. "Cut his throat."

"No, wait!" Cleo shrieked. "Don't hurt him, please! The Temple of Valoria, that's where the crystal is. But know that we have no guarantee that Lucia hasn't already been there and claimed it."

"It's a chance we're willing to take." Ashur gestured toward the guard, who finally released Nic.

She had to speak, she had to tell them what they wanted to know. Nic's life was worth more to her than one crystal.

"Then let's be on our way." Amara went to Magnus, reached up to grasp his chin, and pulled it down until he met her gaze. "Don't underestimate what I'm willing to do to get what I want. And what I want is the Kindred—even one quarter of it will do for now. I will kill to get it. Do you understand me?"

"Oh, yes, princess," he bit out through clenched teeth. "I understand you more than you know."

Amara sent a poisonous look at Cleo. "See how much better it could have been if you'd embraced me as a friend?"

"I'd rather embrace a boil-covered pig," Cleo replied. "Which would actually be a pleasant alternative to you."

Amara laughed, then nodded at the guard holding Lady Sophia. "You stay. The rest of you, come with us. And Cleo, Magnus . . . if you behave yourselves, I may even let you live to see the sunrise."

CHAPTER 30

JONAS

PAELSIA

Immediately after claiming the earth Kindred on behalf of the princess, Jonas, Lysandra, and Felix had set their sights on the next two.

Jonas hadn't sent a message to Cleo yet. He wanted to have all three crystals in hand, to show her he was worthy of her trust.

He wasn't entirely sure why proving himself to her mattered so much to him.

Claiming the air crystal at Chief Basilius's abandoned compound had gone just as smoothly as at the claiming at the temple, even though the compound held memories just as painful. That was where the Paelsian slaves had risen up against the abusive Limerian guards, triggering a massacre just moments before a tornado had torn across the dusty land.

That was in the past now. Jonas knew he had to focus on the future.

Within the compound, dirt paths led off to a labyrinth of small stone cottages with the chief's large villa in the center. They chose to draw the symbol in the clearing where the chief's bonfires, feasts, and nightly entertainment had been held.

"I want to do it this time," Felix had insisted.

He held the blade to his forearm, made a shallow slice, then flexed his arm out, allowing his blood to drip onto the cracked dry ground. He smeared it with his fingertips to create a spiral symbol, then stood up and wrapped his arm with a cloth.

Lysandra clutched Jonas's shoulder as a breeze picked up, circling around them in a sudden whirlwind that made Jonas's breath catch in his chest.

"Over there." Lysandra pointed at the chief's bonfire pit, which was now only a scorched circle in the center of the clearing.

A small sphere had appeared, sunlight glinting off its pearly-white surface.

Moonstone.

The air Kindred.

The sight of it alone was akin to the sweet taste of victory after so many bitter failures.

Felix picked it up without hesitation, grinning from ear to ear. "Nice."

He tossed it to Jonas, who caught it and looked down at the smooth surface of the orb. Like the earth Kindred, there was a sliver of darkness inside, swirling around in an endless cycle.

Lysandra glanced at Jonas. "So where are we headed next?"

"The mountains," Jonas told her, more determined now than ever.

Jonas led them along the path of the Blood Road to the camp he'd attacked along with his group of rebels in the ominous shadow of the Forbidden Mountains, a camp now cleared away with nothing there to remind him of his crushing defeat except for the charred ground surrounding the road.

Here Lysandra insisted on using her blood to draw the symbol for fire.

But nothing happened.

Jonas tried, then Felix.

Nothing.

"Looks like someone beat us to it," Felix said.

But who? All Jonas knew was that he wasn't ready to give up yet. They had to keep trying. And so they did, staying there in the barren and deserted east of Paelsia for two days before they'd exhausted all other options. They finally gave up and headed back to Auranos, disappointed at their failure.

Two crystals out of three, Jonas thought. It would have to do.

Jonas knew they couldn't continue to use the Silver Toad as a meeting place. But he had to pay one last visit there to see if any new messages had been delivered in the week he'd been away.

"I'm starving," Felix said as he pushed the front door open. "Let's stay and eat. There's a nice private table in that dark corner over there. Just keep your hoods up, both of you."

"Wearing our hoods in a tavern won't make us look at all suspicious, will it?" Lysandra replied.

Jonas wouldn't have agreed to this, but the tavern was nearly vacant, save for two tables occupied by drunk and oblivious patrons.

They would eat, and then they'd move on.

"We'll face the wall," Jonas said, managing a grin. "Since you're not lucky enough to be as famous as me and Lys, you can be our lookout."

Lysandra would now be recognizable to anyone who'd been close enough to see her face the day of the attempted executions. And this was their second time in the tavern as a trio.

"Happy to oblige." Felix took his seat and signaled to the bar-keep for drinks. "Tonight we should have a chat about what we're going to do with those two crystals now that we're back in Aura-nos. We could earn ourselves a life's worth of gold with those two pretty pieces."

"Even though we don't know how they work."

"A small inconvenience," Felix allowed.

They'd inspected the two crystals for hours, trying to figure out how to harness their magic. All they'd done was waste time and energy.

Jonas didn't doubt what they were, but accessing their magic was beyond him.

Which was fine with him. Just because he believed in magic now didn't mean he wanted any part of it.

He wasn't looking forward to Felix's chat. He knew that the discussion of whether to sell the crystals to one of Felix's mysteri-ous contacts or hand them over to Princess Cleo would be less of a talk, and more of a heated debate.

He slid his hand over the two crystals in the leather pouch he had tied to his wrist. They wouldn't leave his sight, not for a mo-ment.

Their fate would be his decision and nobody else's.

Galyn, the tavern owner and friend of the rebels, brought drinks—three ales and no wine this time, which pleased Lysandra.

"Welcome back," Galyn said quietly. "It's good to see you again."

"You too." It was a relief to see the younger, heavyset man rath-er than his exuberantly loud, white-haired father, Bruno." Do you have any messages for me?"

Galyn shook his head. "None, although your pretty, young friend has come here several times these last few days. With the recent rumors I've heard about happenings in the City of Gold, I'm sure she has some new information to impart, but she hasn't left a single message with me."

Jonas stared at him. "What recent developments?"

Galyn lowered his voice further. "Apparently, Princess Lucia has run away from the palace with her tutor. The king is furious, and now tears apart every town and village in the kingdom searching for her."

"So the princess's idiotic romantic decisions will mean pain and death for many," Lysandra said with disgust. "The selfish decisions of these vain royals never fail to sicken me."

No one spoke up to argue with her opinion.

"The palace is in disarray," Galyn continued. "Because of this, and, of course, because of the disappearance of Prince Magnus and Princess Cleiona."

Jonas suddenly couldn't find his voice.

"What do you mean, 'disappearance'?" Felix asked.

"I mean, rumor has it they're gone without a trace. Some say that the king went mad and put them both—his heir and his heir's wife—to death. Frankly, I wouldn't put it past him."

Cleo was missing . . . possibly dead? It couldn't be.

Had she been exposed as a spy? She'd sent him two messages, the second only a week ago. Could that be related to this?

Jonas had to know more. If this was true, and if she was still alive, he had to find her.

He lurched up from the table.

"Sit down," Felix said.

His throat was tight and painful. "I have to go."

"Not yet."

"What?"

"Someone just walked through the door and I'm pretty sure you're going to want to talk to her."

Jonas turned, peering past the edge of his hood to see Nerissa entering the tavern. She scanned it, deep relief crossing her face when she spotted him. She hurriedly approached their table as Galyn excused himself

"Thank the goddess you're here," she said, grasping Jonas's hands.

His heart pounded. "I just heard about the princess . . . that she's missing. Is it true?"

"May I speak with you in private?"

Jonas was about to protest, to say that anything that had to be said could be said in front of his friends, but he held his tongue. After all, there could be others listening.

"Go," Lysandra said. "And make haste."

He guided Nerissa out of the main tavern and toward the staircase leading to the inn.

"This is private enough." She looked around nervously at the small alcove.

"Is it true about Princess Cleo?" Jonas demanded.

"She's gone, Jonas. No one knows where."

"And Prince Magnus."

"Him too. It's a mystery, but I know this much. Two guards were slain in the dungeon, including the captain of the guard. It happened while they were on duty . . . watching Cleo, whom the king imprisoned for treason."

The world before Jonas's eyes blurred and darkened. "And now she and the boy she was forced to marry are missing."

"Yes."

"And the king? What is his reaction to this?"

"I have no way of knowing. He's in seclusion. But I have heard that he fears Prince Magnus may have been taken hostage, or murdered, by whoever helped the princess escape. And Jonas . . . well, *you* have been named as the main suspect."

Any other day, he might have found this amusing. Here he was, accused of yet another crime he didn't commit.

Nerissa's face was pale, worried. "I can't stay, Jonas. And I won't be able to meet you again for some time. They're looking at everyone in the palace with suspicion."

"Thank you for sharing what you know. I know how dangerous this is for you." His mind was in turmoil, unsure how to process this information. He'd once hated this royal girl beyond any other . . . yet now he found his world turned upside down at the thought that she'd been in grave danger—that she was *still* in grave danger—and he hadn't been able to do a thing to help her.

Nerissa clutched his arm, drawing his attention back to the present. "There's something else I need to tell you."

"What is it?"

"It's about your new friend, Felix."

"Felix?" Jonas frowned, trying to concentrate. "What about him?"

"Our first meeting gave a bad first impression."

"And here I thought you two hit it off well enough."

"I know men, Jonas. I know when they're hiding something. And I saw that in his eyes. I also saw that you trusted him, which worried me. So I did some digging, and I found some information." She hesitated. "You're not going to like it."

Jonas looked her right in her eyes, steeling himself for more bad news.

"Tell me," he said.

Nerissa shared her information with him, then promptly left.

Jonas returned to the tavern and swept his gaze across the large room. Felix was at the bar, talking to Galyn. Lysandra still sat at the table in the dark corner, studying the wall and sipping from her tankard of ale.

"Lys," he called to her. She glanced over at him and he signaled for her to follow him.

He led her back to the alcove where he'd spoken with Nerissa, only this time he went up the staircase. He found a vacant room on the second floor, and pulled Lysandra into it with him, closing the door behind them.

She eyed him with wariness. "What's happened? Did Nerissa deliver bad news about the princess?"

"Yes, but I can't deal with that right now. We have a more immediate problem."

"What is it?"

"Nerissa doesn't trust Felix."

"That makes two of us," she said, but then grimaced. "Sorry. I know you've come to consider him a true friend. I must learn to respect that. And, really, he isn't nearly as smarmy as I first thought."

He hissed out a breath. "He works for King Gaius."

Lysandra stared at him with shock. "What?"

She looked as blindsided as he'd felt when Nerissa told him. "He said he was raised by a group of cutthroats who worked for a rich boss, right? Well, that rich boss was the king. He's a hired assassin for the King of Blood." Jonas's anger had started slowly, as cold shock, but had built quickly into something practically tangible, something he could hold onto. "That's how he found me. Five weeks ago he was at the palace to receive his most recent assignment—to track me down and bring my head to the king."

"Wait. But—but he didn't do that. You've been with him all this time and he hasn't made a single move, right?" Lysandra gripped Jonas's arms. "Maybe she's wrong."

He was furious with himself for being stupid enough to trust someone he barely knew.

Nerissa's information had resonated with him. It finally filled in the blanks that Jonas had been trying to ignore about his new friend.

He believed Nerissa.

"He's waiting for something." Jonas shook his head. "Now that I have the crystals . . . Cleo told me the king was after the Kindred—after magic. That is his goal. Do you have any idea what the king would pay for even one of those crystals? And do you know what he'd do with that kind of power if he's able figure out how to harness it?"

"Jonas, please calm down. Losing your head isn't going to help."

"Nice choice of words." He groaned and rubbed his hands over his face. "You were right not to trust him. You sensed something, didn't you? Something *off*."

"I did. But—I mean, I'll admit I don't trust easily."

"Neither do I. Not normally. Damn it, I don't have time to deal with this. I need to start searching for the princess . . ."

"Forget the princess for a minute. What do we do now, with Felix? Confront him?"

Jonas began pacing the room. "I will confront him, but not right now."

"Why? What are you waiting for?"

He met her gaze. "Because first I need you to leave."

She looked at him with confusion. "Why would I do that?"

It would be great if once, just once, someone would do as he asked without arguing. "Because he's dangerous."

"*I'm* dangerous too, in case you've forgotten."

She needed to see reason, but there wasn't much time to convince her. "I'm going to just go ahead and say it. I've been worried about you ever since your escape from the palace. I don't want to jeopardize your recovery. I know what happened. It—it was rough for you. And your brother . . ." His jaw tensed. "I know that you'll need to take time to heal."

She stared at him. "I'm fine."

"You're not."

Her face flushed and her eyes flashed with anger. "Yes, I am. I'm *fine*. Stop treating me like a delicate flower, because never, not once in my entire life, have I been one. You don't need to protect me. I can confront Felix with you, by your side. And if he makes any move toward you, I'll kill him."

She was so beautiful when she got all riled up like this. "You never stop arguing, do you?"

She groaned with frustration. "I'm not going anywhere else and you can't make—"

He grabbed her face between his hands, pushed her back against the wall, and pressed his mouth against hers. His emotions were running high tonight, and just then she'd looked so fierce, so gorgeous—

He couldn't resist. He'd wanted to kiss her for ages, actually. And it was just as good as he'd imagined it would be.

She grabbed hold of his shirt as if ready to shove him away from her, but instead she slid her hands over his shoulders and pulled him closer, returning the kiss, and, for a moment, made him forget everything but the salty-sweet taste of her lips.

When they parted, he was panting, certain his face was as flushed as hers.

"Didn't expect that," she whispered.

"That makes two of us."

"Well, it doesn't change a thing. I'm not leaving you."

"Fine." He slid his fingers through her long dark hair, his mind spinning. "We'll confront Felix together. Two against one, better odds."

"Will you, now?"

The words cut through their shared moment like a knife. Lysandra stiffened against Jonas and they both looked toward the entrance. Leaning against the frame in the now open doorway, his arms crossed over his chest, was Felix.

"So confront me," he said, without a trace of humor in his voice or eyes. "What are you waiting for?"

Rage returned, bright as fire before Jonas's eyes. "Where should I begin?"

"You can save the recap. I heard everything through the door. Realized that both of my friends had suddenly disappeared into thin air, so I went searching for them. And here you are."

Jonas stepped away from Lysandra, cursing himself for letting his guard down. The walls here were paper thin; he should have been more careful.

"You lied to me," Jonas growled.

"I never lied. Withheld the truth? Maybe a little."

The smug look in Felix's eyes was enough to incite Jonas. He attacked, grabbing hold of the boy's arms and shoving him backward out of the room and into the hallway.

Felix broke loose easily and smashed his fist into Jonas's face. Jonas stumbled, falling to the ground, but Felix grabbed him by the front of his shirt and yanked him back up to his feet.

"I'm going to kill you," Jonas snarled.

"I'd like to see you try. For all those rumors about you, I've never been too impressed by your combat skills. Me, on the other hand? Professional level."

"I guess that's why the king keeps you in his back pocket."

"Yeah, I suppose it is."

"Stop it," Lysandra snarled. "Both of you."

"No," Felix said, flicking a cold glance at her. "Jonas started this and I'll finish it. Couldn't be any other way. I'm surprised it took this long, really."

The smugness was gone, replaced now by what Jonas saw as pained disappointment.

Without another word, Felix shoved Jonas down the stairwell. He stumbled and fell, unable to right himself until he landed with a crash on his back on the floor. He pushed up and staggered into the tavern, with Felix right behind him.

Jonas grabbed for his dagger, but Felix was there first. He knocked it out of his grip and backhanded Jonas across his face as he tried to get to his feet, then punched him hard in the gut. Jonas spit out a mouthful of blood and found he could barely breathe; the air had been completely knocked out of his lungs.

Lysandra ran down the stairs, a knife in her hand, but Felix turned, grabbed her by her throat, and shoved her backward, sending her crashing into a table.

Jonas tried to get up, but found Felix's knee pressed to his chest and his blade to Jonas's throat.

"So here we are," Felix said. "My little secret's now out. Too bad, I like to keep my secrets secret."

"I trusted you." Jonas growled.

"Trust goes both ways, friend."

"So kill me already."

"Did you consider, for one damn moment, that I'm not as bad as you suddenly think I am?"

"You work for the king."

"I *did* work for the king. I did a lot of bad things for the king, actually, and got paid well for all of them. Ever since I was only eleven years old, I've killed for him. I was a cute kid. I could get into a lot of places his other assassins couldn't. Kept Limeros running nice and tight, no problems. But things have changed since the war. *I've* changed."

Jonas stared up with disappointment—almost heartbreak—at the boy he'd come to consider a friend. "Really."

"I told you how I grew up, just not where or who my boss was. I never had friends. I was raised not to trust anyone unless they were part of my clan. I came to hate those people." Felix's expression grew haunted. "Got my latest assignment from the king, which was to track you down and infiltrate your little group of rebels. Lo and behold, when I found you, you had no group. You were as alone as I was. Call me crazy, but I decided to make a change right then and there. Felt like the right time for me to start down my path of redemption."

Jonas frowned, uncertain what to believe.

"That's right. I wasn't planning to betray you or kill you." Felix voice was thick with conviction. "But the moment you hear something you don't like, *you* betray *me*, *you* decide to kill *me*. Without a second damn thought. Doesn't sound like a real friend to me."

Jonas shot a glance over to Lysandra, and was dismayed to see that she was lying unconscious on the floor. Felix followed his line of sight. "I didn't mean to shove her that hard. But sometimes we hurt the people we love. Life's like that."

Then he plunged his dagger through Jonas's shoulder, pinning him to the floor. Jonas screamed.

"Don't worry, it won't kill you. It just feels like it will." Felix ripped the leather pouch off its ties around Jonas's wrist and pulled out the crystals. He held them as if weighing them to determine their value in gold before curling his fingers around the moonstone.

"My blood, my crystal. It's only fair." He tossed the orb of obsidian at Jonas; it landed heavily on his chest and rolled off to the side. "We're done here."

Jonas watched through a curtain of pain as Felix turned and walked out of the tavern without a backward glance.

Lysandra groaned and began to stir. Galyn emerged from behind the bar and ran over to help her up to her feet.

Jonas lay still, literally pinned to the floor, until Lysandra helped him remove Felix's dagger and patch his wound.

"It's all right," she told him, her expression one of anguish. "We're better off without him."

Jonas wasn't so sure about that. Trust was a fragile thing. And in that moment, he couldn't even trust himself anymore.

He'd learned a few important, but very painful, lessons tonight.

The first was that he'd screwed up.

The second was that true friends were rare. And those with dark pasts didn't always yearn for dark futures.

He could have given Felix a chance to explain, given him the benefit of the doubt after he'd shown his loyalty time and again.

It seemed that Felix wasn't the only one now ready to earn his redemption.

CHAPTER 31

ALEXIUS

LIMEROS

While many of Alexius's memories had grown foggy since Melenia applied her obedience spell to his flesh, one had remained crystal clear. It was of a starry, moonlit night in Paelsia when, in hawk form, he'd watched two sisters use magic enhanced by blood and death to steal a newborn child from her cradle.

He'd watched as they slipped away into the dark forest, the tiny baby swaddled between them. Then, soon after, he watched one sister betray the other in order to deliver the child to the man who'd given her the mission in the first place, a man she believed she loved—a man who would one day be king.

The witch was young and stupid and willing to do horrible things for love—even murder her own sister.

But what Alexius remembered most vividly was the moment he had gazed at the baby's face, wondering if what the witches said could be true: that this innocent child was the sorceress reborn, after all of these years they'd waited.

In his heart, he'd known it was the truth. It was why he'd continued to visit the child for so many years, so he could watch her grow up into the beautiful, powerful, and dangerous girl she now was.

The night Lucia was taken from her birth mother, Alexius had silently pledged that he would always be there to protect her. At the time, he'd meant it with all his heart.

Now, they were together in Limeros. Lucia's hand tightened on his as they drew closer to the temple.

"Oh, Alexius." Her breath froze before her in the cold air as she spoke. "I've missed it here so much."

Alexius didn't have many good things to say about Valoria, so he kept his thoughts to himself. Valoria had believed her opinions were better than anyone else's, never mind that nobody ever shared them. She frowned upon anything that would make a life, either mortal or immortal, more interesting, even reading fables or singing. Cleiona had been the exact opposite: a frivolous, vain creature who cared only about her own amusement.

It was no wonder the kingdoms they'd founded evolved to prize their respective values.

Rising up at the temple entrance was a statue of Valoria, wearing an expression of judgment upon all who entered. Her arms were raised at her sides, and etched into her palms were the symbols of the elements she represented, earth and water.

While this location paled in comparison to the grandeur found at the Temple of Cleiona, which was easily six times the size of this one, it was still very impressive. It was all clean lines of smooth granite blocks, exact angles, sharp edges, with nothing gaudy or out of place. Nothing extra or unnecessary or ornamental. The temple was pristine in all ways, and was open all hours of the day and night to anyone.

But Melenia had sensed great power here—as she had at the three other locations.

He'd thought it would be months, not weeks before he came here.

It had all happened much quicker than he ever would have imagined.

Inside, in the center of the black granite floor, a massive fire roared. This was in some ways ironic, since Cleiona was thought to be the goddess of that element. But in Limeros, one simply needed fire to keep from freezing to death.

The fire, Alexius noted, burned in the center of a long, rectangular pool of shallow water, and was regularly tended by temple attendants dressed in red robes.

There were very few people here tonight—a likely result of both the snowstorm and the late hour. He and Lucia had already secured a room at an inn close by, while keeping her identity well-guarded.

Once the clouds had cleared and the bright moon lit the frozen landscape almost as well as the sun, she had practically dragged him here, excited to show him what had been such a large part of her life before moving to Auranos.

He tried to walk quickly, but, even though the wound Xanthus gave him was healing nicely, his leg still troubled him. It was a harsh reminder of his mortality.

Lucia pulled him down the aisle toward the altar at the front. There she grasped hold of his hands and looked up into his eyes.

"This is where we'll be married," she said, a wide smile lighting up her sky-blue eyes.

"Here?" He raised his brow as he glanced around. "I'm not sure if eloping princesses should be wed in public places like this if they want their secrets to remain such."

"Maybe I don't want it to be a secret. Maybe I want everyone to know . . . even Father." She kissed him, throwing her arms around him and pulling him close. "He'll understand. He *will*."

He wondered if the king was so committed to finding the Kindred that he'd approve this marriage to ensure it. He wasn't so certain. His last meeting had gone well enough, but the king was anxious and impatient about the lack of progress and time.

If only he knew the truth.

"What about your brother?" Alexius asked.

"He might pose more of a problem." But her smile was still intact when she drew back from him. "Magnus will have to accept that I love you. He understands love, whether he'll admit it or not. He'll see in my eyes that this is true and nothing will ever change it. I was always meant to be with you."

His heart a dead weight in his chest, he touched her cheek, trying to sear her image into his memory.

Lucia finally frowned. "Why do you look so sad?"

He shook his head. "I'm not sad."

"This is your happy look, is it? I must say, it has me a little worried. You're not having second thoughts, are you?"

Second, third, fourth . . . millionth. Every decision he'd made, every secret he'd kept. "Not about you."

"Good. I know how different we are. And I know I haven't known you very long at all . . ."

I've known you all your life, he thought. *Watched over you. Protected you from the others. Almost seventeen years now I've waited.*

". . . but this is right," she continued. "I've never been surer of anything in my life."

Alexius took her hand, rubbing his thumb over the large amethyst in her ring. He remembered seeing the same ring on Eva's finger. In the end, for all its power, it hadn't helped the original sorceress against her greatest enemy.

In the first dreams they'd shared, Alexius told Lucia that Eva had perished because she'd fallen in love with the wrong boy. But that had been a lie. Love—at least the love that Eva herself had experienced—had had absolutely nothing to do with the sorceress's demise.

It was such an ironic thought now.

Lucia looked up at the arched ceiling and at the few worshippers filling the hard wooden benches. Then she turned to gaze at the fire that burned to keep visitors warm from the constant chill outside. "Can we claim the crystal here? Now?" she asked.

"Not yet."

She frowned. "What do you mean, 'not yet'? Is it because there are witnesses?"

"No. It's because one last step must be taken here. There's been no blood magic, no elemental disaster. It won't be done in the correct order, but it still must be done. This place"—he gazed around with trepidation—"is the anchor. This place is where it shall all end. And the end will trigger the beginning."

She smiled at his enigmatic speech. "I don't understand."

"I wish I could have explained everything to you, but it's impossible." He rubbed his chest. "But here we are. Here is where destiny has been waiting for us for all these centuries."

She watched him patiently, as if his ramblings amused her. "What do we have to do, then, to accept this destiny?"

She was so curious, insatiably so. He wondered what it would have been like to truly be her tutor—to help her with her magic for years to come. "It's all about blood, princess. Blood is magic. It's the key to everything—the key to life, the key to death, the key to freedom, the key to imprisonment."

She laughed, surprising him, and leaned forward to kiss him. "You're so serious tonight, aren't you? Don't worry, a little blood doesn't scare me."

He wished he felt the same. His chest hurt more with each moment he hesitated—the invisible markings binding him to Melenia's will, controlling him, day and night. "She's making me do this. Please know . . . this is not my choice."

Her smile faded and her expression became cast in shadow. "It's all right, whatever's troubling you. I'm here." Then she hugged him, wrapping her arms around his shoulders to pull him closer. "We'll figure all of this out together and—"

She gasped the second he sank his dagger into her stomach.

"I'm sorry, Lucia," Alexius whispered. "This isn't me. This is something more powerful, controlling me."

He pulled the weapon out. She staggered back and dropped to her knees, touching her wound and staring with shock at her bloody fingertips. Blood flowed from the gash, soaking into her gown and pooling before her on the floor of the temple.

At the other locations, it had taken a great deal of blood to trigger the necessary effect—a tornado, an earthquake, a wildfire. The blood of slaves spilled on the road they were forced to build. The blood of rebel battles in a temple and in the mountains. Blood spilled from scores of mortals, three separate times, to trigger three elemental disasters.

Fate. All of it.

But the blood of a sorceress was more powerful than that of one hundred regular mortals.

Melenia had waited a thousand years for this moment. With Lucia's blood spilled—here, now—the veil between worlds would finally dissipate enough for someone as powerful as the elder to escape her prison and claim what she wanted most.

Through his fog of horror, Alexius heard the screams of those who'd witnessed his violent act. They ran from the temple, leaving him and Lucia alone.

There were no heroes here to step in and save her.

Only a once immortal villain clutching a dagger.

Under Melenia's spell, every rebellious thought he had or word he spoke caused him pain—but all of that was nothing compared to the pain he felt seeing Lucia suffer like this, enduring pain that went deeper than physical.

"What . . ." Lucia gasped. "What are you . . . why did you do this? Alexius . . . why?"

Suddenly, an ice storm gathered, triggered by Lucia's blood, unleashing itself above the Temple of Valoria and shattering every window. Icicles as sharp as swords and as fast as lightning hurtled through the open windows, some impaling the floor and others shattering into a thousand pieces on contact.

Alexius just stood there, silently shaking as he watched Lucia bleed. She stared up at him with pain and confusion etched onto her pale face.

No fury or accusation, only confusion.

All the while the violent storm battered the temple. He had no doubt that anyone who'd set foot outside was already dead. There hadn't been enough time for them to find shelter before the gales struck. Their bodies would be found around the temple, frozen and riddled with ice shards.

But their deaths were meaningless. Only Lucia's blood mattered.

Melenia had been right about so much. But not everything.

Lucia could destroy him with a thought, but she didn't use her *elementia* against him in defense. Right now she was just a girl who'd been betrayed by the boy she loved.

He knelt next to her and took her by her shoulders, struggling to speak past the pain that threatened to block the truth. "That wound won't kill you, but the next one will. You must defend yourself from me while you still have a chance."

Her agonized gaze searched his. "Alexius . . . stop this . . ."

"My mission is carved into my very skin, Lucia. Melenia has compelled me to obey her commands and I can't stop this, I can only delay the inevitable." Each word was a knife in his throat. "Melenia wants you to die, here and now."

"Why?"

"Your blood holds the same magic as Eva's blood—powerful enough to trap her, powerful enough to free her. She doesn't want the Kindred returned to the Sanctuary. She wants it for herself and she's planned this, waited for this, for millennia."

Her eyes grew wider with every word he said. "You lied to me." She drew in a ragged breath. "How could you? I trusted you!"

It took every ounce of his strength to resist the faraway command to run his blade into Lucia's heart and steal her life completely. Melenia's obedience spell burned within him, but he resisted. There had to be another choice . . .

He clutched the blade, his hand trembling violently. "You need to kill me."

She shook her head. "What? No! You . . . you said this wound won't kill me. I'm still alive, I'm here. Please, whatever spell she's put on you . . . you have to resist it!"

"I'm trying," he bit out through clenched teeth. But it was an impossible task.

Melenia would win, just as he always knew she would.

His strength was gone, his small grasp on control slipping. Everything inside him screamed for him to end this, to kill her and be done with it. But he still held on. "She'll do anything to free him," he said. "She believes she loves him and that justifies everything to her."

"What? Who—Melenia? I don't care who she loves. I love *you*. No matter what. I love you, Alexius."

"Why won't you do as I say and defend yourself from me?"

"Because this isn't an *elementia* lesson," she hissed. "And you're not my tutor right now. You're the boy I love and I'm not giving up on you!"

She thought there was still a choice to be made, still hope for a future together.

He wished she were right.

She was so beautiful, this young girl who'd stolen his heart. So beautiful and brave even after he'd done so much to make her hate him. "You still don't understand. She already has won. Now it's just a matter of who will survive until tomorrow—you, or me. And I swear, it will be you."

With that, he tightened his grip on the hilt of his dagger, and with every iota of strength and will he had left, thrust the blade into his own heart.

"No!" Lucia screamed. "Alexius! No!"

The pain was intense, but it was different from the pain of resisting Melenia's spell. This pain would finally free him from the spell that had made him her slave.

The golden swirl on his chest began to glow brighter beneath the blood now masking it. His blood mingled with Lucia's as the ice storm finally began to subside.

She pulled him against her, tears streaming down her cheeks.

"I love you," he said. "And I'm so sorry I couldn't be stronger for you."

She shook her head, pressing her hands against his wound. Her hands began to glow. She was trying to heal him

It almost made him smile. She already knew that earth magic couldn't heal an exiled Watcher, neither his magic nor hers. And yet she still tried.

A ragged cry escaped her throat. "You can't leave me. I need you."

Finally, after so long under Melenia's command, his head was clear of her influence. It meant he didn't have much time left, but he would use that time to help the girl he loved.

He drew her closer to him. "Please, listen to me. Listen very carefully . . ."

Her hot, salty tears fell against his skin as he began to speak, but their warmth couldn't stop the chill that swiftly spread through his body. Throughout his long life, he'd always wondered what the moment of his death would be like—if it ever came. He'd never thought he would be foolish enough to leave the Sanctuary, to risk his immortality for a girl.

But for this girl, he would gladly risk anything.

And before death finally claimed him, he kissed her one last time and told her what she needed to know about what was soon to come . . .

CHAPTER 32

MAGNUS

LIMEROS

As if this trip to Limeros hadn't given him enough problems to deal with, the fact that the Kraeshians were every bit as deceitful as his father believed them to be added a whole new set of troubles. On the carriage ride to the temple, Magnus imagined how he would kill them.

Slowly, he thought. Very slowly.

"Are we there yet?" Amara asked her brother, her usually honeyed voice edged with impatience.

"It won't be much longer," Ashur replied.

Magnus couldn't help noticing that the carriage driver had chosen to take a meandering route to the temple after Ashur informed him of their destination. It had taken nearly twice as long to get there as it should have.

The dawdling ride gave him plenty of time to consider this unfortunate situation, but not enough to figure a way out of it.

He wished he'd seen Amara's threat before now, but he'd been distracted by her beauty and refreshing bluntness. Certainly he couldn't have been the first to make that mistake.

Cleo sat across from him in the carriage, her hands folded on her lap as she quietly gazed out of the window at the snowy landscape speeding past. On the surface, she was so serene, but he was certain a storm raged behind those eyes. There was no way Cleo would have let them kill Nic; he knew that. He didn't even blame her for telling them about the temple while under such pressure.

Well, he blamed her a *little*. But what was done was done.

They finally reached the temple. Magnus stepped out of the carriage, then halted, shocked. An ice storm of a magnitude he'd never witnessed before had ravaged the place. Thick shards of ice protruded from the snow-covered ground. Bodies, some of which had been cut cleanly in half by the gargantuan blades of ice, were scattered everywhere. Blood, black as ink, stained the frosty ground.

Cleo looked around with horror. "What happened here?"

Amara surveyed the scene with her hands on her hips. "An elemental disaster, by the looks of it. I choose to think of this as merely a good sign that we've arrived at the right place."

Magnus crouched next to a body, feeling the man's throat to find it nearly frozen solid. It was enough to tell him this hadn't just happened. At least an hour had passed since this man had died.

The skies were dark but cloudless, displaying nothing but the bright full moon to light the gory scene before them while the rest of Limeros slept.

"Shall we go inside?" Ashur asked briskly.

Magnus hesitated, and a guard shoved him forward. His hands itched for a weapon, but he'd been fully disarmed at Lady Sophia's villa.

Walking inside, Magnus saw that the ice had also penetrated

the temple walls. The floor was covered in a cold, crystal-clear layer, some of which had begun to melt.

The guard shoved him again as they moved down the aisle.

"Careful," Magnus growled, "or I'll make it a point to kill you first."

The guard laughed. "We'll see, boy."

Boy? This lowly Kraeshian guard didn't even bother to use his
royal title. It was an insult beyond any other.

Magnus would *definitely* kill him first.

But Magnus all but forgot about the insolent guard when he
noticed an alarming amount of blood pooled against the black
granite floor by the altar at the front of the temple.

There were no bodies there, not even one. Only blood, lit by
the eternal fire that continued to burn in the center of the temple.

His first troubled thought was of Lucia.

Where are you, sister?

"So we're here," Magnus said, forcing himself to sound calm
and totally in control. "Welcome to the Temple of Valoria."

Amara glanced around, unimpressed. "I'm sure it looked better
before the storm."

"Not especially."

Cleo was hugging herself with her arms crossed in front of her,
as if not even her heavy cloak could keep out the cold. She locked
eyes with Magnus, who quickly looked away.

"Magnus," Amara said, "you should take more pride your little
homeland. My father has always said that Limerians are moral and
very well behaved, for the most part. If nothing else, King Gaius
has managed to successfully control his people through fear and
intimidation."

"Fear and intimidation are tactics that work very well on those
who allow themselves to be afraid and intimidated."

Ashur remained silent, allowing his sister to do the talking. He'd seemed much more disturbed than she had by the dead bodies outside.

"Nothing to say, Prince Ashur?" Magnus asked.

Ashur gave him a tight smile. "Not really. I'd prefer to observe for now."

"That's my brother." Amara looked at him fondly. "An observer. A watcher. I always kid him that at any moment he'll sprout feathers and fly away to join his friends in the Sanctuary."

How painfully unamusing. "Anyway," Magnus began, "this is where Lucia believes the water Kindred to be. Let's start searching. This could take all night."

All night was more than enough time to figure out a way to steal a weapon and lay waste to anyone who got in his way—starting with that insolent guard.

"Yes," Cleo readily agreed with his ruse. "It's like a delightful game of hide-and-seek."

He almost laughed out loud at that. Yes, so delightful, this game.

"I have a better idea." Amara nodded at a guard, who grabbed Cleo's hand and sliced across her palm with a sharp dagger.

She shrieked, yanking her hand back from him.

Magnus fought the urge to break free and run to her. There were guards on either side of him and he knew they wouldn't hesitate to cut his throat.

"We know about the blood ritual," Amara said. "So please, don't waste my time."

Cleo's eyes widened. "How could you learn of . . . ?"

Magnus didn't have to wonder. The answer to this question was tied up back at Lady Sophia's villa.

Thanks to the princess, Nic knew too much. And he had trouble keeping his mouth shut. Although, to be fair, Magnus could only guess the level of duress the Kraeshians had put him under in order to get to the answers they needed.

"Don't keep me waiting," Amara said, tapping her foot. "Or I'll send word to the guard at the villa to bring me your redheaded best friend, one piece at a time."

Cleo exchanged another brief, pained look with Magnus, then knelt on the ground and swept some ice shards away to clear a small area. She took a deep breath in, then let her blood drip to the floor and began drawing the symbol for water: two waved parallel lines.

So much for buying them enough time to figure this out.

"There." Cleo finished, then stood up, glaring at the Kraeshians.

Amara looked around the temple eagerly, as if expecting the roof to open up and magic to stream in.

But nothing happened.

"How long does it take?" Amara asked, her voice sharp with impatience.

"I don't know," Cleo replied just as sharply. "Do you have somewhere else to be tonight? I'd hate to keep you from a prior commitment."

The Kraeshian princess's expression grew sour. "Did you ever like me, Cleo? Or were you only feigning friendship in the hopes that I could save you from the utter disaster your life has become?"

"Despite whatever promises and offers you might have made to me, I could never ignore the sensation I had whenever you were nearby—like spiders crawling on my skin. I knew I couldn't trust you."

"Or maybe you were just jealous of me because of my . . . *connection* with Magnus. You don't like how determined I am to get what I want."

"Determined? No. Pathetic and needy? That's more like it."

"Enough, both of you," Ashur said.

"Not nearly, brother. Cleo should respect me for possessing exactly what she lacks: the strength to get what I want, no matter what it takes. If I were her, I wouldn't merely lie down and accept defeat without a fight. I'd burn with vengeance every day and night looking for any chance I could get to change my situation. We offered you that chance and you ignored it."

"So it's true that alliances were offered between the three of you in an attempt to destroy my father," Magnus said.

He couldn't say he was surprised, but this circumstance did put him in a more awkward position as the odd man out.

"Your father is meaningless in the grand scheme of things," Ashur said. "Barely worth a moment's thought."

"I think he'd disagree," Magnus said. "In fact, I'm sure of it."

"Where is it?" Amara hissed. "Why hasn't the crystal revealed itself yet? How long must we wait?"

Cleo's expression remained impassive. "I have no idea."

Suddenly, a flash of color on the floor caught Magnus's eye. On the black granite between two benches, he saw a smear of crimson.

He drew in a sharp breath.

It was the water symbol, a second one, drawn in blood. It had to have been Lucia, benefitting from her head start.

Was this her blood? Was she all right? Happy with the boy she believed she loved? Or had he only manipulated her to get what he wanted?

There was no way to know for sure until he saw her again.

Magnus's reaction to this discovery had drawn Amara's attention. She followed his gaze to the symbol, her expression darkening immediately. "Your sister, isn't it? Lucia took the crystal."

"It wasn't Lucia," another voice spoke up from the opposite

side of the altar, and a cloaked figure emerged from the shadows. "It was me."

The young man pulled back his hood and, for a brief moment, Magnus was certain it would be Jonas Agallon.

But instead of Jonas's smug rebel face, a flash of messy red hair appeared.

Nic stretched out his hand to show the small sphere of aqua-marine—the same color as Cleo's eyes—that he held in his hand.

Cleo stared at him with unrestrained shock. "Nic! How—how is this possible?"

"Guards, capture him," Amara growled. "Kill him. Take the crystal."

"No," Prince Ashur said firmly before the guards made a move. "You will not. And if any one of you follows my sister's orders for the remainder of the night, you'll deeply regret it."

Unexpected, Magnus thought. *Very unexpected.*

Nic moved forward, his gaze flicking to Cleo's still-shocked expression.

Magnus understood as little about this situation as Cleo did. The boy had been tied up and left under a guard's supervision. A guard who'd been instructed to kill him if he caused any problems.

Magnus decided right then and there to stop underestimating Nicolo Cassian.

CHAPTER 33

NIC

FOUR DAYS EARLIER

Nic fought through the thick fog of unconsciousness, struggling through a tangle of dreams and nightmares to find his way back into the waking world. After what felt like an eternity, he finally opened his eyes.

The potion-induced sleep hadn't been like a normal slumber. It had been heavier, deeper, and he imagined that it was exactly what death felt like.

But he was still alive. For now, anyway.

And he had one hell of a headache.

He pushed himself up and found that he was lying on a cot in a small, dark room. He made his way over to a window to his right, and, ignoring the spinning in his head, gasped at the scene outside. Dark water—as far as the eye could see—under a black curtain of night.

"We're on our way to Limeros," a low voice said.

He spun around to find Ashur standing in the shadows. Without a single thought, Nic attacked. He tried to land a blow on the prince's perfect face, but Ashur grabbed Nic's arm and twisted it behind his back hard enough to make Nic gasp in pain.

"Be quiet, you fool," Ashur growled. "She'll hear you."

"You're going to break my arm."

"Not if you stay quiet."

"Fine."

Ashur held on for a moment longer before he released Nic, who then turned around and punched him in the jaw. The prince whipped his head to the side, but didn't try to retaliate. He rubbed his chin, grimacing. "I deserved that."

Nic glared at him, his fist aching and still clenched . "I'm going to kill you."

"No, you won't. Not after you hear me out."

"Hear you out?" Nic shouted. "Why? Do you have more lies you want to tell me?"

Ashur pressed his hand against Nic's mouth and shoved him back against the wall, his expression fierce and angry. "If she knows you're awake and making trouble, she'll have someone put you back to sleep. Permanently, if she gets her way. You're only alive now because I convinced her we need you."

Nic shoved his hand away. "How helpful. Thanks so much." This time, however, he kept his tone low, barely louder than a whisper.

Ashur nodded. "That's better."

"I aim to please."

"I know you hate me."

"You deceived me, drugged me, and threw me on a ship against my will. I think I have every good reason to hate you. I would have handed King Gaius your arse on a platter if I'd known what you were really like."

"My sister is ambitious. We'd never shared any of the same interests until recently. I've always been more of an explorer than her, and my explorations led me to the legends of Mytica. I found myself fascinated by them, enough to come here personally to investigate."

Nic stared at him, exasperated. "Are you going to tell me your full life history? Seems I have time to hear it, doesn't it, locked up here on this ship?"

Ashur regarded him bemusedly and sat down in a nearby chair. It was the only piece of furniture in the room other than the uncomfortable cot Nic had gotten to know very well. "You need to hear this because it'll help you make your decision."

"What decision?"

"Whether or not you want to help me."

Nic laughed, a sound that was dry and humorless even to his own ears. "You used me. You played a hilarious game of 'trick Nic,' and it worked perfectly."

"It wasn't a game to me." Ashur sighed. "Not all of it."

"Speak. Say what you need to say, then leave me alone. Or kill me. One or the other." He really shouldn't be putting ideas into the prince's mind. Perhaps it would be a good idea for him to just keep his mouth shut and listen.

"It didn't take long for Amara to grow interested in the Kindred. I was a fool to tell her anything about them, or of the legends of the Watchers. But I told her everything. I suppose I was just looking for someone to talk to, since our father had no time for me, and our brothers always seemed to be busy either commanding Father's armada to earn their glory or presiding over court when at home. Amara listened carefully and attentively, but I had no idea how serious she was until she arrived here with a plan to find the Kindred, no matter what it took."

"And here we are," Nic said with distaste. "You two make a fantastic team."

"No, not a team. I don't approve of her tactics. I am quite dis-gusted by her desire for power."

This was hard to believe, to say the least. "And what do *you* want the crystals for? To decorate an empty shelf?"

"That's more along the lines of how I think they should be dealt with. The Kindred are dangerous—collectively and individ-ually. My aim is to keep these crystals from those who would abuse their power."

"If you say so."

Ashur had the nerve to smile at this, which annoyed Nic deep-ly.

"What's funny?" he demanded.

"You are."

"Great. Just what I need right now: confirmation that I can still be a source of entertainment even after having been unconscious for—How long was I out?"

"Almost two days."

"Two days. No wonder I'm so thirsty." Nic raked a hand through his hair, knowing it must be sticking up in every direction. "If you say you're so damn noble—"

A shadow crossed Ashur's expression. "I never said I was noble. I've done unforgivable things in my past, but I'm different now. I'm trying to be better."

He wanted to keep arguing, but the prince was actually getting through to him. He hated that he wanted to believe that Ashur had done this in an attempt to right his sister's actions, but it didn't change anything.

Nic needed to see Cleo again. Whatever he had to do to survive this, he would do. He had to know she was all right.

"Why didn't you let Princess Amara kill me?" he asked.

"You can't die." Ashur looked at him as if this were a crazy suggestion. "I won't allow it. I told you that you're important to me. That wasn't a lie, Nic."

He searched Ashur's face for deceit, but found only sincerity. "How can I ever believe anything you say again?"

"Give me a chance and I'll prove I'm worthy of forgiveness. I have a plan to stop Amara, to show her that what she's doing is wrong. It'll work. She trusts me."

"*Trust* seems to be a common problem with you."

Another smile played at Ashur's lips, but faded in an instant. "I know I broke a bridge between us that we'd only started to build, and I regret that most of all."

Nic stayed silent now, afraid to talk. Talking made him vulnerable. It made him stupid. Especially with the prince, for some reason.

"I'll get you something to eat and drink. You need it." The prince got up from his chair, pausing for a moment at the door. He looked over his shoulder. "You should know that I never planned to kiss you that night. I only meant to talk to you. That was all."

Nic shook his head. "I don't know what to say to that."

"Something about you called to me—your sadness, your vulnerability—and I made a foolish decision. For days afterward, I was certain I'd disgusted you."

Nic had been confused. Uncertain, absolutely.

But he hadn't been disgusted.

Ashur met his eyes. "When this is over, I will ask your forgiveness. I won't ask now; I know it's too soon. But I promise I won't let you down again."

Words failed Nic, until finally he managed, "And what should I do in the meantime? Pretend I'm still asleep?"

"No. Amara's no fool. She'll know you're awake. But stay quiet and don't draw attention to yourself. I'll visit you again to let you know my plan."

"All right."

Ashur paused. "I want to ask you something else when this is over, too."

"What?"

Ashur's smile returned. "You'll have to wait and see."

"Is it important?"

"Very." He left the room and closed the door behind him.

An unexpected twist of hope took hold of Nic's chest. "Then I guess I'll wait and see."

CHAPTER 34

CLEO

LIMEROS

Nic had the crystal. It was real. One component of the legendary Kindred was here, within Cleo's reach, and it was every bit as beautiful as she'd always imagined it would be.

"What's this, Ashur?" Amara's tone was even, but her expression had turned as icy as the frozen shards scattered around the temple.

"I've never been interested in violence, sister," he said. "Except when absolutely necessary. That's where you're more like our father than I'll ever be. If he knew that even that single crystal existed, he'd crush this kingdom to dust to find it, and he'd kill everyone here who stood in his way. I didn't realize how much you have in common with him until now."

They were working together—Nic and Ashur. The thought was sweet relief itself to Cleo, just when she had thought all was lost. She spared a glance at Magnus to find him focused on the confrontation, his fists clenched at his sides.

Amara looked mad enough to spit. "I've killed no one who

didn't directly oppose or threaten us. But I don't understand. How did Nic get here before us? He was tied up!"

"Tied up . . . with the dagger I gave him on the ship."

She hissed out a breath. "And the guard?"

"I took the liberty of slipping some sleeping potion into the flask he always carries with him. And I also asked the driver to take us here the long way to ensure Nic arrived first."

Amara stared at him with disbelief and disgust. "All for what, Ashur? So this *servant boy* could claim the crystal for you, like the loyal minion you've trained him to be?"

Loyal minion? Cleo glanced at Nic with alarm and he gave her a squeamish look and a slight shake of his head, an attempt to rebuke Amara's claim.

Ashur stepped forward, closer to the heat of the fire, all around which the melted snow and ice had formed a moat. "That crystal isn't for me or any other mortal to possess, and certainly not Father in particular. He's already more than powerful enough."

"But I want it," she said.

"No. This magic must stay here and be kept under lock and key. It's too dangerous to be taken elsewhere."

Amara stared at him as if seeing him clearly for the first time in her life. "You're insane, do you know that? I had no idea my brother was insane. I thought he was irresponsible and self-indulgent, but that he could be cunning and deceptive when the situation called for it. I appreciated that, but now you've been cunning and deceptive with me. I thought we were more alike."

"We are in many ways, Amara. But not in this way."

Cleo remained completely still. Was this true? Did he really oppose his sister in her lust for power?

The very thought of Amara having access to the Kindred, even one of them, sickened Cleo. The girl was unpredictable, but she'd tonight she'd also proven that she was ruthless.

"For what it's worth," Nic spoke up, clutching the crystal as he drew closer to Ashur, "and to address an earlier accusation, I'm nobody's minion. But I am helping Prince Ashur—and in turn he will help us too, Cleo. I thought he was using me, betraying me, but he's on our side. None of this would be possible without him."

"Isn't that sweet," Amara hissed. "Brother, you do have real feelings for him after all. I had no idea. You deceived me completely. All for a lowly Auranian guard who isn't worth wiping your boots on."

Real feelings? Nic had told Cleo about the confusing kiss he'd shared with the prince. Perhaps that confusion had cleared way to something . . . more?

Nic wouldn't meet her gaze.

Ashur narrowed his eyes. "Give this up, Amara. You've lost. It's over."

She shook her head, then began to laugh lightly. "Of course. You're right. I've been out of control. I needed someone to shake me like this, to show me the path I'd chosen wasn't right." She let out a shaky breath and drew closer to him, took hold of his sleeve and looked up at his face. "I'm so sorry."

That was a swift surrender. Cleo watched her with disbelief as Amara embraced her brother.

"I forgive you." Ashur kissed her forehead, relief flooding his eyes. "I would forgive my family for anything."

"Unfortunately, I'm not nearly as forgiving." Steel flashed in her grip as she pulled a dagger from the folds of her cloak. Before Cleo could scream or even take another breath, Amara plunged it upward into Ashur's chest.

He stared at her, his eyes wide.

"Father will be so disappointed in you," she said as she twisted the knife sharply.

Ashur grabbed his sister's arms, shoving her back from him. He pulled the dagger out of his chest with a grunt of pain, then fell, hard, to his knees.

"No!" Nic yelled, running to Ashur's side.

Amara nodded at a guard, who slammed his fist into Nic's face. He fell to the ground and lost his grip on the crystal, sending it rolling away across the floor.

Amara leaned over and picked it up.

Nic, his nose gushing blood, scrambled to press his hand against the wound in Ashur's chest.

Cleo and Magnus looked on, horrified.

Ashur clutched the front of Nic's cloak, staining it with his blood. "Please forgive me. I never wanted anyone to get hurt—especially not you."

"I forgive you," Nic whispered, his voice breaking. "I forgive you for everything."

Ashur slumped against him, his gaze going glassy and blank.

Trembling now, Cleo watched Amara carefully for any reaction to having just killed her own brother.

"The emperor won't be happy with this," Magnus said, in a low voice.

Amara sighed. "You're right, he won't. When I tell him that his youngest son was killed by King Gaius's heir, he'll want revenge." She glanced at Cleo, who stared at her with shock and disgust. "Vengeance as it was meant to be—swift and merciless, leaving nothing behind but bones. Now, if you'll excuse me, I must return to Kraeshia, where I can mourn my brother with my own people. But thank you both for leading me to this."

Amara slipped the sphere of aquamarine into her cloak and

pointed to three of her guards. "Stay here and kill them all. Burn their bodies. Leave nothing behind to show we were ever here. And you two," she gestured toward the other guards, "come with me."

She passed close enough to Magnus that, for a moment, Cleo thought he might reach out and snap her neck, but he didn't. That, Cleo felt, was unfortunate. His tendency to use violence to solve his problems would have been perfectly acceptable this time.

She turned to look at Nic holding Ashur's lifeless body in his arms. Nic didn't move, barely breathed, his frozen expression one of pain and grief.

Cleo's heart ached for him.

Nic mourned the prince's death, but he wouldn't have to for long.

The princess had already given her guards the order to make sure the three of them followed Prince Ashur to the everafter.

CHAPTER 35

MAGNUS

LIMEROS

"All right," Magnus said as calmly as possible after Amara and two of her guards had left the temple. "It's time to negotiate. I have every intention of walking out of here with my life, so the only question is: How much gold will that cost me?"

The guard who'd shoved him and called him "boy" stepped closer, inspecting him as if he were a piece of dung he'd found on the bottom of his boot. "Gold?"

"Yes. From what I know of Kraeshians, they enjoy a lavish life-style on par with that of the Auranians. My father is king. He has plenty of gold. I can arrange for a great deal of it to find its way into your possession."

"For all three of you?"

"Amara asked you to kill us and burn our bodies. There are bodies outside that would be sufficient stand-ins for all three of us."

"Interesting proposition. But it's not going to happen."

Magnus's upper lip thinned. "She just killed her brother and plans to blame it on me. Do you really think she's going to let any witnesses live?"

"She needs us."

"She needs no one. Now that she has that crystal, she has everything she came here for. We can't let her board a ship with it. We can't let her leave Limeros."

The attentions of all three guards closed in on Magnus. Out of their eye line, Cleo slowly moved toward Nic and knelt down to pick up Amara's discarded dagger.

She was not helping matters at all. Cleo might have many hidden skills, but Magnus would be willing to wager that the fine art of weaponry was not one of them.

Suddenly her movement caught the attention of a guard, who grabbed her and knocked the blade from her grip. He struck her hard across her face, causing her to shriek and stagger backward. She fell against the altar, striking her head on its edge.

It took all the willpower Magnus had not to move from his spot. He had to wait for the right moment.

The other two guards turned to look at her, laughing.

Magnus struck. He grabbed one guard's arms, seizing the moment of his surprise to steal his sword and stab the Kraeshian in his side.

It worked better than he'd expected. At least until another guard's fist found his jaw, making his head spin and his teeth rattle. He dropped his stolen sword and it clattered to the floor. Magnus ducked in time to miss the swipe of a blade. With the next attempt by the guard to bring his sword down on him, Magnus caught the metal between his hands. It sliced his skin, but he managed to jam the hilt of the sword into the guard's gut, allowing him to yank the weapon right out of his grip.

Without hesitation, Magnus spun and impaled the guard through his throat.

Then something hit the side of his head and he fell to the floor with his arm at an awkward angle. As he landed on it with his full weight, he heard a sickening crack and an excruciating pain shot through his arm.

He was about to rise up to his feet again, but the guard—the same guard who'd shoved him earlier—loomed over him, pressing the tip of his sword to Magnus's chest.

"Stay down," the guard snarled. "And lose the weapon."

Magnus dropped the bloody sword. "You'll notice I didn't kill you first as I previously promised I would," he said.

"No, you didn't. And I haven't killed you yet, either."

"Are you waiting for a special invitation?"

This guard sneered down at him after casting a glance at his two fallen associates. "I think you might be right about Princess Amara. She won't let me live after what I've seen here tonight."

Magnus wasn't dead yet, which meant there was still room for negotiation. "I'm thrilled to be right about something tonight. Truly."

"Where are the other crystals?"

Magnus's jaw tensed. "You want crystals, do you?"

"I don't care about gold. Gold can be stolen, spent, lost. Those crystals . . . that's power I can use."

All Magnus knew about the crystals with absolute certainty was that they belonged in only one person's hands: his. However, this guard didn't have to know that. "I can certainly take you to the next location, since you asked so nicely."

The guard jabbed him with the sword. "Where?"

"Sure, I tell you and you kill me. Doesn't seem like a very good deal." Not to mention Magnus had no idea where the other two crystals were.

The guard's expression twisted into one of greed. "I could kill her, you know. Princess Amara. I could climb aboard that ship, steal the crystal, and throw her body overboard."

"And I wholeheartedly encourage you to attempt that. Go. Leave now while you still have a chance to catch up to her entourage."

"First, I need to take care of the three of you. You don't know anything that could help me. You're no good to me."

Magnus's sword arm was badly injured, probably broken. He had no weapon. He was flat on his back with a blade pressed against his heart.

He'd put up a reasonable fight. Sadly, he'd lost, and his life would be the price he'd have to pay.

Now, later . . . What difference did it make in the end?

Magnus had lied to Cleo. Once the king learned what he'd done—killed Cronus to save Cleo's life—his trust in Magnus would be irreparably broken. The scar on his face was a constant reminder of what happened when he displeased his father. He had received it as punishment when he was merely an innocent, if mischievous, boy. As a man, he'd be held fully accountable for his actions, and another scar would be the very least of what he'd expect to receive. He didn't regret what he'd done, but it hadn't only been an act of betrayal; it had been one of treason.

And he knew very well that the penalty for treason was death.

"Go ahead, then," he growled. "What are you waiting for?"

"Nothing at all, anymore." The guard sneered at him. "Imagine my good fortune of being the one to kill the King of Blood's heir. What an honor."

But then an arm reached around the guard and an already bloody blade slashed his throat, creating a wide crimson line that spilled onto his green uniform.

The guard dropped his sword, staggered backward, and clutched at the gaping wound on his throat before falling to his side in a heavy, twitching heap.

Cleo dropped the dagger and it clattered against the smooth, cold floor.

"That," she said, her voice brittle and shaking, "makes us even. All right?"

Magnus stared up at her, utterly stunned. "All right."

She held his gaze for a moment longer, and then ran to Nic, who'd watched everything from across the temple in a state of shock. He grabbed hold of her and pulled her to him in a tight hug.

It seemed that Magnus had escaped death in the exact moment he'd been ready to accept it.

How unexpected.

He pushed himself up to his feet using his uninjured arm, and glared in the princess's general direction. "We need to find Lucia. And we need to get that crystal back from Amara."

Nic gave Ashur's body a final, pained look before he and Cleo left the temple. Magnus watched as the princess passed him, more annoyed now than he'd been before.

"What?" she demanded.

"Nothing," he growled in return. "Stop wasting time. Let's go."

Magnus had come to a horrible realization. One he knew would cause him nothing but pain and suffering from that day forward.

But there was no changing the truth of it.

He had fallen in love with her

CHAPTER 36

LUCIA

LIMEROS

Lucia spent every last coin she had on a carriage to bring her to the Limerian palace. Her one true home. On the way, she'd used her earth magic to heal her wound. The pain of it was only a memory now. She could heal herself, but she couldn't heal Alexius.

I tried, she thought. *I've never tried harder for anything. I'm sorry I failed.*

By the time she arrived at the palace, it was nearly dawn.

The pitch-dark granite spires stretched up into the sky—black on black. She walked past the palace, ignoring the warmth it might offer her, and moved along the shadowy pathways winding through the still and silent gardens, so different from the light-filled, lively ones at the Auranian palace.

Both so different, but so stunningly beautiful in their own ways.

She was drawn to the cliffs that looked out upon the Silver Sea, lit now only by moonlight. She stood at the very edge and looked down at the glistening black water crashing against the rocky shore.

She held Alexius's dagger at her side. It was still coated in his blood.

His body had vanished from her arms in a flash of light only moments after his death. If it hadn't, she never would have left the temple; she would have stayed right there by his side for eternity. But there was nothing there for her anymore.

Just before he'd taken his last breath, he told her to come here and to wait.

So she waited.

Suddenly she heard the snow crunch behind her, signaling someone's approach. But Lucia didn't turn around. She just focused on the water, on the horizon far in the distance as the moon sank lower and lower.

"Quite a night." A woman's voice, calm and melodious.

"Yes, it was."

"You know who I am, don't you?"

Expecting to see a monster hulking before her, Lucia turned to face the woman who'd destroyed everything. Instead, she saw the same golden beauty she had seen in her frightening vision of the past.

Melenia's eyes were like sapphires with swirls of molten gold. Hypnotic. She wore a gown of platinum and crystal. Her skin glowed and her hair was a cascade of shining gold framed by the ebony darkness behind her.

Her beauty was so vivid—so unreal—it was terrifying.

"I'm sure you're very angry with me," Melenia said, her gaze moving to the dagger Lucia held. "But any attempts at vengeance will be futile. I'm immortal, even here now that the wall has finally weakened between our worlds. That weapon won't work on me."

A fog hovered over and around Lucia, one of grief and pain. She could barely see through it, but she had to try. "This isn't meant for you."

"That's good to hear. But still, I do understand how you feel. I'm sure Alexius told you all sorts of things about me, but you mustn't believe all of them."

"You wanted him to kill me."

"I wanted him to bleed you. Your blood is powerful, so powerful that it broke the curse that has trapped me in my prison for so long. I've now left the Sanctuary for the first time in a thousand years, thanks to you."

Lucia's grip strengthened on the hilt of the dagger. "How wonderful for you."

Melenia smiled. "I know what it's like to love someone, to miss them so much it feels as if your heart will break."

"You've felt that, have you?"

"I have. I've felt that for centuries. But I'll soon be reunited with my love."

"That's why you did all of this, for him. That's why Alexius is dead. That's why hundreds have died to soak your road with their blood. All so you could be reunited with your lost love. With the fire Kindred."

A glimmer of surprise lit the immortal's beautiful eyes. "Alexius was more transparent than I expected in the end."

The dying voice of the boy she loved echoed in Lucia's ears.

"The crystals are not the true magic of the Kindred, princess. The magic is what's trapped inside. An elemental spirit is imprisoned within each sphere. This is our secret. This is what we guarded. This is what we protected from the world . . . and what we protected the world from."

Melenia's gaze hardened, but her smile remained fixed. "One does what one must for true love."

"The god of fire, the most powerful of the four Kindred, trapped with-in a sphere of amber," Alexius had whispered to her. *"To free him, Melenia would destroy the world."*

Lucia shivered. "No. You're wrong. True love isn't selfish."

"Your opinion is noted. Now, there is only one thing standing in my way to reunite with the one I love after all this time."

"Me," Lucia said.

"I'm afraid so. I knew Alexius couldn't kill you. I saw it in his eyes, no matter how deeply I sank my magic into him. I saw that his love for you was true. Lucky girl. Most never experience a love so deep. Imagine, that boy chose to take his own life before ending yours."

Grief blinded Lucia for a moment until she mustered the strength to push it away.

"How will you kill me?" Lucia asked, her voice flat again.

"Similar to how I killed Eva. I stole her magic, which also stole her immortality—although, you're already mortal. This should be much easier a task, but no less satisfying. Now," she said, the hateful smile still fixed on her lips, "let's be done with this."

Something caught Melenia's eye and she glanced down at the ground to Lucia's left.

"That's your blood," she said.

"It is," Lucia agreed.

Melenia looked then to the snowy ground and saw the symbol Lucia had drawn with her own blood. A triangle—the symbol for fire.

Melenia's smile faded and her eyes widened. "What have you done?"

"Alexius told me I could draw this symbol anywhere with my blood to summon him, now that he's been awakened. It's his deci-sion if he wishes to obey."

Melenia's gaze searched the area frantically until she spotted a figure approaching the cliffs.

"It's you," she managed, her voice breaking. "It's really you."

The tall figure wore a cloak. Lucia couldn't see his face, but she knew who he was. The smallest emotion managed to wedge its way into her heart, pushing past her numbing grief.

Fear.

The figure drew back his hood to show dark blond hair and amber eyes. He was as handsome as Alexius was—unnaturally so. All the Watchers were beautiful and eternally young, Alexius had told her.

But this young man wasn't a Watcher.

Melenia seemed uncertain upon realizing he wasn't going to rush to her and take her into his arms.

"Melenia," he said, reaching them and sweeping a gaze over her. "You succeeded. Congratulations."

Finally, her smile returned and she reached for him, but her hand dropped to her side before she touched him. "A thousand years I've waited, my love. I've done everything I could to make this night possible."

"And I'm grateful. Very grateful." He held his hand out to her. She closed the distance between them and pressed her lips to his. It didn't take long before she drew back with a confused expression.

"You didn't return my kiss."

"No, I didn't."

She appeared to compose herself, putting her sheen of perfection back into place, as if the rejection of someone she'd waited a thousand years to kiss didn't bother her in the slightest.

Lucia watched, fascinated. An ancient, powerful, beautiful

woman—as close to a goddess as Lucia had ever seen—rejected by her lover was a rather awkward sight, to say the least.

Had Melenia really believed everything would turn out exactly as she wanted?

The young man turned his gaze to Lucia. She drew in a quick breath at the intensity of his amber-colored eyes. "I can also thank you for this."

"Don't thank me."

"But I must. I'm free because of you. The power of a sorceress, but in the body of a mortal girl . . . how extraordinary." He swept his gaze over her. "You and I, we have much in common."

"No, we don't."

"But we do. We both want to embrace who we are, we both want to stop being used by others and discarded at their will. We both desperately want control over our destinies, and revenge over our enemies."

She didn't reply, so startled she was that she agreed with everything he'd said.

"Unfortunately," he continued, "there are still obstacles in my path to absolute freedom and limits to my current power."

"I've taken care of most of those obstacles," Melenia said. "Of the elders, only Timotheus still lives."

"And you, of course. That makes two elders with the power to imprison me again. That strikes me as two too many."

Confusion crossed Melenia's face, followed by a flash of pain, as if he'd deeply hurt her feelings by saying this.

This really wasn't going according to Melenia's plan at all. Were it another night and another life lost, Lucia might have taken pleasure in that.

"I love you," Melenia said, crossly. As if such words mattered to someone like him. "I've killed for you. And I've done it all to free you so we could be together again."

"And I thanked you," the young man said. He appeared to be no more than twenty, but Lucia knew there was no number for his real age.

He was eternal.

"When she's gone, we'll talk. We'll talk about all of this." Melenia spun to face Lucia, an ugly expression crossing her face, and her fist burst into flames.

So she would use fire magic to kill Lucia.

That seemed appropriate.

Lucia looked at her own hand and held it out. She summoned Melenia's fire into her palm.

Melenia gasped as Lucia stole her magic. "What?"

Alexius has stressed this lesson and, at the time, she'd wondered why. From nearly the moment he arrived, she never understood why he'd been so adamant about tutoring her until she was exhausted and frustrated.

Now she knew that it was all so she could do this.

Melenia held out her hand to form a spear of ice, but Lucia looked at it and melted it with a single thought.

"Stop that," Melenia hissed.

Then Lucia stepped forward, clutched Melenia by her throat, and looked deep into her sapphire eyes.

"Listen to me very carefully," Alexius had said in the moments before he vanished from her arms forever. "Melenia will come for you. She will try to kill you because you are the only one with enough magic to destroy her. She steals other Watchers' magic to make herself more powerful. You can do the same. When her magic is drained, she'll be temporarily mortal."

Melenia summoned her magic once more, and again Lucia stole

it with a thought. Fear entered the elder's eyes as Lucia focused with all her strength and, using what she'd learned from Alexius, drained as much magic—earth, air, water, fire—as she could from this beautiful but evil creature.

Lucia's hands glowed with golden power. The cold wind and stinging snow no longer bothered her. Warmth flowed through her veins and her entire body sang with Melenia's *elementia*.

When she'd taken all she could, Melenia began to tremble.

"Spare me," she whispered, her gaze fixed on the young man who hadn't made a single move to save her. "My love, please, spare me..."

"Kill her," he said, nodding at Lucia.

Lucia thrust her dagger into the Watcher's heart, then pulled it out.

Lucia had lied. The dagger was for Melenia, after all.

Melenia looked down at the wound welling with blood as if hypnotized with disbelief. She reached out for the young man with a trembling hand.

He stepped out of her reach.

"But I love you," she whispered.

"And I hate you."

She stared at him with horror. "Why would you hate me when I did everything for you?"

"You helped to keep me enslaved, Melenia. I'm no one's slave. I never was. And I never shall be again."

As he cast a fearsome, furious look upon her, she took a shaky step back from him before she stumbled and fell off the side of the cliff. Mere seconds before she hit the water, her body vanished in a flash of bright light, illuminating the unforgiving landscape all around them for a long, blazing moment.

Lucia dropped the dagger, her gaze fixed on the black water at the bottom of the cliff.

It felt momentous to witness the death of an ancient and powerful Watcher. This wasn't her first kill—her first had been the malicious Sabina. She'd been wracked with guilt over that moment of uncontrollable fury.

Her emotions tonight were much more controlled. Melenia deserved death and Lucia allowed herself to feel just a small edge of satisfaction that she'd been the one to kill her.

After a moment, she looked up at the fire god she'd summoned here with her blood.

"Are you going to kill me?" she asked, surprised that the thought of it didn't fill her with fear anymore.

"No," he replied simply. "I need your help."

"My help?" The thought was ludicrous. "Why would someone like you need *my* help?"

"Because you can do that." He nodded toward the water below. "You have the power to destroy those that want to control me. And I never, ever want to be controlled or imprisoned again."

She fell silent, her heart pounding.

"My sisters and brother are also out in this land, lost now. They're not as strong as me. They can't as easily take mortal form. They're at the mercy of whoever found them. We must locate them and keep them safe."

This could be her destiny—to be here at the break of dawn with the blood of two Watchers on her hands. Melenia and Alexius. One she hated. One she loved.

There was no one in the world she trusted anymore; no one who didn't want to use her for her magic and cast her aside once they were done.

With Alexius gone, she had no one to guide or teach her.

Her magic burned within her, her ring blazed on her finger,

but despite the pain and suffering of this night, she'd never felt more powerful in her entire life.

"Will you help me?" he asked again when silence fell between them.

He was dangerous—she felt it down in her very soul. The price of this young man's freedom would be forged from pain, death, and fire.

"Yes," she said.

The single word sealed her fate.

Standing there on the steep Limerian cliffs, she was ready to watch the world burn.

ACKNOWLEDGMENTS

My deepest thanks go to Elizabeth Tingue, my wonderful editor, and Ben Schrank, my fantastic publisher. To the incredible Penguin Teen team: Laura Arnold, Erin Berger, Elizabeth Zajac, Jessica Shoffel, Anna Jarzab, and Casey McIntyre, to name but a few. Every author should be lucky enough to get the chance to work with you all. Artsy thanks to Emily Osborne and Shane Rebenschied who outdid themselves yet again with this utterly stunning cover that I just want to stare at all day. A million thank yous to the team at Penguin Canada. And thank you, as always, to my awesome agent Jim McCarthy.

Thank you to my amazing family and friends who are always there to support me in person or online.

And thank you, thank you to the fabulous readers who've embraced the Falling Kingdoms series. I sincerely hope you enjoy the third book in this epic tale!

The turn of a page can open
THE PORTAL *from* OUR WORLD
to MYTICA'S PAST

FROM THE *NEW YORK TIMES* BESTSELLING AUTHOR OF
THE FALLING KINGDOMS SERIES

A BOOK OF

Spirits

AND

Thieves

MORGAN RHODES